THE
LAZARUS
VAULT

Tom Harper was born in Germany and studied medieval history at Oxford University. He has written nine novels, including *Lost Temple* and *The Book of Secrets*. He lives in York with his wife and son. He is Chair of the Crime Writers' Association.

THE LAZARUS VAULT

TOM HARPER

arrow books

Published by Arrow Books in 2010

3 5 7 9 10 8 6 4 2

First published in Great Britain in 2010 by
Arrow Books
Random House, 20 Vauxhall Bridge Road,
London SW1V 2SA

www.rbooks.co.uk

Addresses for companies within The Random House Group Limited can be found
at: www.randomhouse.co.uk/offices.htm

The Random House Group Limited Reg. No. 954009

A CIP catalogue record for this book
is available from the British Library

ISBN 9780099547839

The Random House Group Limited supports The Forest Stewardship
Council (FSC), the leading international forest certification organisation.
All our titles that are printed on Greenpeace approved FSC certified paper
carry the FSC logo. Our paper procurement policy can be found at
www.rbooks.co.uk/environment

Mixed Sources
Product group from well-managed
forests and other controlled sources
www.fsc.org Cert no. TF-COC-2139
© 1996 Forest Stewardship Council

Typeset by SX Composing DTP, Rayleigh, Essex
Printed and bound in Great Britain by
CPI Cox & Wyman, Reading, RG1 8EX

for Jane Conway-Gordon

*better than a poke
in the eye*

'Upon my honour,' said Sir Guiromelant. 'Your tales amaze me. It's a delight to listen, for you tell them as well as any minstrel or troubadour – you're a born storyteller. And yet at first I took you for a knight, and thought you must have done some great deeds of valour.'

—Chrétien de Troyes, *Perceval*

I

London

Ellie told herself she didn't want the job. Didn't need it. She'd just started a PhD in the subject she loved, which was more than a girl like her should ever have dreamed of. Her life until then had been concrete and rust: now she'd stepped through the door into an enchanted world. After nine months in Oxford, she still had to pinch herself at the beauty that surrounded her, the gargoyles and pinnacles, the panelled rooms and immaculate lawns. She had a supervisor who respected her, a boyfriend who adored her, and a mother who almost burst with pride when she told the neighbours how far her daughter had gone.

But none of that stopped her from getting up at six on a grey morning, tugging on some tights that were too thick for May and the tweed skirt she'd bought for her doctoral interview, and taking the bus down the M40 to London. At Marble Arch she got on the Tube with a thousand other commuters, squeezed into the carriage like toothpaste, and wondered how people could endure this every day. She clutched her bag tight to her stomach. Inside was a bottle of water, a sandwich she'd made for the way home, and a letter on thick cream paper with a crest stamped at the top. The reason she'd come.

The Director, Mr Vivian Blanchard, would be delighted if you could visit him to discuss possible career opportunities at the Monsalvat Bank . . .

Sweat pricked the back of her neck as the train swayed into the tunnel. The air in the carriage was thick with body odour and lowest-common-denominator perfume. She felt ill. She didn't even want the job.

The moment she came out of the ground at Bank Station she could feel the danger in the air. A crowd of demonstrators had gathered outside the Bank of England, chanting and clapping and waving their ragged banners. More were expected. Police horses stamped their massive hooves and bared their teeth; stiff-backed riders stared down from behind the opaque visors of their helmets, or over the rim of their shields. They gripped their batons like knights getting ready for battle. Above, the barons of capitalism watched from their glass towers and agreed that this was what they paid their taxes for.

Ellie edged around the demonstration. The crowd jostled her; she almost dropped her bag. A policeman looked her up and down and decided she wasn't a threat. In her tweed skirt and woollen jacket, she didn't look much like a demonstrator. Not much like anyone in the City. Expensively dressed mannequins reproached her from behind the barricaded shop windows, their faces fixed hard in contempt. She wished she hadn't come.

'Look out where you're going!'

An indignant, wheedling shout. She'd walked straight into someone – one of the protesters. Wild, stringy hair hung over a gaunt face with staring eyes and ragged teeth; his T-shirt looked as if he'd lived in it for weeks. The placard on his shoulder said, 'CAPITALISM IS KILLING US'.

'I'm sorry.' She tried to edge around him, but he sidestepped to block her.

'Dangerous times, love.' He thrust himself forward. 'Got to be careful, know what I mean? Got to chop away the dead wood, stop the rot before we get got. Cut out the disease.'

He smelled like week-old rubbish. Ellie recoiled, but the crowd pressed her towards him.

'Society's dying.' Spittle flecked his mouth; his voice was rising. 'There's a disease in this world and it's killing us all. Look around. The bees are dying and the trees are dying. The oceans are rising, but there's no fish in them. It's a sickness.'

Ellie glanced at her watch. She didn't have time. 'I'm sorry, but –'

'No, you listen.'

A hand reached out, grimy nails like talons. He probably meant to grab her arm. But Ellie twisted away, so that the fingers caught the strap of her bag instead. He tugged it off her shoulder; she must have shouted or screamed.

Something blurred the air behind him and the protester sank to his knees with a squeal. A policeman in a fluorescent yellow jerkin stood behind him, baton in hand. He must have been watching, waiting for the excuse. In an instant, two more officers had ziplocked the man's wrists behind his back and dragged him away.

Ellie began to stammer some thanks, but the policeman cut her off.

'*Go away!*' he shouted. '*You aren't safe here!*'

The snarl on his face, half-hidden below the visor of his riot helmet, was almost more frightening than the protester.

Ellie clutched her bag and stumbled away through the crowd.

A few moments later she felt a sickening stab of guilt. The protester hadn't meant any harm. Perhaps she should have taken the policeman's badge number, in case the man wanted to make a complaint. She glanced back, but he'd already disappeared into the yellow-jacketed battle lines.

Ellie arrived ten minutes late, hot and flustered. The encounter with the protester had left her shaken, but that wasn't what made her late. She'd got lost. The map she'd looked at before she came showed nothing but a grey block of space where the bank should have been. On the ground, that translated into a maze of tiny lanes and alleys worming between old buildings: dead ends that turned out to be blind corners, passages that led through houses or slipped through ancient walls. And, just when she was ready to give up, an old stone building with narrow windows and little turrets on the corners, craning out over the cobbled lane.

A gleaming black Jaguar sat waiting outside. *How did that get there?* The moment she came into view, a chauffeur in a peaked cap jumped out and opened the rear door, almost as if she'd been expected. But it wasn't for her. A man in a pinstriped suit and a blue tie strode down the steps and slid into the back of the car. The chauffeur slammed the door and drove off; Ellie had to press herself flat against the wall to avoid being run over. As it rumbled past, Ellie glimpsed a familiar face bowed over the contents of a red leather briefcase. Only for a second, before the Jaguar disappeared round the corner.

Ellie looked back to the bank. A cast-iron sign hung over the door: a snarling eagle framed by a shield, holding what looked like a spear in its claws. It was repeated in frosted glass on the door, and again inside, in brass, on the wall behind the reception desk.

A sour-faced receptionist, with a more-than-passing resemblance to the eagle on the shield, glared her down as she approached the desk. Ellie fumbled the letter out of her bag.

'Ellie Stanton. I'm here to see, um, Vivian Blanchard.'

The receptionist lifted a phone and announced Ellie in a crisp, cut-glass voice.

'He won't be a minute.'

There were no chairs, nowhere to sit. Standing at the desk, not knowing what to do, curiosity got the better of Ellie.

'That man who just left. Was that –?'

The secretary pursed her lips. 'I'm afraid we never discuss our clients.'

Ellie blushed. Had she already ruined her chances? *Pull yourself together*, she told herself. *You don't have anything to prove. They asked to see you.*

The ring of a telephone broke the silence. The receptionist answered without taking her eyes off Ellie.

'You may go up now.'

Vivian Blanchard's office was on the fifth floor, just high enough that you could see the landmark towers of the city skyline through the back window. Ellie barely noticed them. Blanchard filled the room with his presence, welcoming her in, apologising for the delay, offering her coffee, overwhelming her with his energy. When he shook her hand, he tugged it towards him ever so slightly and leaned forward, almost as if he meant to kiss it.

'Enchanted.'

He ushered her into a deep, leather-upholstered sofa. From a box on his desk he took a fat cigar and a silver knife. He sliced off the end of the cigar with brutal economy, then pulled out a gold lighter.

'You don't mind?'

Ellie shook her head, still struggling to take him in. He wasn't like anyone she'd ever met. Everything about him was larger, grander than real life. His tall frame and broad shoulders, and the grey suit that fitted him like armour; the swept-back mane of silver hair, his craggy face and aquiline nose and eyes that glittered like pins. His cufflinks were Cartier, his tie Hermès, and his shoes (though Ellie couldn't know it) were hand-stitched in Paris by a man who only made a hundred pairs a year. When he spoke, there was a hint of a foreign accent behind the words.

'Thank you for coming, Ellie. I can call you Ellie?' He didn't wait for permission. 'I apologise if our approach seemed unnecessarily . . . mysterious.'

'It's not every day you get invited to interview for a job you never applied for.'

'And with a company you have never heard of, no?' Blanchard blew a cloud of smoke towards an oil painting hanging over the fireplace, an imitation Pre-Raphaelite knight.

There was no point denying it. Nobody she'd spoken to seemed to have heard of the Monsalvat Bank. They had a website but it was a joke, a single page with the crest and a phone number. The university careers service had nothing in its files. The sum knowledge of the World Wide Web had amounted to a few references in the *Financial Times*, always in passing; a couple of mentions in *The Economist*. Almost as if the bank didn't want to be found.

'Not much,' Ellie admitted.

'Entirely understandable.' Blanchard bared his teeth in a

reassuring smile. 'Discretion is one of our cardinal virtues. We go to considerable lengths to protect our privacy.'

'I do know that it was established in the sixteenth century by a merchant who came over from France,' Ellie added. 'Saint-Lazare de Morgon. That must make it the oldest bank in England, one of the two or three oldest in Europe. In the Reformation it grew rich handling the proceeds of the dissolution of the monasteries. By the eighteenth century it had established itself as a prime financier to any country in Europe that wanted to start a war.'

Blanchard inclined his head, admitting the charge.

'In the twentieth century it survived wars and depressions as a small but influential merchant bank catering to rich individuals and their companies. In the twenty-first, it's about the last of the old firms that hasn't been taken over by one of the big international conglomerates. Yet.'

Blanchard's cigar had grown a long finger of ash as he listened to her in silence. He tapped it into the crystal ashtray and took another mouthful of smoke. He looked pleased.

'I don't believe that most of that information has ever been placed in the public domain.'

Ellie found herself blushing under his gaze. 'I was curious when I got your letter.'

Curious why a bank no one's ever heard of wants to hire a girl no one's ever heard of, with no experience and no interest in working in the City. She'd spent two days digging through bundles of yellowed documents, crumbling ledgers and arcane forms, trying to work out if the Monsalvat Bank even existed.

'But actually, there is no great mystery how we found you. You remember your undergraduate dissertation? Your *prize-winning* dissertation?'

'The Spenser Prize.' She'd never heard of it until her

supervisor put the entry form in her pigeonhole one day – the only time he'd shown the least interest in her. She'd sent off her essay and forgotten about it. Three months later, back came a letter of congratulations and a cheque for five hundred pounds.

'We administer the prize on behalf of one of our clients. Occasionally, with his permission, we use it to select individuals who may be of interest to us.'

His gaze landed on her like a physical blow. Ellie squirmed and looked away, back to the painting over the mantelpiece. A woman in a gauzy shift, so sheer it hid almost nothing, was tied to a tree in the background. The knight had his sword half-drawn, though whether to cut the damsel free, or to challenge some enemy approaching off the edge of the canvas wasn't clear. Ellie began to wonder if the painting really was an imitation.

Blanchard leaned back in his chair. 'Let me tell you how we are today. We're an unusual firm. Exceptional, I would say. Some call us old-fashioned, and in certain ways we are. But we also know that if we wish to maintain our independence we must keep ahead of our competitors. The most modern practices, the most up-to-date thinking. New furniture in an old building.'

He was obviously speaking metaphorically. The dark, heavy wood of his claw-footed desk had to be three hundred years old at least. It might even have come from one of the dissolved monasteries the Monsalvat Bank had done so well out of.

'Our clients mostly represent old money – some of it very old indeed. They understand that money needn't be vulgar. They require bankers who guard their wealth with a certain . . .'

'Discretion?' Ellie suggested.

'Aesthetic.'

Elllie nodded, though she didn't really understand.

'The *nouveaux riches* – the Arabs, the Orientals, the Americans – we leave them to others. The Jews have their own people.'

He saw the look that Ellie, despite her best efforts, couldn't keep off her face.

'I know this is not politically correct to say, but it is *factually* correct. Money allows nothing else, only facts.'

Blanchard rolled his cigar around the ashtray again.

'I told you we are an exceptional company. But we do not have great assets or vast sums of money invested on our own account. Our wealth is in the minds and hearts of our people. Exceptional people. People like you.'

Ellie sat stiffly on the huge sofa, knees pressed together.

'You think I am flattering you? I can place advertisements in the right universities and next week I will have five hundred impeccable applications. All the same: the same schools, the same degrees, the same thinking. They will all have worked hard – but only within a system that is designed to make them succeed. Whereas you, Ellie – you have succeeded outside this system. And that is exceptional. These others, they think life is a game played between white lines, with rules and scores and referees who blow the whistle if someone kicks them between the legs. You and I, Ellie, we know better.'

Blanchard opened a file on his desk and took out two sheets of paper that looked very much like her CV. How had they got hold of that?

'Tell me about yourself.'

'Why don't you tell me?'

She surprised herself with the boldness of her answer. Perhaps she really didn't want the job. But Blanchard didn't look offended. Somehow, she'd known he'd approve.

'Eleanor Caris Stanton. Born the twenty-second of February 1987, Newport, South Wales. Your mother worked in various industrial jobs; your father . . .' He shrugged. He didn't seem to be reading off any piece of paper she could see. 'You attended an unregarded school and achieved remarkable results. You were offered a scholarship to Oxford university which you turned down in favour of a local former polytechnic of no great distinction. Were you intimidated by Oxford? The privilege and elitism? Did you fear you would be found wanting?'

'No.' Too defensive? 'Even with the money they were offering, I couldn't afford to go.'

'It is no bad thing to be afraid,' Blanchard admonished her. 'Those who think they have nothing to fear usually have nothing to gain.'

Ellie wasn't sure that was true. 'Anyway, I got to Oxford in the end.'

'Indeed. Top of your undergraduate class, a first-class degree in medieval history, you could have walked into any graduate training programme in the country. Instead, you chose to pursue a doctorate. Not many people would have made the same choice. Were you not tempted to go for the money, to escape your background?'

Ellie stiffened. Was he being crass? Or was he testing her? She looked into his face, the handsome lines etched deep into the skin, and thought she saw the curl of a smile. Bastard.

'Money isn't the only way to escape,' was all she said.

Blanchard nodded, rocking in his high-backed chair. 'The poverty of ideas, no?'

'Something like that.'

'But ideas have their own poverty. The ivory tower of academia is an echo chamber, a hall of mirrors. You look at the world through glass and eventually all you see is yourself. Would that satisfy you?'

You aren't safe here. The policeman's words suddenly came back to her.

'Academia's where I am,' she said firmly. 'I'm very flattered you've asked me here, but I've got three and a half years to go and I'm fully committed to the doctorate. I'm afraid there's absolutely no way I could give it up at the moment.'

She'd rehearsed it on the bus, knowing the moment would come and wanting to get the tone right. Don't give offence, but don't leave a scrap of doubt. Like telling your date you had no intention of going home with him.

Blanchard heard her out and looked bored.

'You have worked in banking once before?'

It took her a moment to realise what he meant. The memory was so distant. 'Just a summer job. Very different to this.' Twelve hours a week in the local ex-building society, brown carpets and pebble-dash walls. The only old money there was pensioners drawing their benefits.

'What attracted you?'

Ellie blinked. 'I'm sorry?'

'To that job. Why not a bar, or a clothes shop – the jobs young women do?'

'I thought I should see the other side of the coin.'

I wanted to see where the money came from. To handle it. To be close to it. Just once, to have enough. She'd been poor all her life and hated it. The desperation in her mother's eyes when she came home from the night shift, her terror every time there was a knock at the door. More than once, a sudden departure from a house she'd just started to feel happy in, bundled into a car at night with their few possessions. The injustice of seeing other kids at school coming in with clothes

11

and phones and laptops they'd been given by their parents, while she bought her uniforms second-hand. At university the phones and laptops had turned into cars and flats, while Ellie lived above a kebab shop, sweated over her books late into the night to the smell of chip fat, and filled her spare hours earning minimum wage wherever she could find it.

'Let me tell you a little about our pay policy,' said Blanchard. 'Because we're a small firm, we know we have to offer more than our rivals.' He picked up the silver knife and wiped threads of tobacco off the blade. 'Fortunately, we have deep pockets. As a starting salary, we will offer seventy-five thousand pounds, plus you can expect a bonus that would increase that by about ten to fifteen per cent. As you become more senior, that percentage grows.'

Ellie's mouth hung open. She didn't care if Blanchard saw it. Had he really said seventy-five thousand pounds? The grant for her doctorate was eight thousand, and that was more than she'd ever had to live on in her life. People she'd known at university who'd gone to the top London law firms weren't earning nearly that much. She knew, because she'd heard them bragging about it for months.

'We know London is a difficult place to live,' Blanchard was saying, 'so we try to help the transition. For the first year you work here, you can live in the company flat. The Barbican, the thirty-eighth floor. The views are stunning.'

Ellie nodded thoughtfully. *Seventy-five thousand pounds.*

'Naturally, we provide all the tools you need for the job. A laptop, the latest mobile phone, if that matters to you. A clothing allowance.'

Unconsciously, Ellie rubbed the cheap fabric of her skirt and imagined herself in some of the clothes she'd seen in the shop windows.

'We don't provide a car, because you won't need it. Driving in London is impossible. If we send you further afield we have someone to drive you. And most of your travel will be abroad.'

'Would there be much of it? The travel?'

'Our clients are spread all over Europe. Switzerland, Italy, Germany; France, of course. Sometimes they come to London, but usually they prefer that we go to them.'

Ellie had only left the country once, at eighteen, when she passed her exams. Six months saving the wages from her Saturday job, gone in a week in a Spanish hostel that smelled of drains.

'Naturally, we make it as comfortable as possible. We send you first class and try to find agreeable hotels.'

'I'm sure –'

Blanchard cut her off with a flick of the silver knife.

'Ellie, let us be honest with each other. Most job interviews are built on lies. The candidate lies about how fantastic he is, how dedicated, and the company lies about how great it will be to work for them and they know he will have a glittering career. Really, they will work him until he goes blind on paperwork, and then let him go.'

Ellie listened in silence. The smoke from Blanchard's cigar was making her dizzy.

'We are not like that. We hunt carefully for the one we want and, when we catch him, we keep him. You are an investment for us – potentially worth millions. Like any investment, we want to help you to grow. Yes, the job is demanding. There will be long days – and nights, sometimes – but I promise you, it will be more fascinating than anything you have ever done before. You will come face to face with some of the most powerful and intelligent men in Europe, and they will listen to what you have to say. Eagerly, gratefully. Because you represent the Monsalvat Bank, and because they will recognise in you a kindred intelligence. As we have.'

He clasped his hands together and reached forward over the desk.

'Ellie, we very much want you to come and work with us. Can we tempt you?'

II

Île de Pêche, AD 1142

It's raining on the morning we come to kill the count. The raindrops make rings on the flat sea, a labyrinth of interlocking circles. Our shallow boats glide across the surface and disturb the pattern. The hulls are so thin I can feel the water beneath, like horseflesh through a saddle.

The boats are little more than coracles. In a way, we are pilgrims. My scalp itches where Malegant cut me a false tonsure with his hunting knife last night. My skin crawls where the uncombed wool of the habit chafes it. We took the robes off a group of monks we surprised on the road near Rennes a week ago. The seams stretch around our shoulders: we're broader than the average monk. And we're wearing chain-mail hauberks underneath.

A mist has risen off the sea. It encloses us, a blank tapestry on the walls of our world. There are three hundred islands in this bay, but we can't see any of them. The weather is perfect for us. Dark boats against a dark sea will be almost invisible to the watchmen. Even if they see us, bowstrings soften in the rain. Malegant says it shows God wills it, and we all laugh. We think we understand the joke.

There are eight of us, and each has at least a dozen battles notched on his sword. We have blood on our hands, scars on our faces and prices on our heads. We are not men you would want to meet on the road – as those monks found to their cost. But we all fear Malegant. He stands a head taller than any of us and everything about him is black: his hair and his eyes; the stone in the hilt of his sword; the screaming eagle painted on his shield. Even his armour has been alloyed black.

He pulls out his hunting knife and slices his habit open from neck to hem, as if eviscerating himself. It makes it easier to shrug off the disguise when the battle starts. We all do the same. The sound of tearing cloth rents the silent sea air.

A shadow appears in the mist ahead. I can hear the lap of water on land. The shadow grows over us. A bittern starts its mournful cry. The castle is built right against the sea here, extruded from the rock itself. We're close enough now that I can see mussels and barnacles stippling the walls. Sticks poke out of the water to mark the lobster pots.

We follow the birdcall and find a stone ramp sloping into the sea by a water-gate. The gate has been opened: a Carthusian monk in a robe the colour of mist stands by it. He has his hands cupped over his mouth and is honking like a bittern.

He drops his hands. He has the youngest, cleanest face of all of us: he makes the most convincing monk.

'Did they suspect anything?' Malegant asks. Even his voice sounds black, as dry as soot.

The Carthusian shakes his head. 'The count's in his chapel at prayer.'

We scramble out – our feet get wet, but we daren't risk

scraping the boats on the landing. I take out my sword and unwrap it from its binding. The monks we killed had books with them, and parchment keeps the water out. I drop the pages in the water and watch them float away. The rain tries to drown them.

'Guard the gate,' Malegant tells the Carthusian. 'When the fighting starts, no one escapes.'

He ties his belt in a loose knot over the habit. The pommel of his sword bulges at his waist like an obscenity. We all pull up our hoods and file through the gate.

It's barely dawn, but the castle's already awake. Grooms carry steaming buckets of manure from the stables to the kitchen gardens. Servants sweep out the rushes from the great hall and take them to the bakery to burn. Somewhere, falcons mewl as their keeper brings them fresh meat. A woman in a white dress leans out from a balcony in the keep. I turn my head to see her from the folds of my hood, but the mist wraps itself around her, making her insubstantial as an angel.

For a moment my imagination insists it's Ada. I think I see a red cord tying back her hair, dark eyes brimming with laughter and the brooch, my gift, at her throat.

Don't look, I beg her. *Wherever you are, avert your eyes.* There's no question of asking her to pray for me.

The woman is not Ada. I pull my hood forward so that she disappears from sight.

The chapel's a dark, sunken chamber, half-stone and half-rock. Many feet have worn the floor smooth. A lancet window pierces the rear wall and looks out to sea; three red roundels stain the glass like wounds. There is an altar under the window, and on the altar two branched candlesticks and a reliquary box, all gold.

The count kneels at the altar. He's smaller than I expected:

a thin, wrenlike man, with receding white hair and apple-red cheeks. He reads from a bible on a low lectern, while two rows of monks – real monks – face each other and sing the liturgy over his head.

Have mercy on me, Lord, sinner that I am.

I feel dizzy. I wish I could change my fate. Malegant strides across the room, the cloak slipping from his shoulders. There's no challenge. His sword taps the count on his shoulder like a lord dubbing a knight, and as the count's head turns he smites him.

The weight of the blow slices open the count's collarbone all the way to his lungs. Blood fountains; his head lolls on his shoulders like a pig's bladder on a string. Malegant puts his boot against the dead count's back and pulls his sword free. Blood spills across the book as the count topples forward. One of the monks runs to the altar and smothers the reliquary with his body, but Malegant slits his throat and pulls the corpse away.

Shouts and footsteps sound behind us. Too late, the count's guards have woken to the danger. Malegant picks up the reliquary and holds it aloft like a chalice. His face shines with triumph, while the others butcher the remaining monks.

And I? I know I should draw my sword, perform the service I've been hired for. At least protect myself. But a higher power has me in its grip. I remember the oath I took half a lifetime ago.

To defend the church, my lord, and the defenceless.

How have I come to this?

III

Luxembourg

Lemmy Maartens knew he had the easiest job in the world. A bank inspector in a tax haven – the toughest part of his day, he liked to joke, was choosing where to have lunch. But right now, the job wasn't so easy. Right now, he was sweating.

'You would like more coffee?'

The secretary had reappeared with a cafetière. Lemmy put his cup on the table and pushed it across so she wouldn't see his hand trembling. The cup was fine china – Villeroy & Boch. Lemmy had checked the underside of the saucer while the secretary was out of the room.

'The manager will be with you directly.'

All his life, Lemmy had known that the world owed him more than it gave him. His job, rubbing shoulders with the international financial set, oozing wealth and arrogance, only reinforced the grievance. He wanted the expensive German saloons he saw in the car park; the Italian suits that brushed past him in the corridors. And, he believed, he deserved them.

So Lemmy went freelance. In other countries, regulators were bribed to turn a blind eye. In Luxembourg, turning a blind eye was pretty much Lemmy's official job description. But he was also paid for his discretion – and that was definitely negotiable. Nothing serious, but if you wanted to know whether a rival company was having trouble making its payroll, or if a subsidiary was losing money and ripe for acquisition, Lemmy could find out for you. It earned him a tidy ten thousand euros a month on top of his salary, all carefully hidden where no one would find it. But every time, he sweated for it.

He read the sign on the wall again. *Monsalvat Bank SA*. Even working for the ministry he'd never heard of them, but that didn't surprise him. There were more than a hundred and fifty banks in Luxembourg, attracted by the low taxes and regulators like Lemmy who didn't ask too many questions. Most of the banks didn't extend to much more than a nameplate and a telephone number.

A woman came out of the inner door. She wore a grey pencil skirt and a white blouse unbuttoned to her collarbone. She must be approaching fifty, but with her fine bones and slim figure she had a commanding beauty that the twice-divorced Lemmy could appreciate.

'Christine Lafarge.' She shook his hand. 'I am the manager of this office. I wasn't expecting a visit from your department today.'

'A random inspection,' Lemmy assured her. 'A formality. The new climate, you know. We must be seen to be active.'

Her eyes narrowed. 'Your director usually telephones to alert us. A courtesy, so we can prepare our files.'

Lemmy spread his hands and hoped she didn't notice the sweat on his palms. 'I can only apologise.'

The secretary fetched the printout he needed, a list of

accounts. Lemmy scanned it and pretended to choose one at random.

'This one.'

Mrs Lafarge raised her eyebrows. 'That is one of our most valuable accounts. If the client knew you were investigating his dealings he would be . . .' She thought for the right word. 'Mortified.'

In the delicate world of Luxembourg banking, it was as clear a warning as she could give. *Back off.* Any other time, Lemmy would have apologised at once for his obvious mistake and asked to see a different account, perhaps one that Mrs Lafarge herself could suggest. After three hours of scrupulous inactivity, he'd assure her that everything was in order.

But the people who'd sent Lemmy were paying too much for that. He pressed his fingertips together and looked stern. 'I'm afraid I must insist. Our procedures . . .' He raised his eyes to the ceiling, servant to a higher power.

'Of course,' was all Mrs Lafarge said. 'You will have the files directly. I'll telephone our head office in London to inform them.'

Lemmy smiled his thanks, trying to hide his crooked teeth, and wondered why his mouth felt quite so dry.

London

Ellie arrived for her first day at work late and exhausted. A blanket of grey clouds was smothering the city, packing in the heat and the damp so that everything became sticky. She'd meant to come down the night before; instead she'd stayed in Oxford, up half the night with Doug going over the same argument they'd had all summer. Eventually she'd locked herself in the bedroom and cried herself to sleep. Minutes later, so it seemed, the alarm clock dragged her back.

It would have been so easy to stay in bed. Even now, climbing the stairs to the bank's frosted front door, part of Ellie wanted to turn and run. She felt a fraud in her new suit and shoes, overdressed and shabby all at once. She half expected the receptionist to turn her away, explain it had all been a mistake.

You don't belong there.

Of all the things Doug had said, that was the one that hurt most.

The receptionist rang up to announce her. Ellie didn't catch the reply.

He's forgotten, she thought. *Or changed his mind*. She'd have to trudge back to Oxford, to Doug, admit it was all a mistake. Part of her almost wanted it to be true.

'Ellie.'

Blanchard strode into the reception area. In one fluid movement he shook her hand, clapped her on the shoulder and leaned forward to kiss her on the cheek. 'Welcome to Monsalvat.' He took her elbow and steered her towards the lift. 'I am so glad you have joined us. Your journey was fine?'

'Fine,' Ellie echoed. She felt dazed again, swept up in Blanchard's irresistible aura. It was probably because she was so tired.

Blanchard was apologising for her flat not being ready the night before. 'An electrician was installing new wiring and he took too long, something like this. A mess. But it is all well now. My driver will take you after work. How was your summer? The course was good?'

'I learned a lot.' Courtesy of her prospective employers, Ellie had spent eight weeks of July and August at a country house in Dorset, an exclusive summer camp for would-be investment bankers.

'They send us a report, you know,' Blanchard admonished her. 'They said in the final examination you came first in the class.'

Ellie shrugged, blushing. All her life she'd had to work harder than the others to achieve what she wanted. She was good at it. She hadn't fitted in with the other students, who mostly saw the course as an extension of the boarding schools they'd left not so long before. While they drank and flirted in the bar, she'd sat in her room with her books. The way she'd always done it.

Blanchard gave her a searching look. 'Perhaps you did not mix so much with the other pupils. Maybe they seemed different to you.'

Ellie stared at him, wondering how he could read her thoughts like that.

'But you should try. Our work is not about passing exams and knowing the rules. Of course, you must do this also, but it is not enough. You should socialise with these people. Not because you like them, but because one day, when you negotiate, they will be on the other side of the table. And then you will know their weaknesses.'

A coldness seemed to come over him as he spoke, the remorseless focus of a hunter. Ellie remembered what Doug had said. *These people are predators. The first sign of weakness, they'll rip you limb from limb.* She'd called him melodramatic.

'And here we are.'

Blanchard held the door and let her into a small square office. To Ellie, schooled in the Middle Ages, it looked more like a monastic cell. The floor was dark wooden boards, the walls stark white. A scarred desk stood in the middle of the room, with a leather-upholstered chair and a filing cabinet behind it. There was no computer, nor any phone Ellie could see: only a pile of Manila folders spilling papers across the desk.

'I had my secretary bring the files for some of the major projects we have at the moment. You should familiarise yourself with them before you meet the clients.'

'When will that be?'

Blanchard shrugged. 'Maybe tomorrow? Our job is unpredictable. I said before, it is not something you learn in books. For the next six months you will work as my personal assistant. Because of my responsibilities, you will not concentrate on any particular client, but work on different projects as I need you. Some of the tasks I give you will seem mundane, or irrelevant; others will be almost incalculably important. If you succeed, you will gain a rare knowledge.'

He looked as though he might have said more, but at that moment a middle-aged woman poked her head around the door. 'Mrs Lafarge is on the line.'

Blanchard nodded. 'If you excuse me, Ellie. Destrier will come in a few minutes to give you your passes, your keys and your equipment. He is our security manager. He is very paranoid, but this is why we pay him. Humour him.'

He paused at the door and fixed her with a look that seemed to turn her to glass. 'Remember, Ellie, we chose you. This is where you belong.'

When Blanchard had gone, Ellie sat at the desk and stared at the stack of folders. *The most modern practices, the most up-to-date thinking*, Blanchard had said at her interview. But even the ancient Oxford libraries seemed more modern than this.

She tried the filing cabinet, but it was locked. Her desk had a drawer; she opened it, half expecting to find a quill pen and inkwell. Instead, she saw two rectangular blocks of high-gloss plastic, like jet or polished basalt. One was the size of a pack of cards, the other like a hardback book. In the dusty drawer, they looked like artefacts of an alien civilisation.

There were no markings. Ellie picked up the smaller one to examine it. Her hand brushed the surface: suddenly it started to glow. Red writing hovered behind the mirrored surface.

Enter password.

'You want to be careful what you touch around here.'

Ellie dropped the box. It thudded onto the desk, glowing like a hot coal. A man stood in the doorway. He was tall and broad: his face might once have been handsome, if it hadn't been rearranged by a series of violent events. His grey suit shimmered when he moved. One tendril of a tattoo peeked over the edge of his shirt collar, and a gold stud gleamed in his left ear.

He advanced into the room and picked up the lump of plastic where Ellie had dropped it.

'Destrier,' he introduced himself. 'Never seen a mobile phone before?'

'Mine has buttons.'

'Bin it.' His voice was soft, the accent hard to place. 'This is your new best friend. Your password is in a text message on the phone. Remember it, never write it down. If you forget, or you think it's been compromised, you come to me.'

He typed a number into the keypad which had appeared under the fascia. More symbols glowed into life around it.

'Green to call, red to hang up. It can do other things, which we'll show you later. The company pays for unlimited usage, so make as many personal calls as you like. It works out cheaper for us than trying to work out who said what to who. Same with the computer.' He picked up the other box and tapped in the number again. Ellie heard a click. A clamshell lid swung up on invisible hinges, revealing a keyboard and screen.

'It's a laptop,' she said. Destrier's look made her wilt.

'There's also your cards.' He pulled a cardboard wallet out of his suit and laid it on the desk. 'Company credit card. There's no maximum, but we do check what you spend. No unlimited personal usage on that one. And this is your card for the building. Swipe it wherever you go. If you're not supposed to go somewhere, it won't let you through. In particular, stay away from the sixth floor. It's off limits.'

He sat on the desk and leaned over her. Ellie pushed her chair back.

'We take security very seriously here. We reserve the option to monitor your computer activity, your e-mails and websites, your phone calls, your comings and goings.'

'Of course,' said Ellie, wondering what they thought she might do.

'All our machines carry software to make sure you don't compromise our security. Even by accident.' He slid a piece of paper across the desk. 'Sign this to say you that you've understood and agree.'

Ellie stared at the paper long enough to look like she'd taken it seriously, then signed.

Luxembourg

By quarter to five, Lemmy had found out what his client wanted to know. He'd sweated so much his bedraggled shirt was like a dishrag. His hair was a mess from where he tugged it when he was thinking, and he could feel a spot swelling on the bridge of his nose. But for what he'd earned that day, it was worth it.

He worked another half an hour, just for good measure,

then packed up his briefcase and left. He found his car in the underground parking at Place des Martyrs and his spirits lifted. A silver Audi, his one indulgence. Not a top-of-the-range model, nothing to arouse the envy or suspicion of his colleagues, but fitted with just about every option in the catalogue. Lemmy thought of it as the down payment on his future, a promise of good things to come.

He turned on the engine and let the air conditioning play over his clammy face. He found the hip flask he kept in the glove compartment and swallowed a mouthful of fifteen-year-old Scotch – another indulgence. He leaned his head against the leather headrest, closed his eyes and let ten speakers-worth of music wash over him. He wouldn't do this again for months, he promised himself. It wasn't worth the stress. And for what this customer was paying him, he wouldn't need to.

A tap at the window undid most of the whisky's effect. His eyes snapped open in terror, then confusion as he saw it was Christine Lafarge.

He fumbled for a switch and lowered the electric window, sliding the hip flask into the door pocket. A blossom of perfume blew in.

'Did I forget something?' *Try to be calm.*

She smiled a straight-toothed smile. 'I wanted to apologise. For being abrupt with you this morning.' She'd bent close to the window. 'I was surprised. We are under so much pressure at the moment.'

'It is the curse of the modern world,' Lemmy agreed.

'I know you were only doing your job.' Her hands rested on the windowsill; her fingertips dangled inside the car, brushing his sleeve. Lemmy began to see the possibility of an unexpected bonus to this job.

'Perhaps I can buy you a drink?'

She gave a throaty laugh. 'I could use one.'

She opened the door and slid into the passenger's seat, smoothing her skirt over her legs so that Lemmy would notice them. She could smell the alcohol on his breath.

She fastened her seatbelt and sank back in the seat. She caught Lemmy sneaking a glance at her cleavage and smiled.

This was going to be easy.

London

Ellie's phone rang at five o'clock. She fumbled to find the right place to press the buttonless plastic to answer it.

'Mr Blanchard's car is waiting for you,' the receptionist told her.

Ellie closed the folder she'd been looking at and grabbed her bag. When she peeked into Blanchard's office he was on the phone, listening intently. He smiled her a goodbye.

Blanchard's car was enormous, a midnight-blue beast that filled most of the narrow alley in front of the bank. A suited chauffeur held the door open for her as she slid onto the white leather. She was almost afraid to get in, a child in a shop full of fragile and expensive things. She saw the winged crest emblazoned with the letter *B* on the steering wheel, and it occurred to her it might stand for Bentley.

'Just joined us, Ma'am?' the driver asked. Ellie squirmed. Nobody had ever called her Ma'am before. She nodded.

'I suppose everybody gets this on the first day.'

She saw his smile in the rear-view mirror. 'Not many, Ma'am.'

'Ellie.'

He took the turn at the end of the alley with practised ease, though it looked to Ellie as if the wall must be halfway into the engine block. As they pulled into the traffic, Ellie stared out of the window, watching the crowds of office workers flow up and down King William Street. Most didn't give the Bentley a second look, or only a grudging glance. Only a boy, about ten, dressed in flannel shorts and a baggy red cap, standing perpendicular to the crowds as he stared with innocent wonder at the powerful car inching past. Ellie waved to him. It seemed somehow inconceivable that children existed in the City. He didn't wave back.

'He can't see you,' the driver explained from the front. 'Tinted glass.'

Ellie sat back, feeling foolish.

The car stopped at the foot of a tower – one of three thrusting up out of the concrete fortress of the Barbican, the city's northern rampart. Ellie scrambled out before the driver could open the door for her, and wondered if it was rude.

'Looks like someone's come to meet you,' he said.

At first Ellie didn't see him – she was looking for a suit, assuming it must be someone from the bank. She only spotted him when he started moving towards her. A brown corduroy jacket and a tab-collared linen shirt, half untucked; wavy dark hair and a five o'clock shadow on his cheeks.

'Doug?'

It came out fiercer than she'd meant. Doug was Oxford, her past, her doubts. She didn't want him there. Not today.

His smile faltered. 'I called your office – your boss gave me the address. I . . . I wanted to apologise.' He gazed at the Bentley and tried to look nonchalant. 'Nice car. Is that part of the package?'

'Not yet.' Ellie reached up and kissed him on the cheek. 'Apology accepted.' Behind him, she could see the driver waiting to give her a set of keys.

'Thirty-eighth floor. You'll find everything you need up there.'

The lift seemed to take a long time to get to the top. Ellie and Doug stood in opposite corners, last night's fight still not forgotten.

'Are you sure you came to apologise?' Ellie asked warily. 'Not to rescue me, or steal me back to Oxford?'

Doug held up his hands in innocence. 'I just wanted to make sure you were OK.' They stepped out of the lift; Ellie fumbled with the keys she'd been given. 'And check out the new executive pad, obviously. I – *wow*.'

The moment Ellie opened the door it was as if someone had conjured the interior of a French chateau into this brutalist tower three hundred feet above London: a symphony of dark woods and heavy fabrics, gilded curlicues and lacquered surfaces. Oil paintings in crazily ornate frames lined the walls like a museum – except one wall, which was all glass. Dusk was falling. The city had begun to prepare for darkness, and a carpet of light stretched as far as Ellie could see. She didn't know London well enough to pick out all the landmarks, but she thought she recognised the Houses of Parliament, Saint Paul's Cathedral.

'Look at this place.' Doug was examining a gilded ebony side table. 'I think this is Louis Quatorze. Genuine seventeenth century. And that chair looks like it came from Versailles.'

Ellie wandered through the apartment in a daze. She didn't dare touch anything. In the bedroom she found a vast bed almost waist high, couched in a walnut frame that might have served as a boat. Swagged fabric hung over the head like a pavilion, while more windows looked out to the east, the turrets of Canary Wharf and the ribbon of the Thames stretching to the dark horizon.

A hand reached around. Ellie stiffened, but it was only Doug. She hadn't heard him on the thick carpet.

He leaned into her neck, nuzzling her. He slid the jacket off her shoulders and reached around, fiddling with the buttons on her thin cotton blouse. He guided her towards the bed.

'Maybe you were right,' he whispered. 'Maybe this isn't so bad.'

IV

Île de Pêche, 1142
The count is still kneeling at the altar, but his head lies several feet away. Tendrils of blood stretch out around him, the body desperate to reclaim its missing flesh. His guards are at the door, but even they seem shocked by what they see. The chapel has become a slaughterhouse.

I think of a boy kneeling before a different altar, a different place very far away. A different world.

How did I come to this?

Wales, 1127
I kneel in front of the bishop. My scalp itches where I had my tonsure shaved this morning; my skin itches from the coarse wool of the cassock they have forced me to wear. The stones on the floor are cold and hard against my knees.

A crowd has come to witness this moment: my brother Ralph and my father, his steward and his vavasours in the front rank, as well as the abbot of Saint David's, who hopes I will bring a portion of my inheritance to his monastery one day.

Behind them stand my mother and my sisters; behind them the servants, serfs, their wives and their children. Fifty or sixty souls, all dependent on my father to settle their disputes, protect their homes and collect their taxes. Not all of them are grateful for it. I can feel their bitter stares like knives at my back as I kneel there. I am their enemy.

I know why this is, though I don't understand it. They are Welshmen, Britons, and I am a Norman. But I was born here and so was my father. I have never set foot in Normandy. I have heard the stories, of course: how Duke William claimed the crown of England from the usurper Harold; how my great-grandfather Enguerrand fought with him at Hastings and slew seventeen Englishmen; how my grandfather Ralph followed the Earl of Clare into Wales and was rewarded with the lands my father now holds. I love these stories of knights and battles. I am forever pestering Brother Oswald, the monk who teaches me, to repeat them. He prefers stories of saints and Jesus.

At this age, it has not occurred to me that there is another side to these stories. That every time my ancestors' swords fall or their lances drive home, they land on the ancestors of the men who now stand glaring at the back of the church.

The bishop wears a ring, a thick gold band with a blue stone. The gold presses into my skin as he lays his hand on my forehead. I stare at the stone and try not to cry. I don't want to become a priest. I want to be a knight, like Ralph. Already, I can spar with a wooden sword and gallop my father's palfrey across the meadow by the river. But knights are expensive: there are horses to buy and keep fed, arms and tack to keep in good repair, squires and grooms to pay to maintain them. Priests are much cheaper. My father says a knight only turns a profit in time of war; a priest has his living every year.

The bishop leans forward. His breath smells of onions.

'You are about to take up a holy office. Do you swear these solemn oaths? To reject the snares of this world and turn yourself to Christ?'

I fight back the urge to look over my shoulder. I know Ralph is watching and I hope he is proud.

'To refrain from shedding blood.'

I ball my hand in a fist to hide the bloodstain. I was out at dawn checking the traps Ralph and I had laid in the forest. We'd caught a woodpigeon; I wrung its neck with my own hands.

'To be chaste.'

I'm happy to swear that, though I don't know what it means. I'm eight years old.

'Peter of Camros, the Church claims you as her own.'

That night, I lie on my mattress between my dog and my brother, and whisper the oaths back to myself. They seem so heavy with meaning. It's the first time I have been treated as an adult. I do not like the path that has been chosen for me, but I promise God I will honour my vows to Him.

I cannot imagine, then, how utterly I will break every one of them.

V

Ellie skipped up the steps. The glass doors with their frosted-glass shields parted to let her through, and it occurred to her whimsically that in a bygone age they would have been considered magic doors. She hadn't got lost this morning, but she was still later than she'd planned. The vast bed in the apartment had proved hard to escape, especially with Doug using all his wiles to sabotage her departure.

She nodded good morning to the receptionist and crossed to the lift. And stopped.

There were no buttons.

'You have to use your card.'

A suited sleeve with gleaming gold cufflinks reached past her and slid a card into a discreet recess beside the lift. Ellie half turned.

'Are you the new girl?'

'Ellie.'

'Delamere.'

She'd already noticed that nobody used first names at

35

Monsalvat – though Delamere looked too young to have picked up the habit. He had sallow skin and dark eyes, with a mouth that tended naturally towards a certain hangdog grin, as if he was embarrassed about something. His dark hair was flecked with grey at the sides, though he couldn't be much older than Ellie.

'Do you work in Mr Blanchard's department?'

He gave a conspiratorial laugh. 'Everyone here works for Blanchard. I'm on the legal side. Very boring.'

They got into the lift together. Delamere pressed the button for the second floor and then, unprompted, the fifth floor for Ellie. She looked at the button above and remembered what Destrier had said. *Stay away from the sixth floor. It's off limits.*

'Who works on the sixth floor?' she asked, trying to be casual.

Delamere seemed to flinch slightly. He fiddled with his tie. 'Monsalvat's a very devolved sort of place. Half the time you've no idea who's doing what, even the man next to you. Drives us mad, but Blanchard insists. Says it's good for security.'

The lift chimed its arrival. He swiped his card again to open the lift doors.

'Security seems to be a big thing here,' Ellie said. 'Are they scared of bank robbers?'

'Blanchard likes to say you can steal more from a bank than its money. An old place like this has plenty worth hiding. Plenty of secrets.' The door was closing. He stuck his arm out to hold it and looked at her, with a strange sadness behind his involuntary grin.

'You don't seem like the sort of girl they usually go for.'

The words hit Ellie like a punch. She felt tears pricking around her eyes, and prayed she wouldn't start crying. That would really finish her. Delamere seemed to realise he'd said something wrong.

'I'm sure you'll do fine,' he said. 'Fine,' he repeated. 'Just – be careful.'

He looked like he wanted to say something else, but the closing doors cut him off. He didn't try to stop them this time.

By the time the lift reached the fifth floor, Ellie had recovered enough composure to believe she wouldn't start sobbing at the first colleague she saw. *Idiot*, she told herself. *Of course you're not like them.*

She still needed another minute before she faced Blanchard. She crossed the empty hall and leaned against the windowsill. The building stood around a central courtyard, like a school or a prison: from the internal window, she could look right down into it. A dove preened itself on the rooftop opposite.

It made her realise something. Pushing her nose against the glass to see down, she counted the floors of the bank. Ground, first, second, third, fourth, fifth – but when she looked up, there was only a flat roof.

No sixth floor.

She shook her head to clear the confusion. *An old place like this has plenty to hide.* She found a tissue in her bag and dabbed her eyes, just to make sure no rogue tears had crept out to betray her. Then she went to find Blanchard.

Blanchard was out. He'd left a note on her desk apologising: a cream notecard with the bank's crest stamped into it. His handwriting was a quaint, Victorian cursive that slanted across the page in spidery lines. The paper had absorbed his scent: when Ellie picked it up to read it she caught a breath of something floral, and a darker, bitter note underneath. Overnight, the stack of files on her desk had grown several inches higher.

She tapped her passcode into the laptop and opened it. Locked, the seam between the lid and the body was all but invisible. There was no brand or manufacturer's mark on the anthracite-black shell – only the smudges of her own finger-prints. She opened the e-mail program, the way Destrier had shown her.

93 new messages.

But I only just started. Apart from Blanchard, she didn't recognise any of the senders.

The door blew open without a knock. A man in a blue suit and a pink shirt barged through and deposited three more inch-thick files on the front of her desk. His eyes were puffy, his cheeks raw-veined from drink. His hair was parted down the middle and swept back, clustered into fronds by the gel.

'Lockthwaite,' he barked. 'I need two copies of each by lunchtime.'

Without elaborating, he spun on his heel and walked out.

Ellie stared at what he'd left, at the wall of folders already barricading her desk, then back to her computer screen.

99 new messages.

She felt the blood rising in her cheeks again. *Calm down*, she told herself. But her pulse only raced faster. *Think.*

The photocopier had its own room down the corridor. It didn't seem to be on; Ellie wasted several vital minutes trying to open it, until she noticed the slot just under the rim. She slid her card in. Red lights flashed on the console; a green glow seeped out from under the lid as the machine growled into life, like a dragon woken in its cave.

Whoever put the file together hadn't meant it to be copied. Most of the papers were stapled together; many were irregular sizes, small notes or flimsy carbons that blew off the copier if Ellie so much as breathed. She had her laptop balanced on the edge of the machine to work on her e-mails, but it was impossible. The copier devoured the paper and spat it out faster than she could keep feeding it. After twenty minutes she'd hardly dented the first file, while rereading the same paragraph of the same e-mail three times over.

'What are you doing here?'

Blanchard stood in the doorway. He had a cigar in his mouth; a small mound of ash at his feet suggested he'd been watching her for some moments. He looked angry.

'Who told you to do this?'

'I think his name was Lockthwaite.'

'Sachervell. Lockthwaite is the client. Can't you read?' Blanchard pointed to the label on the front of the folder. He swept it up one-handed and stormed out of the room. By the time Ellie had grabbed her laptop and followed, he was in an office halfway down the corridor delivering a furious lecture about the proper use of resources. Ellie hung back. A minute later, Blanchard reappeared.

'Come with me.'

Through the open door, she saw the man whose name wasn't Lockthwaite standing behind his desk. His face had grown several shades redder. He shot her a murderous look as she passed.

Blanchard marched her to the lift.

'Many things have changed in our profession, but some unenlightened attitudes persist. They will make things difficult for you; they will see you are a woman and assume you must be a secretary. They are conditioned to think that way: you cannot change it, any more than the mouse can charm a cat. So you must resist them. Force them to accept that they cannot dictate to you. Power is the only language they understand.'

They'd come out in the lobby. Blanchard's car sat waiting outside.

'We're late for the meeting.' He saw Ellie's blank look and gave an exasperated click of his tongue. 'Didn't you read your e-mails?'

Luxembourg

Once, the city had been called the Gibraltar of northern Europe. From the moment in the dark ages when Count Siegfried built his castle on the cliffs above two dizzy ravines, eight centuries of human ingenuity had made it impregnable. Now most of the walls were gone; tourists manned what was left. The city's best defences were the invisible ramparts that protected its banks, complex laws and absolute discretion, hoarding the riches safe inside.

But the ravines remained. Pleasure parks filled the bottom, while traffic thundered overhead across the high Romanesque spans of the Viaduc and the Pont Adolphe. Which was where, on a wet evening in early September, two men walked and argued.

One was a tall man, in a long black coat and a black homburg hat that, even in Luxembourg, was at least forty years out of date. It cast a deep shadow over his face. The other was shorter and rounder, in a shapeless blue mackintosh that did nothing for his figure. He had no hat, and had forgotten his umbrella. The rain slicked his hair against his scalp and ran down the side of his nose like sweat.

'Why did you change the meeting?' the tall man asked.

Lemmy Maartens wiped water from his eyes. He was trembling.

'I thought I was being followed.'

The tall man glanced up and down the long pavement. They

were walking with the flow of traffic, so that the headlights of the passing cars only shone on their backs. A hundred metres back a man was straggling behind them, his face hunched over a sodden map. He wore a white plastic poncho, the sort that tourists buy if they get caught out by the weather. It made him look like a ghost. About twenty metres ahead, a homeless man sat on a piece of cardboard wrapped in a blanket. Otherwise, the bridge was empty.

Lemmy gestured to the man with the map. 'Do you think he's watching us?'

'Don't worry about him.' The tall man quickened his pace. Lemmy glanced over his shoulder again, almost as if he was expecting someone.

'What did you find?'

The question was urgent, verging on desperate. Lemmy, a keen student of human weakness, saw his opportunity.

'The money first.'

The tall man didn't try to argue. He pulled a packet from inside his coat and passed it to Lemmy. A brown envelope – *Jesus*, Lemmy thought, these people had no imagination. He rubbed it between finger and thumb, feeling the thickness of the wad inside.

As a rule, Lemmy preferred electronic transfers. With the Internet, he could conjure money in and out of sight in seconds. Cash was more substantial. But for this amount, it was worth the effort.

They'd come to within a couple of metres of the homeless man. Lemmy stopped and tore open the envelope. If he felt any shame counting so much money in front of a man whose entire wealth sat in a Styrofoam cup by his feet, he didn't show it.

'It's all there,' his companion said. 'Keep moving.' He

glanced back. A hundred metres behind, the figure in the white poncho had stopped to study his map under a streetlight.

'You didn't have to risk your career going into that place,' Lemmy grumbled.

A black minivan with a taxi-company number on the side drew up and stopped on the kerb.

'You look wet,' the driver shouted through the open passenger window. 'You need a ride somewhere?'

'We're fine,' said the man in the hat.

But he wasn't. In the second he was distracted, the van's rear door slid open. Three men in black sweatshirts and black jeans leaped out, straight for him, while a fourth stayed inside and held a gun.

The tall man saw them and acted instantly. He didn't think of trying to fight: he ran straight to the rail and tried to heave himself over the edge. But this had been predicted. Before the man could get over the rail, the tramp had sprung up and wrapped himself around his legs. He clung on; the man kicked and flailed, but it was too late. The men from the van piled in and pulled him down. One took a needle and jabbed it into the side of his neck. He slumped and lay still.

Two of the men carried their victim into the van. Through the open door, Lemmy saw a pair of slim, feminine legs and bright red shoes sitting on the back seat.

The third man picked up the homburg hat off the pavement and tossed it into the car. Then, for the first time, he looked at Lemmy.

'Well done,' he said.

Lemmy stared at him in utter terror. He had a terrifying face, broken in so many places, with a tattoo curling up the back of his neck. A gold stud gleamed in his ear.

'Of course, you didn't see anything.'

Lemmy nodded. He realised he was still holding the open envelope.

'Can I keep this?'

The man shrugged. 'Sure.'

Without warning, strong arms grabbed Lemmy from behind and hugged him tight, pinning his hands to his sides. Before he could draw breath to scream, they dragged him to the edge of the parapet, lifted him up and dropped him over the rail. He fell fifty metres and landed in the concrete canal that was all that remained of the Pétrusse river. The men, including the tramp, drove away in their minivan. The tourist in the white raincape had vanished.

Lemmy's body was discovered half an hour later, by a French businessman jogging through the park. It didn't take long for the police to gather the basic facts: his name, his address, his occupation and the envelope stuffed with five-hundred-euro bills still clutched in his hand. Further investigation added the information that he drove a high-specification German sedan and held documentation for a number of bank accounts in the Cayman Islands, Liechtenstein and Switzerland. The fact that he had visited the Monsalvat bank the day before was noted but not thought relevant. There were no next of kin.

A passing driver came forward to say he might have seen a taxi pulled up, and a gang of men in a brawl on the pavement. But the taxi company in question could prove that none of its drivers had been nearby at the time, and the descriptions of the men were so vague as to be meaningless.

Two days later a small notice in the newspapers reported that Lemmy Maartens, a respected civil servant in the Ministry of Finance, had leaped to his death off the Pont Adolphe. He left no note. The police speculated that he had been under a lot of stress, brought on by the financial crisis and the recent wave of bank failures. Perhaps he felt responsible. He was, his colleagues all agreed, devoted to his work.

VI

Wales, 1128

You can conquer the Welsh, but you can't defeat them. My father says it's because of the land: mounted knights can't pursue the rebels up mountains and through forests, or into the deep marshes. My mother also says it's because of the land – but she doesn't mean it the same way.

My mother is a Breton – which, she says, makes her a cousin to the Britons who plough fields and cut wood for my father. She says Brittany is like Wales, a wild realm on the rim of the world. In these places, the borders between worlds grow thin and permeable; we scuttle across the surface like a spider on a pond. In England and Normandy, rocks are rocks and trees are trees, or they are iron and firewood. In Wales, every rock and tree might hide the door to an enchanted land. Once, when I was playing on the mudflats by the river estuary, I saw a shimmering wall of air, as you get over a fire. Another time, I put my ear to a crack in the rocks and heard laughter far below.

Last August, three of my father's hayricks burned in the

45

field. In October, someone broke into the stable and cut the hamstrings on his warhorse. My father had to slit its throat himself: when he came out of the stable, up to his elbows in blood, it was the only time I ever saw him cry. He blames brigands, but behind his back the servants whisper about the faerie people.

My mother knows many stories of the faeries. Sometimes, when the fire has burned low in the hall and my father has drunk his fill, she takes out her little harp and sings the tale, while I sit by the fire and the dogs lick fat off the hearth. Sometimes we sit together on the grassy bank under the willow by the river. All the ones I like best begin the same way: 'A long time ago, when Arthur was king . . .'

I ask my mother when Arthur was king, but she just frowns and repeats that it was a long time ago. I ask Brother Oswald, who has been teaching me history. Was it before Duke William? Before Alexander? Before King Solomon? I think he will cuff me and tell me another story about Jesus or Saint David, but he chews his reed pen and tells me how Arthur was descended from Aeneas and Brutus; how he lived some six hundred years ago in the time of Saint David, when the Romans had gone and the Normans hadn't yet come. He says he killed a giant on Saint Michael's mount, and grew so powerful he even overthrew Rome. Some men, he whispers, say he is not dead but merely sleeping in a cave, and will come again in Britain's deepest hour of need.

A light comes into Brother Oswald's eyes as he tells this. Then he remembers himself, and sends me back to my declensions.

I sit in the sun and listen to my mother.

'A long time ago, when Arthur was king, a knight went hunting. He spied a white stag and gave chase, following it until he found himself deep in the forest.

'Suddenly, on the evening air, he heard a scream that made his horse rear up in fright. He spurred through the trees, and presently came out in a leafy glade. A hawthorn grew there, and tied to it stood a maiden, the loveliest he had ever seen. She wore a plain white shift and a plain white dress, nothing else. Her golden hair was so fair even Isolde the Blonde would have looked like a Moor beside her.'

I stir. 'Who was Isolde the Blonde?'

My mother shushes me. 'I will tell you that story another day. When you're older.

'The knight drew his sword to cut her free. But the moment he dismounted, the ground trembled with the approach of rushing hooves. The lady groaned. "Now you must flee," she warned him. "That noise is Sir Maliant, the wicked knight who holds me prisoner. If he finds you here he will surely kill you."

'"Upon my honour, I have never fled from any man," said the knight. He remounted his horse and spurred towards his enemy. Their lances bent like bows and shattered; they drew their swords, laying about each other with such fury that wood splintered, iron split and both horses were killed. The knight pummelled his opponent until every lace of his armour was broken. At last, he struck off his helmet and knocked him to the ground.

'"Mercy," his enemy pleaded.

'But the damsel demanded his head, and the knight obeyed. His blow fell hard; the head flew out onto the heath and the body crumpled.

'Heedless of his wounds, the knight approached and cut the cord that bound the lady.

'"Thank you, Sir Knight," she said. "You have saved me from a grievous fate. What reward would you have?"

'"Only a token, and perhaps a kiss."

'She laughed. "I will give you better than that." She took his hand and led him around the back of the tree. "This is what the wicked knight sought from me."

'The good knight saw nothing. But the damsel reached into a hollow in the tree and pulled open the bark like a curtain. Within, the knight beheld a tree-root stair twisting down into the earth.

'"This is my realm," said she. "Come down, and I will give you your full reward."

'But the knight delayed, for he saw that the lady was an enchantress, and he feared what might befall him in her kingdom.

'"Have no fear, Sir Knight. You may depart whenever you choose. All you must promise is that whatever you find, you must leave behind when you return. There is a great treasure in my castle, and many are the thieves who have tried to take it."

'Then the knight swore, and eagerly followed her down the twisting stair. And he was not disappointed, for the lady's kingdom was just as she had said. She had a fair castle with a great hall and galleries, and every room was piled with treasure. Servants came to dress his wounds; they served wine in golden cups, and a haunch of venison cooked with hot pepper. And the knight thought there had never been a place so wondrous.

'He stayed there a year and a day. At night he feasted and took his pleasure with the lady, and in the daytimes he hunted and never came home empty-handed, for she had hounds who never lost the scent, and a bow whose arrows always hit their mark.

48

'But eventually he grew weary of this constant leisure, and thought he would return to his own world. And as he took his leave, he spied a goblet of fine, pure gold, set with precious stones. And though it was small and plain next to the other treasures in the castle, yet he thought it was the most beautiful piece he had ever seen.

'"She has so much treasure here she will not miss this one small cup," he said to himself. "And they will never believe me at Arthur's court if I do not take back some proof of where I have been."

'So he slipped the cup inside his tunic and stole out of the castle. He climbed the twisting stair, hurrying until he reached the top. He could see sunlight through the hole in the tree and the green leaves beyond. For the first time in a year he could smell the air of our world.

'But he had forgotten the cup in his tunic. The moment he set foot on the threshold of our world, the earth began to tremble. The jaws of the tree snapped shut; the tree-roots withered to dust, and he fell back to the ground. And when he limped back to the castle, the towers were torn down and the rooms empty; the treasure had vanished.

'The lady received him in her great hall. Her eyes were like drops of ice, her skin white as bone. "You have broken your oath," she told him. "Now you can never leave my kingdom." And she cast him into a dungeon, and whatever he ate tasted like ash in his mouth, and whatever he drank never slaked his thirst.'

'Go on,' I say. 'What happened next? How did the knight escape?'

My mother puts down her harp and folds her hands in her skirt. 'He never did. He had broken his promise, and he could not return to this world.'

49

I haven't told this story as well as my mother told it. Perhaps because I don't like it. Surely, I think, there is always a way back?

VII

London

Ellie's first week at the bank felt like the longest of her life. On Friday night she ordered a pizza and ate it in bed, trying not to drip grease or tomato sauce on the eighteenth-century woodwork. She slept for twelve hours and was still tired when she woke. She stayed in bed with her laptop and her phone, grinding down the week's backlog and watching the clouds hang over London. Doug was at a conference in Nottingham, which had seemed like a pity when he arranged it, but was now a relief.

At four in the afternoon, she realised she was starving. She got out of bed, reluctantly, and pulled on an old sweatshirt and a pair of jeans. After five days of skirts and stiff jackets, all she wanted was comfortable clothes. She took the lift thirty-eight floors down and went out, surprised by the smell of the outside air. The city had become a ghost town. The streets were empty, the office buildings dark and blinded. It took her half an hour to find a corner shop that was open, where she bought a box of cereal and some milk, and a selection of crisps and chocolate.

She'd meant to go further, to walk down to the Thames or St Paul's, but the empty city frightened her. She retreated to her flat, skulking past the concert-goers who had begun to gather outside for the Barbican's evening performance.

By Sunday evening, Ellie had fought back her e-mails to half a dozen outstanding. She'd written one report on the privatisation of the Government's share in a bank, and another on a Belgian conglomerate that wanted to acquire a cement company. She'd learned a whole new vocabulary, using words like *leverage* and *synergy* and *capital optimisation* promiscuously. She felt like an impostor, a student bluffing an exam in a language she barely understood. And the next morning it would start all over again.

There were only two files on Ellie's desk on Monday. She still had no idea who put them there – Blanchard? the secretaries? – or how they knew so accurately what she would need for the day. Even before she took off her coat, she skimmed the summary pages. She'd learned very quickly it was important to have at least a vague idea what was in your in tray.

She'd arrived early, fighting her way through the Autumn rain. Doug was coming down that evening, and she wanted to be back in good time for him. She'd bought two fillet steaks from the butcher in Leadenhall Market and spent half an hour on the Internet finding out how to cook them. They'd cost thirty pounds, which in Oxford had been a week's food budget.

The building was almost empty, but when she went into Blanchard's office to drop off her reports his jacket was already draped over the back of his chair. She could smell his scent in the air, mingled with the ever-present cigar smoke. A folder lay on his desk, red leather with gold writing stamped in the cover.

Leather bands tied it shut, and the knots had been covered in something that looked like dried blood. Sealing wax?

Ellie read the gold lettering upside down. *LAZARUS*.

'What are you doing?'

Blanchard's voice, behind her and sharp. Ellie spun around and tried not to look guilty. His hard jaw softened into a wolfish smile. 'You're dripping all over my carpet.'

He advanced into the room until he was almost touching her. He reached out and pushed a damp lock of hair back behind her ear.

'You look like a drowned mouse.'

'I didn't have an umbrella.' The rain hadn't looked so bad from the thirty-eighth floor, but it had wormed its way through her clothes almost as soon as she stepped out the door. 'I couldn't find a bus.'

'Have you heard of such a thing as a taxi?' Blanchard sounded appalled. Ellie shrank: it had never occurred to her.

Darting around, her eyes fixed on a blemish on Blanchard's bone-white shirt cuff. She tried not to stare, but Blanchard's eagle gaze missed nothing.

'What?'

'Nothing.' Embarrassed. 'There's a spot of blood on your cuff.' No response. 'I wondered if you knew.'

'A shaving cut.' He didn't look. 'Listen, Ellie. Appearances matter in our profession. The apparel proclaims the man. I know it will take you time to learn the intricacies of this work. I expect it. But please do not let down this company by your presentation.' A cold smile. 'I think we pay you enough that you can afford an umbrella. Maybe even a taxi.'

Despite the damp clothes clinging to her skin, Ellie felt prickles of heat all over her body. 'I didn't think I'd be meeting clients today.'

'You never know what the day will bring.' Blanchard ran his eyes down her, stripping off her sodden clothes with his gaze until she felt entirely naked. 'There is a shop just off King William Street, a gentlemen's outfitters but they also cater for women. Take your credit card and buy something dry to change into, everything you need. I will see your statement. If you spend less than a thousand pounds, I shall be very disappointed with you.'

Ellie nodded mutely.

'And be back within the hour. We have a meeting to attend. The files are on your desk.'

Ellie read the files standing in front of a mirror, while a stooped old man with a tape measure around his neck hemmed and pinned until he was satisfied. The shop next door sold leather goods: on a reckless impulse, she went in and bought a new pair of shoes and a new handbag. Let Blanchard complain about *that* if he wanted.

The Rosenberg Automation Company occupied a dilapidated factory somewhere east of Woolwich, near the river. Ellie arrived looking like a thousand pounds. Part of her felt sick when she thought how much she'd spent on this single outfit; part of her was giddy with the extravagance. And the clothes were immaculate. Every time the skirt's silk lining brushed against her legs, or the jacket's smooth seam hugged her shoulder, confidence surged through her.

From skimming the file, she knew that the company had been founded in the 1930s by a Russian émigré Jew. It manufactured control systems for industrial machinery. Ellie didn't know what that meant, but she knew it didn't matter. *They make baked beans, they make space satellites, it's only details*, Blanchard had told her. *They have capital, they have debts, they have shareholders and liabilities. All that matters is they have a price.*

In this case the shareholder was an old man, son of the founder and no less Russian in his obstinacy. After three hours locked in a meeting room, drinking black tea out of Styrofoam cups, they were no closer to finding his price than when they'd walked in. When it came to negotiations Blanchard seemed driven by an animal spirit, a hunger for the deal that cajoled and encouraged, threatened and harried the opposition towards conceding. At times he would jump out of his chair and prowl around the room; other times he leaned forward on the table and listened with half-closed eyes as the old man banged his fist and repeated himself for the umpteenth time. But the old man soaked up the pressure and never flinched, while his son – a sullen, dark-eyed forty-something – sat by his side and glared.

'The patrimony is the pillar of the family,' Rosenberg senior said yet again. 'It is a father's duty to protect it. We have rationalised our workforce, invested in new equipment, consolidated our supply chain, everything the consultants tell us. We are an old company, but everything is state of the art. This is how we have always been and this is what my son will inherit.'

Blanchard was in a foul temper when they left. 'This patrimony is garbage,' he raged. 'Did you see his son? He would sell the company, take the money, in five seconds if he had the chance. But he is a coward, he does not dare tell this to his father.'

Ellie flipped through the file. 'The old man must be almost eighty. How much longer can he hold on?'

'To life? Too long.'

'I didn't mean . . .'

'If this deal does not happen in the next two weeks, the logic will no longer exist and the client will pull out. We will lose the fee, the dozens of hours we have already invested in it. And all because of a frightened child and a stubborn old man.'

'The old man's frightened too.' She surprised herself by saying it out loud, though she was sure it was true. She'd grown up surrounded by fear. Fear of losing your job, your house, your dignity. She knew the signs, the false pride and chippy bravado, the darkness in their eyes.

'Frightened of what?' A stillness overtook Blanchard. 'His son?'

'A vulnerability.' Ellie stared at the back of the driver's seat and thought furiously. 'Not his son – he knows he can control him. Something in the business. Every time we got close to discussing it he closed us down.'

'Find it.' Suddenly Blanchard was alive again, feeding off the hope she offered. 'Pull this company apart, look for anything we missed. Find it, and give it to me by Wednesday.'

Back at the office, Ellie switched off her mobile phone and hid from her e-mails. She pulled up everything she could find on the company: their accounts, their customers, their products. She dug out the notes from her course and looked for all the telltale signs she'd learned: underperforming divisions, foreign subsidiaries bleeding cash, investments gone wrong. There was nothing. Rosenberg managed his company as conservatively as his father.

We have rationalised our workforce, invested in new equipment, consolidated our supply chain, everything the consultants tell us. There'd been bitterness in his voice, the shame of a proud man being told how to run his business. But also something else.

The world outside grew dark. The lights in the great office

towers she could see through her window began to blink off. Numbers swam in front of Ellie's eyes.

And then she found it. One line in the accounts, nothing more. Not even definite – just a suggestion, the end of a thread that she might unravel.

A discreet knock broke her concentration. She looked up, annoyed, but it was only the night porter.

'I tried to ring, but your phone was off,' he apologised. 'There's a man downstairs to see you. Says you were supposed to meet him an hour ago.'

Doug. Ellie swore under her breath. She'd completely forgotten. 'Tell him I'll be right down.'

She gathered up the files and put them in her bag. She'd have to do more work after dinner, though she knew Doug would be cross. She passed Blanchard's office and saw his light was still on, though when she tried the door it was locked.

Doug was waiting in the lobby. Ellie took one look at his face and knew he was furious.

'I'm so sorry.' She threw her arms around him and kissed him on the lips to show she meant it. 'Big project.'

'No problem.' He was trying to be gracious, though he couldn't hide the scowl on his face. He looked her up and down, trying to work something out. 'You look nice.'

'I bought a new outfit.' It was already beginning to feel like hers, though she wouldn't tell him how much it had cost. 'Let's go.'

She put her arm in his and squeezed against him. They didn't speak much. Doug was still angry; Ellie's mind was still deep in the books of the Rosenberg Automation Company.

They'd just reached the main road when she realised she'd left the steaks in the fridge on the fifth floor.

'I've got to go back. I've left our supper at the office.'

'We'll get something on the way.'

'No.' *A thousand pounds on a suit and I'm worried about thirty quid's worth of beef.* 'It's supposed to be special. Just wait here.'

She hurried back, her heels clicking on the pavement. An unmarked white van had pulled up outside the bank; she just glimpsed two men in black jeans and black coats manhandling a large box, as big as a coffin, through the doors. She hesitated. For a moment she imagined it was a bank robbery in progress. But people didn't rob investment banks, and when she reached the lobby the night porter was safe behind his desk.

'What was that that just arrived?' she asked while she waited for the lift.

The porter studied his crossword and didn't meet her eye. 'Delivery for Mr Blanchard.'

But when she looked at the old-fashioned dial above the lift to see where it had gone, the needle was pointing at the sixth floor.

VIII

Wales, 1129

My home is a castle. Not like the ones in Pembroke or Caernarvon, with their stone walls and high donjons. Our castle is mostly mud: an earth rampart topped with a palisade, ringing the compound of mud-and-wood buildings inside. There is a thatched barn and a thatched hall, and it is hard to tell them apart. In winter the grassy banks trap the rain and turn our courtyard into a swamp. My father calls it our moat; my mother tells us the story of a knight who grew up in a lake.

That spring, my father hires a Flemish engineer to build a watchtower. He sharpens the stakes in the palisade, and fills the gaps where the livestock have knocked them down in the winter. There have been disturbances again: a man was killed in Brandennog. Nobody believes that will be the end of it. The Welsh love their honour and they love fighting. Ralph says we'll be safe in our castle, but my father looks grim. He says that when you keep behind castle walls, your enemies know where to find you.

I think: if our sheep can break through the palisades, what would the Welsh do?

It often rains in Wales, but in my memory it is always the last day of spring. My father and Ralph were away last night and haven't returned; Brother Oswald has been called away to his monastery, and I have taken my horse into the forest. I think I might visit the fields by the chapel, where the harrowers are working, but I am in no hurry. The trees are in flower and the shrubs in leaf; a gentle sun dapples the lush meadows. I get down from my horse and walk barefoot through the grass, which is green and velvet against my skin. I slip off my horse's bridle and let him graze freely.

I have brought a javelin with me, and I amuse myself throwing it at knots in the trees. My brother teases me that the javelin is a Welsh weapon, ignoble. Ralph says the only way to fight with a spear is couched under your arm. But Ullwch, my father's herdsman, has been teaching me, and I can knock a gamecock off its branch with one throw.

I don't aim at birds that morning. Their songs light up the forest; my heart leaps to hear them. I don't want to spoil it with bloodshed. Each throw takes me further from home, but I don't mind. I can find my way back, and my horse is so docile he won't stray far.

A noise echoes through the trees – a strange staccato clatter like drums. I follow the sound, clutching my javelin and crouching low. As I draw closer, I can hear the high ring of metal, like bells or cymbals. I know from my mother's stories that the faerie folk love music, and I wonder if this might be them.

I peer over a rotting tree stump and see them: five knights, helmed and armed, riding through the forest. They aren't faeries, though the way the sun flashes on their armour makes them look like angels. Nor is there music. They're riding in a trackless place: the oak and hornbeam branches slap their armour, their lances knock against their shields, the steel rings of their hauberks jangle and chime together. They're a splendid sight. I ache with the longing to be a knight.

I almost hail them, but something makes me hold back. Why are they riding so far from the road? Why are they armed as if for war? I press myself into the moist earth. With my javelin and my buckskin cloak I look like a small Welshman, and there are many stories of knights ambushed on the road. I don't want them to mistake me for an enemy.

The knights pass by. Behind them, a company of men creep through the trees. In their brown leather hauberks and grey-green tunics, they're almost invisible. They don't speak or laugh, as men on the road usually do. Some carry bows, and some spears or axes – but the blades are uncovered, and the bows strung. They mean to use these weapons soon. As I watch their progress I realise they're following the stream.

I know where that stream goes. It flows to my father's castle.

I crawl, then I run, then I ride. Well before I reach the house, I know it's too late. I can see the smoke rising from the thatched roofs – my father said they were no good for a castle. The watchtower hasn't saved us. When I get to the brow of the hill and look out, to the open plain and the sea shimmering behind the smoke, the battle's already lost. The knights have surprised us utterly. The gates stand open, and the defenders I can see have had no time to arm. Some of them are fighting with rakes and wood-axes; several already lie dead. One of them has a sickle in his hand and is using it to fend off a mounted knight. With a lurch, I realise it's my father.

My old mare is no warhorse. I jump off and run down the hill, sliding and tripping on the uneven ground. No one sees me coming – or, if they do, they think I'm one of them. I cross the bridge over the stream and enter the gate unmolested. The smoke stings my eyes. The battle must nearly be over – some of the foot-soldiers have already turned to plunder – but in the far corner, under the pilings of the watchtower, there's still resistance. Two of the mounted knights are circling a figure who's trying to hold them off with a billhook.

It's Ralph.

I run towards them. Ralph doesn't see me. He lunges at one of the knights who blocks the blow with his shield and chops the billhook out of Ralph's hand. The other darts forward. He stabs with his spear, and Ralph collapses in the mud.

I scream; the knight turns, and the moment I see his face I let fly my javelin.

But I'm only ten years old, and though I'm accurate I'm not strong yet. The javelin sticks in his shield like an arrow. He laughs, pulls it free and drops it in the mud. He walks his horse towards me, not knowing whether to spear me on his lance or just trample me into the ground. I grab a smouldering brand that was once a cruck beam and swipe it in front of me.

The other knight rides up and touches his captain's arm.

'Look at his head.' He's seen my tonsure. He wheels his horse to face his captain. 'It's a sin to kill a priest.'

'And folly to leave a son alive.' The captain is a huge man, taller than the roof of the hall – or so it seems to my ten-year-old imagination. He wears a chain ventail laced on to his helmet so I can't see his face; his helmet puts his eyes into shadow. I stare at him unblinking. I've heard that if you see the man who kills you, you haunt him ever afterwards as a ghost.

It's only afterwards that I realise he was speaking in French.

At the time, I don't notice. The captain is deciding whether to kill me. His horse paws the ground. Warhorses are not bred to stand still in battle.

Somewhere in the distance a horn blows. I don't know who has sounded it, but it speaks to the captain. He pulls his own horn from his saddle and repeats the call. Around me, I sense the tide of the battle ebbing.

The captain pricks his spurs without warning. The horse springs forward and thunders towards me – I know I should jump out of the way, but I can't move. Perhaps the greater part of me wants to die. The ground trembles under my feet, as if the earth is opening itself to receive me. I close my eyes and wait for death.

And then the ground is still and the horse is behind me. I haven't moved. I look down, and realise I'm still holding the brand. At the last moment, the horse must have swerved away from the fire. Whether the knight chose to spare me, or whether he missed his opportunity, I'll never have the chance to ask. If I ever see him again I'll kill him on sight.

The other knight rides by. He doesn't want to kill me, but as he passes he swings the butt of his spear into my ribs, knocking me back onto the ground. By the time I get to my feet, the battle's over.

I stagger to the gate and see the departing raiders streaming back across the bridge with our livestock, my father's horses, whatever bits and pieces of our household they can carry. One has a duck under his arm; another is carrying a stack of our silver plates as if he's just cleared them from the table. A goblet wobbles on top of the pile.

My mother runs after them, screaming a cry that tears open my soul. She catches up with the knights at the head of the bridge. One of them turns; he makes a movement I can't see, and my mother collapses to the ground. She looks as if she's fainted, but she'll never get up. My father is dead, run through his thighs with a lance and then beheaded. My brother Ralph died beside him. Wandering through the ashes, I see the crows and rooks coming to pick out his eyes. I run towards them in a fury, but I'm so feeble that day they barely move. They flutter onto a broken plough and watch, waiting for their chance. There are no buildings where I can hide Ralph's body, so I dig his grave right there.

The Welsh love their feuds, as ready to avenge a hundred-year-old insult as one suffered this morning. They're vindictive, bloodthirsty and violent. Perhaps, living among them, I've learned something of their ferocity, for now I have sworn revenge.

I am the oldest son now. Knighthood is my right, and my duty.

IX

East London

A fog hung over London that morning. The streetlamps were still lit, casting a false dawn over the cobbled alleys and brick warehouses. If not for the lights of the burglar alarms winking from their gables, it might have been a hundred years ago.

Ellie stood waist deep in boxes and wished she'd worn gloves. The rain the day before had turned the cardboard to pulp, which came away in long strips when she touched it. The skip stank of damp and urine; the ground squelched underfoot. On the wall above, a scarred sign advertised the Rosenberg Automation Company.

Delicately, as if she were handling medieval parchments and not the refuse in a back alley behind a factory, she peeled the boxes apart to find the names written on them. She wrote them down on a pad of paper. Some had telephone numbers or web addresses, and she wrote those down too with shivering, sticky fingers.

When she was done, she clambered out of the skip and went round to the café across the street from the factory entrance. A

Chinese woman brought her greasy eggs and coffee while she watched the morning shift arrive. Some of the workers came in to get breakfast or a cup of tea, and she listened carefully to their conversation. If any of them had seen her the day before, they didn't connect her with the young woman who'd arrived in the Bentley and the thousand-pound suit. That morning, Ellie had scraped her hair back into the tightest ponytail she could manage, and put on an old tracksuit she hadn't touched since she left Newport. She wore no make-up. She wondered if this was how she'd have looked if she'd never left home, never gone to Oxford, never written an essay for the Spenser Prize and never come to the attention of Vivien Blanchard. *All I need is the baby*, she thought.

She sat there most of the morning, pretending to read the *Sun* and observing the delivery vans come and go. At eleven o'clock she drained her last cup of coffee and found a bus to take her west. She showered at her flat and tried to scrub the dirt from under her fingernails. She looked longingly at the new clothes from the day before: would it be wrong to wear them two days in a row? She was sure Blanchard would notice.

'I wondered if you would join us this morning,' he said, when she finally reached the office. It was half-past twelve and he looked angry. Ellie didn't care.

'I've got it,' she announced. 'Rosenberg. *We have consolidated our supply chain*, he said, remember? They went too far. There's a component in their products, a logic board, and they only have one supplier. They're completely dependent on them.'

Blanchard leaned back in his chair and drew on his cigar. Ellie already recognised the trick: to lure you on with

66

indifference, ready to snap back at a moment's notice. 'How do you know this?'

'The accounts. Last year they spent a quarter less on components than the year before, but their sales stayed constant. I went down to the factory and looked around. There are only two companies in the world that make these logic boards, and only one of them has boxes going into that factory.'

Blanchard stared at the painting on the wall, at the helpless damsel tied to the tree.

'They can insure against supply-chain disruption.'

'Their premiums haven't changed.' Ellie could hardly control her excitement. 'The old man hasn't told them. He's driving without insurance and praying he doesn't get in an accident. I made a few phone calls.' Pretending to be a buyer from a rival firm, trembling with the deceit and the fear of getting caught. 'It would take him six months to arrange a new supplier, and the business doesn't have the cash to survive that long.'

She stopped talking and realised she was shaking. For the first time, she began to understand the energy that drove Blanchard.

'And you propose . . .?'

'Buy the supplier as well. It's owned by a private equity firm who are sitting on a lot of losses. They'd bite your hand off. Then merge the two companies and make the business properly viable.'

Blanchard knitted his fingers together and stared at her, as if she were a work of art he was slowly coming to appreciate. His cigar burned untouched in the ashtray.

'Ellie, this is good. Very good indeed. Our client will be delighted when I tell him.'

When I *tell him.* Ellie tried not to look disappointed. Blanchard saw it anyway.

'I am not trying to steal your glory, Ellie. Not at all. But I cannot spare you. I need to send you on an assignment straight away. There is a company in Luxembourg that one of our clients wishes to acquire a stake in. It is a complex arrangement and there are other bidders. At the moment we are performing due diligence. I want you to dig through their files and see if you can find anything that would affect the value of the company, anything they are trying to hide from us.'

In Luxembourg? What would she tell Doug? 'When do I leave?'

Blanchard consulted his watch. 'A car will take you to the airport in ten minutes. You are booked into the Sofitel. Not the best hotel in Luxembourg, I am afraid, but it is where the other bidders are staying. Perhaps you can get to know them. I'm sorry there is no time to pack. Buy whatever you need at the airport, or when you get there. Our local manager is a woman called Christine Lafarge. She can help you.'

Ellie turned to go. Halfway out the door she remembered something.

'Why does the Rosenberg deal have to be completed so quickly? That was the one thing I couldn't work out.'

Blanchard smiled. 'I am glad there are some secrets we can keep from you, Ellie. In a month, the Government will announce an inquiry into the possibility of building a new freight distribution terminal in Woolwich. Major infrastructure investment. The Rosenberg factory will double in value. Six months later, the Government will decide in favour and it will double in value again.'

He sounded so certain it would happen, as if he could lift the veil and peer into the future at will. Ellie remembered the ministerial Jaguar she'd seen outside the bank on the day of her interview.

The adrenaline was draining out of her; guilt had begun to set in. She thought of the old man's stubbornness, the weight of the generations on his shoulders. 'I suppose it'll be good for the business,' she said hopefully.

Blanchard stubbed out his cigar. 'Very good for business.'

Three hours later Ellie landed in Luxembourg. It was hard to believe the day had started waist-deep in rotting cardboard. She breezed through immigration, had no bag to wait for, and walked straight past the man in the arrivals hall holding a sign with her name on it. He had to run to catch up with her.

'This way, please.'

He led her out the front, where a long black Mercedes sat carelessly parked across a pair of double-yellow lines. A woman slid out of the back seat. Slim, elegant and agelessly beautiful, in a grey Chanel suit and diamond earrings, she held Ellie by the shoulders and kissed her on both cheeks.

'Christine Lafarge – welcome. Vivian has told me all about you. He speaks very highly. Your journey was not tedious? Air travel is such a bore these days.'

It was the second time in her life Ellie had been on a plane – and the first that included free food and drink, let alone an executive lounge and dedicated check-in. She said it had been fine, and watched Luxembourg glide past the window as the car headed for the city.

'I am sorry this is very unexpected. The work is going so slowly, and today one of my team has disappeared – *pouf* – off to a new job. Vivian has told you the situation?'

'I read the file on the plane.' Talhouett Holdings, a mining and chemicals concern. The Luxembourg government held a

69

stake which it was trying to divest. Two bidders had been shortlisted, and were now frantically combing through the records trying to uncover any dirty laundry before they finalised their offers. There were two weeks to go.

They crawled through the outskirts of the city, a long strip of square apartment blocks and neon signs. Ellie had expected something grander.

'There wasn't much in the file about the bidder,' she said tentatively.

'Groupe Saint-Lazare. They are our biggest client, both here and across the company. They are also a shareholder in Monsalvat, so there is much pressure on us for success.'

At last they were approaching the heart of the city. The street widened into a grand boulevard lined with handsome neoclassical buildings, then swung along the edge of a vast ravine filled with trees. Ellie could see houses spilling down the steep slopes of the gorge, as if the city could no longer contain itself. Across its depths, glass office blocks faced vast stone bastions, impossibly high. The setting sun shone off the ramparts and cast them in a fiery, medieval light.

The car dropped Ellie outside the Sofitel. A porter appeared to take her luggage, but all she had was a black shoulder bag she'd bought at the airport with a few toiletries and a change of underwear.

'Vivian said you had no time for baggage.' Christine clicked her tongue. 'This is my fault. Tomorrow I will show you some shops where you can buy clothes.' She gave Ellie an appraising, motherly stare. 'I think they will be very good on you. But now, I am sure you are tired after your journey. My number is in your phone if you need anything. I hope the hotel is not disagreeable.'

If Ellie hadn't had the Barbican flat to compare it to, she'd have thought it was the most perfect room she'd ever seen. The bed alone was wider than her old bedroom; the towels in the marble bathroom were almost as big as the sheets. She ordered a gin and tonic from room service, shutting her eyes to the price, and went out on the balcony. Her room looked straight across the ravine to the old city perched on its plateau. She could see spires, and the turrets of the ducal palace, with the green waves of a forest rippling behind. It looked like a fairy tale.

The beauty of it made her feel lonely. She thought of Doug. She'd tried to ring him before she left, but he'd been in the library, his phone switched off. With a pang of guilt, she realised he didn't even know she was in Luxembourg. She got her phone and hesitated. Unlimited calls, Destrier had said. Did that include calls from abroad?

It didn't matter: Doug's phone was still off. The library stayed open until eight – nine in Luxembourg – and Doug was quite capable of staying until it closed without coming up for breath. It was something they'd had in common.

She undressed and ran herself a bath. The gin had warmed her blood; she felt drowsy. She'd call Doug in an hour or two. She closed her eyes and let the hot water cover her.

Six storeys down and half a mile distant, the Mercedes prowled along the Boulevard de la Pétrusse. Christine Lafarge sat in the back, upright in the deep leather, and spoke softly into her phone.

'She has arrived. She seems very sweet, Vivian; I can see why you like her so much. But are you sure she is suitable?'

She listened while Blanchard summarised the Rosenberg Automation deal. She smiled.

'Perhaps your little kitten has claws. Did you get my package?'

71

'Destrier has him on the sixth floor.'

'I hope he gets what he wants.'

'He is very thorough. But be careful, Christine. There will be others. Watch Ellie closely.'

X

Normandy, 1132

I lie on my mattress and listen to the night. I hurt all over. My arm aches from practising my sword strokes, and my chest and shoulders from being practised upon. My hands are raw from cleaning other men's armour, working the bristles of my brush into the thin holes between the rings. I smell of sweat, oil, blood and straw.

It's been three years since I crossed the sea, puking into the bilge as the storm battered us. I've taken service as a squire in the household of Guy de Hautfort. He's my uncle's cousin: my uncle arranged that I should come here to learn the skills of a knight. There are half a dozen of us, some from England, some from Normandy. I think Guy is a good man, but he has little concern for us. We're thrown together like a litter of whelps, to snarl and chase and bite each other until we've found our places.

I'm not happy here. When I arrived, the other boys teased me for my accent and my tonsure. They called me 'monk' and 'Welshman'; they stole my food and threw my clothes in the

73

latrine. I cried a lot in those first months. Now I've learned to hide my feelings. Even when I'm naked, I have my armour.

I knew the history of the Normans before I came here: how they conquer everywhere they go like a plague. First their own duchy, then Sicily, England, Antioch. Now that I'm in their heartland, I understand why. There are no safe havens in Normandy: their entire kingdom is a frontier. There are Bretons to the west, Angevins and Poitevins to the south, French to the east and Flemings in the north. Hautfort is in the north, a particularly troublesome region near Flanders. It breeds hard men. Guy de Hautfort is a squat, barrel-chested man, a flint protruding from the chalky Norman soil. He sparks easily if struck.

Guy's seneschal is called Gornemant. His arms are a quartered shield, each a different colour, like a fool's coat, so we call him the jester. It's ironic: he's a grim, stern man who never smiles. His beard is grey as steel, and his eyes as hard. He rode with Duke Robert and the Army of God on crusade; he was there when Jerusalem fell. We often beg him to tell us those stories, but he never does. His face stiffens and he blinks, as if a speck of that desert dust is still lodged in his eye.

Gornemant takes charge of our instruction. Day after day, he teaches us when to rein in the horse and when to prick him with our spurs; how to hold the shield so that it rests on the horse's neck and how to fewter a lance so that it doesn't glance off the enemy. He watches our swordplay and tells us how we would have fared with real weapons: this blow would barely have scratched his arm, that one would have stuck him through or taken off his head. Very rarely, he lets us gallop through the orchard and tilt at the bladders he has strung from the apple trees, or crouch in the branches and try to leap on to a passing horse. These are my favourite days. For the rest, we practise on each other. We wear quilted cloth armour, but I think its only benefit is to mimic the cramping effect of chain mail.

If it were only practice at arms, I might enjoy it more. But there are other duties. My lord Guy must be dressed and undressed, armed and disarmed; he needs his food served, his meat sliced, his cup filled. I have to fight even to win the right to perform these chores – all the squires want the privilege, to attract his attention. You must be first outside his bedroom door in the morning, the first to his stirrup when he rides in, last to leave the great hall at night. Then you must attend to your own chores: sew up the tears in the cloth armour and try and stuff more rags inside, hoping it will hurt less tomorrow; wash clothes; sweep the grate. The other squires have servants of their own, but my uncle says there is no money for servants for me. He has my father's castle to rebuild, after all. I think he means to build it in stone.

When I lie in my bed, I tell myself stories to get to sleep. My adversary is always the same – the black knight as tall as a house. In my stories I meet him in a glade, in a waste forest, a withered heath: I shatter his lance, break his shield, dent his armour and finally cut off his head with a single blow and mount it on a stake.

I always defeat him. But he returns in my dreams, and there he has the upper hand.

Guy has a son called Jocelin, two years older than me. If he wasn't there, I'd be less unhappy. Guy may be as cold and hard as quenched steel, but his son is still in the crucible, hot as the fire that surrounds him. His mood changes with the wind, the same way iron flushes and pales under the bellows. You touch him at your peril.

Indisputably, Jocelin is the leader of our pack of dogs. Like all leaders, he affirms his power by exercising it on the weakest – me. He encourages the other boys to play pranks on me. One night he hid a rat in my bed. Another time, when I'd spent two hours painting a boar on one of Guy's shields, he walked by and tipped the bowl of paint across it so that my work was ruined. If I achieve anything, a few words from him can make it feel worthless. If I fail, which I do often, I never hear the end of it.

I hate all the other boys, but I hate Jocelin the most.

My one solace, in my few spare moments, is reading. It's something else they tease me for. Guy's chaplain is supposed to instruct us in the rudiments of reading and writing: most of the boys ignore him, or threaten to practise their swordplay on him. I have no need of him – I'm already more literate than I'll ever need to be as a knight – but I still seek him out. He gives me books. Not prayer books and breviaries, but proper stories. One day, when I've saved him from a cruel prank that Jocelin was planning to play, he rewards me with a particularly rare book. The pages have been worn thin by many hands, the binding's frayed and one of the gatherings has come un-stitched, but the words are like honey on my tongue. The author is called Ovid, and the stories are fantastic concoctions of myth and wonder. I wonder how I have lived this long and never heard them, why they are not as common as water. I think even my mother didn't know them.

One afternoon, I'm lying on my mattress reading when Jocelin comes in. The story's captivated me: I don't notice him enter until suddenly the book is snatched out of my hands, tearing the corner of the page. I leap up, outraged, but Jocelin's already running out the door. If I let him get away, he'll throw the book down a cesspit or into the moat for sure. I race after him, brandishing my wooden sword: along the corridor, down the twisting stair and across the courtyard. A flock of geese squawk in alarm as I push through the door into the great hall – straight into the back of someone.

He's too big to be Jocelin. It might be a servant laying fresh rushes on the floor, but servants don't wear camelin coats trimmed with fur. He turns angrily. He's used to collisions on the battlefield, but not in his own hall.

I stammer an apology. 'Jocelin stole my book.'

Guy's eyes switch to his son. 'Did you?'

Jocelin, standing by the hearth, shuffles in his place and flushes. He's embarrassed his father has not immediately taken his side – and angry. He opts for defiance.

'Perhaps you want me to kneel down, put my hands between his and swear fealty. Become his liegeman.'

'I want you to give back his book.'

'If he wants it, he can fight me for it.'

He's six inches taller than me, broader and stronger. Whenever we spar, he beats me. But on a battlefield, you can't choose your adversary. I put up my wooden sword.

Jocelin grabs the blade and twists it out of my hand. He throws it into the fireplace. 'If you want to fight me, fight like a man.'

Gornemant goes to the armoury and fetches two small bucklers and two old swords. They're iron, immensely heavy: their point and edges have been made blunt, but the weight alone could break someone's neck. The other boys push back the tables and stand on them, an impromptu grandstand. The servants forget their chores and gather at the back of the hall.

One of them tries to take wagers, but he doesn't get any offers. The result isn't in doubt.

We face each other down the length of the hall. Jocelin swings first; I block the blow with my shield and my arm goes numb. It leaves me too dizzy to counter-attack. I step backwards and Jocelin advances. I see the smirk on his face and wish so desperately I could wipe it off. I sway to my left then drive forward. He thinks I'm going for his sword-arm and turns; instead, I swing the flat of the blade like a club, right across his face.

Blood swells from his cut lip. I wanted to break his nose, but perhaps I've dislodged a tooth. Some of the crowd gasp. Gornemant scowls: if I'd done it on the training ground, he'd call me a Welsh savage and hit me.

Jocelin spits out a gob of blood. His eyes are wild, but he knows how to control himself. With terrifying force, he gets his shield rim inside my guard and pushes my sword out of the way. It opens me up: he batters my ribs with three hammer blows, then punches me in the gut with the pommel.

There's no point resisting – it'll just hurt more. I let my legs go and fall to the floor. Jocelin's poised for another blow. He looks as if he's ready to break my neck, but his father steps in and puts his hand on the blade.

'That's enough.'

Give me a javelin, I think, *and I would make you regret it.*

It's not the last time Jocelin and I fight. But later, the swords are sharper – and the consequences catastrophic.

XI

Luxembourg

'You're where?'

Doug's voice, hazy and confused. A silence followed, so long Ellie thought she'd lost the connection. 'Sorry. For a moment I thought you said you were in Luxembourg.'

'They gave me ten minutes' notice. I tried to call but you didn't answer.'

'What are they – the Gestapo? Nobody has to go that quickly.'

'I know it's mad. It's just the way it works.'

A yawn came at her down the phone. 'Did they put you up somewhere nice, at least?'

Ellie glanced at the designer wallpaper and the fifty-inch television on the wall. 'It's OK.'

'That's good. You know where I spent the night?'

'I thought you'd go back to Oxford.'

'I spent it on a chair in the lobby of your tower in the Barbican. I must have rung you twenty times. I tried the bank, the college in case you'd gone back. I was about to call the police.'

'I fell asleep,' Ellie admitted. She'd finished her bath and lain down on the bed, waiting for Doug to get out of the library. The next thing she knew it was six-thirty and the hotel phone was ringing with an alarm call she hadn't ordered.

'Did you sleep well?' Exhaustion slurred his words, but the sarcasm came through sharp and clear.

'Listen, I'm so sorry. I swear I'll make it up to you. We knew it was going to be like this in the beginning.'

'That's why I told you not to do it.'

'I promise it'll settle down.' She looked at her watch. 'I've got to go.'

'It's six in the morning.'

'Seven in Luxembourg. I'll call you tonight.'

'When are you coming back?'

'I don't know.'

His voice became more distant. 'It's like you've stepped through a door and I don't exist any more. You're in your world, and I'm nowhere.'

'I'll make it up to you,' she repeated.

'I'm going back to Oxford. You know where to find me if you want me. Whenever you're back in England.'

'I love you.' But he'd hung up.

Ellie's textbook defined due diligence as the careful examination of a company's records to ascertain all the material facts regarding its financial position. *Pry before you buy*, the lecturer on her course had called it. In fact, Ellie thought, it was more like trawling your hand through a haystack and seeing how many needles pricked you.

Talhouett Holdings SA occupied one of the big glass blocks overlooking the gorge, just up the street from the hotel. The views might have been stunning, but Ellie didn't see them. The moment she arrived, a guard led her like a prisoner to a windowless room at the back of the building, the data room. The Monsalvat team – five men and an empty chair – huddled around a plastic table at one end of the room piled with files and cups of coffee. The rival bidder's bankers had the other end. In between, and all around, stood racks of steel shelving, overloaded with boxes, folders, discs and papers. The entrails of the company for capitalism's priests to pick over, and read the signs as best they could. They took up so much space that there was no room for aisles between the shelves: instead, the company had invested in library-grade rolling stacks, digitally controlled shelves on wheels, which rolled and rumbled apart like magic doors to open a path to the shelf you needed.

It was like being stuck in a mundane corner of hell. After an hour, Ellie wanted to run screaming from the room – except the door was locked, monitored by a security guard who picked his teeth. By lunchtime, when a sullen girl brought sandwiches and soft drinks, she would have paid back her entire salary to be out of there. Her colleagues all came from the local Monsalvat office: they ignored her, and talked amongst themselves in the Luxembourgeois dialect. She got more attention from their rivals. One in particular, a thin man with a greying ponytail and a tie that drooped well below his collar, seemed to be staring at her every time she looked up. He chewed gum incessantly. That afternoon, as Ellie was coming back from the toilet, she met him going the other way. She tried to brush past with a smile, but he angled himself across the corridor to block her path.

'Lechowski,' he introduced himself. He took a pack of gum from his pocket and offered her a stick. 'I must apologise if I stare at you, but you are the only beautiful thing in that room to look at.'

Ellie had heard similar propositions in every walk of her life, from the streets of South Wales to the hallowed quads in Oxford. She knew she wasn't extraordinary to look at, but she had some unwanted aura that gave men the impression they had a claim on her. *It's because you look kind*, her mother had said, tart as ever. Whatever it was, she still hadn't got used to it.

'There's a lot to get through,' she demurred. She tried to edge forward, but Lechowski stood firm. He wore a cologne that he'd probably bought in Duty Free. It made a sickening confection with the minty air blasting out of his mouth.

'You are staying at the Sofitel?'

Her heart sank. Blanchard had said the other bidders were staying there too. *Perhaps you can get to know them.*

Reluctantly, she nodded.

'Maybe I see you in the bar this evening. Luxembourg is a graveyard at night, but I know some places to have fun.'

He wouldn't let her pass without some concession. She offered a false, desperate smile.

'That would be nice.'

London
Like the City itself, the Monsalvat building had grown and spread over centuries. You could pick out individual items and date them – a twelfth-century stone still bearing the marks of the chisel that cut it; an eighteenth-century brick baked in the kilns at Southwark; a twenty-first century steel beam designed by computers – but the whole, the way it knit together and functioned, was indivisible, the sum of its history.

In one of its oldest, darkest corners, a filthy figure lay huddled on the floor. His hands were chained together and so were his feet, and those chains were themselves chained together to keep him in an awkward, doubled-over position strung up like a puppet. He couldn't move one limb without moving them all – and to do so was agony. Both his arms were broken. His legs were a mess of scars and dried blood; the only places you could see skin were where they'd swabbed it clean to attach the electrodes.

But he wasn't defeated. They'd thrown everything they could at him and he hadn't broken. He'd held firm to his training, his cause. He hadn't given them what they wanted.

The door swung open. The thick-set man with the broken nose and the tattoo creeping out from his collar stood in the opening, framed by a wall of sodium-orange light. The face from his nightmares.

'Let's try this one more time.'

The knife glimmered in his hand as he advanced into the room.

'Tell me about Mirabeau.'

Luxembourg

Ellie left at six thirty, the last of the Monsalvat team to go. She'd packed up her files fifteen minutes earlier, but sat and waited until Lechowski had disappeared into the stacks before she slipped out. Dusk had already fallen; an autumn chill nipped her cheeks, biting life back into her. She couldn't face the hotel, so she strolled across the Pont Adolphe to the old town. Far below and out of sight, police tape flapped in the evening breeze.

Ellie hadn't heard anything from Christine Lafarge, so she assumed their shopping trip was off. She didn't mind. She wandered through the streets, looking at the bright windows and the passers-by. Many of the shops were familiar, the same chain stores and fast-food franchises you'd find in any major city. But somehow, filled with people speaking other languages, they felt foreign.

The lights and crowds faded away as she moved east, into the oldest part of the town. Here the cobbled streets were narrower and the walls taller, with high-set windows far above the street, as if they still distrusted the world outside. Remnants of the old fortifications began to appear: the stub of a rampart hacked off like a limb; a gateway without gates arching across the road.

The night was getting cold and Ellie had no coat. She decided to go back. She'd reached the bottom of the hill, a small enclave in the ravine where gabled houses peered over a still river. She wasn't sure if she could get up on the other side; she turned to retrace her steps. And that was when she saw him.

A dim figure stood on the bridge at the bottom of the hill. He wore a white plastic rain cape with the hood pulled up, though there was no rain about. She didn't know how long he'd been there.

You're in the middle of a big city in the heart of Europe, she told herself. *Of course there'll be other people about.* Except he was the only one, and the bright lights on the plateau above seemed far away, like passing aeroplanes.

The man lifted his head. He seemed to be staring straight at her, though in the shadows of his hood it was impossible to tell. He raised an arm as if in greeting. The plastic cape spread like a bat's wing. Slowly and deliberately, like a child stalking a pet, he began walking towards her.

Ellie turned and ran. Back up the hill, back towards the lights and safety. Her shoes were impractical: the heels skidded and teetered on the uneven cobbles. She pulled them off and ran in stockinged feet, feeling the damp ooze between her toes. There was no one to see her. Through the gateless arch that was no protection, along undefended ramparts, until she came out in a square between the looming blocks of some government ministry. She glanced back, but there was no one, no rush of pursuing footsteps or shadows advancing along the wall.

She looked around to get her bearings. Which way was the hotel? It couldn't be more than a quarter of a mile away, but she was desperate for a cab. She had a cramp in her side; her legs burned and her feet ached.

And there he was.

She couldn't believe it. He'd appeared like a ghost, like a vampire out of the air. The spectral white coat flapped in the breeze as he walked towards her across the square.

Ellie's brain was in meltdown. All she could think was that it was impossible. Impossible. How do you escape a man who can scale a cliff in the blink of an eye?

She ran.

'Wait,' a voice called from behind her.

She ran. Past an unmanned guard booth, round a corner and down a windowless alley. At the far end she could see street lights and cars flashing by on Roosevelt Boulevard. If only she could make it. A crack echoed off the walls like a shot. Did the man have a gun? Did ghosts need guns? A split second later she realised it was one her shoes: she'd dropped it. She left it in the gutter where it had fallen.

She reached the main road. A taxi was coming round the bend and its light was on. She waved frantically to flag it down and almost threw herself onto the back seat.

'Sofitel.' She had to repeat it three times to make herself understood.

The driver didn't want to take her. It was only a few

hundred metres, she was wasting her money. She pushed a twenty-euro note into his hand and he stopped complaining.

As the car pulled away, she looked back. Condensation blurred the windows; the lights of the cars behind dazzled her. She thought there might be a figure standing under the lamp at the end of the alley, but she couldn't be sure.

Ellie made the taxi do a full circuit of the city centre before it dropped her at the hotel. She wasn't sure who she thought she would fool. She kept her face pressed to the window, but didn't see anyone. At the Sofitel, she hurried into the lobby and made straight for the lifts. All she wanted was to be in bed behind a locked door. Unless the ghost could walk through walls.

'There you are.'

A hand clamped down on her shoulder. She would scream, she decided: call security, the police, anyone. They couldn't just grab her in a public place. But the air wouldn't come out of her lungs.

'You left work without me,' an aggrieved voice complained.

It was Lechowski. He'd lost his tie. Could he have been the ghost? He looked too short; he certainly smelled as if he'd spent the evening in the bar. He looked her up and down in a way that was supposed to make her feel sexy, but only made her cringe.

'What happened to your shoes?'

She managed a weak smile. 'They were giving me blisters. I walked up from the bottom of the valley.'

'You should have taken the lift.'

Ellie stopped trying to edge past him and stared. 'What?'

'The public lift. It takes you up from the valley to the city. By the *Cité Judiciaire*.' He laughed, assailing her with another blast of mint-edged alcoholic vapour. 'Only in Luxembourg are they so lazy. Maybe we go tomorrow, ride it together? For now, I buy you that drink I promised.'

He made a swipe for her elbow. But Ellie hadn't run for her life through the streets of Luxembourg to be cornered by a creep like Lechowski. She pirouetted away, stepped neatly past him and was inside the open lift before he could move.

'Maybe another time.'

XII

England, 1135

Jocelin's mother – my lord Guy's wife – died some years ago. It's something Jocelin and I have in common, though it doesn't bring us any closer.

Guy has decided to remarry. I think, cruelly, perhaps he's so disappointed in his heir he wants to try again. But in fact, Jocelin will be a perfectly acceptable heir. He'll keep his boot firmly planted on his vassals and tenants; he'll collect their tithes and their taxes enthusiastically; if there's a war, he'll fight energetically for his Duke and probably win lands and favour.

But Guy can't wait for a war to expand his territory. Jocelin has three sisters, and they'll need dowries soon. For a long time, Guy has had his eye on an estate across the river: good pasture, forests with rights of hunting and firewood, fields to grow corn and a mill to grind it. The land belongs to the Beauchamp family, but they are rarely there. Most of their interests are in England now: crossing the sea each time one of their tenants demands justice, or if the King decides to visit, has become tedious. They have a daughter, and they are willing to endow her with the Normandy estates as her marriage portion. Messengers go to England with a proposal, return with a price, risk themselves at sea once more with a counter-offer. Guy holds two farms in Berkshire whose rent he never sees: they become part of the bargain too.

At last the contract is agreed. Gornemant the seneschal sails to England to collect Guy's new bride. He takes four knights, three grooms, six servants, a butler, a cook – and me.

When I left England I was a boy with the tonsure raw in his scalp. Now I am sixteen: a man, in some ways. My hair has grown out, though my companions still call me 'monk', and I have a credible beard. I will never be as big as Jocelin, but I occasionally beat him in the training ground. Every time I do, it feels like one step nearer my revenge.

We step ashore in Dover, a mean little town at the mouth of a river. High cliffs loom over us. I only ever saw England on my way to Normandy, and that through my tears. But I can tell the country is prospering. King Henry has been on the throne some thirty years, and peace makes England flourish. When I meet my uncle in Windsor, he wears a scarlet cloak and a vair mantle, fresh from the furrier. When he rests his elbows on the table, it leaves a residue of chalk dust.

He serves me larks' tongues and capons, and wine he has brought from Burgundy. Then he tells me the king has appointed a new castellan to my father's castle. I don't know, but I guess, that my uncle has profited in some way from this arrangement. It's quite clear that I'll never claim my inheritance.

'But look at you,' he says, with gruesome joviality. He hasn't looked at me properly all day. 'You're a man, now. You can make your own way.'

I know what he means. I've grown up; his obligations are discharged. He's rid of me.

I stare at my plate. 'I'm still a squire,' I mumble.

'You'll be a knight soon.'

'What about the men who killed my father?'

My uncle shifts uneasily on his stool. Once a year or so I write him a letter reporting my progress, and each time I ask this question. He has never answered it.

'It was impossible to find them. There were no witnesses.'

'I witnessed it.'

My uncle wipes the gravy from his mouth with a napkin.

'Wales is a dangerous place. Many die violently. It's impossible to bring all the perpetrators to justice.'

Afterwards, I'll always wonder what that signified. Did my uncle connive in his own brother's destruction? I could believe it. *Wales is a dangerous place; many die violently.* It would be easy to arrange one more death – and the men who killed my father spoke French, not Welsh.

From Windsor, we follow the Thames upriver to Wallingford, then strike west. It takes three days, but it's a pleasant journey. There are frosts at night, but at dawn they dissolve into spring mists. The sun shines from a creamy April sky and makes the world mellow gold. Up on the hills, the trees are in bud. I've never seen a country more at peace with itself.

The Beauchamps live in a fortified manor house in a broad valley west of Wantage. It's a handsome house that, like its owners, has sprawled away from its original military purpose over the past decades. Handsome outbuildings and new wings almost completely obscure the stout fortress at its centre. A mound still lifts up the tower, but it seems less formidable when surrounded by terraced vegetable gardens. Its builder once diverted the river for a moat, but the current generation have constructed weirs and dykes to make fishponds.

That evening, we dine on carp and trout, stuffed with raisins from the local vineyards. Walter Beauchamp doesn't need to impress us much: the marriage benefits Guy more than him. Ada is his youngest daughter, and he could always send her to an abbey if needs be. But he sets out the table in his great hall and brings in his household to entertain us. In the gallery, a minstrel plucks his psaltery.

I have no place at the table. I stand in the folds of the heavy fabrics which line the wall, like a green man half buried in foliage. Every so often, I emerge to refill Gornemant's cup, or recharge his plate. Otherwise, I listen and observe, always learning.

As a result, I'm probably the first man in the hall to notice Guy's bride. Her father has waited to unveil her until the first two courses are under our belts, until wine has softened our eyes. While servants clear dishes, I glimpse a flash behind a curtained doorway, a head peeping round to see the men who've come for her. All I can make out in the gloom is the gleam of precious stones, the pearls she wears in her hair and the gems at her throat. At least, I think that's all I see. Later, she'll tell me that I stared straight into her eyes without realising it.

The psaltery falls silent. The men at the table look up as Guy's bride makes her entrance. She carries a silver dish in front of her, humble as a servant, but she's beautiful, noble and richly attired. Two squires escort her. Beauchamp has them carrying candelabras, ostensibly replenishing the lights at the table, in fact casting a shimmering nimbus around their mistress. The candles make her skin as soft as ivory, her hair like gold leaf, her jewels a bright constellation.

I'm transfixed. The moment she enters the hall, it seems to

me that the room grows so bright that the candles and the fire lose their brilliance, like stars washed away in the sunrise. I feel like the knights and wanderers in my mother's stories, encountering their wayward damsels and enchantresses. I'm gripped by magic.

At the end of the table, Gornemant's reaction is more businesslike. The stars haven't dimmed for him. He examines her with clear-eyed purpose, like a cook appraising a doe brought in from the hunt. Will she do? Will she please Guy? Was she worth surrendering the Berkshire estates for?

She puts down the grail-dish she's carrying and curtsies. A poached lamprey swims in its own juices in the silver platter. Her father's steward carves it and serves the portions on whole flatbreads, while Gornemant asks her a few trivial questions. She answers demurely, her eyes downcast. So as not to stare, I make myself watch the other knights. They can't believe Guy's luck. Even if she looked like a horse, he'd have taken her just for the land. As it is . . .

Ada Beauchamp curtsies and retreats. The candles stay, but the light goes with her. On the pretext of fetching more wine, I follow. I find her in a courtyard, leaning against the wall with her head tipped back to the stars. Her breath makes small clouds in the chill night. Through the kitchen window I can see the cooks preparing a sugared cake in the shape of a boar, Guy's emblem. But here, we're alone.

'When you're the lady of Hautfort, you'll have servants to bring the fish.'

She laughs. 'My father says that men like to know a woman can serve.'

Her voice is deeper than I expected, mellow. She looks at me as if she expects me to say something, but every word I ever knew has suddenly flown out of my head.

She says, 'How long have you served Guy de Hautfort?'

'Six years.'

'What sort of man is he?'

I want to talk about her, not Guy. 'Fair.'

She's looking at me intently. For a moment I think she's disappointed, then I realise she wants to hear more. She wants reassurance, to know that she isn't being led across the sea to some ogre.

'He's a good man.' Maybe. 'Kind and gentle-hearted.' Less plausible. 'Handsome.'

She smiles. I wonder if she's seen through my lies. 'And his son?'

She holds my gaze. I try to think of something to say about Jocelin, any benevolent lie, but I can't. Her eyes seem to dare me to speak the truth.

'He's a pig.'

That makes her laugh. I'm glad I said it; it forges a bond between us.

'I'm Peter.'

'Ada.'

Now that I'm close, I can see that her hair doesn't really shimmer like the sun. It's a trick: she's braided it with thread-of-gold. Absent-mindedly, she pulls out a strand. She winces; she's pricked herself on one of the pins holding her braid in place. A drop of blood beads on her fingertip. She presses the finger between her lips and sucks out the blood. I watch her mouth and tremble: a revelation. I don't have much experience of women, beyond a scullery girl who lets me unlace her bodice and touch her breasts in Guy's woodshed. Only now do I understand how the men in my mother's tales felt, why they risked all for the love of a lady.

'I should go,' she says. 'My mother will want to hear

93

everything.' She gives me an earnest smile. 'Thank you for introducing yourself. It's nice to know there'll be at least one friendly face in Hautfort.'

'More than one, for sure,' I mumble.

I watch her disappear into the lighted doorway. The enchantress has vanished: I'm the forlorn knight alone on the hillside. I remember her sucking her finger, the ruby lips and the luminous skin.

She's pricked me – and I know that instant the wound will never heal.

XIII

Luxembourg

'I've found something.'

Ellie cupped her hand over the phone. She was standing by the bandstand in the Place d'Armes, scanning the crowd for any sign of a man in a white raincoat. For the past ten days she'd confined herself to the data room and her hotel room, growing fat on room service and running up an exorbitant bill on bad movies. She didn't even dare go to the bar, for fear Lechowski would be lurking there.

'Talhouett have a Romanian subsidiary which might have some pretty huge liabilities. I only found it by chance: there's nothing in the accounts. One of their directors resigned in protest at the way they were handling it. For some reason a copy of his letter made it into the personnel file.'

'Have the others seen this?'

'I don't think so.' Not judging by the collection of dried-out Post-it notes which had fluttered out like dead leaves when she opened the file.

'Can you remove the letter?'

Ellie thought of the dull-eyed security guard reading his dirty magazines, the perfunctory bag searches at the end of the day. The biggest risk was Lechowski.

'Maybe.'

'Do what you can.' Blanchard's voice was quiet; Ellie struggled to make it out over the blare of a street artist's boom box in the square behind her. 'One other thing. Did you find any reference in the files you looked at to something called "Mirabeau"?'

It sounded familiar – a budget item, maybe? – but her head was so full of names and figures she couldn't remember where or what it had been. And she'd already learned you didn't say anything to Blanchard without being sure of your ground.

'I don't think so. What is it?'

'Not important. When will you be back in London?'

The due diligence period was almost over. 'I'm flying home tomorrow night. I'll be in the office on Monday.'

'This is excellent work, Ellie. Again you have surpassed yourself. Our client will be impressed. Do you have plans this weekend?'

The street artist had started banging a steel drum. 'I'm sorry?'

'Michel Saint-Lazare – our client – has invited me to Scotland to hunt. I wondered if you would like to come with me. He would be very interested to meet you.'

For a moment, Ellie was captivated by a vision of lochs and forests, a turreted castle with a roaring log fire, snuggling into an eiderdown in a four-poster bed late at night. She bit her lip. 'I promised Doug I'd go to Oxford this weekend.'

'Then you must go, of course.' At once, Blanchard was brisk and businesslike. Was he offended? Disappointed?

He probably doesn't care one way or the other.

'I'll see you on Monday.'

Oxford

Ellie took the train to Oxford, staring out the window as it chugged up the Thames valley. An autumn haze covered the fields; the sun shone from a vivid October sky and made the world golden. Up on the hills, the leaves were turning. There would be a frost that night.

On a Saturday morning, the carriage was almost empty. Ellie scanned the faces she could see: a mother with two daughters, a man with a bag advertising antiquarian books; two students talking with self-conscious earnestness about Kant and Heidegger. She was invisible to them, which suited her well.

Doug had rugby training that morning; she'd told him not to meet her. She still felt an irrational stab of disappointment when she scanned the waiting faces at the station hall. Just being in Oxford made her apprehensive. She'd only lived there for nine months before Monsalvat approached: long enough for it to be familiar, but not to feel she'd ever belonged. The sense of unfinished business soured the taste, like an ex-lover.

It took her ten minutes to walk to Doug's place, a small mews house provided by the college near the Ashmolean. She still had her key; she let herself in. A pair of muddy rugby boots lay in the hall. From upstairs, she could hear the sound of running water. Books and papers filled the living room, stacked on shelves and sills. After three weeks in the glassy altitudes of high rises and hotels, it felt dim and dingy. Empty screwholes pocked the walls like machine-gun fire. The paint had peeled above the doorframe, and the carpet was threadbare. She'd never noticed it before.

She climbed the stairs and opened the bathroom door

without knocking. Doug stood in the shower, his face flushed from the fresh air and hot water, his dark hair slick against his skin. Ellie was struck, as she had been their first night together, by his long, rangy body and muscular arms.

He opened his eyes and started. 'Practice finished late. I was going to come and meet you at the station.'

'I told you not to bother.'

'You know I never listen to you.' He grinned and held out the soap. 'Are you going to scrub my back?'

Afterwards, they walked hand in hand along the towpath towards Abingdon. Oars slapped the water as the new eights crews flashed by; the damp smells of mud and rotting leaves filled the air. For the first time since she'd started at Monsalvat, Ellie felt she could breathe again.

'How's your research coming along?' She'd held off asking until now. In the first six months of their relationship, work had been a shared passion. Now it was a faultline.

'It's good.' Doug frowned. 'Really good. I had a letter last week, totally out of the blue. A guy up in Scotland, reclusive millionaire or something. Apparently he'd read one of my papers on early medieval romance and wanted to talk to me.'

Ellie glanced at him. 'In Scotland?'

'We met in London. At his *club*.' An ironic emphasis. 'Huge place off Pall Mall, lots of Victorian busts and deep leather chairs and not a woman to be seen, except the one taking your coat. Anyway, he was waiting for me. An old man in a wheelchair, strapped in to some sort of respirator. He never said a word. He laid out this leather folder on the table. He had a minder with him, a tall guy in a long black coat. He looked like an undertaker. The first thing he did was make me sign a confidentiality agreement – which I'm breaching, telling you this, by the way. The minder said that the old man had found something in his attic recently and thought it might be interesting.'

'What was in the folder?'

'A sheet of A4 paper.' Doug smiled at the anticlimax. 'But there was a poem on it written in Old French. Twelfth or thirteenth century, you'd think from the style. The minder said it was a transcription of this piece of parchment they'd found in the attic. I read through it – I'd never seen it before.'

He said it lightly, but Ellie knew what he meant. If Doug didn't recognise the poem, the chances were it had never been published.

'Obviously I wanted to see the original, but he said it had been put in a bank vault for safekeeping. I asked if anyone else had looked at it. He said not since it came out of the attic. He didn't know how long it had been there. They gave me the printout to study and asked me to let them know what I thought.'

They were approaching the weir at Sandford lock. A red sign on pilings in the river warned DANGER AHEAD. Despite the sun and her snug coat, Ellie shivered.

Doug checked his watch. 'We should head home. I've invited Annabel and Mark for supper.'

Ellie tried not to look disappointed. She squeezed his hand. 'I thought we could be on our own tonight.'

'I invited them ages ago. It'll be fine.'

Annabel was a wispy woman who always seemed vaguely surprised to find herself in the twenty-first century. Mark was the sort of man who came to Oxford with certain stereotypes and did everything he could to live up to them. He was the only person Ellie had met who wore a cravat. He had also been her doctoral supervisor.

'Mark'll be a nightmare. He still hasn't forgiven me about the bank.'

'He's looking out for you. He wants the best for you.' Doug stared at a bird's nest couched among the willows. 'We all do.'

'I've got what's best for me.'

'I just thought – the way they packed you off to Luxembourg like that, no word of warning. You didn't seem very happy there. I thought maybe . . .'

His voice trailed off. He snapped a twig in two and threw the pieces in the water.

'Maybe I would come running back to Oxford?' A cold fury was building inside Ellie. 'I've just helped decide a deal worth seven hundred million euros. I'm earning more in a year than you and Mark and Annabel combined.'

'There're others ways to value what you do,' Doug said quietly. 'You're a great researcher. Don't waste it as a cog in some great money-making machine.'

'So I can waste it gathering dust in a library?' She remembered her first meeting with Blanchard. *Academia is an echo chamber, a hall of mirrors.* 'I'm out in the real world, doing real things and earning real money.'

'Numbers on a computer. It's not real.'

She was trapped in a nightmare, reliving all the arguments they'd had that summer, the ones she thought she'd buried when she went to London.

'You can't change this,' she said flatly. 'It's who I am.'

'It's not –'

The nightmare always ended the same way. Hot tears and rushed steps and Doug calling after her, too late. Leaves and twigs squelched underfoot. She didn't look back until she'd rounded a bend. She knew Doug wouldn't follow. He'd wait at the house, and eventually she'd go back. They'd skirt around each other like wary dogs, until eventually they'd pretend they'd forgotten. Until next time.

Except there *was* someone coming after her. A short man taking long, hurried strides, his face flushed from the effort. He wore green rubber boots and a green jerkin, whose numerous pouches and pockets bulged with all manner of reels and bright flashes of fabric bound onto hooks. He didn't carry a fishing rod.

The path was narrow and overgrown; Ellie stood aside to let him pass. But he didn't. He stopped a few feet away and half-lifted a hand, almost as if he recognised her.

Ellie froze. She'd never seen the face before, but his pose was utterly familiar.

'Ellie Stanton?'

She couldn't run: the towpath was too muddy. Branches and brambles blocked the way. There was no one else in sight.

'Who are you?' She sounded faint and terrified, a little girl lost in the woods.

Metal flashed as he pulled something out of the pouch at his side. Ellie steeled herself to scream – but it was only a hipflask. He unscrewed the cap and offered it to her.

'You look like you could use a drink.'

'No thanks.' She couldn't keep the trembling out of her voice.

He took a swig and refastened the cap. He didn't look dangerous. He was short and tending to fat; he had tousled sandy hair and bright blue eyes and ruddy cheeks that fitted his fishing gear perfectly. He seemed to have genuinely enjoyed the drink.

'You're a hard woman to track down.'

A motor launch droned by. Ellie thought about calling for help, but the engines were so loud they'd never have heard. A little girl sat on the bow and waved at her.

101

Keep him talking. 'Was it you in Luxembourg?'

'Yes.'

'You took the lift to get up the hill in front of me.'

He glanced down at his stocky frame and short legs. 'I wasn't going to overtake you on foot.'

'Why didn't you call me at the hotel, if you wanted to speak to me?'

'Too difficult. They were watching it.'

His easy manner had let Ellie begin to relax; now she snapped back into reality. She looked at the barbed row of hooks looped onto his jerkin. Was he insane? Dangerous?

'I know I must sound mad.' Didn't all mad people say that? 'But you're in tremendous danger at Monsalvat.'

You aren't safe here. Ellie peered closer, wondering if he had been the man at the demonstration in London as well. She didn't know what to think any more.

'Why do you think they let you use your phone for personal calls? They're listening, Ellie. All the time. Watching as well, as often as they can.'

'Why –?'

'They're not what they seem. Underneath all that twenty-first century capitalist veneer, there's a medieval heart that's all darkness and malice. Look in their vaults sometime. They want something, and they're using you to get it.'

Ellie thought she'd be sick. 'Why are you telling me this?'

'Because–'

'Ellie!'

While he'd been speaking, Ellie's world had shrunk into a tiny sphere bounded by mud, water and wood. A place out of time. Now the barriers receded as Doug came running around the bend in the path, his long coat flapping around his legs.

'I'm so sorry. You're right – I shouldn't have said any of

that. I've rung Mark and Annabel to cancel tonight. Let's just go home, open a bottle of wine and curl up on the couch.'

He looked at her again, misreading the anguish and confusion written all over her face. Drops of blood beaded on his hand like a string of pearls where brambles had torn the skin.

'I'm so sorry, Ellie.'

She kissed him, but only to stop him talking. Her eyes sidled over his shoulder down the path. The fisherman had vanished.

Doug had followed her gaze. He pulled back a little. 'Who was that man you were with? He wasn't giving you any trouble was he?'

'He just wanted directions.'

He accepted the lie. Ellie let him take her arm and escort her back towards Oxford, pretending that the fight was all that had upset her. Delicate ridges of pink clouds furrowed the blue sky; an owl hooted from somewhere in the thicket.

She'd never felt so lost.

XIV

Gornemant can tell I'm on edge. He says I show too much anger on the practice field. When we spar, I fight wildly and lose often, which only makes me angrier. Gornemant thinks it's impatience. He's seen it happen to all squires left kicking their heels too long, waiting for their spurs. He thinks I need a war to lift me. But God smiles on his people that year: all Christendom is at peace. I could take the Cross and go to fight for Jesus in the Holy Land, but I don't have enough money for the journey.

And the truth is, I want to stay in Hautfort. All the hours of drudgery are worth it for my glimpses of Ada. To leave her would be desolation. At dinner, I can stand behind my lord Guy's table for hours, just to be close to her. If she speaks to me, I carry her words with me like a treasure boxed in my heart. If she ignores me, I despair. I recall everything I have ever said or done to her, wondering what might have offended her. I tear my mind out wondering if she'll ever forgive me. And the next morning she gives me a smile, or her hand brushes mine as I help her mount her palfrey, and I'm insane with hope again.

I know I'm deluding myself. Ada has no idea: she'd be horrified if she knew what I'm thinking. Neither of us would ever betray Guy: my lord, her master. But I'm trapped in a dream, an enchantment, and for the moment I have no will to break it.

An August day, a cloudless sky. The whole world is limp with the heat. Gornemant had us in the lists all morning in full armour, charging and skirmishing until we were ready to drop. My hair's as wet as a dog's; my hands are sticky with the pine resin I rubbed on so my damp hands wouldn't drop my sword. I stink of sweat, horse, leather and oil. If I don't cool off soon, I think I might boil away.

I strip off my clothes and dive into the stream by the apple orchard. The first fruits are beginning to ripen on the trees, but there's no one here to pick them. The labourers are all in the fields bringing in the harvest. Guy's gone to inspect the new mill he got with Ada's dowry. Apart from the birds, I might be the only person alive.

When I've washed, I haul myself out and lie naked on the grass. The sun dries me quickly; bees and hummingbirds flit about over my head. Black spots dance in front of my eyes.

I'm hungry. I pull on a clean tunic and walk along the stream, looking for an early apple, or perhaps some mushrooms. I haven't gone twenty paces when I see her, sitting alone at the edge of the water in a plain green dress. I didn't notice her arrive; I wonder how long she's been there. Did she see . . .?

To hide my embarrassment, I study the undergrowth on the far side of the stream. I see a hazel and a honeysuckle, their stems and branches twined and knotted together, and I say, 'Do you know the story about those?'

She shakes her head.

'They grew on the graves of Tristan and Yseult. King Mark burned them down three times, but the hazel and the honeysuckle always grew back.'

She rolls over on her stomach and peers at her reflection in the water. 'That sounds like the end of the story. Tell me from the beginning.'

I might as well not have bothered with the swim. I'm sweating into my clean tunic more than I ever sweated under my armour. I should go, plead some chore that Gornemant has for me. I can't trust myself.

I sit down on the bank, what I hope is a respectful distance away.

'Long ago, when Arthur was king . . .'

The words are a key, unlocking my anxiety. They relax me; I find I can go on. My mother never told me the tale, but I have heard it many times in Guy's hall. I'm surprised Ada doesn't know it.

None of the troubadors I've heard entirely agreed with each other, and mine is changed again.

'Tristan was a knight from Lyonesse, who served his uncle, King Mark of Cornwall.

In my mind, uncle Mark is a fat oaf in a vair-fur cloak that leaves powder on the table.

'Mark sent him to Ireland to fetch his bride, Yseult the Blonde. Yseult was the fairest maid in all Britain.'

From the corner of my eye, I see Ada winding a lock of her golden hair around her finger. Is she seeing Yseult as I do, with soft blue eyes and a dimple on her chin, lying on a riverbank among the camomile?

106

'Yseult's mother was a sorceress. To ensure a happy marriage, she concocted a love potion and gave it to Yseult's maid for the wedding night. But on the ship from Ireland, Tristan grew thirsty. He found the bottle and thought it was wine; he drank it. Yseult found him in the cabin and asked to share his drink. She didn't know what it was.'

'Where was the maid?' Ada asks archly.

'The story doesn't say. Tristan and Yseult stared into each other's eyes, and at that moment they fell headlong in love. The walls of the boat seemed to melt away and all they knew was each other.'

I don't know where Ada's looking. At that moment, I am very deliberately not staring into her eyes. I'm dizzy; the sun is hot on my skin; I drank too much beer at lunchtime. I'm desperate to make her understand, to tear down the cautious walls of protocol and speak truthfully.

Ada pulls the petals off a daisy and tosses them onto the water. 'It must have been a strong potion.'

'When they reached Cornwall, Yseult was married to King Mark. But on her wedding night she crept away from the marriage bed to be with Tristan. She had her maid take her place with the King. In the dark, he didn't know the difference. Before dawn, Yseult stole back.'

'It sounds horrible. So dishonest.'

'She was in thrall to the potion. They both were.' I'm quick to defend them. In the stream, a brown trout noses against the current. He doesn't move; he barely twitches his fins. I'm the same, forcing myself to be still in the face of the vast currents swirling about me.

'Eventually, the lovers grew careless. Rumours circulated. King Mark's advisors went to the king and warned him he was being cuckolded by his nephew. So Mark set a trap. When

Yseult went to bed, he had his servant scatter flour on the floor. He thought it would show up any footprints left in the night.'

'Clever.'

'Yseult saw the trap and warned Tristan. But his love was so strong he couldn't resist her. He leaped from the doorway and landed on Yseult's bed in a single bound.'

'Was that love?' Ada's sceptical. 'It sounds more like plain lust.'

I blush. I'm furiously aware that she's far more experienced than I am in this area. Suddenly my story of the lovers seems false, like an ill-tuned harp. Embarrassment ties my tongue. I turn away.

'Go on,' Ada says gently. 'I want to hear how it ends.'

'In his leap, Tristan had opened a wound he was carrying from his last battle. He cleared the flour, but three drops of blood fell and landed in it. When Mark found them next morning, he had the two lovers arrested for treason.

'He imprisoned Tristan in a tower on the edge of a high cliff. But Tristan managed to pull open the bars on the window and leap down onto the beach. Because he was innocent, God made sure he was unhurt.'

Ada raises an eyebrow. She doesn't think Tristan was innocent.

'His squire found him and fetched his horse. Just as Mark was about to set the pyre under Yseult, Tristan galloped into the courtyard. He cut Yseult free from the stake and pulled her onto his saddle. They rode away into the forest where King Mark's men couldn't find them.'

'And?'

'And they lived happily ever after.'

She throws a pebble at me. 'Cheat. That's not the ending I know.'

It's not the ending I know either. That has a poisoned wound; Tristan lying in agony waiting for a ship with white sails to announce Yseult has come to heal him; Yseult dying over his corpse as she arrives too late. But I don't want that ending on a summer's day that smells of honeysuckle.

I throw the pebble back at her. 'If you're the storyteller, you get to choose how it ends.'

XV

London

'Talhouett Holdings SA owns a thirty-five per cent stake in a Romanian mining operator which is currently on trial accused of massive arsenic spillages into the Danube basin.'

Ellie sipped her water. Her mouth felt dry as dust. In the conference room in front of her, a dozen men stared at her from around an oval table. These were the board of Monsalvat Bank: a monochrome conclave of white men and black suits, grey hair and hard grey faces. Blanchard's tie, deep crimson, was the only colour in the room, as if a vandal had splashed paint across an ancient photograph. Some watched from behind hooded lids, half closed; others pored over the table and wrote indecipherable notes. Several eyed her as if she were something on a menu.

'The stake doesn't appear anywhere in their published accounts because, under Luxembourg law, it isn't considered a controlling stake. But under Romanian law, as the largest shareholder, they're liable for any damages.'

'Do the other bidders know this?' demanded a balding man

with liver spots on his skull. Flecks of spittle flew as he talked.

'I don't think so. The only reference I found was a letter in an unopened personnel file.'

'The letter is no longer there,' Blanchard added. Ellie cringed. She remembered the hard corners of the paper tucked in the waist of her skirt, the terror it would rustle or fall out as the data-room guard looked her over. If the men in the room guessed what she'd done, they didn't seem troubled by it.

'What are the chances of a conviction?' fired in a hatchet-faced man on the other side of the table.

'Romania's under a lot of pressure from Europe to prove that they're getting serious about environmental regulation. A high-level prosecution team from Germany have flown out to help them secure a conviction. If they find out Talhouett's involved it'll make a politically attractive target. It's not a local firm, and it'll send a message internationally.'

'How much?'

Ellie blinked. 'I'm sorry?'

'How much money?'

'Based on recent rulings, the fines might run to several hundred million euros.'

'And to make the problem go away?'

'I don't –'

Blanchard stood, uncoiling like a snake. 'Thank you, Ellie. I think you have given us all the information we need.' He ushered her out into the corridor. 'You did very well. The board are hard men to impress.'

Did that mean she'd impressed them? It was hard to believe from those stony faces.

'We will take the Talhouett project from here. We need you on another job now. You'll find the files in your office.'

Ellie walked down the corridor and sank into her chair. New

files had appeared like magic on her desk – even the sight of them made her sick. She'd spent most of the last forty-eight hours preparing her presentation and she was exhausted. At least it had allowed her to put off thinking about the other questions hammering at her mind.

Her phone rang. She stared at the glowing numbers written like runes under the plastic shell. *Why do you think they let you use your phone for personal calls?*

'How did you get on?'

It was Delamere, the lawyer she'd met in the lift on her second day.

'I survived – thanks to you.' It was Delamere who'd taken her through the intricacies of European corporate law, hour after hour until her head swam. 'I owe you.'

'How about lunch?'

Ellie glanced at her laptop. *Thirty-eight new messages* – to add to the couple of hundred she'd barely read while she prepared her report. And those new files. She thought the pile might have got taller while she sat there, though of course it was impossible.

'When was the last time you ate?'

She tried to think. 'There was a pizza yesterday afternoon, I think . . .'

'That does it. You're coming with me.'

He took her to an old-fashioned inn down an alley off Cornhill. A shield hung over the door: a black vulture emblazoned on a red cross. Inside, a marble bust watched possessively over the heavy tables and upholstered chairs that looked as if they hadn't been changed since the nineteenth century.

'Boarding-school food, I'm afraid,' said Delamere, and Ellie

112

nodded as if she knew what they ate in boarding schools. She ordered fish and chips and a glass of water. Delamere ordered a steak and kidney pudding and a bottle of red wine. The waiter poured two glasses without asking.

'Cheers.' Delamere raised his glass. 'Ellie Stanton. There aren't many people who present to the board inside their first month here. Blanchard must see something pretty special in you.'

She blushed and sipped the wine, not wanting to look rude. 'How long have you been with the bank?'

'A year and a half. Halfway through my tour.' He saw Ellie's quizzical look. 'No gold watches in this company. Monsalvat only hires on three-year contracts. Pay you a fortune then turf you out on your ear – or rather, into some plush job with one of the big boys. I assume Blanchard told you that?'

Ellie was pretty sure he hadn't. She gave a vague smile.

'So how are you finding it?'

'Hard work. But rewarding,' she added hastily, so as not to give a bad impression.

'It's hard all right.' He wasn't paying much attention. 'Monsalvat's a queer place. Rumour has it there's a vault under the building stuffed full of treasure. You know, until the seventeenth-century goldsmiths acted as bankers? They had to have strong vaults anyway, so they offered them as secure storage for their customers. You took your gold cup or plate or whatever to the goldsmith, and he'd lock it up for you.'

'You think it's still there?'

'Why not? The bank's been rebuilt umpteen times, but the foundations go way back. It was built on the ruins of an old Templar lodge. Who knows what's buried in the vaults?'

He raised his glass again, less steady this time. 'To the de Morgon family, our illustrious founders.'

Ellie toasted them without enthusiasm.

'You know about the de Morgons? They were Normans, probably been around since the Conquest. They keep a tight grip. You know Michel Saint-Lazare?'

'I've heard the name.'

'He owns Groupe Saint-Lazare, our client. Apparently he's the umpteenth descendant of the original Saint-Lazare de Morgon – still has a stake in the bank.'

Their food arrived. Ellie picked at her fish, while Delamere sawed into his steak and kidney pudding.

'I did my dissertation on the Normans. Scary people. They conquered Sicily before they conquered England, did you know that? There's a theory that the Mafia grew out of their feudal structures. It's just another racket.' He speared a kidney on the tip of his knife and waved it at her. 'You've got the king, the *capo dei capi*; his barons, who are like the captains, and then the knights and so forth who go around extorting protection money from the villagers so they can live high off the hog. The whole thing's steeped in violence; every so often it breaks out into a full-fledged war.'

He grabbed the bottle of wine and topped up her glass. Ellie was alarmed to see that she'd drunk most of it while he talked.

They're not what they seem. Ellie lowered her voice. 'Do you think Monsalvat's involved with the mob?'

'God no – nothing so crass.' Delamere's face was flushed with the alcohol; he was speaking in an exaggerated whisper that only drew attention from the neighbouring diners. 'It's the *attitude* I'm talking about. *Droit de seigneur*, the right to rule.'

Ellie drank her wine and tried not to make eye contact.

'We wear suits instead of suits of armour, and we go into battle with laptops instead of lances. But it's the same

114

mentality. In their minds, people like Blanchard are still riding around the countryside sacking and pillaging. You and me, we're the squires. We run around fetching their armour, grooming the horses and sharpening the swords, and hope that one day we'll get tapped on the shoulder.'

He gave a rueful smile. 'Sorry. Shouldn't drink in the middle of the day. Listen, what are you doing this evening?'

Ellie was so tired she almost missed the subtext. She tried to frame a considerate smile and fought back the nausea rising in her throat.

'I'm afraid I have to call my boyfriend.'

But when she rang Doug that night, he didn't answer. She left a message and waited for him to call back. An autumn gale was blowing through, howling around the heights of her tower like a pack of wolves. Rain pelted the windows and made a mess of the view. She worked through some e-mails and watched TV, but she couldn't concentrate. At ten thirty, she tried again. Still no answer. There was a landline at the house which he never used: she dug out the number and tried that. It rang for what seemed an eternity. Then:

'Hello?'

A woman's voice, soft and fragile, as if interrupted in the middle of some private tragedy.

'Is Doug there?'

'I'll just get him.'

A hundred questions boiled up inside her in the time it took Doug to come to the phone. She could hear murmured voices in the background, which quieted some of her questions and demanded others.

'Ellie?'

'Are you OK?' She could tell from his voice he wasn't.

'Fine. I was going to call you as soon as the police left but they're taking ages.'

Her heart took another lurch. 'What–'

'I've been burgled. They took my laptop, my phone, the telly. Turned the place upside down. Must have thought I had something valuable squirreled away. They found my passport, which is a real bugger. I was booked to go to France tomorrow.'

'France?' Ellie clutched the handset. She felt as if she'd dialled into a world she no longer recognised.

'Something's come up with that poem I told you about. There's a manuscript in Paris I want to look at.'

A voice in the background called something Ellie couldn't make out.

'They want me to sign the statement. I'd better go.'

'Who answered the phone?'

'Lucy. One of my students. She'd come round to drop off an essay and saw the broken window.'

I was one of your students, Ellie thought.

'I have to go.' More quietly, tinged with embarrassment: 'I love you.'

'I love you too.'

For the next month, the walls of Ellie's world were rain and numbers. Numbers on paper, numbers on phones, numbers on screens as she worked and reworked the spreadsheets that Blanchard sent her. In the evenings, and in the pre-dawn darkness when she went to work, rain curtained off the windows through which she saw the world. It never seemed to stop. At night she dreamed of windows on screens and screens on windows, rivulets of numbers running down them and collecting in pools at the bottom. Sometimes she woke with tears on her face. In the 4 a.m. silence she imagined that the

116

rain had drowned out all of London; that she, alone on the thirty-eighth floor, was the only person who had survived.

The weather put everyone on edge. Even Blanchard's impeccable good manners stretched to breaking. He snapped at her for minor mistakes; her reports came back covered in red ink. When she stumbled out of her nightly taxi – she never walked any more – it was all she could do to take her supper out of its packaging and collapse into bed. At least she saw nothing more of the man from the towpath. She puzzled over his warning until it grew so old she dismissed it. She didn't tell anyone, certainly not Doug. He didn't need any more reason to distrust Monsalvat.

She began to dread their nightly phone calls. Whether it was the distance or the weather, they could never agree, grinding on each other like the wrong key in the wrong lock. Doug went to Paris on a new passport, but wouldn't tell her what he'd found. Once, she heard a woman's voice in the background and spent a long, furious night lying awake and wondering. When she asked Doug about it the next day, he said it had been a radio play and called her paranoid.

One Thursday in early November, Blanchard invited Ellie to lunch. Some of his good humour seemed to have returned: he told her she needed fattening up and pinched her cheek like a wicked uncle. To her surprise, when they stepped out the door his car was nowhere to be seen.

'The restaurant is just around the corner. The exercise will do you good.' He raised an umbrella and made a chivalrous gesture with his arm; Ellie took it and clung close, struggling to dodge puddles and keep pace with his long strides. Some children from a local school had put out a stuffed straw man on the pavement and were collecting for their bonfire. Ellie couldn't imagine how they'd find anything dry enough to burn.

He took her to the Coq d'Argent, an exclusive restaurant on the top floor opposite the Bank of England, all walnut panelling and red leather chairs. Ellie ordered smoked ham with roasted figs; Blanchard asked for *Marennes d'Oléron* and something called Imperial Al Baeri. Ellie sneaked another look at the menu while he studied the wine list. Marennes were oysters; Imperial Al Baeri was caviar. Price: £118 for fifty grams.

She closed the menu and looked away to hide her shock. Beyond the windows the building tapered like the tip of a spear, supporting a roof garden which was as sodden as the rest of London. And sitting at a table by the windows overlooking it, a briefcase by his knee, a face she'd have been happy never to see again.

She almost grabbed Blanchard's arm. 'That man over there. I know him.'

'It's the City. Most of the men in this room, I have done deals with them.' He sat back and let the waiter pour two glasses of champagne.

'Pol Roger. Churchill's favourite.'

'His name's Lechowski,' Ellie bore on. 'He was in Luxembourg doing due diligence on Talhouett.'

Blanchard looked amused. 'Did he ask you to go to bed with him?'

That brought Ellie up short. She blushed crimson; she began to stammer a couple of different answers, but none would come out right. She took a long draught of the champagne to buy herself some time. Blanchard never took his eyes off her.

'Lechowski has a reputation. In the world of investment banking, he's known as "the letch". You know, he once offered

Christine Lafarge to give her his client's complete defence strategy if she would sleep with him.'

The waiter had come back and was setting out the food. Ellie sat in awkward silence until the business of plates and napkins and cutlery was concluded. Blanchard paid him no attention.

'What did she do?'

Blanchard squeezed lemon over his oyster, then picked up the shell and tipped it into his mouth. He licked his lips with a smile so carnal it made Ellie blush all over again.

'Who knows? But next morning, Christine had the document and we completed the takeover.'

Across the room, Lechowski stood. His jaws mashed reflexively on a piece of gum. For a horrible moment, Ellie worried he'd seen her. But he was looking elsewhere, towards an older man with brusquely chopped white hair and a sharply etched face striding towards him. They shook hands; Lechowski gestured the older man to sit.

'Who's that?'

Blanchard suddenly seemed much more interested in Lechowski's table. 'His name is Lazarescu. He is a judge in Romania. He is in London for a conference.'

His dark eyes fixed Ellie, laying down a challenge. Choosing her words carefully, she said, 'I thought we abandoned the Talhouett deal.'

Blanchard smiled, pleased. 'The management of Groupe Saint-Lazare considered your presentation very carefully. Ultimately, they felt that Talhouett holdings is too important strategically to abandon the acquisition.'

He spread caviar on a piece of toast and popped it in his mouth. Ellie tried to count the little black globules and wondered how much each one cost.

'This puts us in an awkward position. We know that the

company is worth less than it appears, but our rivals do not. If we bid the correct value, we will lose.'

By the window, the briefcase had somehow migrated from Lechowski's side of the table to the judge's.

'So you're telling Lechowski?'

Blanchard swallowed another oyster, chased down with a mouthful of champagne. 'Did they teach you the efficient market hypothesis on your course? In an ideal market the price of an asset will reflect all available information about its future prospects. All we are doing is correcting an inefficiency in the market.'

'I thought market inefficiencies were where profits were made.'

Blanchard acknowledged the point. 'It was a superb piece of work you did, Ellie. I know you do not want to see it thrown away to our enemies. But – *c'est la guerre*. Sometimes we must sacrifice a pawn to capture the king.'

Ellie wondered which she was.

'Do you have plans for this evening?'

His question caught her off balance.

'I have tickets to the opera and my client cancelled. Wagner – *Tristan und Isolde*. Do you know it?'

Ellie shook her head. Opera, like caviar, wasn't on the menu much in Newport.

'It is sublime. Perhaps the most shattering work of art ever created. The tenor who sang the first performance died two weeks afterwards. The composer was so afraid of its power he banned all further performances in his lifetime.'

'It sounds dangerous.'

She only said it for lack of anything more intelligent to say. Blanchard took her seriously. 'The music takes you across the threshold to another place – a place governed by obsession.

That is to say, without boundaries. Sometimes it is difficult to return.' He waved to get the waiter's attention. 'Of course, if you have other plans . . .'

She caught his glance, daring her, and held it. She was still angry about Lechowski. She didn't even think she liked opera. But the thought of another evening alone in her tower, combing her e-mails while she waited for the inevitable squabble with Doug, filled her with a sudden, palpable dread.

She drained her champagne. 'What time does it start?'

Brenner Pass, Austria

Two men sat in a café at the *rästhof* on the autobahn, watching the trucks labour up the high pass. They called each other Harry and George, though they didn't attach a lot of weight to those names. George was tall and lean and stooped, with a white beard and white hair that grew in woolly curls. Harry was shorter and wider, with tousled, sandy hair and a friendly face that always seemed to be apologising for something. At the moment he was studying the inside page of a three-day-old Italian newspaper. A handwritten translation had been taped next to one of the articles. It didn't make it any easier to read.

'Can they trace him back to us?' Harry asked at last.

'They won't even try. Italian police get so many of these they probably class it as natural death.'

George grimaced. Both men knew there had been nothing natural in the way their friend had died. The newspaper detailed it with weary dispassion: the burns and broken bones, the minor amputations, the scars that had had time to form before he finally died.

'We have to assume he gave them Mirabeau. God knows I would have.'

121

George sipped his coffee and made a face. 'This whole operation was a mistake. All we've done is put them on the scent. Saint-Lazare won't stop now until he's pulled that company inside out.'

'He has to buy it first.'

'We'll fight him.' George tipped a second packet of sugar into his coffee. 'Drexler might help; perhaps Koenig. We'll give it everything we can.'

'So will they.'

They sat in silence for a moment. On the autobahn, a truck crested the pass and gathered speed as it began the descent towards the Italian border.

'What about Ellie Stanton?'

Harry studied his fingernails. 'Difficult. They're working her hard. Evenings she mostly spends in her apartment. Doesn't even walk to work.'

'Has she told Blanchard about your encounter in Oxford?'

Harry shrugged. 'I don't think so.'

'We need to get her on her own. Tell her more. If she could get into the vault for us . . .'

'I thought we agreed we wouldn't try that again,' Harry said quietly. Perhaps George didn't hear him.

'Where is she now?'

London

In a bare room, a woman in a white strapless dress wandered among long, empty tables. The lights were dim and smoky: it must be late, or very early morning. She stroked her hand along the tables, as if the touch brought back memories. She looked lost.

Ellie settled into the plush velvet seat. Her new dress, bought that afternoon, was tight against her skin. Under the lights, the woman in white hesitated under the false proscenium, then stepped through onto the raked stage sloping towards the orchestra pit.

Afterwards, Ellie found she couldn't recall the evening with any sort of precision. She had memories, vivid memories, but they were disordered, pages plucked from a book that couldn't be reassembled. Hours in the warm womb of the theatre that passed like a dream, a woman in white and a man in black and a love so immense that only music could properly describe it. The cup meant to kill them that instead made them fall in love – or did he only fall in love because he thought he was dying? Drinking champagne in the glass hall where girls like her had once sold flowers; and, later, on the roof terrace, watching the tourists and the street artists far below while a full moon rose over London. Blanchard's hand slipping over her seat-arm to rest on her thigh somewhere in the darkness of the second act, his touch hot through the thin silk of her dress. The lovers who surrendered themselves to night because they couldn't bear the starkness of day, careless of the wounds they inflicted on those they loved less well. The faithful, unheeded friend: *Take care, take care. Soon the night will pass*. And always the music, more beautiful than she had ever imagined music could be. Circling, overlapping, rolling in like great ocean waves and breaking over her as if it would dash her to pieces.

She left the theatre in a daze. She felt limp, bruised by the music and yet desperate to hear more. She clung to Blanchard's arm and he told her it was called *Tristan*-intoxication, that it was a well-known phenomenon of the opera. Part of her was glad to know it wasn't just her; part of her resented it. The emotion was so strong she couldn't bear to share it.

The Bentley was waiting for them on Floral Street, a faithful dog who always knew where to find its master. Blanchard held the door open for her.

'Would you like to come back to my home? It is not far.'

Ellie's world had shrunk again. All her choices, her past and her future, had reduced to this single point, a fulcrum. To move would tip the balance irrevocably. She could taste the champagne sweet on her tongue, smell the scent of her own perfume intoxicatingly strong. She looked at Blanchard for reassurance and saw only intent.

Take care, take care. Soon the night will pass.

The car drove down Shaftesbury Avenue, past theatre-goers emerging from the shows with their souvenir T-shirts and shopping bags held over their heads against the rain. Down Piccadilly where wet crowds huddled in the bus shelters, and right into Mayfair, to the brightly lit arcade of Claridge's hotel.

Ellie stiffened. For a moment, the spell flickered.

'I thought you said we were going to your house.'

'My home. This is where I live.'

Ellie didn't question it. A doorman held an umbrella and escorted them to the lobby. She saw Blanchard slip something in his pocket and wondered if he did that every day. The lobby was golden and bright. A man in a white dinner jacket sat at a piano playing Cole Porter and Gershwin. The concierge nodded to Blanchard and smiled respectfully at Ellie. The lights from the crystal chandelier winked back from the chequerboard floor, polished like a mirror.

Stars of bliss shine smiling down.

Blanchard's suite was on the third floor, a dimly lit world of heavy fabrics and elegantly outsize furniture. He took a bottle of champagne from the fridge and poured two glasses. The liquid was so cold it hurt. Ellie drained it in one gulp. There was nowhere in reach to put down the glass, so she let it fall on the carpeted floor. Blanchard stepped behind her to turn out the light; for a moment she felt the giddy illusion of being alone in unbounded space.

Blanchard's hands, surprisingly gentle, slid the straps of her dress off her shoulders. It slithered to the floor. He leaned around and kissed her throat, while his hands traced out her silhouette: her thighs, her hips, her taut stomach and her breasts.

Ellie sank onto the bed. Darkness enfolded them.

XVI

Normandy, 1135

October brings rain. Rain chews up the roads, rusts iron, spoils fodder. You can't build a campfire with wet wood, or a siege engine. There will be no more wars this year, and no more wars means no more knights. It will be a long winter of regret and resentment, listening to water drip through the roof and trying to keep our quarrels from spilling into violence.

All the squires feel the disappointment, but I think I feel it worse than others. I'm tired of waiting. Waiting for my spurs, waiting for my revenge, waiting for Ada. The hope that flowered in the summer has withered. Now I stand behind my lord Guy at the table and scowl. I still contrive excuses to bump into Ada in the courtyard or the corridors – I can't help myself – but when I see her I'm curt to the point of rudeness. I always regret it afterwards. Worse, it doesn't seem to bother her.

One day, I'm passing by the door to Guy's chamber when I hear Ada's voice. I pause, lurking in the impenetrable winter shadows. To my surprise, I hear my own name spoken.

'Don't leave me with Peter. If I have to be chaperoned, let Jocelin do it.'

A draught blows through the open window. My heart turns to ice. I edge further along the corridor so that Guy and Ada come into view around the doorframe. She's kneeling in front of him, lacing up his leather gauntlet. It looks obscene.

'I want Jocelin beside me for the kill.'

'Peter looks at me as if I'm something that fell down the chimney.'

Guy strokes her hair. His hands are clumsy; he'd take more care brushing his horse.

'He's obedient and trustworthy. You'll be safe with him.'

It flashes across my mind: *he doesn't trust his own son with his wife.*

Ada stands and turns away, frustrated. 'As you wish.'

If we can't make war on each other, we make war on the animals. Hunting keeps our arms strong and our aim true through the winter: it also keeps us out of mischief. Normally I enjoy it, but not today. Ada's words were like a knife through my heart – the sharper for being so private, so true. I wish Lady Death would take me.

But if Hautfort's taught me one thing, it's to bury my emotions. I keep my eyes tight on my tasks as we gather in the courtyard. I fasten my riding cloak; I saddle Ada's horse, tightening the girth and the breast-straps; I remember to look surprised when Guy tells me I'm to accompany her. It's no risk. Four of her ladies will be with us.

We ride into the woods. One of the foresters has seen boar, and Guy wants one for his table. The hounds bay and sniff about the bushes; behind them, the kennelmen walk with the mastiffs on tight leads. I think I see a resemblance to Jocelin.

I can see dark clouds gathering. The rain will return, but it doesn't put off Guy. Two of Ada's maids return to the castle; we ride further, deeper. It isn't like the Welsh forests of my childhood. The trees are more spread out, the stretches of heath and scrubland broader between.

We're in one of these open spaces when the hounds catch the scent. The wind's rising: it snaps their baying away through the long grass. I can't smell the boar but I can smell rain in the air. The unleashed hounds bound away towards the line of trees at the edge of the heath. Guy spurs after them, followed by Jocelin, Gornemant and his retainers. I stay with Ada and her ladies and watch them go. By the time they reach the trees, they're already well dispersed. In this weather, it might be hours before they raise the boar.

A plump drop of rain lands on the back of my hand. The sky looks as if it's about to fall. I gesture to the trees on the near side of the heath.

'We should get under cover.'

Ada nods, though she doesn't look at me. She looks as if she wishes she were back at the castle. We walk the horses towards the forest. I glance back, in case the hunters have changed their minds, but there's no sign of them. Thunder rolls across the heavens.

We're halfway there, riding past a lone beech tree, when the lightning strikes. It sears the air; the thunder pounces so fast that it masks the sound of cracking wood. I only hear it when a heavy branch, half a tree's worth, crashes into the grass in front of me. The lightning's blasted it clean off the trunk.

My hunter rears up with a shriek of terror: it takes all my strength and practice to rein her in. By the time I've mastered her, the other horses have scattered. I can see one galloping up a hillside without a rider; another's vanished completely.

Ahead, through the rain, I just glimpse Ada's piebald mare disappearing into the forest.

I canter after her, oblivious to the wet branches clawing and pawing at me. Ada's horse seems to be following some sort of path, though I don't know where it goes. All I can see is the flash of her cloak flitting through the trees, leading me on. We're climbing; the trees thin, oak and ash giving way to pine and fir. The ground becomes steeper and stonier. It slows the horses. Now she's only a few dozen paces ahead of me. If she were a doe, I'd risk the shot.

Ada emerges into a high clearing and halts. The rain pounds through the scrawny trees; a pile of twisted rocks makes an ominous backdrop. I slide down from the saddle and run to take her bridle. I whisper in the horse's ear to calm her, then look up at Ada. 'Are you hurt?'

'No.'

Her eyes are glazed; she's shivering. I look at the rocks and find a place where an overhang makes a rudimentary cave. In my mother's stories it would be the door to another world; here, it's just somewhere to get out of the rain. I tether the horses to a fir tree, letting the reins out loose, and join Ada under her shelter. Thunder roars over us. The storm doesn't seem to be moving.

'It won't last long.'

Ada doesn't answer. She sits with her arms around her knees, staring into the rain. She looks as if she's thinking hard. I put my cloak around her shoulders, careful not to touch her. Her dress is soaked through, plastered against the curves of her body. I try not to notice.

'What are you thinking about?'

'Things I wish I could change.'

I shift, trying to make myself comfortable on the hard

129

ground. The rush of the chase is still in my veins. It makes me say things I normally wouldn't dare.

'Do I really look at you like something that fell down the chimney?'

I'm not prepared for how furious she looks. I thought *I* was the wounded party. Now I feel compelled to defend myself.

'I was passing the door.'

'You don't understand. And you do – look at me – like that.' I think she's sobbing. The cloak's slipped off her shoulders, but when I try to rearrange it she almost slaps me away.

'You treat me like a criminal.'

'You treat me like a serf.'

'Each time you look at me, I feel I've done something unforgiveable.'

'Then what do you want me to do?'

She hesitates, closes her eyes. I think: she's going to say something so terrible it will change everything between us.

She reaches across, ever so gently, and kisses me on the lips.

I'm lying propped on my elbows. I'm so stunned I lose my balance, sliding backwards. Her eyes widen: she thinks I'm recoiling in disgust or loathing, and I reach out an arm to keep her from pulling away. I only mean to reassure her, to make her understand, but my clumsy movement brings her down on top of me. Or perhaps she comes willingly. I feel the weight of her body against mine, her flesh stiff through the sodden fabric.

After that, I hardly know what happens. She's kissing my face, my lips, my neck; she's pressing me into the damp ground; she's running her hands through my hair. She unlaces her bodice and I bury my face in her breasts. I roll on top of her, scraping my back against the low-lying rock. I fumble with her skirts, and she guides me gently inside her.

Thunder rolls its warning across the sky, but we don't heed it. The rain curtains off the world and hides us from the day. I smell rock and wood and wet earth; I feel her damp skin against mine. I imagine I hear a hunting horn and pull back, but Ada says it's only the trees creaking in the wind. She draws me back in.

At last I understand what the poets' songs mean. The walls of the world seem to melt away. All we know is each other.

XVII

London

'Where were you last night?'

Doug's voice, like water dripping down the back of her neck.

'I went to the opera.'

Ellie stood in the check-in queue and endured Doug's surprise, the obvious questions and the false answers she'd prepared. She knew she should feel guilty, but – against the enormous act of betrayal – these subsidiary lies simply irritated her.

'Just a client. It was pretty boring, actually. Went on for five hours. I forgot to turn on my phone when I came out.'

A tannoy announcement shouted down the rest of her story, as if the airport itself were ashamed of her.

'They're sending me to Brussels. I'll probably stay the weekend, meet a few people.'

She waited while the tannoy repeated its announcement.

'They're calling my flight.' Another lie. 'I'll call when I get there.

'You too.'

*

Somewhere in the depths of the night, Ellie had woken and crept to the bathroom. She splashed water on her face and stared at her body in the mirror. Moonlight flooded the room, so that her naked skin became like the marble on the walls. She felt devastated, her limbs like wax. Blanchard's love-making had been an all-out assault – not physically, but on her very being. Tenderly, delicately, he had stripped her defences until she was reduced to pure sensation, utterly in his power. It had been terrifying, but also ecstatic, a sense of utter abandonment. Even the memory made her shiver.

The light was on when she went back into the bedroom. Blanchard was sitting up in bed, his head tipped back against the pillows. His eyes slid onto her as she crossed the room, admiring her nakedness. She was surprised to find she enjoyed it, the sense of power it gave. She curled up under the duvet beside him and rested her head on his shoulder, running her fingers through the wool of white hair on his chest.

A small gold key hung on a chain around his neck. He'd stripped off everything, but not that. Ellie lifted it up and examined it. The teeth were so intricate they looked as if they'd snap off if they touched a lock; the handle was in the shape of a cross, set with a red stone.

'What does that open?'

'My heart.' Gentle but firm, Blanchard prised the key out of her grip and relocated her hand onto his stomach. He stroked her hair and said, 'You have to go away tomorrow.'

Ellie pulled back and stared at him. She tugged the duvet up to her shoulders.

'This is not because of what happened between us tonight. That changes nothing. Nothing at work,' he corrected himself. 'Between us, everything. If you want.'

Ellie no longer knew what she wanted. But Blanchard was waiting, and it seemed to matter to him. She nodded.

'I need you, Ellie. You are an extraordinary person. Together . . .' He blew air out of his mouth, as if smoking an imaginary cigar. 'We are right together. We can accomplish so many things.'

He gripped her arm and pulled her around so that she was inches from his face.

'Perhaps you think I do this every night, bring back a beautiful young woman to my bedroom. Perhaps you think it is nothing to me – or that it is too much, that I am embarrassed or ashamed. This is not the case. I am in love with you, Ellie. If others talk at the bank, it means nothing to me. But you are young and new: if your colleagues are jealous, it will hurt you.'

He leaned forward and kissed her, pressing her against the mattress, pinning her down with his body. Ellie put her palms against his chest and pushed him back. The key dangled on its chain, tickling the skin between her breasts.

'What about . . .?' She pulled a face, mock sensible. Blanchard understood.

'I'm clean.'

'I didn't mean – you see – I'm not on the pill.' Two weeks earlier she'd been so busy she'd forgotten to take it three days running. After that, she just hadn't bothered. She hadn't needed it with Doug.

'You do not need any protection with me.'

He spread her hands and buried her beneath him.

Brussels

It was Joseph Conrad who described Brussels as a whited sepulchre of a city, Ellie remembered. After two days there, digging through the accounts of a minor industrial concern, she felt she'd stepped into a grave herself. The narrow streets and imposing houses with their blinded windows; the silence; the low cloud and constant smell of rain; the Belgians themselves, every face a locked door. She would have given anything to go home for the weekend. But home meant Doug, confrontation and farewell, and she couldn't deal with that yet. She had to do it face to face, she told herself. He hadn't said anything when she stopped signing off their conversations with 'I love you'; she wondered if he'd noticed.

On Saturday morning she ordered breakfast from room service and decided to spend the day in bed with a book. If she couldn't escape Belgium, at least she could pretend it didn't exist.

She'd just got out of the shower when she heard a knock from outside. She pulled on a dressing gown and opened the door, realising how hungry she was. But there was no breakfast, and the corridor was empty. All she found was a complimentary newspaper she hadn't ordered. She picked it up; she was about to throw it straight in the bin when she felt something surprisingly solid inside.

She tipped the newspaper over. A book slid out from the central fold, a guidebook to Brussels. She wondered if it might be a free gift. But the spine was already broken, and she could see the irregular edge of a pink Post-it note poking out of the pages.

With rising anxiety, she opened the book to the marked page. A piece of paper, a folded sheet of yellowing newsprint, sat tucked into the crease. Feeling as if she was delving into some strange kind of Chinese box, Ellie opened it.

It was a single page from the *Evening Standard* dated 19 February 1988. Among the antiquated news, a small column at the bottom of the page had been asterisked.

BIZARRE DEATH IN TUBE TUNNEL

Central Line Underground services suffered severe disruptions this morning after a man was struck by a train in the deep tunnel between Bank and Liverpool Street stations.

London Underground officials expressed surprise that the man could have wandered so far, given overnight cleaning works and regular services passing through the tunnel earlier in the morning. CCTV images from the stations gave no indication of how he had managed to evade platform security and enter the tunnel.

A spokesman for London Underground said: 'Thankfully, incidents like this remain astonishingly rare. The tunnels on the Underground network are dangerous places. No member of the public should ever attempt to enter them on foot. This tragic accident only serves to illustrate the perils.'

The deceased has been identified as John Herrin, 38, of Reading, Berkshire.

Ellie sat down on the bed, trembling. There was nothing shocking in the article, beyond the faded tragedy. She had never heard the name John Herrin. It was simply the date. A date she had seen so often, gold lettering in black granite on a damp hillside near Newport.

In loving memory
ANEURIN STANTON
12th May 1949 – 19th February 1988

She flipped through the rest of the guidebook, looking for any clue to who had sent it. Various sights had been highlighted in fluorescent marker, or tagged with asterisks in the margin. The marks looked fresh.

All thoughts of reading in bed were forgotten. She pulled back the curtains, letting in the dirty autumn light, and dressed quickly. Then she went sightseeing.

'*Any tour of Brussels should start with the Grand Place.*' That line of the guidebook was highlighted and starred, so Ellie began there. She dutifully admired the fifteenth-century Hôtel de Ville with its needle spire; the baroque guildhouses with their allegorical carvings of Prudence, Faith, Justice and other virtues that the burghers had arrogated to themselves. She saw the House of the Swan, where Karl Marx had written *The Communist Manifesto*, and which was now a restaurant where you could pay thirty euros for a starter.

She spent an hour wandering through the Musées royaux des Beaux-Arts, lingering particularly in the Bosch and Breugel rooms which had drawn marks in the guidebook. Several times she spotted a man in a fawn trenchcoat behind her, always just turning away, as if a painting had suddenly interested him. By the time she reached Magritte she had almost persuaded herself to approach him, ask if he was the source of the book. But by then he'd evidently grown bored of the art and she couldn't find him.

She ate lunch in a café that the book highlighted, wondering if the whole thing was insane. She watched the other patrons carefully, waiting for one of them to pull up a chair and introduce himself, offer an explanation. None did. There was one more site marked in the book and it was the furthest away: she almost decided not to bother. But she'd come this far, so she got on the tram and rode out down the long, tree-lined avenue to the quiet suburb of Tervuren.

The Royal Museum of Central Africa stood in an imposing, lead-domed building that looked like a mausoleum. It was a place out of time, an anomaly in the fabric of history. Built as a monument to King Leopold's vanity, it had opened the year his vicious reign in the Congo finally became too much even for his countrymen to stomach. In the 1960s the winds of change had blown in just enough to shake loose the 'Congo' from its name, but not enough to disturb the dust on the old collections. Lions and elephants stood rigorously stiff in glass cases, poised as their killers had posed them. The only reference Ellie found to the savagery of the Belgian occupation was in a brief display in a gallery at the far end of the building, an apologetic footnote tucked at the bottom of the page. She thought of Conrad again, and wondered how many of those profits had poured into accounts at Monsalvat.

The horror, she murmured to herself.

'We meet again.'

She spun around. A short, tubby man with tousled hair and an apologetic expression was watching her from across a cabinet of ivory tusks. Perhaps she'd half expected him, but she was still shocked. It occurred to her that he'd bided his time, waiting until she reached the furthest, emptiest place in this distant, empty building. There were no guards here. The whole long corridor leading away from the room was deserted.

'I'll scream,' she warned him.

'Please don't.' He stepped away, holding up his hands, as if she were pointing a gun at him. It unnerved her.

'Why did you send me that newspaper article?'

He looked out of the window, at the green lawns and grey sky. 'Let's go for a walk.'

*

London

There was nothing special about the building at No. 46 Lombard Street, unless you looked at the roof. On four floors it housed an insurance company, a firm of headhunters who preferred the term 'executive search', a commodities trader and a small consultancy. But on the roof, unseen and unnoticed, there grew a forest of antennae, dishes, aerials and masts. They twitched in the wind, feeling out the least ghost of information.

If you could have followed your way through the tangle of holding companies and blind trusts that owned the building, you would eventually arrive – by way of Liechtenstein, Monaco, Luxembourg and the Channel Islands – almost back where you started. And if you could have followed your way through the tangle of electrical cables coiled up in the basement, they too would have led to the same place: out of the building, a hundred metres underground along Lombard Street, and up into a dark room on the fifth floor of an old building behind King William Street, filled with the hum of electronics. In that room, if you could have peered through one of the many screens that lit it, you would have seen two men staring at a map overlaid with red lines like a child's scribble.

'It's too easy,' said Destrier. 'In the old days we'd have needed six men to keep tabs on her – backup vehicles, disguises, the lot. Now her phone tells us every step she takes and it's not even illegal.'

Blanchard examined the map. 'She's been busy.'

'All the tourist sites.' Destrier made a gesture on the touchscreen and the map zoomed out. Now the red lines looked a tangled ball of string, with a single thread trailing off the end. 'Right now, she's at the Congo Museum.'

'Show me the time profile.'

Destrier pushed a button. The lines changed again, swelling or contracting so that the thickness showed the length of time spent in any given place. Stringy veins where she'd been travelling, broad pools where she'd lingered in the museums. It made the overlay look like a giant blood splatter.

'She's spending a long time at the Musée d'Afrique.'

'Maybe she likes dead animals.'

Blanchard stared at the screen. 'Do you have watchers?'

'Two guys followed her for a couple of hours this morning at the art gallery. Saw a thousand pictures of fat women and nothing else, then buggered off. Not very cultured, my guys. Koenig's in town; Saint-Lazare said he was a higher priority.'

'Of course. How about phone calls?'

'Not many.'

'Any to Oxford?'

'One a night. Talks for about ten or fifteen minutes.'

'Were you listening?'

Destrier gave him a sly look. 'She hasn't told him about her night at the opera, if that's what you're wondering.'

Blanchard didn't rise to the bait. 'Keep monitoring her.'

Brussels

Outside the museum the grounds descended in a series of severely geometric terraces towards an ornamental lake. The pale gravel crunched like bonemeal underfoot, powdering Ellie's shoes white. At least there were more people here, families with dogs and children roaming about on a Saturday afternoon. Ellie said nothing, waiting. But her companion seemed in no mood to speak either. He slouched along with his hands in his coat pocket, darting little glances over his shoulder.

140

'Who are you?' Ellie said at last.

His face brightened. He looked glad for the opening, and it occurred to Ellie that perhaps he was as nervous as she was.

'You can call me Harry.'

'Are you a spy?'

He thought about that. 'Not in any political sense. I belong to a group that prizes secrecy.'

'Like the Freemasons?'

'Not really.'

He paused, examining his reflection in the pond. 'I'm sorry about all the cloak-and-dagger. I tried to get you at the art gallery, but they were watching.'

Ellie could feel herself skating on a thin layer of credulity, talking and nodding as if this were a perfectly normal conversation. 'Who's *they*?'

'Your employers.'

'Of course. The medieval heart of darkness, spying on me all the time.' She rounded on him. 'Why did you give me that newspaper article?'

'Because I thought you should know the truth.' He held her gaze. 'John Herrin was your father. John Herrin was Aneurin Stanton.'

'My dad died in a car crash,' she said numbly.

'That's what your mother told you.'

They turned left, along a long rectangular lake. Everything here was straight lines: the horizontal banks of the lake and the path running parallel; the perpendicular bars of a row of poplars.

'What's your version?'

'Pretty much what it said in the paper. He was hit by a train in an Underground tunnel. Died instantly.'

Ellie felt dizzy. 'Can we sit down?'

'It's better if we keep moving.' Harry glanced over his shoulder. 'He died trying to break into the Monsalvat Bank.'

'Is that what you are? Bank robbers?'

'Monsalvat have something in their vaults that belongs to us – something they stole a long time ago. Nye Stanton died trying to get it back. Now you're their star young banker.' He pouted, feigning surprise. 'Coincidence, no?'

'So – what? You rigged the competition to get me in there? You thought I'd unlock the vault to let you go in and get what you want?'

'We didn't have anything to do with it.'

They passed a small boy feeding bread to a flock of ducks. The birds pecked and jabbed and half-drowned each other to get to the crumbs. Harry glanced at his watch.

'We haven't got much time. You've been working on the Talhouett takeover.' It wasn't a question. 'Has anybody mentioned Mirabeau to you?'

'No.'

'Do you know the Lazarus account?'

Ellie remembered the red folder she'd seen lying on Blanchard's desk. 'No.'

'Please think, Ellie. This is more important than you can imagine.'

'Important to who?' The thin ice that had supported her belief, that had allowed her to play along with the charade as if it made any sense, suddenly shattered into a thousand pieces. She flailed, drowning in the rush of doubt. 'You say I'm being spied on, but the only person I've seen spying on me is you. You come here with crazy stories about my dad that can't be true. I don't know who you are, but if I see you again, I swear I'll call the police. I'll tell Blanchard.'

'If you do that, you'll never see us again.'

'I don't want to.'

'No. But you might need to.'

He thrust a business card into her hand and hurried away. No name or logo, just a phone number and a scribbled note. *If no answer, leave a message for Harry from Jane.*

'Do you expect me to use this?' she shouted after him. He didn't look back.

She thought about tearing the card into pieces and scattering it on the wind, or dropping it in the long reflecting pool. Being rid of him for good.

But just the same, she put it in her pocket.

XVIII

Normandy, 1135

It's getting dark by the time we ride out of the forest. The rain's stopped; the clouds have moved to the horizon. They hover over the sunset, bruising it like a fist. I let Ada ride half a length ahead of me, as befits my lord's wife. Neither of us speaks. There is more inside us than we can possibly say.

When I thought Ada hated me, I longed to know what she was thinking. Now that I think she loves me, not knowing is almost unbearable. An hour ago there was nothing between us, but the doubts have already started to set in. *Does she regret it? Has she changed her mind? Is she thinking about Guy?*

The thought of Guy sinks my spirits. Suddenly, what we've done seems less like the fulfilment of my dreams, more like a monumental error.

I'm still thinking about it when the clashing of steel rings into the evening air. It's coming from a thicket that stands like an island in the middle of the next field.

'Wait here.'

I kick my horse and canter across the field. The earth

beneath his hooves is white with ash from the burned stubble. I can't find a way in to the copse, so I dismount and push through the briars and brambles on foot. It's so dark inside I can barely see the branches, but there's no mistaking the urgent sounds of battle. Sparks light up the small clearing in the middle of the thicket: I can make out two dim figures lunging and retreating from each other like dancers. One's a knight in full armour, a shield on his arm and a sword in his hand. He's dismounted; the weight encumbers him. It's just as well for his opponent, who's got nothing more than a brown tunic and a fur-trimmed mantle to protect him. He doesn't even carry a sword: he's desperately parrying the knight's attacks with a straight-bladed hunting knife.

It's Guy.

It's like watching a dog baiting a bear – except that the bear's claws have told. Guy's limping from a cut in his thigh; he can't run. The knight swings, and the strength in his blow knocks the knife clean out of Guy's weakened grasp. It flies away into the bushes, lost. Guy's helpless.

He has his back to me; he hasn't seen me. In a flash, I see how easy it would be to slip away into the undergrowth. He's wounded and unprotected: he'd never leave this thicket alive. Ada would be a widow and could remarry who she liked.

It all rushes through my head in a split second. Is God tempting me, or has He granted me this golden opportunity to set right all the sufferings of my life? But I'll never know what I'd have chosen. The knight lunges to his left and Guy staggers out of the way, turning. His head comes up and he sees me. I know he does, because his face changes so much even his enemy notices. Quick as a rat, the knight pivots to meet me.

I'm committed – and all I have to defend myself is my knife. I reach for it, but only feel cloth. It's not in my belt where it should be – in fact, my belt isn't there either. I must have left it in the forest. I feel the dizzy terror of being utterly defenceless.

The knight's confused – he must take me for some page or peasant who's wandered into the battle. He doesn't know whether to kill me now or wait until he's dealt with Guy.

Guy moves. The knight, knowing he's the real threat, turns and lifts his shield.

I feel a stone against my foot. Unnoticed, I bend down and scoop it up. It's about the size of an apple, snug in my hand. With an instinct I've been honing all my life, I hurl it at the knight's head.

I have a good throwing arm. It strikes him clean on the back of the skull, just below the rim of his helmet. He staggers; I haven't knocked him out, but I've stunned him. It's all the opening a veteran like Guy needs. He steps forward, twists the knight's sword out of his hand, and has it at his throat in a trice.

'Who sent you?'

The knight doesn't answer. Perhaps he's still dazed. Guy doesn't think so: he reverses the sword and slams the pommel into the knight's face. Blood gushes from his broken nose.

'*Who?*'

He mutters something I can't make out. Even Guy isn't sure. He says, 'Athold?'

The knight nods and doubles over. He spits out a wad of blood. Guy takes a step back. I remember what Gornemant taught me. Never kill a knight who surrenders to you. Always think of the ransom.

Distracted by my thoughts, I barely see the movement. There's a hiss and a squelch: the next thing I see, Guy is pulling the sword out of the knight's throat. I hear a patter like raindrops as the knight's blood drips onto the leafy floor. Guy wipes the sword on his mantle. He glances at the blade, then at me: for a thrilling moment I think he's going to dub me there and then.

He scowls, and jams the sword in his belt.

'Where was your knife?'

'I dropped it in the forest.'

I can't meet his gaze – but it doesn't linger on me. He's already striding away.

'Will you make me a knight?' I call after him. It's an impertinent question, but I've just saved his life. I'm not prepared for the look of fierce hatred he answers me with.

'You saved me with a rock. Any boy who's ever shied at pigeons could have done the same.'

We find my horse at the edge of the copse. Without asking, Guy swings himself into the saddle and rides ahead. I stumble after him through the ashen fields. When we reach the road my heart lurches: Ada's not there. I can see hoofprints in the mud heading down the road, just one set, and I hope it means she rode back to the castle. Guy, thankfully, doesn't see them.

Much later, I realise why he was so ungrateful to me – and why he killed the knight when he could have had the ransom. He's an old man, with an old man's vanities. He doesn't want anyone to know how close he came to being killed.

XIX

London

'Have you ever heard of a man called John Herrin?'

Ellie covered the phone with her hand, though her door was shut. For all she dismissed Harry's dark hints and allegations, she felt uneasy calling from the office. But her mother went to bed so early these days it was hard to catch her any other time.

'Herrin?' Her mother sounded weary, too old for a woman who hadn't yet reached retirement. Perhaps it was the line, which hissed and clicked like a shortwave radio. Ellie would have to get the phone company to look at it next time she visited. 'Like the bird?'

Ellie spelled it out. 'I think he might have known Dad.'

'Ah . . .' A sigh, like a willow rustling in the wind. For as long as Ellie could remember, a distance had entered her mother's voice whenever the subject of her father came up. 'Nye had so many friends. I didn't know them well, you know. Things were different then.'

148

Ellie drew a deep breath. 'When Dad . . . died . . . it was just a car accident, wasn't it? No one thought there was anything suspicious.'

A long pause.

'It was a long time ago.' She closed the door, gentle but absolute. 'When are you coming home, Eleanor?'

'Soon,' Ellie promised, ashamed. 'Work keeps me so busy. But I'll be there for Christmas.'

'And Douglas?'

'He's fine.'

'Will he come for Christmas too?'

Ellie bit her lip. 'I don't know.'

'It would be nice. You make such a lovely couple together.'

When she'd hung up, Ellie logged on to the bank's main system and looked up the account for the Spenser Foundation. She remembered the name from the cheque they'd sent when she won the essay competition: she'd wasted half an afternoon enjoying the sheer possession of it, touching the stiff paper that spoke of wealth, admiring the bank's crest stamped in the corner. The first time she'd crossed paths with Monsalvat Bank. She'd even let herself imagine not depositing it – keeping it as a trophy. But in the end, five hundred pounds was five hundred pounds.

The account information appeared on-screen. Ellie stared.

In the entire history of the Spenser Foundation, there had only ever been two transactions. In March of last year, five hundred pounds had been transferred in electronically. Two months later, it had been withdrawn in the form of a cheque – made out, though the system didn't record it, to Ellie Stanton. Nobody had touched the account since then.

So where did the money come from? She could see from the

prefix it was another Monsalvat account. She clicked to get its details.

Legrande Holdings. This account was much busier, a steady stream of comings and goings. But while the money travelled out in all directions, it seemed to come from one principal source. Saint-Lazare Investments (UK) Ltd.

Her pulse was racing, though there was nothing wrong about what she was doing. She clicked to view the Saint-Lazare account.

ACCESS DENIED

Ellie tasted cigar smoke in her mouth and looked up. Blanchard was leaning against the door, watching her with his usual inscrutable expression. How long had he been there?

'I didn't hear you knock.' Trying to be casual, she brushed the computer's trackpad to close the open window.

'You were concentrating very hard. I did not want to disturb.'

'I'm just tired.'

For a moment, she imagined telling him everything – Harry, Brussels, John Herrin. All she wanted was for Blanchard to wrap his arms around her and reassure her. Harry was a fantasist, a lunatic worming his way into the gilded life she'd been given.

But there was just enough in his story to give her pause. Not the bald facts, which were unbelievable, but the spaces around them. Her mother's silence when she mentioned John Herrin. The Spenser foundation's accounts. A sense of ACCESS DENIED, secrets she wasn't privy to.

You don't say anything to Blanchard without being sure of your ground.

Ellie's face had pinched in thought. Blanchard read it as tiredness. 'Perhaps you need to rest. I was going to ask if you wished to join me for dinner tonight. There will be clients there,' he added apologetically, 'but they are quite civilised.'

Once again, his frank stare seemed to look right through her, as if he could see her heart somersaulting inside her chest. She knew she shouldn't. She'd spent three weeks in Brussels persuading herself that it had been an aberration, a one-off mistake she could redeem by forgetting it. But Blanchard aroused a hunger in her, an animal instinct that dislodged all right and reason.

'I'd love to.'

And even as she said it, she knew she would go to her flat beforehand and put some clean clothes and bathroom things in her bag. Just in case.

Footsteps in the corridor released her from Blanchard's stare. Destrier's thick frame filled the doorway. He shot Ellie a furious look that made her wonder what she'd done.

'Got a minute?' he asked Blanchard.

'They've got to her.'

Destrier paced his office. He was angry and sweating, though the air conditioners kept the room at a steady twenty degrees and the monitors bathed the room in a cool soothing blue. 'She tried to access the Saint-Lazare account.'

'So? She knows she's working on a deal for them.'

'Look at the history.' Destrier pointed to the screen. 'Spenser Foundation, Legrande Holdings, Saint-Lazare. She's following the money. She's also just called her mother, which she hardly ever does, and started asking some odd questions.'

He pressed a button. Ellie's voice filled the room through the recessed speakers, as real as if she were standing beside them.

'*When Dad . . . died . . . it was just a car accident, wasn't it? No one thought there was anything suspicious.*'

'Now where would she have got an idea like that?'

'You're supposed to be able to tell me,' said Blanchard acidly.

'Well, we can both guess who it was. How and when, I don't have a fucking clue.'

'I told you to watch her.'

'You also told me to keep a light footprint and not let her get suspicious. She's a smart girl: she'll notice if we go in too hard. One of my chaps already thinks she might have made him in the art gallery in Brussels.'

Destrier thought for a moment.

'We can fix her phone. There's a toy we can install that turns it into a microphone, broadcasts even when she thinks it's off. Kills the battery quick, though, which she'll notice. Might miss some important calls.'

Blanchard nodded. 'Do it. If she stops for five minutes, if she is not in her office or the apartment and you do not have sight of her, turn it on.'

'Even at night?' Destrier gave him a sly leer, which Blanchard affected not to notice.

'Especially at night.'

'She still hasn't told the boyfriend, in case you're wondering,' Destrier called after him.

Oxford

She almost pleaded ill and called it off. Even though it was his birthday, arranged for weeks, she almost persuaded herself it would be kinder on him not to go. But that would be unforgivable cowardice. Her only consolation in the whole affair had been that Doug didn't know how badly she'd betrayed him. To do something to hurt him, however minor, was more than her conscience could bear. So she went.

In the second week of December, Oxford became a ghost town. The students left, taking their noise and confidence and sense of ownership; in their wake came the hopefuls, interview candidates hoping one day it might belong to them. Desperate for companionship in their solitary ordeal, they clustered together and roamed the streets in groups twenty or thirty strong. Five years earlier that had been Ellie. She scanned the faces as she passed them and wondered what would become of them.

Doug could tell that something was wrong. She kept on catching him giving her anxious looks. He asked ten times if she was feeling OK; each time Ellie gritted a smile and said fine, just working too hard. Eventually he took the hint and stopped asking, but she could see the concern on his face. Every time he opened his mouth, even to clear his throat, she had to stifle her terror. *Is there someone else? Are you cheating on me?* But he never asked.

On Saturday night, she took him for a birthday meal at a restaurant on the Banbury Road. She'd looked at the menu once or twice when she was a student and laughed at the prices; now they only seemed average. The dining room sat inside a wrought-iron conservatory, filled with fronded plants and fairy lights, a true winter garden. Ellie thought it was magical; Doug just looked uncomfortable. When the waitress arranged his napkin on his lap, he sat stiff as a corpse until she'd gone. If she came and poured more wine, he'd break off whatever he was saying and stare awkwardly at his plate. Ellie barely noticed her.

Doug tried to order risotto, the cheapest dish on the menu. Ellie overruled it and ordered him a rib-eye steak, with a bottle of Saint-Émilion, which she thought she remembered from one of her dinners with Blanchard.

'It's your birthday,' she reminded him. 'We should celebrate.'

She handed over the small box and watched anxiously as he opened it.

'A watch.'

It was Omega, bought from Brussels Duty Free for a price that owed more to guilt than value. Without much enthusiasm, Doug slipped off his own watch to try it on.

'You didn't have to,' he murmured. 'The old one works fine.'

She remembered it had been a present from his father when he graduated.

'A change might be nice, once in a while.' To her guilty ears, even that simple sentiment was heavy with double-meaning. She cringed. Had Doug noticed?

I am not going to ruin his birthday.

He raised his glass. 'It's nice to see you.'

'Happy birthday.' They chinked their glasses tentatively, as if afraid of breaking something.

'I was thinking about Christmas,' Doug said. 'I know it's late, but perhaps we could go away, get a cottage somewhere. Maybe even go abroad. The college gave me a travel bursary for Paris and there's some money left over. I suppose you could afford it.' He reached across the table and put his hand on hers. 'We could use some time together.'

Ellie squirmed. *I'm sleeping with someone else.* She wanted to scream it, so loud the glass walls would shatter, the roof fall in and the cosy warmth blow away into the night.

'I promised Mum I'd spend Christmas with her.'

By Christmas, you'll never want to see me again, she thought.

She couldn't bear to see his disappointment – a proxy for all the ways he didn't know she'd let him down. 'Maybe in February, for our anniversary.'

I am not going to ruin his birthday.

Doug fingered the metal strap of his new watch as if it itched.

'How's your work going?' she tried.

His face brightened. 'Very well. You remember the poem I told you about, the old guy in the wheelchair? I sent him some preliminary thoughts and he liked them a lot. Invited me up to Scotland to see the original. Offered to pay for my train fare and everything.'

'When are you going?'

'I went. Last weekend. He said I could bring my girlfriend, but you were in Brussels or somewhere.'

Always the reproach. In a way, she drew strength from it. It made it easier to think about what she had to do.

'How was it?'

'Amazing. You should have seen this place. I had to change trains at Edinburgh and again at Inverness. This gnarled old gillie type picked me up from the station in his Land Rover, drove me about an hour into the mountains. Just when I thought we must be completely lost, we came over the ridge and there's this castle on a hill rising up out of the forest. Forget Scots Baronial revival – this was the real thing, probably fourteenth century. You could still see the moat, though someone had tried to turn it into a ha-ha when they landscaped the gardens in the eighteen hundreds.'

The waitress brought their food.

'It was almost dark when we got there. The gillie led me into this great medieval hall, tapestries and hammer beams and a fireplace you could park a car in. There was a table with twenty chairs and one place set – for me. Apparently, Mr Spencer couldn't make it for dinner but would join me afterwards.'

He saw the flash of surprise on Ellie's face. 'Mr Spencer's the chap in the wheelchair. Anyway, it was all kind of eerie. There were about a hundred dead deer on the walls and they all seemed to be staring at me while I ate. Venison, to make it worse. And after supper, Spencer rolled in with his minder and brought out this leather case. Inside was a single leaf of parchment with the poem on it, hand-written in gall ink.'

'Was it genuine?'

Doug sliced off a piece of steak, relishing it. 'I'm no expert, but it looked pretty authentic to me. You could see where the acid had etched into the parchment. I asked if he'd had any tests done and the minder said the parchment had been authenticated as twelfth century. *Twelfth century*, for God's sake. He hadn't had the handwriting done, because he didn't want anyone to read it. Fair enough. I told him I didn't know much about palaeography, but the text certainly rang true for that period.'

'So what did he want you to do with it?'

'Mr Spencer thinks the poem's a riddle. He thinks it leads to buried treasure or something.' Doug rolled his eyes. 'At least, that's what the minder said. The old man never says a word. Just sits there sucking on his respirator.'

Ellie topped up the wine glasses. 'So what do you think?'

'There's a riddle all right, but it's nothing to do with lost treasures.' He leaned across the table, cupping his glass in his hand. 'The real question is, who wrote it?'

It was obvious from his face he had an idea, that it excited him very much. Ellie played along with a wide-eyed stare. 'And?'

'I can't tell you.'

She slapped his wrist across the table. 'Cheat.'

He gave a shamefaced grin. 'I'd love to. But I signed a confidentiality agreement.' He inclined his head towards the next table, where a group of dressed-up young men and women were laughing loudly. He lowered his voice to a mock whisper. 'You never know who could be listening.'

They're listening, Ellie. All the time. Suddenly, the glass room felt more like a cage than a garden. She pulled her shawl over her shoulders. Doug didn't notice.

'I stayed up half the night poring over the parchment. The poem's only eight lines long, but I wanted to remember every detail, every fibre in the parchment. I drank it up. In the morning the housekeeper rolled it up and put it away, the gillie drove me back to the station, and I was trundling back to Oxford.' He shook his head in wonder. 'Sometimes I wonder if I dreamed the whole thing.'

Talking about the trip to Scotland had warmed Doug up. He no longer looked offended by the restaurant. He tucked into his steak with unfeigned enthusiasm; the wine flowed out of the bottle until it was empty. When the waitress took their plates and asked if they wanted pudding, Ellie glanced across the table and saw a familiar suggestive smile on Doug's face.

'Just the bill.'

Afterwards, Ellie knew it was unforgivable. She should have told him the truth. But somehow it was never the right time. On Saturday night they slept together for the first time in weeks – a birthday present and a farewell all wrapped in one – and when she woke on Sunday morning Doug was already in the kitchen cooking her breakfast. They walked through the University Parks, pale with frost and winter sun, and each time Ellie thought she'd summoned her courage the moment seemed too good to spoil. Maybe it was nervous energy, or the delicate knowledge it was almost over, but she felt closer to him than she had in months. All her senses were heightened: the smell of his coat when she snuggled against him on a park bench; the touch of his lips when he kissed her; the laughter as they sat outside the Turf Tavern drinking mulled wine. The intensity reminded her of their first few weeks together. Before she knew it, she was sitting on a train pulling out of Oxford station and she still hadn't told him.

And when she went back to the Barbican flat after work on Monday, the Bentley was waiting at the kerb. The driver lowered his window.

'Mr Blanchard wanted to know if you'll be joining him tonight.'

She didn't blink. 'I'll just get my things.'

It happened the same way the following night. When the car didn't appear on Wednesday she almost panicked; she spent a lonely night replaying everything that had happened that day, wondering what she might have done to upset Blanchard. But on Thursday the car was there again. By Friday, it felt routine.

Soon after that Ellie realised she had become . . . what? Blanchard's mistress? He wasn't married, and she was barely attached herself any more. His girlfriend? That was a ludicrous word to use with Blanchard, who probably hadn't had a girlfriend since he was twenty-five, if in fact he'd ever been that young. It was hard to imagine; he felt ageless.

Eventually Ellie decided on 'lover'. It sounded continental and sophisticated, which she liked, and a touch old-fashioned, like Blanchard himself. It was also accurate. However many dinners and concerts she sat through, however many clients she met, there was always a sense of biding time. The heart of their relationship remained where it had begun, in the bedroom.

Or perhaps she was more than that. Otherwise, the following Monday, Blanchard might not have summoned her from her office and taken her to the sixth floor.

XX

Normandy, 1135

The storm drove water into the woodshed: the fire smoulders red, and smoke fills the hall. Guy paces angrily, while Gornemant, Jocelin, and the half-dozen knights he's managed to summon stand attendance. I lean against a tapestry, woven in with the wool figures. I know I should be concentrating on their council, but all I can think about is Ada. I know she came back safely, alone, but I'm desperate to see her. I try to remember the soft skin of her breasts, her taste on my tongue and her body enclosing me. I clench my fists with frustration.

Guy is talking about Athold du Laurrier, his neighbour. I've never seen him, but I know his reputation. If sheep disappear from a field, or a hayrick burns, or someone steals the blades of a plough, Guy blames Athold. It occurs to me that Athold probably says the same about Guy.

'While we were hunting, they raided Massigny,' says Gornemant. Massigny is a village near the edge of Guy's fiefholding. 'They killed three men and drove off a dozen more.'

Guy slams the palm of his hand against a pillar. He's not grieving; he couldn't care about the lives of a few peasants. He's furious about the insult to his authority – and the cost. Those men will need ransoms, and if Guy doesn't contribute the peasants will start to think about switching their allegiance.

'If he wants a war, I'll give him a war.'

It's a small, vicious war. There's a lot of suffering, though not many deaths. It's harder to kill someone when your arm's chilled to the bone, your tunic's soaked through and your sword is blunt with rust. It will never make a great tale. Sometimes I wonder if I brought this calamity down on Guy – if this war is God's punishment for my sin. It doesn't stop me sinning more. It's hard to have an affair in a castle in a state of war – routines are unpredictable, corridors busy, eyes sharp. But we manage. Each encounter is brusque, the physical pleasure attenuated by the terror of discovery. Sometimes Ada cries and says she can't go on. I cradle her head to my chest and tell her I love her.

When I'm alone, I sit and list the times and places. *There* in the stables behind the winter fodder; *there* in her own bedroom while Guy was away; *there* in the storeroom at the back of the tower, while mice scuttled around the grain sacks. I chart the encounters compulsively, surveying the battlefields of this invisible war we're fighting against the world. I remember the press of her body against mine. I feel the wounds.

Guy's war ends in March.

A misty morning: the world caught between winter and spring. Leafless trees seem to float in the fog; the rising sun makes a line of gold in the sky. Three of us are riding across a hillside meadow. We're supposed to be patrolling for Athold's

161

men, but in this mist they could ride past a hundred yards away and they'd be invisible.

Jocelin rides in front; I follow a few paces behind with William, one of the other squires. Jocelin and I will never be friends, but as we've grown up, we've found ways of ignoring each other. We're all fully armed, except for the spurs which none of us has won yet. The weight of the armour feels natural now, a second skin, and I'm grateful for the quilted undercoat which keeps me warm.

Ahead, Jocelin pulls up and stares at the ground. A muddy scar cuts across the turf. Hoof prints. It rained in the night – these tracks are fresh.

'Just one of them,' William mutters. Jocelin shoots him a withering look.

'Only if he was riding a ten-legged horse. Look how close the prints are. They were riding single file, to hide their numbers.'

We follow the tracks down the hill to the river. They go in as one, but emerge individually: it's hard to keep a strict line through water, hard to scramble up a bank where it's already been trampled down. We count five or six sets of hooves, all pressed deep into the ground. Whoever's riding them is carrying a lot of weight.

'We should ride back, warn Guy.'

This time it's my turn to feel Jocelin's scorn. 'Warn him that someone's left footprints on his land? He'll want more than that.'

Down in the valley, the fog's thicker than ever, but I know there's a village a few hundred yards upstream, around a bend in the hillside. It was part of Ada's lands, now Guy's, though Athold covets it for the mill. If he can sell flour, rather than the corn his tenants give him, he can raise more money, buy more land or men to conquer it. He has four young sons and an ambitious wife: he needs to expand.

We tether our horses in a stand of willows and make our way upriver towards the village. We cross on the weir. Usually, the miller charges travellers to use it as a footbridge, but there's no one here now. We crawl across, clinging to the boards, which are slick and slippery from the spray. White water foams beneath us.

The village straggles along a rough track, pitted and furrowed. Wood-framed houses line the road: their thatched roofs pitched so low they almost touch the ground. Creeping from house to house, we come to a small church with a roofed gallery surrounding it. Once, my mother told me, they were built to keep the graves dry: now the dead are left to soak in the churchyard, and the roof shelters the commerce of hawkers, vagrants, friars and young lovers. This morning it's empty. All the villagers have been gathered on the triangle of grazing land in front of the church, herded there by the quartet of mounted knights who rest their swords across their horses' shoulders. A fifth, wrapped in a red cloak and with a red shield on his shoulder, sits astride his warhorse and addresses them from on high.

Jocelin tugs my sleeve. 'Athold,' he mouths to me. 'Go back to Hautfort. Fetch my father.'

I'm trembling, but there's no way I'm going to leave. 'Send William.'

Jocelin scowls, but it's no place to argue. William's two years younger, with spindly red hair and a face like a cheese. He'll do as he's told.

'Ride to the castle. Tell Guy that Athold is here, with a small force and vulnerable. Bring him as quick as you can.'

William slips away. Sheltering behind the church wall, Jocelin and I listen to what Athold is saying. All we can see is the cone of his helmet, and the point of his spear.

'From now on, your tithes and your taxes come to me.' He

walks his horse back and forth in front of the villagers. The helmet traverses the top of the wall. One of the villagers must say something: all of a sudden, the helmet stops and Athold shouts.

'Guy de Hautfort is no longer your lord. Can he protect you? *Can he protect you*?' The spear rises and swings down. I hear a grunt and a scream. He must have cracked it over some poor unfortunate's head.

'Where is the miller?'

A shuffling in the crowd as the man comes forward.

'You are *my* tenant now. For supplying my enemy, Guy de Hautfort, your mill is forfeit.'

I remember the miller, I've seen him before. An old man with white hair and white skin, as if flour had been ground into every pore. His voice is strong and clear. 'The mill is my patrimony. My family have always kept it.'

'Until now.'

A desperate note. 'What will my son inherit?'

'Your son? Is this him?' The helmet turns a fraction, tilts forward. 'Is it true you're worried about your inheritance?'

I don't hear the answer. Athold doesn't either. 'Speak up.'

'Yes.'

'Yes . . .?'

'Yes, my lord.'

'So.' Athold considers this. Then, so fast I barely catch it, the spear spins around and stabs down. I hear a woman's screams. An angry chatter rolls through the crowd, but Athold's knights advance their horses and the noise stops. Everything but the screams, which subside to a low sobbing, as if someone's heart's been torn out.

'Now you don't need to worry about his inheritance.'

The helmet moves away. The spear-tip rises again, streaked with blood.

164

One by one, the villagers come forward and swear fealty to Athold. I can't see, but I imagine they have to take it kneeling in the mud beside the still-bleeding corpse. A terrible dread hangs over the village. It's not Athold they fear any more, but Guy. In a month or a year's time, if he wins this war, he'll sit on his horse in front of them and demand fealty, and someone else's son will have to die as an example.

The gallery floor creaks. A gap-toothed man in a floppy cap has come round behind and is staring at us in shock. I put a finger to my lips and wave him to be quiet.

But he still has mud on his knees from swearing loyalty to Athold. He knows how to impress his new lord.

'It's Guy's son.'

We race across the road and down a lane to the mill. Hooves pummel the ground behind us. I'm running so hard my heart might burst, but the weight of my armour holds me back. I see the river in front of me. The hooves drum in my ears. Then we're on the weir, running across the treacherous planks so fast we don't have time to fall. A spear clatters off one of the stone piers, and I look back.

Athold's men have pulled up at the water's edge. The river's too fast and deep to cross, and their mounts would never manage the weir. They'll have to go down to the ford, cross, ride back. It gives us a head start.

But the ford isn't far, and by the time we've gathered our horses from the willow stand we've lost precious minutes. We follow William's tracks, back up the hill and out of the mist towards Hautfort. It's open heathland here, good riding country.

A horn sounds behind us. Looking back, I see five horsemen coming over the crest of the hill. They rise out of the mist like waves from the sea. The tips of their lances glint in the sunlight. Athold's seen Jocelin: he knows if he can catch him now, he'll have Guy checkmated.

I know where I fit on this chessboard – a front-rank pawn, blocking the way to the more valuable pieces. I turn my back and ride. I'm galloping, standing in my stirrups crouched low over the saddle. The horse's mane billows back in my face. Something flies through the air to my right, an arrow. I'm riding so fast I could almost outpace it: they won't get through my armour, but they might yet injure the horses. I kick my mount again, though he's giving everything he can.

A low wall approaches. My mount clears it with a clean bound, but the horse behind isn't so lucky. I hear an animal scream and the clatter of stone; when I turn back, a black horse is writhing on the ground, hooves flailing. Jocelin lies outstretched behind him.

I only have a split second to make the choice, and I don't hesitate. I would happily see Jocelin trampled into the mud under Athold's hooves, but Guy would never forgive it. I rein in my horse, turn, and charge towards the pursuing riders.

There are four of them, with another further back. I aim for the smallest and lower my spear. The knight draws his sword and spurs his horse faster.

It's different from practising in the orchard. Apple trees don't move: here, everything happens twice as fast. The wind makes my eyes tear; I can feel the ash-shaft hard against my palm. He lifts his shield. I aim my spear. I try to remember everything Gornemant said.

And then I'm past. *I've missed him* – I don't know how. Was it cowardice? Did I shy away at the crucial moment, fail my first test as a knight? I've no time to think. There's another rider ahead. He wasn't expecting me to break through: his shield's on his back and his sword still in its scabbard.

I'm not going to fail again. I raise my spear and try to hold it steady against the rise and fall of the horse. Everything is aligned: my eyes, my breath, the spear tip, the knight's exposed face. Gornemant wouldn't approve – he says you should aim for the body, the biggest target – but I don't want to unhorse my enemy. I want to kill him.

This time I don't shy away. The spear strikes and sinks in, so deep there's no chance to pull it free. I have to let go or I'll be yanked off my horse. My arm's numb, shivering. It's only later I realise that the lance went clean through his skull and struck the back of his helmet. I wheel my horse and look back.

The knight's slumped over in his saddle, the spear still implanted in his head like a heron's beak. Now I can see the device on the shield strapped to his back – a red field and a white bar. Athold's arms.

The other knights are leaping down from their horses, casting their weapons to the ground, pulling off their helmets. I think Athold's death must have broken them: then I see a dozen knights cantering towards us. Guy's at their head on his chestnut charger, his banner floating behind him. He slips out of his saddle and runs to Jocelin, who groans and rubs his head. He'll live, at least long enough to tell the story of how I saved him.

Surely now Guy will make me a knight.

XXI

London

'Come with me.'

There was no preamble, none of the small compliments he usually offered on her dress or her hair. His tone gave nothing away. She couldn't even see his face as she hurried after him to the lift. Walking out of her office, she saw a small mound of ash on the carpet by the door, and wondered how long Blanchard had been standing there.

They're listening, Ellie, all the time.

In the lift, he took his keycard from his pocket and slid it in a small slot that Ellie had never noticed before, not the one she normally used. A new light appeared on the panel. For the first time Ellie had seen, the button for the sixth floor was illuminated.

'Push it.'

Ellie did. Perhaps it was her heightened expectations, but it seemed stiffer than the other buttons, as if there was a great weight behind it. The lift began to move – not up, but down. The lights blinked out their descent. First Floor . . . Ground

Floor ... Basement 1 ... Basement 2 ... and suddenly, back at the top of the list, 6.

'Not everything is where you would expect.'

The lift shuddered to a halt. The moment the doors opened, Ellie could smell the age in the air: a damp, dark smell of something that had been buried for centuries. How far down were they? The light from the lift crept over a square of flag-stoned floor; everything beyond was in darkness.

And suddenly it was golden. The moment Blanchard stepped out of the lift, hidden lights faded up to reveal a small square chamber bounded by ancient stone walls. Shelves had been cut into them, but even the stone seemed to sag under the weight of the treasures it held: plates and bowls, tureens and salvers, goblets, chalices and candlesticks. They sparkled under the lights, throwing off overlapping arcs of silver and gold that rippled across the floor like water.

Entranced by their lustre, Ellie found herself moving towards them. She stretched for a particularly ornate piece of plate, decorated with relief images of jousting knights.

Blanchard's hand closed around her wrist and stopped it mid-reach. 'Don't touch. Every piece triggers an alarm.'

'Where did all this come from?'

'Orphan assets. We have been collecting for centuries.'

In the middle of the room, four stone columns supported the vaulted ceiling. At their centre, on a stone plinth, a golden cup sat spotlit in a glass case. It was the only piece in the room behind glass, though Ellie couldn't see why it should be more valuable.

Blanchard loosened his tie and unbuttoned his collar. He reached inside his shirt and pulled out the golden key on its slim chain. He advanced towards the cup. Snarling stone faces adorned the four corners of the pedestal, strange monsters out

169

of legend. Blanchard reached inside the mouth of one, a horned serpent, and turned the key.

Ellie blinked. Nothing had happened. Blanchard stepped away and let the key drop back inside his shirt.

'Behind you.'

Ellie looked back to the lift. The doors still stood open – but on the far side of the lift, where previously there had been a mirrored wall, a heavy oak door had appeared.

They stepped back through the lift. Blanchard took out the same key as before and slid it into the wooden door. The black iron of the lock seemed far older than the bright golden key. In the corner of her mind, Ellie registered that he turned it clockwise this time, as if locking it.

The door swung in – no hint of rust on the hinges. Blanchard gestured Ellie to enter.

She crossed the threshold and paused, swaying in the darkness like a feather in a breeze. She reached out, stroking the void for hidden obstacles. She felt nothing, but the movement must have touched some invisible beam. Hidden lights glowed into life, just as they had before, revealing a long gallery with low-vaulted ceilings. Twin rows of square pillars ran its length, dividing it into three aisles. There were no shelves, no golden treasures on display. Instead, the bays of the side walls were studded with iron doors like bread ovens. Each had a different shield painted on it.

'It was an ossuary for the monks.' Blanchard's voice, breathing over her shoulder as if the old monks still haunted this place. 'We removed the bones when we fitted the vaults.'

She felt a flash of pity; for a moment she imagined she heard the anguish of the unburied dead crying out. She shivered. This far down, in a city that was – for all its skyscrapers and fibre optics – indisputably ancient, it was easy to get carried away.

She turned. 'Why did you bring me here?'

'I wanted you to understand how deep the bank's history goes. Monsalvat have occupied this site for five centuries. You have heard the story that we built on the ruins of an old Templar lodge?'

Ellie nodded.

'That was built on the foundations of a Norman church, which in turn had vaults that were Saxon.' His arm swept down, from crisp blocks of masonry to the smaller, crudely dressed stones beneath. 'Where they built, who knows? Here, time becomes space.'

Blanchard led her further in, to a place where a sunken mosaic sprawled between a gap in the flagstones. 'We think this might be Roman. Naturally, no archaeologist has ever been down here.'

Two thirds of the way down, a second corridor intersected the main aisle at right angles. It must mirror the shape of the church it had once underpinned, Ellie realised. She tried to imagine the floorplan of the Monsalvat building, and wondered if it still bore any relation to the buildings buried underneath, the pattern inscribed on every age of history.

At the far end – the east end, Ellie supposed, though it hardly mattered that far down – an iron door lay set in the floor. In the dim light she made out the bank's crest stamped into the metal, the ravenous eagle with the spear in its talons. Blanchard took almost reverential care not to step on it as he approached one of the vaults in the wall. He moved his hand over the surface in a series of brisk gestures, then turned the handle and opened the door. Ellie peered over his shoulder, but couldn't see inside.

'There is another reason I brought you here.'

He removed a small leather box from the vault and

presented it to her. She fumbled with the leather strap that bound it. The moment she had it off, the two halves of the box fell open like wings. Cupped between them, resting on a cushion of raw wool, lay a gold ring. A red stone the size of a hazelnut bulged from its setting.

'I wanted you to have this.'

Blanchard slid the ring on to her hand. It was too loose on her ring finger, but fitted her middle finger perfectly. Ellie stared at the dull gold against her white skin, the way the smouldering ruby trapped the light deep inside. Her guts churned, she felt faint. Could he be . . .?

'This is not a proposal of marriage, or something like that,' said Blanchard, in such a way that mere engagement sounded trite. 'This is an old ring of my family's. It solemnises our attachments, brings us luck.' He smiled. 'A ring of power.'

A roar filled the chamber, as if a long-dormant dragon had woken in his lair to find a piece of his hoard missing. The walls shuddered. Ellie grabbed on to Blanchard in terror. He put an arm around her and grinned.

'The Central Line travels very close to this place. When they dug the tunnel in the nineteenth century we had to lodge a special application to re-route it so it would not disturb our vault. As Mr Saint-Lazare likes to say, the present always intrudes on the past. And vice versa.'

He leaned forward and kissed her. His cold lips made her tremble, but his mouth was moist and warm. She tasted tobacco on his tongue. He hugged her tight and pulled her against him, so that the hard points of his body dug into her.

'Do you like the ring?'

Ellie lifted her hand, enjoying the weight on her finger. 'I don't know what to say.'

'I will not tell you how old it is. But – keep it safe.'

The vault door clanged like a bell as he closed it. He took her hand and began to lead her back to the lift, then paused.

'The Finance Ministry in Luxembourg will announce the Talhouett decision next week, December twenty-second. Michel Saint-Lazare has invited me to spend Christmas with him afterwards at his home in Switzerland. He has asked specifically if you would come too.'

He said it casually, but the whole weight of his gaze suddenly switched on to Ellie. She felt caught, an exotic butterfly on the point of the collector's pin.

'It would mean a lot to me,' he added. He'd dropped the detachment he usually wore; his words were almost painfully frank. 'Christmas in the Alps is magical. To share it with you would be . . . perfect.'

Ellie had never seen a white Christmas. She tried to think of her mother, the promise she'd made and the disappointment if she didn't go. But Blanchard's stare had a hypnotic power, a gravity that skewed everything beyond its field. Other obligations seemed only dimly important. She started to answer, and realised she'd already begun composing the excuses to her mother.

Luxembourg

Christmas brought out the German side of the Grand Duchy. In the Place d'Armes in the heart of the city, a giant fir tree loomed over the Christmas market that filled every corner of the square. Wooden cabins festooned with lights and fake snow offered a psychedelic array of brightly coloured sweets, obscenely long sausages, carved nativity scenes and ornaments. Steam rose from vats of mulled wine, mingling in the air with the smells of gingerbread and frying onions, the sound of carols and fairground music and laughter.

Inside the conference room at the Ministry of Finance, the only concession to the season was a plastic tree with a few tired baubles at the back of the room. No one paid it any attention. There were no smiles in that room, only tense faces and brittle anticipation as the rival bidders milled about, waiting. Blanchard was there, Christine Lafarge as well, and a number of the bankers she'd met doing the due diligence. Across the aisle, Ellie saw Lechowski. His jaw rose and fell as he worried at a piece of gum.

An official called the meeting to order. The Ministry people sat at a long table across the front of the room, fat men with thin hair and shiny suits. No one looked at them. All eyes were on the double-padlocked metal box that stood on a lectern in front.

The official invited representatives of the two bidders to come forward. In turn, Lechowski and Christine Lafarge each went up and undid one of the locks. The official opened the lid and turned the box upside-down. Two sealed envelopes fell on to the table.

The president of the panel handed one envelope to each of the men beside him. They ripped them open and read the letters inside, then swapped with each other. The audience waited. The president collected both letters and confirmed their contents for himself. They conferred. Ellie twisted Blanchard's ring on her finger. She hadn't expected to be so nervous.

The president switched on his microphone. 'The winning bidder is Groupe Saint-Lazare, three hundred and forty-seven million euros.'

In an instant, the Monsalvat team were on their feet, applauding and congratulating each other. Across the aisle, Lechowski and his backers sat stony-faced, the glares of men narrowly beaten and suspecting a foul. The men from the privatisation commission didn't look much happier: they must be wondering why the sale had failed to attract a higher offer.

'Well done, Ellie. Without you, we could not have done this.'

Blanchard kissed her full on the lips, the first time he'd ever done that at work. He must be pleased. Embarrassed and surprised, Ellie kept her eyes open, and so saw Christine Lafarge watching in the background with a knowing smile on her face. She remembered Blanchard's story about Christine and Lechowski, and wondered if Christine and Blanchard had ever been lovers. The thought made her absurdly jealous.

Blanchard turned to murmur a few words to the commission president. Christine took her arm.

'Vivian tells me you are going to Mont-Valois for Christmas. Michel Saint-Lazare's chateau.' Ellie nodded. 'You are very lucky. It is a magical place.'

Ellie must have drunk more champagne that night than in all her life previous. The Monsalvat team drifted from bar to bar, hotel to hotel, ordering by the magnum. The group became a living organism: new faces appeared whom Ellie had never seen before; others disappeared, only to reappear two stops later with yet more hangers-on. The hotel clock had turned past 3 a.m. by the time she and Blanchard returned to their room. Blanchard ordered more champagne from room service, then set about demonstrating that it did nothing to impair his physical functioning. Ellie didn't get to sleep until five. At eight, the telephone rang with an alarm call. When she opened her eyes, Blanchard was standing in front of the mirror tying his tie, shaved and dressed already.

175

'What time is our flight?'

'As soon as we get there.'

The airport was crowded with families heading off on holiday and ex-pat workers trying to get the last flight out before Christmas. Ellie thought she might faint if she had to queue for more than five minutes, but Blanchard pushed past all of them to an unmarked door at the back of the terminal. Inside was a parallel airport universe of friendly staff and no queues: an immigration official who glanced at their passports and wished them merry Christmas; a security officer who carried their bags to the gate; and finally a simple door that led straight on to the tarmac, up a flight of stairs and aboard a small jet.

It was like no other aircraft Ellie had seen. The eight seats looked more like leather armchairs than anything that belonged on an aeroplane, with seatbelts discreetly recessed out of sight. Ellie sank back into the chair and fell asleep to the sound of turbines and Blanchard talking on the phone in French.

At Lausanne a black Range Rover was waiting for them on the runway. They climbed in, their bags were thrown in the back, and before Ellie realised it they were on the motorway climbing towards the mountains.

'Shouldn't we have shown our passports or something?' she wondered.

'Mr Saint-Lazare has an accommodation with the Swiss authorities.'

Ellie supposed that he would. According to *Fortune* magazine, he was Switzerland's seventh richest man. Despite diligent research, that was almost as much as she knew about him. The combined weight of *Who's Who*, the *Lexis/Nexis* database and the World Wide Web supplied little more than a reputation as a generous charitable benefactor and a ruthless corporate raider, buying and selling companies the length and breadth of the continent. '*Who is Michel Saint-Lazare?*' a plaintive article in *The Economist* had asked a few years ago. 'Behind an impenetrable wall of shell companies and cross-holdings, Groupe Saint-Lazare is reputed to be one of Europe's largest privately held companies. Yet its owner, Michel Saint-Lazare, is so reclusive some claim he died years ago.' The only photograph she'd found was fifty years out of date, a black-and-white playboy on a post-war beachfront. Nowhere did it mention his connection with Monsalvat Bank.

The Range Rover turned off the highway, following a twisting road ever-upwards. Mountain peaks loomed in the near distance. Snow began to appear – at first small patches in the hollows of the bends, then spreading across the landscape until it drowned it completely. It dazzled Ellie; she wished she'd brought her sunglasses. In the grey, tired atmosphere of London, it hadn't occurred to her.

The car turned again, this time onto an unploughed road through a forest. The chauffeur engaged the four-wheel drive. The trees started to fall away: when Ellie looked out the window, she saw they were on the edge of a precipice that plunged to a foaming river far below. She looked the other way for reassurance, but the mountain had disappeared. They were driving along a ridge, a thin spine of land along the top of a promontory. Ellie peered anxiously through the front window, looking for any glimpse of the house, but the low winter sun shone straight in her eyes. She hoped the driver could see where he was going.

And suddenly they were there. They rattled over a bridge,

through a gate where portcullis teeth still pricked out of the arch, and into the courtyard of Michel Saint-Lazare's home.

Christine Lafarge had called it a chateau. Blanchard described it, wryly, as a chalet. In plain fact it was a castle. It rose from a fist of rock at the end of the ridge, half severed from the mountain's arm by a narrow ravine. A wooden bridge was the only access: on every other side, the rock face dropped three hundred feet sheer to the valley below. The whitewashed walls stood almost invisible against the snow: the steep black roofs seemed to hover in the clouds.

All of which Ellie only saw later. For the moment, she had only the vaguest impression of high walls and lofty turrets looking down on her; attendants hurrying out of what had once been stables to take their bags; a butler bringing cups of steaming wine almost before they were out of the car. The sun shone through an arch in the western wall, reflecting on the snow to fill the courtyard with light.

A dark-suited servant led them into the house, up a spiral stair to a long corridor. It looked like a museum: spears and shields hung on the walls, side by side with the trophy heads of long-dead game. But behind the doors the rooms were warm, with thick carpets and heavy curtains and an enormous four-poster bed swagged with lace. Peering out of the window at the snowbound valley below, Ellie felt she'd landed in a fairy tale.

'Do you like your room?'

Blanchard had appeared. For a second Ellie thought he'd stepped out of the tapestry on the wall, until she saw the door beside it leading to the adjoining bedroom. She put her arms around his waist and linked her hands behind his back.

'Do we need two rooms?'

'Sometimes it is good to have your own space.' He leaned forward, burying her in his embrace. 'But not too much.'

'Michel is away tonight,' he whispered in her ear. 'We will have to amuse ourselves.'

Ellie nodded, happy. Over his shoulder, she saw a stuffed wolf's head set over the doorway, its jaw open and its eyes staring down.

She closed her eyes.

XXII

Normandy, 1136

I kneel in front of Guy. The stones on the floor are cold and hard against my knees. On the altar, a burnished sword gleams in the candlelight. The white linen shift is smooth against my skin. Gornemant has drilled the symbolism into us since the day I came to Normandy. White for purity, for the law of God you will defend.

White as naked skin in moonlight. In the depths of the night, when I should have been keeping my vigil, I crept through the castle to the storeroom by the orchard. Ada was waiting for me. It's never warm enough to remove our clothes, but we pulled my tunic and her dress down to our waists to feel each other's bodies, nothing between us. The room smelled of last year's apples, sweet and cidery. The barrels were almost empty, but the ripeness lingered in the air.

When we'd made love, we lay on a piece of sackcloth on the floor. The moon shone through the grated window; shadows criss-crossed Ada's back. I stroked her bare skin, breaking the shadow bars. I heard snuffles in the darkness – her crying. The tears made tracks down her cheeks, a silver cage. I wiped them off.

'We'll be all right,' I whispered in her ear.

Gornemant steps around me and fastens a red cloak over my white shift. Red for the blood I will shed in the service of the Lord.

Ada shed blood last night. Just a scratch, a cut on her finger where the scab had torn off. As she fumbled with my tunic, a few spots smeared on the white wool. I panicked; in a few hours I'd be standing in the chapel, the entire household watching me. Ada crept to the kitchen and fetched vinegar, a rag. By the time she'd finished, the stain was little more than a watermark.

A narrow belt girds the shift around my hips. Gornemant says it's to remind me to shun the sins of the flesh. I loosen it so it hangs lower, covering the worst of the stain. When the priest comes to the part of the oath where I swear myself to a life of purity, I hope he doesn't look down.

You swear by almighty God to defend the church, your lord, and to protect the defenceless from the mighty.

I repeat the oath. Guy lifts the sword off the altar and holds it above my head while the priest says his blessing. For a second I see the image of Guy as he was in the copse that day, the hiss of air as the sword cut through the knight's windpipe, the drip of blood falling on leaves. If he knew what I've done with Ada, he'd cut my throat right here in the chapel. Instead, he slides it into the scabbard and buckles it around my waist. I stand, so that Gornemant can fix my gilded spurs on to my boot.

My leggings are brown, brown for the dust that is every man's destiny, proud or humble. I'm no stranger to dust and earth these days. Dust on the flagstones in the storerooms and cupboards; dust in the stable straw; damp soil under the rock where we first kissed. We are creatures of earth, and the gold rings or spurs we wear to flatter our nobility mean nothing but vanity. The spurs aren't even mine, only borrowed for the day. Tomorrow they'll be iron.

Guy swats my shoulder with the palm of his hand.

'Receive this blow in remembrance of Him who ordained you and dubbed you.'

I don't need to be taught the symbolism to know what it all means. It means I am a knight.

Gornemant suspects. Last week, he told me a long story about a Flemish count. One of his knights had been sleeping with the count's wife: when the count discovered them together, he had his butchers beat the man raw, then held him upside-down in a latrine until he suffocated. Or choked on effluent – no one could tell afterwards. Gornemant gives me a heavy look. 'A lord must be able to trust his knights in all things,' he says, 'as much as his own right arm.'

In the Bible it says, 'If your right arm offends you, cut it off.' We both know that.

I want Guy to be able to trust me. I want to honour my oaths. I thought that sleeping with Ada might be an ending, that possessing her body would cure my desire. Instead, it's only made it worse. From the moment I met her, my love has been a wound. Now, a fever is spreading. The more often I have her, the more often I want her. Instead of being grateful for the times we have, hasty and snatched, I resent the times we're apart. On the nights when I see Guy leave the hall to follow her to her room, I want to snatch a candlestick from the table and ram it through his eye.

*

My frenzy makes me reckless. Last week, one of the grooms surprised us in the stables as he came to fetch a cropper. Thankfully, the hinge on the stable door squeaks. We were able to cover ourselves, and made a great production of having come to show Ada Guy's new colt. But servants gossip. I know I should rein myself in, temper my passions unless we can be absolutely safe. Next time, we wait until Guy's away visiting one of his outlying tenants. We meet in the guard room at the top of the north tower: you can bolt it from the inside, and since Athold's death Guy hasn't bothered with a sentry there. It's as safe as can be had.

I get there first. It's a cloudless night and the moon is full: it shines through the windows and arrow slits, gleaming off the heads of the spears in a rack on the wall. The whole room is filled with silver light. I spread a cloak on the floor and wait.

I see Ada's approach by the candlelight creeping up the doorframe. The stairs are steep and uneven: she doesn't trust them in the dark. When she appears, she's wearing a spotless white shift. No coat or dress, just a mantle of marmot fur.

The candle she carries lights up the tower like a beacon. Anyone could see it. I pinch out the flame with my fingers and hug her close, pressing my mouth into hers. She doesn't reciprocate. There's a stiffness in her, a withdrawal. I step back.

'Are you all right?'

She stands so still that in the moonlight she looks like a statue of herself, a stone Ada. It reminds me of a telling of the Tristan story I've heard, where Tristan builds a wooden likeness of Yseult in a cave so he can stand and watch it hour after hour while she's separated from him.

'We have to stop.'

Perhaps Tristan was wise. The statue would never have said that. They're words I've dreaded hearing since our first touch.

'Why?' I'm not sympathetic; I sound like a child.

'Guy. Of course.'

'Do you love him?' I know she doesn't.

'He's my husband.'

It's not the 'husband' that offends me: it's the 'my'. I hate any implication that Guy belongs to her, or she to him. She belongs to me.

She reaches out a hand to console me, but I shake her off. I don't want to make this easy for her.

'We can't go on,' she insists. 'Would you kill him? Fight all his knights and vassals, defy the world just so we can lie together? It's impossible. You can't write a happy ending to this story. If you love me, let me go.'

If I love her? Let Guy come, let him beat me and drown me or burn me at the stake – I'll fight for her with every breath in my body. Only never deny our love.

A noise sounds on the stair. I look at the door – Ada didn't bolt it. I start towards it, but before I'm halfway across the room it flies open with a crash. A figure stands in the entry, a burning brand in one hand and a naked sword in the other. The glare of the light blinds me.

'Peter?'

It's Jocelin.

XXIII

Mont Valois, Switzerland

Ellie woke on Christmas morning, naked and warm under the fur-trimmed coverlet. For once, Blanchard was still asleep; she lay beside him, feeling the chasm of hot air between their bodies, listening for his breathing. He slept as quietly as a cat, no snore or murmur. Cold clear sunlight streamed through the mullioned window; in the courtyard, Ellie could hear the staff tending the castle as they must have done for centuries. She thought she'd never been happier.

She caught sight of the wolf above the door and turned away to hide it. The movement woke Blanchard. He leaned over to kiss her, twisting back as he did to reach under the bed. His hand came up holding a small fat package wrapped in gold paper.

'Happy Christmas, Ellie.'

She sat up in the bed and slit open the paper with her nail. It was a book, bound in crimson leather with a crest stamped in gold on the cover.

'Is this another one of your orphan assets?'

'It belonged to the Saint-Lazare family. Michel sold it to me.'

She could tell it was old. She'd handled enough manuscripts in her year at Oxford to recognise the smell of vellum. She opened the cover.

Le Conte du Graal.

And underneath, in Blanchard's familiar copperplate:

For Ellie, a great romance.

She couldn't believe he'd actually written on the ancient parchment. As she touched the page the book's history seemed to flash through her imagination: the parchmenter racking the calfskin until it was paper thin. A young boy climbing in a tree, trying not to get stung, while he removed the gall-wasp's nest to get the acid which would sear the ink into the page. The scribe sharpening his reed pen, sitting very straight at his angled desk as he copied the text. And now her own name, graffiti on their monument.

Blanchard read her expression.

'The past was once the present, Ellie. History is merely the accumulation of all the presents that have ever been. Those who lived in the past have no better claim to it. You lived, you owned this book. You are part of its story also.'

Ellie turned to the first page. The script was tiny, only a few millimetres high, laid out in three well-ordered columns with a boxed, gilded initial at the top. It looked like some sort of list, or an index: only if you peered closely at the minuscule text could you see that each was a line of poetry.

'Do you know Chrétien de Troyes?'

'Only by reputation.' There must have been some lectures at university, but she didn't think she'd gone.

'He was the first and greatest of the romance writers. He took folk tales and legends, stories of the common people, and turned them into poetry for kings.'

'Thank you.' She rolled on top of him, rubbing her body against his as she plied him with kisses. 'And all I got you was a pair of socks.'

While Blanchard showered, Ellie rang her mother. She knew she should be guilty, but it was Christmas morning and she refused to let herself feel bad. She let the phone ring a full minute, but her mother didn't answer. She remembered it was an hour earlier in Wales: her mother would probably be at church.

Ellie glanced at the bathroom door, debating with herself. She could still hear the shower running. She hated calling Doug in front of Blanchard, though occasionally it had been unavoidable. It brought them into the same room, put her lies in such sharp focus it hurt. And she hated the way Blanchard looked: never jealous, or even embarrassed, only vaguely amused. Perhaps, being French, he thought it was normal.

Doug answered straight away, like someone who'd been waiting for her.

'Happy Christmas, sweetheart.'

'Happy Christmas.'

'How's Wales?'

Was there an edge in his question? A trap? Had he guessed?

'Fine. Mum's gone to church, I'm peeling potatoes.'

This is the last time I'm going to lie to you, she promised silently. The weeks since his birthday had slipped by in a blur; then it was almost Christmas, and she didn't want to ruin it. January was the time, she'd decided. The worst time of year: Janus the two-faced god, looking forwards and backwards. She'd tell him in the New Year.

'How's the weather? Have you got a white Christmas?'

Her mind raced. She should have checked online. 'Probably just the same as you've got.'

Behind the door, the shower had stopped.

'I think I heard Mum coming in. I'd better go.' She endured the usual sign offs with mounting impatience, staring at the door, willing it to stay shut.

'I love you.'

She'd barely hung up when Blanchard walked out in his dressing gown. He gave her a quizzical look.

'Were you talking to someone?'

'My mum.'

Blanchard took a shirt from its hanger in the wardrobe. 'You should get up. We have to earn our Christmas lunch.'

By the time Ellie got downstairs, a dozen men and women had assembled in the courtyard. If she'd met them in real life Ellie would probably have run a mile: tall and flatly handsome, dressed in fur hats and tweed jackets and riding boots, they looked like a species apart. She wondered if they were all Saint-Lazare's guests, or if some might be family. Blanchard mingled with them, making small talk and introductions which Ellie immediately forgot. She kept waiting to meet Michel Saint-Lazare, but apparently he wasn't there.

A convoy of Land Rovers took them halfway down the mountain, to an upland meadow studded with trees and hedges. Another Land Rover was already there with its boot open. From inside, Ellie could hear a high-pitched chirrup.

It came from a cage. A tall bird sat on a perch, clutching the wood with sharp, wizened claws. It had a tuft of white feathers at its breast, broad wings tucked up to its shoulders, and a curved beak like a cutlass. Ellie didn't need to know much about birds to recognise the lethal power in its body. A predator. A heavy chain shackled it to the cage.

Blanchard pulled on a leather gauntlet and laced it up to his elbow. Murmuring soothing words, he opened the cage and slipped the chain off the perch, over his wrist. The bird hopped on to his outstretched arm, preening the white feathers on its breast. The assistant – a falconer? – pulled a small leather hood over its beak and fastened it around her head.

'It's beautiful,' Ellie said. 'So noble.'

'A peregrine falcon. Falconry has always been the true sport of kings.' Blanchard took out a lure tied to the end of a long string and held it in his right hand. 'It requires infinite patience and deep pockets.'

Blanchard strode across the field with Ellie in tow. A black hound trotted at his feet, while the other guests followed at a wary distance, watching Blanchard and sipping coffee that the driver had brought in the Land Rover. The falcon wore a bell tied to its tail feathers which trilled whenever it moved.

They stopped in the middle of the meadow. Blanchard pulled off the hood and unclasped the chain. The falcon looked around, its head twitching. For long moments man and bird stood absolutely still, dark figures against the white field.

With a trill of the bell and a clap of feathers, the bird rose off Blanchard's arm. Its wing almost caught Ellie in the face. It shot into the air so fast she barely saw it, climbing to a point above a small copse at the end of the field.

'She's seen something.'

From the deep pocket of his fur coat, Blanchard took what looked like a miniature radio and turned it on. Through a burst of static, it began to emit a regular low-pitched tone. When he pointed it towards where the bird was hovering it grew louder.

'The bird has a radio beacon attached to its leg. If we lose sight of it, this will help us find it.'

The falcon hovered, flapping its wings against the breeze to stay in place. Ellie squinted at the sky. The air was so clear she could see everything: the black feathers under its wings and the fleck of white at its breast; the curved point of its beak. She almost imagined she could see its eyes, scanning the air. Waiting, waiting –

– And down. It happened so fast Ellie didn't even see the prey. The falcon swooped and vanished behind the trees.

'Come on!' Blanchard shouted. In an instant they were running across the field, staggering through the deep snow. Blood rushed in her ears: the wind, the crunch of snow, the baying of the hound. They scrambled over a fence and pushed through a hedge into the copse. Blanchard waved to his right.

'The trees disrupt the signal. It is better if we keep apart.'

She veered away through the virgin snow, pushing into the undergrowth. She crossed a narrow stream, tripped on a buried tree-root and just caught herself on the trunk of a birch.

You'll never find it like this. She stopped, resting her hands on her thighs to ease the cramp, breathing hard. Heavy branches creaked under their coat of snow; a robin called. Away to her left she could hear distant barking. And somewhere ahead, not far off . . .

There. The trill of a bell, like a sleigh harness.

Moving more slowly now, Ellie crept through the trees. The bell grew louder. She peered round a bush.

The falcon sat triumphant on the grey carcass of a goose. The goose's wings had cratered the snow like a bomb blast, though it lay still now. The falcon leaned over, mewling softly as it pecked out the bird's heart. It was very clean – the only evidence of death were three drops of blood spattered on the snow, so cold and precise beside the corpse.

Ellie stared at them. She suddenly felt dizzy. The snow dazzled her, so bright that the drops of blood seemed to lift off it and swim in front of her eyes. She thought she'd never seen such a colour.

Through her daze, Ellie heard another trill. It was such an alien sound it took her a second to realise it was her mobile phone. She fumbled it out of her pocket.

'Eleanor? It's Mrs Thomas. From No. 96.'

Ellie knew her: a short woman who lived down the road from her mother, with round cheeks and a terrier. But why –?

'I knocked but you weren't at home. I got your number from your mother's bag. I didn't know if you were down – or if you were spending Christmas somewhere . . . Such a shock. Such a terrible thing.'

She was babbling, talking around something too awful to come at directly. Ellie stared at the falcon gobbling the heart out of the bird it had killed.

'What's going on?'

Mrs Thomas was saying something about ambulances, about hospitals and doctors and whether she'd be all right. Her words made no more sense to Ellie than the falcon's mewl.

'*Who?*' But she already knew.

Snow shivered off a cluster of branches as Blanchard pushed into the clearing. He held the radio receiver like some sort of remote control, pointing it at the bird. He looked at it with delight, something almost approaching rapture, then saw Ellie.

'What has happened?'

From down the mountain and across the sea, a voice in her ear said *it's your mother*.

Saint-Lazare's plane was in Vienna for maintenance and a storm had closed the runway. Ellie spent the night at the airport and took the first flight next morning, a budget airline filled with screaming families and returning skiers. The cabin blazed aggressive colours; it smelt of sweat, old sunscreen and fresh beer. Two rows back, a child was sick all over the floor. At Bristol, she waited an hour for the skeleton-staffed airport to produce her baggage.

No trains were running on Boxing Day. Ellie took a cab from the airport all the way to Newport – forty miles that cost almost a hundred pounds. She stared out of the window at the tired city, the few high-rise towers that struggled above the skyline and the tangled attempts at public art. She hadn't been back since she started at Monsalvat. She'd forgotten how grey it was.

To enter a hospital, even as a visitor, is to surrender yourself – as if the only way to manage so much human suffering is to build something incomprehensible to humanity. The Royal Gwent was no exception. The moment Ellie stepped through the doors she became a captive: to unwritten schedules and rules, Byzantine hierarchies that never came to a head. Even the architecture seemed designed to dislocate. She remembered something Blanchard had said in the vault about time becoming space. By the time she reached the room in the stroke unit, both time and space had compacted into a fluorescent-lit void.

Her mother lay in a curtained-off corner of a four-bed ward. There was a window, but the only view it offered was a brick wall. Her mother couldn't even see that. Her eyes were closed; there was something subtly asymmetric about her face, though Ellie couldn't say what. Needles and tubes probed her body, while screens and monitors brought second-by-second news of what was happening under the skin.

Ellie sat and fished out the box of Swiss chocolates she'd bought at the airport. She laid them on the plastic bedside table.

'She can't eat at the moment.'

A doctor had appeared, a tall man with fair hair and a smile that offended Ellie.

'What happened?' Ellie heard the crack in her voice and realised how close she was to falling apart completely. 'I'm her daughter,' she added.

'She went to church on Christmas morning. Apparently, she'd gone to light a candle after the service when she collapsed.'

Ellie could imagine the scene. The grey austerity of Saint David's, whose vicar would never allow a Christmas tree inside his church. The white-haired ladies – they were mostly ladies – drinking their Christmas morning sherry, the news going through them like a panicked flock of birds. Father Evans pushing through, calling for calm. The ambulance in the churchyard. How long did you have to wait for an ambulance on Christmas day?

'They brought her straight here. She hasn't regained consciousness yet.'

'Will she . . .?'

Ellie couldn't finish the sentence. Her mind rebelled; her imagination refused to supply the necessary possibilities.

'I don't know. Her signs are good. It depends if there's any, ah, underlying damage.'

He means brain damage, Ellie thought dully. She looked at her mother's face again, the thin bones and sharp creases. In a horrid way, she looked more at peace than Ellie could ever remember seeing her.

The doctor gave a subtle glance at the clock on the wall.

'She's in the best possible place. We'll take good care of her, I promise.'

*

Ellie didn't know how long she sat with her mother. The doctor said it might help to talk, and so she spoke. Halting and awkward, often tearful – honest in a way she'd never dared when her mother could hear. She told her about Doug and his poem; about Blanchard and the ring he'd given her; about the cities she'd visited and the places she'd stayed. She described Saint-Lazare's fairy-tale castle, and the dead goose with its blood so bright on the snow. It made her realise how little there was in her life any more that wasn't connected to the bank. Sometimes her thoughts drifted away; she didn't know she'd stopped speaking until uncounted minutes had passed.

Visiting hours ended. Ellie made her way out of the hospital, trailing her suitcase down the corridors like guilt. *I should have been here*. She'd found a set of house keys in her mother's handbag. With nowhere else to go, she went home.

Ellie slept in her mother's bed that night. As soon as she woke, she phoned the hospital. No change, better or worse. They told her it was a Sunday: no visitors until the afternoon. She picked through the impractically formal clothes in her suitcase until she found a pair of jeans and a woollen jumper. The house was freezing, and when Ellie went to have a shower the water wasn't much better than ice.

With vague memories of a tank in the loft, Ellie unhooked the ladder in the ceiling and clambered up. A sign nailed under the rafters warned that the joists wouldn't support her weight, though perhaps that was just because every inch already had to contend with the mass of boxes stacked as high as the roof would allow. The hot water tank, she thought, lay somewhere at the back.

There was no way through. With a sinking heart, Ellie pulled on one of the boxes nearest to her. The old tape holding it together was brittle and dry: the moment she touched it it snapped like rice paper. The box fell open, spilling papers and photographs across the floor.

Ellie wanted to cry in frustration. For a second, she imagined walking away and checking into a hotel downtown: abandoning this cold, broken past for functional anonymity. But something in the sprawl of old documents caught her eye. It was a photograph of her mother, younger than Ellie could ever remember her, with long straight hair and a skirt so short it made Ellie cringe. She was standing in front of a cathedral with her arm around a man: the camera must have snapped just as something distracted him, for his head had turned and he was staring off-camera. He looked handsome in profile, with strong features and a deep, questioning look on his face.

Aneurin Stanton. Ellie recognised him at once, though she'd only ever seen half a dozen photographs of him. She turned over the photograph and saw her mother's small neat handwriting, efficient as ever.

Bressanone, Italy – March, 1987.

So far as she knew her mother had never left the country, never even had a passport.

Curiosity took hold of her. She delved into the boxes, sorting through the papers. It reminded her of the data room in Luxembourg – due diligence on an unfinished life. Two lives, in fact, for among the bank statements and electricity bills was a fair sampling of Ellie's past. School photographs and exercise books; drawings and paintings; report cards, certificates, school concert programmes. And slipped among them, the faintest shadows of a third life that had defined them both. An army discharge certificate; an old life-insurance policy; postcards from the continent. She'd never imagined her father travelling so much. *The weather is fine. I've seen some beautiful things. Not much luck here. I love you. Nye.*

She looked at her watch. Past twelve – visiting hours would start soon. She gave up on trying to get to the hot water tank and steeled herself for an icy shower. There was one bundle of papers left in the box she'd been working on. On top, tucked under the rubber band, was what looked like an unused airline ticket. Ellie pulled it out, wondering why the journey had never happened.

The ticket was for a British Airways flight from London to Munich. February 20th 1988.

She felt a wave of sadness as she realised why the ticket had never been used.

Aneurin Stanton: 12th May 1949 – 19th February 1988.

Except the name on the ticket wasn't Aneurin Stanton. It was John Herrin.

XXIV

Jocelin stands in the doorway holding the burning brand. The flames spit and hiss like a demon; his face is etched with fury.

He raises his sword. Ada's nearest the door, and I think in his rage he'll cut her down just to get to me. Instinct takes over. I snatch a spear from the rack on the wall and lunge at him. He dodges the blow the way Gornemant taught us, twisting away, but the tip catches a fold of his tunic and flings him back, into the space where the stairs drop away. He falls down the stairs, thudding and clattering on the treacherous spiral, his sword ringing like a dropped coin. The torch goes out.

I put an arm around Ada's shoulder and hug her to me, trying to impress the urgency.

'If you stay here, Guy will kill you.'

She nods. I take her hand and lead her down the stairs, feeling my way with the butt of the spear. We find Jocelin in a heap on the next landing, blood oozing from a wound in his skull. I don't stop to see if I've killed him. Somebody must have heard the noise.

But no one's raised the alarm yet. We reach the bottom of

the stairs and creep across the courtyard to the stables. I find a groom curled up in a stall and shake him awake. He rubs the straw out of his eyes.

'Jocelin had an accident – a fall in the dark. I have to go to Guy. Saddle my horse, and the grey palfrey.'

I leave him and run to the gate, while Ada goes inside to fetch some things. I feed the watchman the same half-truth, and together we crack open the gate wide enough for a horse to pass. I glance at the buildings, wondering if Ada will come. What if she's changed her mind?

Ada emerges dressed in a stout travelling dress and cloak, with a small bundle tied over her back. Whatever misgivings she has, she's mastered them for the moment. Her face is invisible under the hood: I can't guess what she's thinking. She puts something cold and sharp in my palm.

'Don't forget these.'

My spurs. The groom buckles them on around my boots. He sees Ada climb into the grey mare's saddle and gives a bewildered stare. Has he begun to wonder why the house is so dark, so quiet, if Jocelin's in such distress?

'She needs to be with her husband.'

We slip out the gate. The moon's strong, lighting our way. The rhythm of the horse under me calms my nerves. Ada rides beside me. Her hood blows back and her hair flies behind her. I gaze across the fields where we practised our swordplay and made mock charges. Past the orchard, where I told Ada the tale of Tristan, and the low-roofed barns where we met by night. These places have been my world for the past six years. It's a strange thought that I'll never see them again.

I feel free, but I know it's an illusion. I saw the look on Jocelin's face. If he's alive, no power on earth will stop him coming after us.

XXV

Newport, South Wales

Nothing had changed at the hospital except the staff. Two nurses were dressing the bed, rolling her mother first one way and then the other, like a corpse. Ellie couldn't watch; she waited outside the curtain. A sign on the wall reminded her that she should switch off her mobile phone. At least it would save the battery. In the last few weeks, it had been running down surprisingly fast.

When the nurses had gone, Ellie took up her vigil. She'd brought the old postcards from the attic and she read them aloud, giving life to a voice she'd never heard. She hoped her mother could hear, that somewhere behind that still face she was remembering happier times. What was Dad like? Ellie wondered. In her eyes, he'd only ever been a source of sadness to her mother. It was strange to think of them happy together. Like most children, she couldn't imagine her parents having an existence without her.

The hospital closed early on a Sunday. With a stab of guilt, Ellie realised she almost felt glad. It had only been twenty-four hours, but she was already sick of the hospital, the low light and random interruptions and long hours of nothing. Was this how she'd spend the rest of her life?

The moment she got home, she found herself climbing back to the attic. She looked at the flight coupon again, half-hoping she'd imagined it. But the name was still there. John Herrin.

Now that she knew what to look for, she went through the loft systematically. She found her old school atlas and plotted her father's travels using the postcard dates and places, ticket stubs, any receipt in a foreign currency. She looked for anything to do with John Herrin, anything to do with London and the Underground, any references to a tubby man called Harry. Working in libraries on her dissertation, she'd trained herself to disconnect the analytical half of her brain, to inventory the goods without appraising them. Only when she had all the pieces would she let herself think about how they fitted together.

At half-past midnight she was done. The hot water tank stood revealed at last. Her clothes smelled of dust, her arms and face itched from rubbing the rockwool insulation. She found the switch on the tank and treated herself to a long shower, lingering until the hot water supply started to fail again. She rummaged out a tin of soup and some cheese biscuits from her mother's cupboards and made herself a late supper – she hadn't eaten all day. Only then did she examine the evidence she'd accumulated.

She had the atlas. A scattering of dots marked across the double-spread Europe, trips taken every two or three months from 1984 through 1987. The furthest east was Istanbul; the furthest west Santiago de Compostela, but most of the dots clustered between the Rhine and the Seine, the fault line where France and Germany had pushed against each other for centuries, throwing up statelets like Belgium and Luxembourg in their tectonic struggle. Another string of dots ran along the Alps, from northern Italy to southern France. Several clustered in Switzerland around Lausanne.

Then there was the plane ticket for John Herrin – to which she had added a hotel bill and an application to Somerset House for a duplicate birth certificate, both in the same name.

Finally there was the letter, typewritten on thick cream paper, inviting John Herrin to a job interview on Thursday November 22nd 1987. The letter that made Ellie gasp when she saw it.

The Director, Mr Vivian Blanchard, would be delighted if you could visit him to discuss possible career opportunities at the Monsalvat Bank.

London

Ellie couldn't believe anyone used phone boxes any more. But, like Cliff Richard and Harvey's Bristol Cream, they still seemed to exist. Huddled inside the glass box on the corner of Moorgate and London Wall, she was glad for it. She knew Monsalvat could monitor the calls from her phone – she'd signed a piece of paper that let them do just that. Until two weeks ago, she hadn't imagined she'd have anything to say worth listening to.

The phone rang and rang until an answering machine kicked in. Ellie looked at the card Harry had given her in the gardens in Brussels – a phone number with a London prefix, and a scrawled message. *If no answer, leave a message for Harry from Jane.*

'Hi Harry, this is Jane.' She stammered for something to say and couldn't think of anything. 'Give me a call.' But he wouldn't call on her mobile, and there was no phone at the flat.

A car drove by, flooding the phone box with light. Ellie

turned away. Could it be the Bentley? She tried to catch a glimpse, but it was already nothing more than a pair of red brake-lights glaring back at her.

She looked at her watch. In Newport, the hospital reception desk would close in ten minutes. Hoping no one was watching, she stepped out of the phone box and got out her mobile. A soft voice, as familiar and unworldly as the talking clock, told her the same news it had told her every day for a week. No change.

All she could do was wait.

In most of the City, January was one extended hangover from the year before: slow days, long lunch breaks and early finishes. Even the junior analysts sometimes made it home before eight. But at Monsalvat, the phones rang and the corridors hummed and the e-mails flew about as quickly as ever. Ellie found out why on the Friday after New Year, when Blanchard called her into his office.

'How is your mother?' he asked at once.

'Stable. Still unconscious.' She didn't meet his eye. Each night when she went back to the Barbican, she held her breath for fear the Bentley would be waiting outside. Each night, it wasn't there. It was almost as if Blanchard could smell the reluctance that had come over her. She'd barely even seen him in the office.

'You are satisfied with the care she has? She is getting everything she needs?'

'As much as you can expect.'

'She has family to visit her?'

'Not really.'

Blanchard toyed with his cufflinks. 'I was speaking to a friend of mine, a doctor. He is an expert in stroke recovery, perhaps one of the four or five best in the world. He has a

202

private hospital near Harley Street. He is willing to accept your mother as a patient, if you like.'

Ellie shook her head. 'That's so kind – but we'd never afford it. My mother doesn't have any insurance.'

'The bank will pay.' Blanchard leaned forward over his desk, staring so hard Ellie couldn't look anywhere else. 'I know you do not want charity – nor would I. But you must do what is best for your mother. When she comes out of her coma she will need intensive therapy. The Health Service is a machine; one life is nothing to them. Especially in winter. For the care your mother needs, London would be better.'

She couldn't argue; she knew he was right. But she couldn't agree – not because she was proud, but because she was terrified. Bringing her mother to London, to stay in Blanchard's hospital tended by Blanchard's doctors, would be surrendering her into his power.

Blanchard misread her doubts. 'You forget, I have an interest in this too. I do not want you to suffer unnecessarily. It will be easier for you if you do not spend half your life on the train between here and Newport. Better for your mother if you can visit her every day. For coming out of a coma, I am told, the presence of loved ones is very important.'

He picked up a gilded letter-opener and spun it on its point on the desk. 'And there is business. Always business. I understand your thoughts must be with your mother, but I need you here. Now.'

Ellie waited.

'Michel Saint-Lazare was delighted to win the Talhouett auction. The company are not so pleased. The management refuse to accept our nominee to the board, or give us any access to the company. So Michel has decided to launch a bid for outright control.'

'A hostile takeover?'

'It will be a monumental battle. Both the French and German governments own stakes. If the French sell to us, the Germans will refuse; if the Germans sell, the French won't. In fact, probably neither of them will do business with us, because they will suspect us of being a Trojan horse for the other. Between them, they own 40 per cent of the company. That makes it difficult for us. All the cards must fall our way. But Michel is determined.

'We need you for this, Ellie. Your mother's condition could last for months and you cannot put your life on hold all this time. It goes on.'

He pressed the letter-opener into the desk, pushing a dent in the leather blotter. 'It would be difficult, I think, to keep working for Monsalvat if your mother remains in Newport.'

A week later she got a reply. The message was so well hidden she almost missed it: slipped into the folds of a free newspaper handed to her on the street as she walked towards the Barbican. The distributor thrust it into her chest; then, when she took it, held on a moment longer, so she was forced to look up. The yellow cap was pulled low over his face, but she recognised Harry's worried features below it. The next moment, he spun away to press another newspaper on an unwilling commuter. She looked out for him again the next day, but he wasn't there.

Two nights later, she got off the bus on the Fulham Road and walked back to the corner, checking to make sure no one was following. *Old Church Street*, the message had said, though there was no church Ellie could see: only an antiques shop and a plain brick wall disappearing around the corner. But there was a churchyard, an orphaned parcel of land long since forgotten. Ellie had seen it from the top deck of the bus, behind the wall she was now approaching.

Paint peeled from a green door in the wall: it looked as though it must have rotted shut years ago, but when Ellie pushed, it opened with barely a squeak. Ahead of her, a dozen rows of gravestones stood half-sunk into the soil, like some Neolithic monument.

'I'm sorry we couldn't find somewhere more convivial.'

In other circumstances, a lone figure loitering in the shadows of an abandoned graveyard would have made her jump. Today, she was too tired. Harry stood against the wall where the bus passengers couldn't see him, watching through the arms of a moss-covered cross. He beckoned her over.

'Are you trying to scare me?'

He shook his head. 'You have no idea how difficult it's been. Blanchard has you covered every second you're out of the office. Seems to know where you're going even before you step out the door.'

'That's not hard. I go to the office, I go home. That's about it.'

Ellie thought back, trying to picture any unexpected coincidences, recurring faces. As ever, Harry sounded like a polite, soft-spoken lunatic. *Except now*, she thought, *I have to believe him*.

If he was right, she didn't have much time. 'Tell me about my father. Did he work for Monsalvat?'

Harry scratched a hunk of moss off the cross, exposing the white stone underneath. His finger came away black.

'He didn't get the job. In Brussels, I told you that I belong to an organisation. Call it a brotherhood, though we've nothing against women. We've been fighting a war against Monsalvat, on and off for almost nine hundred years.'

It was an extraordinary statement, but all Ellie could think to say was, 'The bank's only existed since the sixteenth century.' *Only.*

'As a bank. As an entity, it goes much further back. Saint-Lazare de Morgon, who founded the bank, was a descendant of a Norman warlord called Lazar de Mortain. Even by medieval standards, he was a particularly vile piece of work.'

'Why did my father apply for a job there?'

'He was reconnoitring. You remember I told you he died trying to break into the vaults?'

'It's not the sort of thing you forget.'

'Nine hundred years ago, Lazar de Mortain stole something that belonged to our brotherhood. So far as we know it's still there, locked deep in the vault.'

Ellie remembered the vault shuddering as the train roared past. She imagined the bright headlamp reaching round the corner. A figure caught in its beam, no time to react. The screech of steel, burning metal, an impact. Sometimes, when she was working late and the office was quiet, she could feel the floor shiver, echoing the faint rumble far below.

'Monsalvat, for all its lip-service to the modern world, is effectively a feudal household. Michel Saint-Lazare's the king, and Blanchard his loyal seneschal. He's also Saint-Lazare's nephew, did you know that?'

Ellie shook her head.

'Saint-Lazare can't have children. We met up with him once, left him paralysed from the waist down.' Absent-mindedly, Harry played with the button on his overcoat.

Something Blanchard had said popped into her mind, that night after the opera. *You don't need any protection with me.* She tried to imagine these old men – so much money, so much power – yet denied the most basic, creative power of all.

'What about Talhouett? What have they got to do with you?'

'With us, nothing. They're just what they seem, a mid-ranking European industrial concern. But, by an accident of history, they own something that belongs to us.'

Ellie remembered his question in the park in Brussels, and Blanchard interrogating her after the due diligence. 'Mirabeau.'

'You don't need to know what it is. But somehow Saint-Lazare found out about it. When we heard he was prowling around Talhouett, we sent someone in to find out what he knew.'

Ellie saw a shadow move on one of the gravestones. Perhaps she wasn't too tired to be frightened after all. But it was only a squirrel.

'It went wrong. One man died, another got captured. He's dead too.'

'Captured by . . .?'

'Blanchard? Saint-Lazare?' Harry shrugged. 'Doesn't matter. Blanchard's got a henchman who probably did the dirty work, a nasty chap called Destrier.'

'I've met him.'

A bus rumbled by on the Fulham Road. The lights of its upper deck seemed to hover in the night, men and women floating past with no conception of what was happening in the darkness below.

'Why did Blanchard recruit me?' Ellie asked.

'We don't know. We didn't think he knew you existed, or we'd have protected you better. We never meant for you to get mixed up in this. But now that you have . . . *Damn.*'

He'd twisted the button on his coat so hard the threads had snapped. He looked at it ruefully.

'That was new last Christmas.'

Ellie didn't care about his coat. She didn't care about a nine-hundred year-old knight, or a brotherhood who wanted to bring down the bank.

'What do you want me to do?'

Never ask a question if you don't already know the answer, they'd taught on her negotiating course. But you always knew. Even speaking to Mrs Thomas in the thicket in Switzerland, she'd known what was coming. It was as if, in the intake of breath, you could hear the words that would re-emerge.

'We want you to break into the vault.'

'What's in it?'

He dropped the button into his pocket. 'You wouldn't believe me if I told you.'

'You want me to risk my life for it, but you won't tell me what it is?'

'I can't.' Harry shoved his hands in his pockets. 'When you've got it – when you're safe – I'll show you everything.'

'But my dad knew what it was.'

'Your father had devoted his life to it.'

She tried a different tack, pretending she hadn't already decided. 'You said you didn't want me mixed up with this.'

So often, she'd thought there was something incurably apologetic about Harry: the downturned mouth, the jowly face and eyes that drifted naturally towards his shoes. But there was nothing apologetic when he next spoke: only hard inevitability.

'You're already mixed up. I'm trying to get you out.'

XXVI

France, 1136

The next two months are the happiest of my life.

We head south, towards the lands of the King of France. Nowhere's safe for us, but at least that'll be dangerous for Guy's men too. After two days we sell our horses. It's a wrench, surrendering my status so soon after I won it, but they're too easily recognised and we attract too many looks. We might just pass as a knight and his lady, but people will wonder where our servants and baggage have gone. They'll remember us.

On foot, we're almost invisible. As spring turns to summer, the people of Christendom pour on to the roads in their thousands. You could travel from Canterbury to Compostela and never be alone. After the first week, when every bump in the road has me looking over my shoulder for the dust of galloping hooves, the crowds start to relax me. The more people who see us, the fewer who'll notice.

You can see the change in both of us. I grow my hair long, and let my beard grow out. Ada's beauty's harder to disguise, but after two months her skin is harder and darker. We present ourselves as husband and wife, and live accordingly. After so long lurking in shadows, it's a joy to have it out in the open. It feels right, honest. I can almost forget that Ada has a real husband.

She never talks about him, but there's a look she has whenever we pass a church, a quietness, that reminds me she took a vow before God. It still binds her, however much I wish it away.

For a time, when we stop being children, we wish the world could be other than it is – that wounds could heal without scars, that every love could be a first love, that past sins could be undone with a single confession. I learned the truth when I was young: we can never shed our sins and regrets, only accumulate more, a burden that we grow and carry until our deaths. The best we can do is learn to live with ourselves, to accommodate our pasts.

At the shrine of Our Lady of Tours, I give Ada a wooden brooch, two birds drinking from a cup. I can't marry her, but I get down on my knees and promise her, 'I'll always love you, I'll always protect you.'

But summer fades. One day, I realise the road isn't as busy as it was the week before. It's easier to find space at the pilgrim hostels and almshouses; the queues at the town gates aren't as long. Travellers have begun to return home for the harvest, to wipe the dust off their shoes and lay up stores for winter. The questions that I've kept firmly over the horizon now seem urgent. When everyone goes home, where will we go? How will we support ourselves? We've stretched the money from the horses as far as we could, but it's almost gone. On the road, it's easy to pretend to be a glovemaker and his wife from London, but that won't feed us through the winter. Ada can sew and weave, but so can every woman. The only trade I know is fighting.

It's late August when the answer comes to me. We're in Burgundy, near Dijon; dusk is falling, earlier and earlier these days. We arrive at an inn. Usually we avoid them because of the cost, but it's been raining all day and we slept under a hedge last night. Passing the door, I notice a tall blue shield painted with a golden star leaned against the wall. When I've haggled with the innkeeper for a bed and some food, I ask him about it.

'Etienne de Luz.' He jerks his thumb to the back room, where I can hear laughter and singing from behind a curtained door. 'The Count of Dijon is holding a tourney in three days at La Roche.'

The innkeeper slouches off to attend to something. Ada grabs my wrist. She can see what I'm thinking.

'It's too dangerous.'

'No one will recognise me. We're a long way from Normandy.'

That's not what she means. 'Men die in the tourney all the time.'

I know she's right. There are no blunted edges and filed-down points in the tourney. When lances shatter, splinters fill the air like swarms of arrows. But next morning, after a long night arguing with Ada, I'm standing in the stableyard when Etienne de Luz comes to get his mount.

It's obvious at once that he's no warrior. For a start, he's fully armed: a real fighter would save his strength for combat. His gleaming hauberk and jewelled scabbard can't hide the fact that his mail coat only has a single layer of rings, and his sword would probably snap in a strong wind. But the men who trail out of the tavern behind him look useful enough.

I step in front of him. 'I hear you're taking a company to the tournament at La Roche.'

He looks me up and down, then turns to his seneschal. He wants a second opinion. He's vain, but he knows his limitations.

The seneschal sees enough to be interested. 'What can you do?'

I look around the yard. My eye alights on a dove, perched on the edge of the roof, pecking grubs out of the thatch.

'Give me a spear.'

The seneschal obliges. I heft it in my hand, testing the weight, finding the balance. It doesn't have the poise of a Welsh javelin, but it will have to do.

I crouch, take a half-step back, and let fly. The javelin strikes the dove clean in the breast and goes through, burying itself in the thatch. Blood stains the white feathers. Etienne and his seneschal look impressed.

Guy would say it's hardly a knightly skill. But on the tournament field, all that matters is how many bodies you bring in.

'Can you do that on horseback?'

I don't tell him how the dove got there – that I snared her last night in the stables and tethered her to the roof-beam with a loop of thread; that I've paced out the distance exactly. The storyteller doesn't have to tell his audience everything.

'Give me a horse, and I'll show you what I can do.'

XXVII

London

If it wasn't for what came afterwards, the next month would have been the hardest of Ellie's life. Every morning she was up at five, at her desk half an hour later chewing on a cereal bar and digesting the overnight news stories. At eight she met with Blanchard and the rest of the bid team, then straight on to twelve hours of meetings, conference calls, e-mails and spreadsheets. Every night at nine a taxi came to ferry her to the hospital, where she'd spend an hour at her mother's bedside: at least, having gone private, there were no restrictions on visiting hours. Then another taxi home, poring over the messages coming in on her phone, and perhaps a final hour's work before two or three in the morning.

She lived in darkness, a world of constant night where she never seemed to sleep. She began walking to the office again, even when it rained, just for ten minutes in the open air. Soon she came to recognise the people who were up at that hour: the streetsweeper on the corner of Gresham Street,

213

making the world new again; the newspaper delivery driver who honked as he drove past; the newsagent lifting the shutter on his shop who never looked at her. Sometimes she remembered to be careful, to watch for following footsteps or shadows in doorways. Most of the time she was too tired to think of it.

She was in limbo, a tight-stretched canvas on which other men wrote their desires. Some days she thought it would tear her in two. She couldn't leave Blanchard, not while her mother lay sick in his hospital; she couldn't ignore Harry. She didn't even know if she was still going out with Doug. She'd told him about her mother, much later than she should have, garbling the story to hide the fact she'd been in Switzerland for Christmas. He'd wanted to go down and visit, but Ellie told him not to. She could tell he was hurt – he started to say something about the state of their relationship, but bit it back. After that, he called once a week to ask how her mother was doing, but otherwise left her alone. The calls were so formal, so measured, she sometimes wondered if she'd broken up with him in a sleep-deprived moment and forgotten it.

As the month wore on, Blanchard began to give her unusual new assignments. One night, she found herself outside an office block in Wapping slipping a stiff-backed envelope through a letterbox. Two days later, a newspaper not usually known for its business coverage printed a story about the Finance Director of Talhouett UK. Under the headline BANKER SPANKER it described, with excellently reproduced photographs and eyewitness testimony, the Soho habits he hadn't thought to reveal to his wife. He threatened to sue, then resigned to spend more time with his family.

Another day, Ellie spent a morning sitting in the lobby of

a hotel on Knightsbridge, watching for the trustee of a well-known pension fund. When he arrived, she followed him into the lift. By the time he reached the seventh floor he owned a new Gucci briefcase so heavy that simply carrying it left him lopsided. A week later, his fund announced that it would use its shareholding to vote in favour of the Saint-Lazare takeover.

If Ellie had stopped to think, she might have considered the implications of what she was doing. But she didn't. Her working mind had become a balance sheet: things that progressed the takeover; things that impeded it. Cause and effect barely entered the equation; right and wrong not at all. She was too tired.

At least she didn't have to travel much. Talhouett's head-quarters and most of its business were on the continent, but a quirk of history had left its principal share listing in London. There was only one trip, and like most of her travels, it happened unexpectedly, when Blanchard stormed into her office one afternoon. Ellie had never seen him look so furious.

He knows, she thought. *Harry, Newport, everything.*

She shuffled papers and tried to look cool. 'What is it?'

'A white knight.' He slammed a folder on her desk. 'What do you know about the Koenig Group?'

Ellie swallowed as she tried to pull her thoughts together. 'They're private equity, aren't they? Mainly infrastructure and communications deals.'

'They have tabled a friendly offer for Talhouett. The management is keen – even the German government may consider supporting the bid. One of their politicians thinks we are the unacceptable face of global capitalism.' He pulled a face.

215

'That makes no sense.' Ellie frowned. 'We're already offering more than the accretion/dilution numbers say. Koenig don't have any complementary businesses to create synergies, and if the German government are on board they won't let them sack workers or break up the company. What's in it for them?'

'This is not a coincidence, Ellie. Michel Saint-Lazare has enemies: one of them has put Koenig up to this. We must go to Paris at once.'

'I thought Koenig were in Frankfurt.'

'There is no point speaking to them.' He picked up his file and turned to go.

'Koenig want to play the white knight. You know the easiest way to stop a charging knight?'

Ellie looked blank.

'Kill his horse.'

The Bentley purred down Commercial Road towards Limehouse. Traffic was light, but Blanchard ordered the driver to take a detour. When Ellie glanced up from her laptop, she was surprised to see long rows of warehouses crawling past.

'Is this the way to the airport?'

Blanchard murmured something about roadworks. Ellie went back to her work. When she looked again, the car had stopped at a dead end in a mazy industrial estate. She assumed they'd taken a wrong turn – but Blanchard was staring out the window with purpose, waiting for something. Had he spoken?

Ellie followed his gaze, through a chain-link fence topped with coils of razor wire. Behind it lay a wasteland: charred bricks and twisted metal beams, the remnant of a warehouse gutted by fire. The breeze blew up flakes of ash, as if the fire still lingered, though it must have happened some time ago. The rubble had been bulldozed into heaps, and the scorch marks on the adjacent buildings painted over. At the back of the plot, a derelict sign advertised *Logical Components*, a monument to the fallen company.

But she'd seen the name before. She remembered her first week at work, a proud old man defying Blanchard's offer so that his son could inherit a business he didn't want. The Rosenberg Automation Company, which had streamlined its supply chain to remain competitive. A skip behind the factory, waist deep in cardboard looking at logos on boxes. *Logical Components – the choice is Logical.*

'That was the company that sold logic boards to Rosenberg. Their key supplier.'

'Their factory burned down three months ago. Without their components, Rosenberg were unable to continue manufacturing. Their customers deserted them, the bank denied them credit. They were about to declare bankruptcy when we made one final offer to acquire them. Reduced, obviously. The company was almost worthless.'

Ellie forced herself to look him in the eye. 'Why did you bring me here?'

'Rosenberg was your first deal. I thought you would want to know how it ended.'

'Not like this.' She stared at the wreckage, imagining the flames consuming the building. 'Did you do it?'

'Of course not.' He parted his lips, baring his teeth. Daring her to contradict him.

'But if I did – is it wrong? A company, fundamentally, is merely the sum of its assets. An accumulation of value. Let us say I order our trading division to take an aggressive position regarding a certain corporation. They dump the stock, or short-sell it. A rumour goes around the market and others follow suit. In a matter of minutes I have destroyed hundreds of millions of pounds from a company's assets. All perfectly legally. Why is it any different if I destroy those assets in the form of buildings and machinery, rather than paper? If I use fire rather than the telephone?'

'It's illegal.'

'Nobody dies. We have a sentimental attachment to physical property, but it is nothing more than an incarnation of wealth. And wealth is the material of capitalism. We create it or we destroy it; we work to acquire it and deny it to our enemies.'

'And what does all that wealth buy you?' Ellie murmured – more audibly than she'd intended. Blanchard looked surprised.

'Power, of course.'

Paris

Ellie had always wanted to see Paris, but not like this. They landed in darkness; half an hour later, a limousine was sweeping through the post-rush hour traffic. She felt on edge. Every time she looked back, a black Range Rover with dark tinted windows seemed to be behind them. If they changed lanes, it followed; when they turned, it turned. When a taxi tried to nip in front, it roared forward to close the gap, almost taking off the taxi's front bumper. The taxi veered away with a squawk of outrage.

'Is someone following us?'

Blanchard glanced back and smiled. 'Destrier has arranged a babysitter. He says there is a gang of anarchists who have made threats against us. Nothing specific, but Destrier worries. He's like a grandmother.'

The Range Rover melted away in traffic as the limousine

drew up in the Place Vendôme outside the Paris Ritz. At check-in, their room keys came with a message.

'Mr Lechowski is awaiting you in the Elton John suite.'

Ellie's heart sank. 'Is he advising Koenig now?'

'He was a natural choice. He already knew the company inside out from trying to buy it.'

'Is that ethical?'

'It's efficient.'

The Elton John suite was more tasteful than Ellie had expected, a soft-lit symphony of pink and ivory. The heels of her shoes almost lost themselves in the carpet. Lechowski was waiting for them in the sitting room. Through an open door, Ellie could see an eight-foot-wide bed capped with a pink canopy.

'You are looking as beautiful as ever, Ellie,' he complimented her. 'May I get you a drink?'

'Just water.'

He picked up a pink telephone and ordered.

'This is an unexpected meeting. Your assistant would tell me nothing on the phone, but I assume you have come about Talhouett? You did very well in Luxembourg; we were disappointed not to win. Our bid was only five million euros less than yours.' He watched Blanchard carefully. 'But perhaps you knew that already.'

Preternaturally quickly, the waiter came with the drinks – mineral water for Ellie, a brandy for Blanchard and a Jack Daniels for Lechowski.

'This is about Talhouett,' Blanchard confirmed.

Lechowski spat out his wad of gum. 'Off the record?'

'That depends what we agree.' Blanchard took out his knife and sliced the end off a cigar. 'Koenig gains nothing by buying Talhouett. Ellie?'

As briefly as possible, Ellie outlined the case. Lechowski listened without interest, staring the whole time at a point six inches below her throat.

'And even if Koenig win the company, we will still own ten per cent of it. You will find we can be a very disagreeable shareholder.'

'I thought Groupe Saint-Lazare owned that stake.'

Blanchard swatted the objection away. 'We think the same on this.'

'As ever.'

'Koenig have no shares to offer, so they will have to pay cash. In this market, only a fool pays cash. Especially one with debts to service.'

A pause. Lechowski sipped his whiskey. Blanchard exhaled a cloud of smoke.

'*Eh bien.*' Blanchard gazed at one of the pictures on the wall, an extravagant painting of a space rocket. 'When I was a child I loved astronomy. Orion, Pegasus, Andromeda – I could plot every one. Back then, space seemed so exciting. Now, it seems more about bureaucracy than heroism. Did you hear about the landing craft NASA sent to Mars?'

Lechowski shook his head.

'A vehicle the size of a vacuum cleaner, but they spent more to build it than you or I would spend on a whole company. Ten years to prepare it, three more to fly however many hundred million kilometres through space. And when it arrived, it crashed into the planet at three hundred miles an hour. Do you know why?'

If Lechowski knew, he wouldn't deny Blanchard his punchline.

'Because the scientists made their calculations in centimetres, but programmed the lander in inches.'

They both laughed. Ellie looked between them and wondered where Blanchard was going.

'There is another story like this, which perhaps you know,' Blanchard continued. 'A German private equity firm who wanted to buy a Hungarian property developer. They opened the books and did the due diligence. They put it into spreadsheets, models, valuations – all by the book. They bought the company for a handsome premium – they were so eager to get into the booming Hungarian property market. And then –' Blanchard smiled. 'They found out that the assets they paid for in euros had actually been quoted in forints.'

He laughed again. This time, Lechowski didn't join in.

A long roach of ash dangled from the end of Blanchard's cigar. He rolled it off in the ashtray and took a sip of brandy.

'Of course it is just a story. I mention it only because Michel Saint-Lazare has always wanted to expand into Hungary. If any of your clients had assets they were looking to sell, he would be eager to deal with them.'

Lechowski had gone very still, like a cat watching a bird in a tree. Ellie could almost see his jaw trembling.

'How much does Saint-Lazare have to spend?'

'Maybe two, three hundred million euros. Of course, he would be relying on the profits from Talhouett to fund it.'

Lechowski took a long sip of his Jack Daniels. The glass came away empty. Ellie refilled it from the bottle that room service had thoughtfully left on the sideboard. Playing waitress seemed to be the only reason she was there.

'I will tell you a secret,' Lechowski announced. He had recovered some of his poise. 'The Koenig management do not want to buy Talhouett. They are only doing it because the board have ordered it. But the board do not really want it either. There is one man, Herr Drexler, who has forced this

221

deal on them. Unfortunately, he is the chairman. It will take forceful advocacy to persuade them to change course. It can be done, but it will take a *personal* appeal.'

'Your bank will get its commission.'

'My bank, yes.'

'Three per cent could be six million euros. If you originate the deal, most of that will find its way into your pocket. You will certainly be able to afford your new Porsche.'

'Actually, I prefer Aston Martin. My colleagues say I am perverse, but there is something so oxymoronic about English craftsmanship.'

Lechowski drained his glass again. When Ellie went to fill it, he held it so she had to bend low in front of him to reach. His knee brushed her leg.

'I am a romantic, Blanchard. I prefer English cars to German, and American bourbon to Scotch. And a warm bed to a cold one.'

He smiled at Ellie. For a moment, even the smoke seemed to freeze in mid-air. Ellie gave Blanchard a desperate look and found no comfort in his eyes. He lifted himself out of his chair.

'I think I will go to bed. It has been a long day. He gave Ellie a bleak smile. 'I will leave you two to sort out the details of the agreement.'

Lechowski stood to shake his hand. 'I must just excuse myself for one moment,' he told Ellie. 'I hope you will be here when I come back.'

Blanchard delayed until Lechowski was out of the room.

'Lechowski was never meant to play the white knight,' he observed.

The smoke was making Ellie's eyes water. She felt hot, unwell. 'Do you really –?'

'Do whatever you have to.'

222

*

London City Airport

Blanchard's phone started buzzing the moment they were off the plane. He listened, smiled, said a few words and hung up.

'That was the office. Koenig have just issued a press release to retract their bid. They say the market conditions are not favourable. The Talhouett board will meet tomorrow, and everyone expects that they have accepted our bid. I don't know how you did it.'

He slid an arm around Ellie's waist and leaned in to kiss her. But she twisted away, slipping out of his reach.

'Would it bother you if I said I'd slept with him?'

'Of course.' Blanchard met her gaze frankly. 'I am a man; I feel jealousy. You are very precious to me. But that is personal. This is business. And in business a certain ruthlessness is admirable.'

He inclined his head, waiting for her to speak.

'I didn't sleep with him,' she said. 'I told him I found him attractive, but I knew his reputation. I told him if I went to bed with him and then he broke our agreement, no one would ever take me seriously again. I said he could have me when the deal was complete.'

An admiring smile flickered across Blanchard's face. 'He will hold you to that,' he warned.

I'm not planning on being around to find out.

She let him kiss her as they waited outside the airport for the car. When they'd got in, she took her phone out of her bag and turned it on. Even in the short time she'd been in the air, a few dozen e-mails had come through. She read through them, half-listening to Blanchard as he talked about celebrations, about where they could get a table at such short notice.

223

'When the contracts are signed the whole bank will celebrate,' he told her. 'Tonight it will be just you and me.'

The last message told her she had a voicemail waiting. She dialled in and listened in silence.

'Probably it's Lechowski asking you out,' Blanchard joked. He stroked a strand of hair back from her cheek; he reached across to kiss her again, then paused. He must have read it in her face.

'What is it?'

XXVIII

Torcy, France, 1136

They say the ground shakes when two lines of horsemen come together. If you're one of the riders, you don't notice: your whole world is a shaking anyway. The rise and fall of the horse, the sway of the lance, the creak of leather and the rattle of shifting armour. Some of the knights wear knotted cords tied to their helmets, to snap and crack as they blow behind them. It's vanity: just one more thing for an enemy to grab hold of.

But for now, everything is still. The drums and horns have fallen silent. The crowd are hushed. I sit in my saddle, feeling the cantle dig into my back. A cold wind catches the pennon on the tip of my spear. The horses stamp and blow hot air through their nostrils. Across the field, some two hundred mounted knights wait in line in front of a grandstand. It's draped with cloth which spreads and billows in the wind, so that the whole construction seems to wobble.

A herald calls '*laciez*'. Four hundred men pull their helmets on. I tie my chinstrap tight under my chin. From under the brim, I scan the opposing line for any sign of Guy de

Hautfort's banner. It's part of my ritual, part of the danger. We're far from Normandy, but men travel a long way for the tourney.

Something at the far end of the opposing line catches my eye. A familiar shade of blue, or perhaps the shape. It's too far away to see clearly: the device is hidden behind another knight's banner. But it worries me. Usually we get there with enough time to ask the heralds who's on the other side, but we were delayed on the road from Poitiers and only arrived last night.

A trumpet sounds. We charge.

This is my fifth tournament in Etienne's company. In my first, at Dijon, I captured three knights and five horses. Etienne sold four and let me keep one, a chestnut charger. I was just getting used to him when I lost him again, in the next tournament. It happened in the first charge: a lance caught me plum on the boss of my shield and bowled me out of the saddle. I was lucky I only lost my horse.

Since then I've been more successful. Ada tells me to be careful, that the last thing I want is a reputation, but if you hold back in the heat of battle – even a mock battle like the tourney – you'll probably find yourself on the ground. *Do you want me to do my worst?* I ask her. *Wheel and flee rather than face the other knights?*

She never answers, but I can see it in her face. *If you loved me, you'd flee.* I don't know how to make her understand that the two aren't incompatible. I do love her – but I have to fight.

I survive the first charge, though only just. I'm still worrying about the banner I saw, and don't have my lance properly sat in its fewter. But they call it the tourney because the true test is when you hear the shout of *tournez*. Turn again. Any fool with enough courage can risk the first charge. It's turning to go back that really tests your mettle, when your arm's shivering and your lance is a splintered stump, when you no longer have your comrades riding knee to knee. Reining in a horse from full gallop, bringing him round and spurring him to the next charge is no easy feat. If you're too slow, you'll get broadsided by the enemy who turned faster.

I wheel about and spur forward, trying to edge down the line to my left. I can't see where the banner's gone. There are no blunted weapons on this field: if Jocelin's here, it would be easy to kill him.

A knight on a bay charger comes galloping at me, heading me off. I put the banner out of my mind and draw my sword. It's always more dangerous the second time. Neither of you, man or horse, is as focussed. The worst injuries happen now: the shield you don't hold high enough, the piece of armour that's come unlaced, the dazed horse who staggers at the crucial moment.

I prick my spurs and return to the battle.

It's a good day for us. By the time the bugles end it, we've taken a dozen prisoners, including a castellan's son who should fetch a good price. My body aches all over, though nothing compared with what it'll be like tomorrow. I've got a cut above one eye where a splinter caught me, but otherwise it's only bruises.

Yet I still feel uneasy. I watched for it all day, but I never found the banner I'd spotted. After the second charge, the tourney splintered into scores of skirmishes and individual combats, gradually spreading over miles of fields. I had to stay close to my company; I couldn't risk myself alone.

227

I tell myself it's probably nothing. Lots of knights carry blue banners – and even if it was Jocelin, he could have broken his lance on my shield and never recognised me. But I'm eager to get back to our camp and find Ada.

The tent's empty; she's not there. Etienne and the men have gone to feast in the Count's castle, but one of the grooms is sitting by the fire, drinking wine we took as ransom for a Burgundian knight.

'Where's Ada?'

He wipes wine from his mouth. 'She went to meet a horse-dealer at the chapel of Saint Sebastian, near the forest.'

Why not the horse market? I hurry down between the rows of tents, trying not to snag my spurs on the guy ropes. I'm so busy watching my footing I don't see the young squire approaching. I barrel clean into him. It's only as I draw back, murmuring an apology, that I see his face. The red-brown hair in loose curls, the mouth that droops down at the corners, the cheeks that never quite lost their youthful fat.

'William?'

'Peter?'

He's not happy to see me. He knots his hands together and twists them in his tunic. He doesn't know what to say.

'It's good to see you again.' I have a fixed smile on my face; my mind's racing. *How much does he know? Who can he tell?*

'Have you taken service with another knight?'

He shakes his head. 'I'm here with Jocelin.'

I should kill him – cut his throat, sink him in the town ditch. But we lived in each other's pockets for six years: sparred, played, joked and fought together. He isn't my enemy.

I put my hands on his shoulders and force him to look at me.

'Where can I find Jocelin?'

228

William stares at the ground. He mumbles something – I probably wouldn't have caught it, but I heard the name just five minutes ago.

'The chapel of Saint Sebastian.'

The chapel stands on the edge of a mown field, with a walled crypt beside it. I arrive on my charger, armed and helmed. I don't see anyone there.

A cry comes to me on the evening air. I follow the sound, around the churchyard wall to the place where the forest comes hard up against it.

She's tied to a birch tree wearing nothing but her shift, so badly ripped that there's barely a palm's breadth of cloth intact. Rasping blows have lacerated her skin, and there are burn marks on her arms that look like the tip of a heated sword.

Her eyes open, tiny points of light against deep wells of shadow. 'Peter?'

I jump down and run towards her, my sword drawn to cut the ropes.

'Go away.'

They're the last words she speaks to me and I wish she hadn't said them. I want to remember her voice as it was, full of life and spirit. Not this cry, dragged out of her in agony.

A harness jangles to my left. I turn. A knight rides out of the shadows of the forest, flanked by four or five men on foot with spears. One of them runs to my horse and grabs the bridle.

'What have you done to her?'

'Not what you think. Not yet.'

I can't see Jocelin's face, but I know his voice. It's rich with triumph.

'She's still my father's property, for all she's whored herself to you. Perhaps when he's finished with her, he'll give her to me. And when I'm finished, I'll give what's left to the stable boys for their sport.'

I wish I hadn't dismounted. I wish I'd never come to this tournament. I wish I'd killed Jocelin that night in the tower.

'Let her go. Let her go and take me.'

He laughs. 'I don't have to choose.'

They're paltry words. But in that clearing, with blood in my mouth and guilt flooding through me, they make me snap. I'm back in Guy's hall fighting over a stolen book. I know I can't beat him: he's on horseback, fully armed, but it doesn't matter. I put up my sword and charge at Jocelin. One of his men drops into a crouch and hurls his spear at me. Out of pure instinct, I duck.

The spear sails over my head and makes a soft, clean landing, barely a sound. I turn, though I already know what I'll see. It struck Ada clean through the breast, pinning her to the tree. Her hands clutch the shaft: she's trying to pull it out. She doesn't have the strength. Her arms go limp, still gripping the spear; her head drops. Blood flows down the ash, touches her hand and drips onto the ground.

Even Jocelin didn't mean that to happen. His surprise is a fraction slower than my fury. I fly towards him and get inside his guard: he pulls his boot from his stirrup and kicks the sword out of my hand, but I grab his arm and sink my teeth into his exposed hand. He screams and loosens his grip. I grab the sword by the blade and wrest it out of his hands. It cuts my fingers and I let it fall. He wants to bring his shield round, to chop it down on my head, but the straps get caught on the pommel.

I cling on to his leg, trying to wrestle him out of the saddle. Something comes away in my hand – his spur. Gripping it like a knife, I plunge it into the exposed leg just above his knee.

There's a howl of agony. I want to keep hold of the spur, to keep stabbing him until all the blood drains from his body. But surprise makes the horse move. My frenzied thrust misses Jocelin's leg and sinks into its flank.

The sound of a screaming horse is worse than a screaming man. The horse rears up; its hooves drum the air inches from my face. It lurches forward, trying to outrun the agony of the spur stuck in its side. I fling out my arms to grab on to Jocelin, but a hoof strikes my chest, kicking me back onto the ground. Then he's gone.

The other men flit about me, shadows on the edge of the clearing. I can hear a couple running after Jocelin; the other two wait, wondering what to do. They could kill me easily, but perhaps they don't know if Jocelin wants me alive.

Shouts and hooves in the falling darkness decide them. If I twist on my side, I can see fire on the meadow, horsemen with torches riding towards us. They're calling for me.

Jocelin's serjeants melt into the forest as Etienne and his men gallop up to the clearing. It's as well they're carrying torches or they might have ridden straight over me.

'Peter?'

They're all staring at Ada, speared to the tree. The weight of the shaft has prised open the wound: her white shift is drenched in blood that's black in the firelight. Shock's written on their faces. They all liked her.

I fall on my knees and vomit onto the ground. Etienne puts a tentative arm on my shoulder, but I shake him off.

He thinks he's saved me. But Ada's dead, my mother and father and brother are dead, and the men who did it haven't been punished. I've failed everyone I ever loved.

Nothing can save me now except revenge.

XXIX

Newport, South Wales

According to the hospital, her mother died while Ellie was on the plane somewhere above the English Channel. Ellie didn't think anything could make her feel worse, but somehow it did. She should have been on hand, at her mother's bedside – not drifting up in the clouds. It felt like a metaphor for something: lofty, blinding, insubstantial.

Doug didn't come to the funeral. She sent him a text message telling him the news, but ignored all his replies asking when the funeral would be. Blanchard didn't come either, though he sent his representatives: two men in a blacked-out Mercedes, parked across the road from the crematorium with the engine running. The wipers never stopped, presumably so that the soft rain gathering on their windscreen wouldn't obscure the view. Ellie almost considered inviting them in, offering them the chance to do their job properly, without pretence. There were plenty of seats.

Afterwards – after Mrs Thomas had said a few words about what a kind lady Mrs Stanton had been; after a choir had

232

sung 'Men of Harlech' out of the CD player in the corner; after she'd watched the coffin conveyed onto its gas-jetted pyre – they went to the tea shop on the corner. No one stayed long. By two thirty, when Mrs Thomas picked up her terrier and announced she had to go and collect her grandson from school, the low clouds were already threatening a premature dusk.

Mrs Thomas kissed her on both cheeks and gave her a hug. 'Do be careful,' she said. 'You're on your own now.'

Ellie went back to the house and fetched a few things from the attic. She supposed she'd return some day, even if only to sell it, but she said goodbye anyway. Just in case. She turned off all the lights and the heating, and made sure the doors were locked. Outside, the black Mercedes was struggling to reverse into a parking space on the narrow street. Ellie waited until it was wedged in, then left the house and hurried down towards the station. She knew they'd catch up with her – but not before she'd had time to use a payphone. She let it ring three times, then hung up.

I'm on my way.

London
Ellie took a taxi straight from Paddington to Claridge's. It was only seven o'clock; Blanchard wouldn't be back from the office for hours. The final details of the Talhouett takeover agreement had proved elusive; for the last two days, teams of lawyers had been working around the clock, garrisoning every spare corner of the Monsalvat office. Ellie had barely noticed them.

She lay on the bed and thought about what she had to do. She opened the brandy decanter and poured in the phial of liquid Harry had given her. She stared at the paintings on the

233

walls and they stared back: a gallery of callow knights and flimsy damsels, in dark forests or empty wastelands. It surprised her that Blanchard subscribed to this romanticised, Victorian take on the middle ages. Somehow she'd thought, with his far-back ancestry, he'd prefer a more authentic view.

Blanchard came in at eleven, smelling of coffee and cigar smoke.

'You should have called. I would have come straight away.' For the first time she could remember he looked tentative, unsure what to say. He sat down on the bed beside her and undid his tie.

'How was it?'

'It was my mother's funeral.' *What do you expect?*

Blanchard took a decanter of brandy and poured two glasses. 'This will help.'

Ellie didn't touch it.

'If you want to be alone tonight . . .'

'No.' She spun around, pushing him back on the bed. She stood in front of him. Staring down, she unclasped her necklace and earrings and laid them on the dressing table. She shrugged off her jacket. Without artifice, as if she were in a shop changing room or the gym, she unzipped her skirt and unbuttoned her blouse, Blanchard lay there, watching and sipping his brandy. She held his eyes as she unclasped her bra and laid it over the other clothes on the back of a chair.

The lights in the suite were low. From the corner of her eye she glimpsed herself in the mirror, the curves and shadows of her naked body. Her raven hair hung down her back; her breasts were hard and cold. She looked like one of Blanchard's pre-Raphaelite maidens, transported by ecstasy or death. She wondered if she had the strength for what she had to do. For

234

the first time in her life, she felt utterly alone in the world. In a strange way, that made it easier.

Blanchard began unbuttoning his shirt. 'We don't have to –'

She got onto the bed and knelt over him. Her hair brushed his face.

'I need you.'

She had never made love like it before. A frenzy possessed her: grief, guilt, fear, hatred – a storm of pent-up emotion cracked open like a thunderhead. She prised his lips open and pressed herself inside him: her tongue, her breasts, her fingers. She bit and pinched and raked her nails down his back, raising welts like burns wherever she touched. She forced him into her; she rocked back and forth against his hips, moaning and gasping as if exorcising a demon, careless of who could hear it in the corridor or the world outside. Blanchard finished before she did, but she made him go on, holding him inside her until she screamed. She fell forward on top of him, pressing herself against him. She was sobbing, though she didn't know what the tears were for. Their faces were so close the tears wet them both. Blanchard wrapped his arms around her and told her he loved her. For the first time since she'd known him, he sounded frightened of her.

She didn't know how long they lay there. Somewhere in their passion the clock had got knocked over. When she heard Blanchard's breathing soften, she pushed herself up and looked down.

Blanchard's face was still. In the hollow of his throat, the small gold key hung where it always did.

Ellie blew on her hands to warm them, then reached down and lifted the key. There was no clasp: she had to loop it over his neck.

The chain brushed his ear and he stirred, murmuring

something in his sleep. Ellie went still as stone. If he caught her now he would surely kill her. She waited, not daring to breathe.

The doctored brandy had done its job. Blanchard settled back and let dreams reclaim him. Ellie pulled the key free and rolled away off the bed. She dressed quickly: not in her funeral clothes, but in an old pair of jeans and a tight-fitting jumper. She rummaged in Blanchard's suit and found his access card, then pulled the cufflinks out of his shirtsleeves.

She grabbed her backpack and tiptoed out of the room. Her watch said half-past midnight. Harry had said the spiked drink should last for about eight hours, but she thought six was safer. And she had a lot to do.

For the first time all week, the bank was dark. The bid teams must finally have gone home. Foil wrappers and wire cradles from champagne bottles littered the lobby floor; she assumed it meant good news. Even the security guard seemed to have indulged: he was nowhere to be seen. She let herself in with Blanchard's card and went straight to the lift.

From high in the corner of the foyer, a camera's black eye recorded her entry. The pictures travelled instantly to the fifth floor, where a computer analysed them and compared the face coming through the door with the card that had been used to open it.

Ellie arrived on the fifth floor half a minute behind her image and let herself in to Blanchard's office. Down the hall, the computer recorded the fact. She pulled a small laptop out of her bag, bought for cash on the Tottenham Court Road. With an electrician's screwdriver, she prised the mother-of-pearl inlay off the cufflinks she'd taken from Blanchard's shirt. A small circuit-board, the size of a five-pence piece, lay nestled inside.

236

'*Is there a video camera or something in there?*' she'd asked when Harry gave them to her. They'd been in the changing rooms at a clothes shop on Oxford Street, pressed into awkward intimacy behind the curtain.

'The sleeve would obscure a video camera. This is a gyroscope and accelerometer. It measures the pattern of his movements, the distance and direction, and the software can correlate that with the keypad to work out which buttons he's pressed.'

Ellie had looked doubtfully at the small cufflinks. 'It sounds like science fiction.'

'These things are everywhere now – mobile phones, laptops, music players.' He'd given a sheepish grin. 'We actually got these from a video-game controller.'

'And that's supposed to make me feel better?'

She slid a nail under the circuit-board, pulled it out of the housing and connected it to the computer using a plug that Harry had given her. A window opened on-screen with a picture of a telephone keypad. The virtual buttons flashed; a second later, a number appeared superimposed.

918193.

She swung pack the painting that covered the safe.

Contrary to the office joke, Destrier didn't live at the bank. His home was a mock-Tudor mansion near the A12 in Essex, which he shared with two Rhodesian Ridgebacks and whoever could be paid or persuaded to share his bed. That night, she was a skinny girl with vacant eyes and no chest; she barely looked thirteen, though the agency had assured him she was old enough. Whatever his impulses, he knew what his employers would do if he got caught out with an underage girl.

And now his phone was vibrating in the darkness. He fumbled for it on the bedside table, rubbing his eyes as he stared at the screen.

INTRUSION ALERT

He tapped the screen to call up the details.

Card 0002 >> facial verification failure

He didn't have to check the registry to know who card 0002 belonged to. He stared at the picture underneath. The Stanton bitch. Every suspicion he'd entertained for the last six months – every doubt, every worry, every fear – crawled over his skin like lice.

Calm down, he told himself. He knew she'd been fucking Blanchard that night – had listened to it through the mic concealed in her phone. Her moans had still been in his ears when he screwed his own girl, who'd been limp and undemonstrative by comparison.

Maybe she picked up the wrong card. Perhaps Blanchard sent her to the office to get something.

He left the girl and went to the computer in the room next door. He connected to the office and brought up the security log.

01:09 >> Card 0002 entry to BUILDING

01:11 >> Card 0002 entry to ROOM 5-1

Blanchard didn't allow cameras in his office, or Destrier could have had a look at what Ellie was doing. All he could do was watch the log to see what happened next.

While he waited, he dialled Blanchard at Claridge's. He let it ring until the voicemail picked up; hung up; tried again. No answer. He swore, though silently. Blanchard wasn't the sort of man you cursed out loud, even from thirty miles away.

A new line appeared on the security log. Destrier stared at it in disbelief.

238

Ellie lifted the red folder out of the safe and laid it on Blanchard's desk. She hesitated for a second, reading the gold-lettered LAZARUS on the cover and wondering what she would find inside. She felt the leather cords; she tested the seals between her finger and thumb. The wax flexed in her grip: it must have been resealed recently.

No way back from here, she told herself. On the wall, the damsel tied to the tree tipped her head back in a plea to the knight advancing on her. *Save me? Don't hurt me?* The paint was silent.

Ellie snapped the seals. Crumbs of wax spilled over Blanchard's desk, but she didn't bother to wipe them away. He'd find out soon enough.

She'd never seen a file like it. The earliest pages were sheets of parchment, still supple and smooth to the touch; they gave way to a stiff and brittle paper with an ivory sheen, that gradually softened into creamy writing paper and finally to regular A4 office paper. Some of the paper felt thin and grey, and she supposed that came from wartime. It was like looking at tree rings, history written in cross section.

But she needed the present – and she found it almost at once, a sheet of paper at the back headed 'Vault Access'. Underneath was a list of strange words, foreign and archaic. *Or, argent, azure, gules, vert* . . . Each had a four-digit number beside it.

She closed the safe and jogged down the hall to the lift. When she slid Blanchard's card into the invisible slot in the panel, the button for the sixth floor started to glow.

Her hand hovered in front of it, trembling. The ruby on her finger smouldered like a dragon's eye. On her wrist, the seconds ticked by.

She stabbed the button.

With the merest tremor, the lift began its descent. Past the basement and the sub-basement, then a long eternity when it was nowhere. Ellie began to wonder if it had stopped, if some hidden sensor had betrayed her deception. Her heart twitched with panic; she gazed at the buttons, overcome with a desperate urge to push them and turn the lift back to the world above. But it was too late.

She didn't feel the lift stop. The doors glided open, revealing the golden room with its treasures so tantalisingly unguarded. *Every piece triggers an alarm.* But what else might trigger it? She approached the jewelled cup on the plinth in the centre of the room. A movement in the glass made her flinch, but it was only her own ghostly reflection. She unzipped her top and pulled out the key.

Four carved beasts peered from the corners of the plinth: a dragon, a horned serpent that she thought might be a cockatrice, a griffin and a basilisk. Ellie knelt and peered in their mouths. At the back of each stone throat, a small keyhole invited the key. She slid it into the serpent, just as Blanchard had done. Her arm tensed as she reached in, as if the stone jaws might come to life, spring shut.

Nothing happened. The key fit the lock perfectly. She felt the mechanism bite as she began to turn. It was working.

Or was it that simple? It occurred to her that all the vault's defences were built on illusion. It didn't block your way: it invited you in, tempting you to betray yourself. The sixth floor that lay three storeys underground; the unprotected treasures on the shelves around her; the door hidden back where you'd come from.

Every piece triggers an alarm.

She eased off the lock and withdrew the key. Trying to stand

240

where she'd stood before, she examined the cup in the case. It looked different to last time. Halfway up, the stem swelled out in a golden bubble, decorated on four sides with inlaid coloured stones. Ellie was sure the stone facing her before had been emerald green; now it was white, a fat pearl.

The cup had turned.

She circled the plinth, poring over the cup. The other stones in the stem were yellow – she thought it might be amber, though in fact it was a diamond – and a blood-red garnet.

She tried to remember a lecture series she'd been to at university, a wizened old professor who might have come straight from a monastery scriptorium.

Griffins were the guardians of gold.

Basilisks had a white spot on their head like a diadem.

The cockatrice had black eyes. Or were they red? Her memory faltered; she looked to her phone, but of course there was no reception down there.

You don't even know that any of it corresponds at all.

Her heart thudded inside her chest; with every beat, she felt time racing away. She had to make a decision.

She put the key in the basilisk's mouth and turned.

Perhaps, somewhere else in the building, an alarm went off or a light began to flash. In the deep vault, Ellie had no way of knowing. Behind her, she heard the hiss as the false door in the lift slid back to reveal the rugged wooden portal behind.

She checked her watch: almost two hours gone. She'd have to hurry.

The Aston Martin raced down the A12 towards London. The road was almost empty at that time of night; the needle hovered well above a hundred miles an hour. Inside, Destrier was barking orders to a chastened security guard. He'd gone to

Blanchard's office but found nothing, the door locked, the light off. That worried Destrier even more.

The line beeped to announce a new message. 'Just find her,' he shouted. He hung up, then glanced down to read the message.

He nearly drove off the road. He slammed the brakes and the rear end started to fishtail on the slick tarmac. He spun the wheel and swerved back, almost into the path of an oncoming lorry. Its horn blasted through the cold night, falling away like a dying breath.

Destrier eased his speed down to ninety while he gathered his thoughts. He glanced at the message again, hardly believing his eyes. Where the hell was Blanchard?

01:29 : Card 0002 entry to FLOOR 6

Ellie had brought a head-torch, but she didn't need it. The hidden lights glowed into life the moment she crossed the threshold. She moved down the ancient aisle, scanning the vaults above for watching eyes, cameras or beams that would trap her. She saw nothing.

She crossed the transept and reached the back of the vault, under where the old church's altar must once have stood, before the religion of wealth replaced the religion of charity. She thought of the mosaic half-buried in the floor, and wondered what older, darker faiths had flourished here before that. The iron doors glared at her like dead eyes in the furrowed walls.

Here, time becomes space.

She knew, without ever having being told, which vault it was. She remembered it from her visit with Blanchard: the two double doors in the floor painted with the Monsalvat crest and a steel keypad beside it. A black eagle on a red shield with a white chevron, clutching a golden spear. She looked at the piece of paper she'd taken from the Lazarus file.

Or, argent, azure, gules, vert . . .

Her last contact with Harry had been a CD and a book, delivered in a free newspaper again as she walked past Moorgate Tube station. She bought a portable CD player and sat outside in the Barbican listening to it. High walls of pebbledash and distressed concrete soared all around her. Ornamental water gushed out of a pipe into a series of ponds; wells sunk in the concrete revealed fragments of the medieval walls deep below the twentieth-century monument.

Harry's voice spoke through the headphones. 'All the vault codes at Monsalvat are based on heraldry. Each colour in the crest is allocated a number, which changes weekly. You'll get the numbers from the file. Then you have to determine the correct formulation of the crest, which gives you the order. You'll find everything you need to know in the book we've given you.'

Ellie had read the book like an eight year old, hiding under the duvet with a torch long after she should have been asleep. It taught her a new language, a new grammar – escutcheons and lozenges, charges and tinctures. She learned the difference between engrailed and enfossed, between metals and furs. She marvelled at the precision of it, even as she despaired of its intricacy. But she learned it.

Gules a chevron Argent, overall an eagle displayed Sable, armed and holding a spear both Or.

She consulted the paper from the file and found the numbers that corresponded to the colours. Each had four digits, sixteen in total. She entered them on the keypad, praying she'd remembered the medieval terminology correctly.

For a moment nothing happened. Then, with a creak that sounded as old as the stones themselves, the doors swung in.

XXX

Troyes, County of Champagne, November 1141

The town is packed: All Souls was two weeks ago, and the Cold Fair is in full swing. Merchants have come from all the corners of Christendom to trade their wares. The Count of Champagne has built vast warehouses on the edge of the town to accommodate the trade; his guards are everywhere in their blue and white livery, shepherding the money as it changes hands. You can buy furs, wool and linen cloth, pepper and spices, leather and silk – anything you can imagine.

It's also a good place to buy men.

The square in the centre of the town has become a cockpit. Four rings have been roped off, where squires and serjeants take turns testing their strength in combat. I manoeuvre my way to the front. A fat man in a leather cap and armour is taking on a young squire, whose face is a mask of concentration. The boy dances and skips, jabbing and parrying. The fat man barely moves, content to swat and bat the boy back. On the far side of the ring, I can see a one-eyed, grey-haired man in a black coat trimmed with gold. He's watching the fight, but he looks bored.

With a sudden movement that belies his size, the fat man darts forward. Two strokes and the boy's clutching his hand in agony, his sword on the ground. He reels away, towards a girl who looks as if she's having second thoughts.

The crowd applaud; money changes hands. While they're talking, I duck under the rope and pick up the fallen sword. The weight feels good.

The fat man looks at me. 'Did you lose your armour?'

I shrug. If I were more extravagant, I'd make some bragging retort.

The crowd are getting interested. There's nothing they like more than an entertaining mismatch. A proven champion in leather armour, against – what?

They're waiting to see if I'm just a fool who's drunk too much, or if I can surprise them.

I stand as stiff as I can and take a couple of awkward, artless strokes. The fat man relaxes. Another novice, he thinks. I retreat from his attacks, skittering around the ring like a frightened fawn. The fat man follows, taking his time. The crowd bay encouragement. From the corner of my eye, I see the man in the black coat watching intently. He's not deceived.

I start to slow down. The fat man sees his moment and comes in for the kill. He's agile, but he's got a lot of weight to carry – and I've watched how he does it. I see him coming and drift back. He lands heavily and staggers forward, off balance. I get inside the reach of his blade and grab his arm. I twist it until it's about to snap, then chop down the hilt of my sword against his wrist. He drops his sword: he's trying to pull away, but I won't let go. I knee him in the gut, and for good measure, slam the pommel of my sword into his nose. I don't think I've broken it, but I've made it bleed. The crowd like to see blood.

Another man gets in the ring. He's taller and leaner, full of confidence. I don't waste time with this one. Inside a minute, he's lying on his back with my sword at his throat.

I've made my point. I clamber out of the ring and wipe the blood off my hands.

'If anyone wants my services, I'll be in the Black Bull,' I announce.

There's a tournament at Ressons in a week, and somebody will be looking for a lance. I'll fight under a borrowed standard, take my winnings, then disappear again.

This has been my life for five years.

I feel a hand on my sleeve and spin about. It's the one-eyed man who was watching the fight, a grey face in black and gold livery. He doesn't ask my name. Perhaps he knows I wouldn't give it to him.

'You fought well.'

I nod, accept the compliment.

'I work for a man who rewards good fighters.'

He opens his hands, making me an offer.

'I don't have a horse. Or arms.' I lost them in Hainault, fighting a brutal little border war for a count who never paid me.

'The man I work for can provide them.'

'For a tournament.'

'For . . .' He weighs his words like a spice merchant counting peppercorns. 'He can tell you himself.'

He brings me to a goldsmith's shop. At least, I think, he'll be able to pay me. A black eagle hangs on the sign above the door, its greedy claws outstretched. While I wait, I eye up the cups

247

and plates that line the room, dull gold behind iron bars. I wonder if I could steal one.

I remember the story my mother told about the man who stole a cup from an enchanted land. His punishment was that he could never leave. When I was young, I thought it was a cruel ending, but at least I thought it was an ending. Now I understand that the story continued. I think of that knight, trapped in the underground kingdom. Every day, he must have woken thinking, *Perhaps this will be the day*. Devising ever more elaborate plans, straining for the roof of his world, piling frustration on misery. Always out of reach.

Death is the only ending, and I crave it. Sometimes, especially in darkness, I run my finger down the blade of my sword and think how easily I could do it. It would be a sin, but no worse than others I've committed. I think how sweet the release would be.

But I'm not ready to die. Every morning, I wake and think, *Perhaps this will be the day*.

At the front of the shop, three clerks sit behind a table facing the square. I watch the coins move across the chequered tablecloth, like pieces on a chessboard. Men bring them, rearrange them on the table, take some back. Gradually, I begin to see the patterns. Many of the customers are merchants from the fair who want to change their own coins for the livres of Troyes. A group of Italians bring him twenty of their silver coins, and receive a gold livre in exchange. But when an Italian who's going home brings him his own gold livre, he gets only eighteen silver coins.

Do they know they're being cheated?

I lean forward on the edge of my seat, fingering the hilt of my knife. Surely a fight's going to break out when one of the merchants notices. But there's no complaint, no argument.

The steward comes out of a door at the back of the shop and beckons me in. I expect him to take me upstairs: instead, we descend. At the bottom of a tight stair, he lets me in to a low crypt. The stones are cold, the room lit only by candles. Ironbound boxes line the walls. At the far end, a hunched figure sits at a table, though I sense him more than I see him. He's robed in darkness. A silvered mirror hangs on the wall behind him, reflecting back the candlelight like a moon.

A pale hand seems to beckon me forward. Closer as I come, I can still barely see him. He's wrapped in a black cloak, black wool with a sable fur collar. The skin's been taken off the animal in one piece, so that the toothy snout and tiny claws clasp around his throat. All I can see of the man is his face: a high forehead, a hooked nose and stringy white hair poking from under a black cap. His skin is pale as scraped parchment, and shrunk in on itself like a plum left to dry in the sun. The only colour comes from his eyes, which are blue as a May sky. They stare at me so hard I wonder if he's blind.

For the first time in five years, I feel afraid.

'You are a fighter?' His voice is strong, granite hard.

I nod, but I can't meet those eyes. My gaze drifts downward to the table, a beautiful thing. It's the chequered tablecloth from upstairs made solid, ebony and ivory inlay.

'I'm assembling a group of fighting men.' He twitches his hand. It makes an unnatural, rasping sound as it moves across the table. I look, and see that it isn't skin: it's silver, metal wrought in the shape of a hand blistered with black gemstones. It looks like a reliquary.

'This is a private matter. Not a tournament – a real fight. I need men who aren't too proud to fight on foot, nor too noble to bury a knife in someone's back if need be.'

I don't blink. It's nothing I haven't done already.

'It will take six weeks, maybe two months. For this, I will pay you a hundred livres.'

It's been a long time since I smiled, but now I do. I glimpse myself in the silvered mirror on the wall and realise what a terrifying sight it is. *A hundred livres.*

For that, I could hire enough men to overrun Hautfort and burn it to the ground, Jocelin inside. I can almost hear his screams.

Perhaps this is the day.

There's a noise behind me. A man's come through the door, though if he wasn't standing by a candle I wouldn't see him at all. Everything about him is black: his hair, his eyes, his tunic and his boots. He stands so tall his head's almost hidden behind the roof-vault.

'Malegant de Mortain will be your captain,' the old man says. 'You will do whatever he tells you.'

'Where are we going?'

'West.'

Île de Pêche, Brittany. Six weeks later.

The raindrops make rings on the flat sea, a labyrinth of interlocking circles. Our shallow boats glide across the surface and disturb the pattern. The hulls are so thin I can feel the water beneath, like horseflesh through the saddle.

It's been a hard ride from Troyes. It's winter: even the main roads can be impassable, and most of the time Malegant kept us on shepherds' paths and animal tracks. He wouldn't tell us where we were going, though every day the sun set ahead of us. The landscape changed as we headed west. Open farmland gave way to dripping forests and dark mountains, deep gorges and wild rivers. Sometimes it took a whole day just to cross one valley. It reminded me of my childhood, a magical place where the edges of the world grow permeable.

A shadow appears in the mist ahead. I can hear the lap of water on land. We scramble off the boats on a ramp by the water gate. I take out my sword and unwrap it from its parchment binding. I drop the pages in the water and watch them float away.

These are the pages of my past. Once I thought I could write them myself, fill them with romance and happy endings. Now I know better. I watch the rain try to drown the pages, and wish I could do the same for myself.

'Guard the gate,' Malegant says. 'When the fighting starts, no one escapes.'

XXXI

London

The vault was a pit, five feet deep and three feet square. All she could see at the bottom were shadows.

There shouldn't be much in there, Harry had told her. *Get everything.*

It was too deep to reach: she'd have to get in. She sat on the edge of the hole and prepared to lower herself down.

But something about the edges of the open doors had caught her eye. They were serrated, sharp triangular teeth that fitted together seamlessly when closed. She touched one of the points, and grabbed it away as a thin bead of blood welled on her fingertip.

Perhaps there's a reason they're called trap doors.

Painfully conscious of time, she got up. She'd seen two tall iron candlesticks lurking in the corners of the vault: she fetched one, dragging it over the stone floor, and wedged it across the mouth of the hole. She remembered the head-torch and turned it on. The white beam searched the pit.

Was it all for this?

In spite of her terror, she found herself strangely disappointed. There was nothing that she had imagined: no treasures like the ones in the antechamber; no ancient books of magic or wisdom; no hoard of gold. It looked more like what you'd leave behind after cleaning out an attic. A battered leather tube that might have held a telescope, and a square cardboard box sitting on a low plinth.

She dropped down to the pit floor. The tube was lighter than she'd expected. She shook it gently, but nothing moved inside. Was it empty? She put it in her backpack.

She put her hands on the box. It was cold to the touch, even through the cardboard. She could tell it would be heavy. She edged her fingertips underneath it and lifted it off its pedestal.

She'd never know what she'd done wrong – only that, for all her precautions and preparations, somewhere, somehow, she'd missed something. The trap doors sprang together: if not for the candlestick wedging them apart, their sharp teeth would have bitten Ellie in two. The iron shivered; for a terrifying moment she thought the candlestick might snap. A second later the lights went out.

Barely aware of what she was doing, Ellie shoved the box into her backpack and threw it out of the pit. She hauled herself out, slung the backpack over her shoulder and ran for the door. Behind her, the chamber echoed with a noise like a gunshot as the candlestick holding the trap doors fell loose.

She reached the end of the aisle and stopped dead. The torch played over the door, casting a ghostly orb on the ironbound wood. It must have closed automatically.

She was trapped.

'Knock the fucking door down if you have to.'

Destrier gunned the car down Cable Street. Ahead, he could

see the crenellated outlines of the Tower of London – and the real towers of London, the towers of banking and finance, rising beyond.

'I've been trying to reach him all night and he's not answering his phone,' he told the Claridge's concierge. 'I'm worried there might be an emergency.'

There's an emergency all right, he thought grimly. The latest update had come a minute earlier

01:44 >> FLOOR 6 : VAULT 32 : THEFT ALARM

He still couldn't believe she'd got that far. With any luck, the trap doors would have ripped her in two by now. If not, he'd do it himself.

The phone rang again. A foreign number, not Claridge's, and an accented voice.

'Mr Saint-Lazare wants to know what is happening at the bank.'

This side of the door had neither handle nor keyhole. Ellie scanned the walls for anything that might open it, a monster's head like the one in the chamber or a thin slit for a card. There was nothing.

Panic rose in her throat. She kicked the door; she hammered her fists against it until her skin was raw. It didn't move. She cursed herself for being there, for listening to Harry. She cursed Blanchard, her father –

Nye Stanton died trying to break into the vaults. He was hit by a train in an Underground tunnel.

There must be a way out.

Not that it did Dad any good.

She stepped back from the door and took a series of long breaths, forcing herself calm. She didn't know what commotion the alarm might have unleashed in the rest of the bank, but the underground chamber was silent as the grave. She looked at the row of vaults in the wall, the iron doors where monks' bones had been dragged from their rest to make way for worldly treasures. She imagined the rattling of the bones as they tumbled out of the alcoves to be hauled away in sacks. The screams of their ghosts. She listened to the darkness.

The grave wasn't silent. The air throbbed; a low rumble pulsed through the chamber. At first she thought it was only the blood in her ears, but the longer she listened the more distinct it became.

She looked at her watch. The first Tube wouldn't pass for hours yet. And it didn't sound like the train that had shaken the vault when she was down with Blanchard. It was less intense, more constant.

As Mr Saint-Lazare likes to say, the present always intrudes on the past. And vice versa.

It was hard to pinpoint the sound: the whole vault was an echo chamber, and that far underground she'd lost all sense of direction. But if the crypt was built to the plan of a church, then the far end, where the Saint-Lazare vault lay, must be east. The door would be west, and the right side of the aisle – looking towards the door – would be north.

Ellie was pretty sure the Central Line ran to the north of the Monsalvat building.

She ran to the crossing where the four arms of the church came together and listened, turning slowly, testing. The noise was definitely loudest from the north transept. She walked along it to the far end. There were three vaults here, each with a coat of arms painted on its door and a steel keypad embedded in the wall beside it.

Choosing at random, she examined the crest on the centre

vault. A blue shield divided by a wavy line, with silver crosses above and below.

Azure a fess engrailed Or between four crosslets Argent.

She consulted her paper again, matching the colours with their numbers, then punched them into the keypad. A bolt clicked; the door loosed. Ellie pulled it open and shone the torch inside. She saw a narrow room about six feet deep, ironbound boxes piled on the floor. The throbbing noise was louder in here – but the walls remained strong, unyielding.

She tried the door to the right. *Ermine two chevrons Argent.* The code didn't work the first time: you needed to count the two chevrons separately, she realised. She tried again, and this time the door opened to her tug.

She knew at once it was the right room. The noise was louder, carrying through the bricked-up hole in the rear wall. A skein of red light played over it from a sensor screwed to the ceiling. *An alarm*, she thought. But she wasn't worried about alarms now. She wondered if her father had got this far, if it was he who'd smashed the original hole.

She found the pair of the candlestick she'd used in the trap doors and used it as a battering ram, swinging it against the wall until her arms ached. The bricks were strong, but not impenetrable – and she was desperate. Whoever had sealed the hole had obviously trusted more to the alarm than the barrier – or perhaps they'd meant it as a trap, another snare to tempt the unwary. The wall cracked; the bricks crumbled. A dark tunnel loomed beyond. She squeezed through, crawling on her stomach and pushing the bag in front of her.

After a few metres, the passage ended in a slitted grille, alternating bars of greater and lesser darkness. Ellie wriggled herself around and kicked at it until it came loose. She pushed off, slithered through the mouth of the hole and landed on her feet.

She looked around. By the light of her head-torch, she could see twin rails curving into the darkness, with a third rail gleaming silver between them. She stepped back, pressing herself against the wall. Somewhere nearby, the throb of a jackhammer filled the tunnel.

The tracks hissed and began to glow. A white light appeared from around the bend, bearing down on her.

By the time Destrier reached the bank, he was as close to panic as he'd ever been in his life. He left his car in the alley, behind the two Range Rovers that had already arrived, and went straight to the fifth floor. He'd no sooner reached his office than he had the Claridge's concierge on the line, wringing his hands down the phone as he described finding Mr Blanchard passed out on his bed. 'He is breathing normally,' he assured Destrier. 'We have summoned the doctor as a precaution and he will be here very soon.'

'Any signs of violence? A burglary?'

The concierge sounded shocked. 'Of course not.'

Destrier rang off and despatched two of his men to Claridge's to get a better picture. 'If he can open his eyes, bring him here at once.'

He was about to check the security log, when the phone rang again. He almost ignored it, but the sixth sense that had kept him ahead of trouble so long warned him to check the number. The moment he saw it, he knew it couldn't wait.

A mechanical voice, inhuman. 'Do you know who this is?'

Destrier swallowed. 'Yes.'

'Tell me what has happened.'

Destrier told him as much as he had guessed. 'I can't be sure until we speak to Blanchard. And get hold of Ellie Stanton.'

At the other end of the line, there was a sucking sound like a valve opening and closing. 'There are only two keys to that vault, and one of them is around my neck. Presumably the other is in Miss Stanton's hands. Inside the vault.'

'Can you –?'

'I will be on my plane within half an hour. Stay there.'

Even deadened by the electronics, the threat in his words was evident. Destrier felt a sudden, urgent need to justify himself.

'If Blanchard hadn't –'

'Blanchard knew what he was doing. You were supposed to protect us.'

The line went dead. Destrier was still staring at the phone when one of his men walked in.

'We can't get into the vault until the old man gets here,' Destrier told him.

'Don't we have a plan for if someone gets in?'

'The plan is anyone who actually reaches the sixth floor doesn't make it past the fucking booby prize. There isn't a plan for this.'

'At least she won't be going anywhere.'

Destrier turned back to his computer and opened the security log. In the monitor's pale glow, his face was blue as a corpse.

'Oh my Christ.'

02:01 >> FLOOR 6 : VAULT 26 : OPENED

02:02 >> FLOOR 6 : VAULT 27 : OPENED

02:04 >> FLOOR 6 : VAULT 27 : INTRUSION DETECTED

'Another intrusion?'

'It isn't an intrusion, you stupid fuck. She's broken out.'

Steel hissed on steel. The white light brightened, rushing forward along the tangle of dust and cables that ribbed the tunnel walls. Ellie knew she should move, but there was nowhere to go. The shaft she'd crawled out of was too high to get back in; the deep tunnel too narrow to get out of the way. She stood on the track and let the light blind her with its brilliance. It seemed to be taking a long time. Was this the last thing her father had seen?

She closed her eyes. The light drummed through her eyelids. She heard a screech and the heavy protest of metal – the driver must have seen her, but she knew it would be too late.

The noise faded away, echoing down the tunnel. Was this what dying was like? She hadn't felt the impact – but then, she supposed at that speed she wouldn't.

She opened her eyes and winced. A few metres away, an angelic radiance shone straight at her face. Was this her judgement? What should she say?

A shadow moved in front of the light, blocking it out.

'What the hell are you doing? You almost got yourself killed.'

Ellie shielded her eyes with her hand. A black man in yellow overalls and a white helmet was standing in front of a flat-bedded dolly. He sounded angry, though there was a softness in his voice that evoked warm places far away. He looked her up and down.

'Where's your vest and helmet?'

'I –'

'Bloody contract staff.' He turned away. 'You can explain this to the Bank manager.'

The Bank manager was a grizzled man with a sharp face and a badly fitted suit. Ellie had prepared a story while she waited outside his office, but he wasn't interested. He just pointed to a shelf above his head, sagging under a collection of vinyl-bound booklets.

'Do you know what that is?'

She shook her head.

'That's the contract for this job. It tells me everything: how long the screws have to be, how many rats I have to kill, how many sheets of bog roll I'm allowed to wipe my arse.'

He pressed his fingertips together and stared at her.

'It also tells me how many staff members I'm supposed to get killed. You want to guess how many?'

Ellie stayed silent.

'Goose-egg. Zero.' He sipped a plastic mug of coffee. 'You got lost and almost ran into a train. That's a safety incident, and the contract says we can't have those. They want me to report it – but if I do, that's three days I'll spend up to my tits in paperwork. We'll get behind on the job – except the contract says we can't do that either. So I'll spend another three days writing a report to explain why that's happened. Then we'll be a week behind. The contract says we have to pay compensation if we get a week behind. I'll get a bollocking from my boss, and I'll have to write another report. Two million commuters will be cursing my name, and all because some silly cow took a wrong turn down a tunnel. You read me?'

She did.

'What's your name?'

Ellie was too tired to invent something. She stared at the map on the wall behind him.

'Hainault.'

'Hah. Born to do this job, were you?' He didn't want an answer. 'What did they hire you for?'

'Cleaning.'

'It's always the bloody cleaners,' he observed, to no one in particular.

*

Above ground, a new day would be beginning. All the chorus of Ellie's old life would be there – the streetsweeper on the corner of Gresham Street, the delivery driver, the newsagent lifting the shutter on his shop – but they would find other people to wave to, honk at, ignore. The old day hadn't finished for Ellie: she was trapped in the night that would never end. She wandered through the darkness with the cleaning crew and the rats, scraping away the human residues that accreted on the station walls, fluff and hair, cloth and paper. It felt like stripping a corpse.

Her shift ended at five. She took off the overalls and took her bag from the locker they'd given her. A foreman led the crew up the silent escalators to the gates, but Ellie hung back. She'd spent all night in the tunnels, and ended up no more than a few hundred yards away from Monsalvat. They must have worked out how she'd escaped by now – surely they'd check the Central Line stations when they opened.

She waited until the others had left, then summoned her courage and stuck her head around the Bank manager's door.

'How do I get home?'

For a moment she thought he'd bite her head off. But something in her face, desperation or exhaustion, seemed to spark a rare flash of pity in him.

'Where do you need to go?'

As far away as she could – the end of the world if possible. She looked at the map on the wall again.

'Ealing.'

'There's a ballast train coming through in five minutes. It can take you as far as Acton.' He scowled, though she thought he meant it kindly. 'Otherwise, you'll probably try and walk it and I'll end up with another incident on my hands.'

Ellie rode with the ballast to West Acton. In the cold pre-dawn mist, she found a payphone on the platform and dialled the number she'd been given. Harry answered at once.

'Are you OK?'

'I've got it.' There was no triumph in her voice, only the flat line of exhaustion. 'Where do we meet?'

Monsalvat staff called it the war room, though they usually meant it metaphorically. Screens on every wall brought in newsfeeds, financial information, graphs and spreadsheets; they could also be used to extend the room into infinite space for video conferencing. The cleaners hadn't been in yet: at seven o'clock that morning it was still littered with the detritus of the Talhouett takeover battle: folders and papers, coffee cups slowly curdling, pizza boxes and stale doughnuts. A dozen men had gathered around the table, with Blanchard and Destrier at their head. At the far end, removed from the others, an old man sat in a wheelchair. His body was skeletally thin, hunched over as if against the cold: the skin on his face was white and scarred with wrinkles, though his clear eyes were blue like a baby's. Tubes and wires trailed from a metal collar around his emaciated neck, binding him to the wheelchair. Each time he breathed, a small arsenal of pumps and valves wheezed into action, pushing and sucking the air from his lungs. Yet there was no doubt that every man in the room deferred to him. Not out of pity or respect, but from fear.

'We put men on the platforms at Bank and Liverpool Street stations the moment they opened,' Destrier was saying. 'Somehow, she got away.'

He glanced at the man in the wheelchair, like a dog expecting to be kicked. The blue eyes stared back unblinking.

'The good news is, she's still got her phone on her. We got a trace on it an hour ago. Acton, of all places. Must have taken

262

the Tube. We sent a team, but by the time they'd got there she'd gone underground again. Heading east, back into the city.

On the walls, the graphs and numbers had been replaced by maps and satellite images, with the Underground network superimposed. The security log was displayed behind Destrier, hanging over him like a death sentence.

From his wheelchair, Michel Saint-Lazare made a coughing noise. Everyone turned. He must once have had a natural voice, but no one there – except, perhaps, Blanchard – had ever heard it. When he spoke, it was really the machine behind him speaking.

'She must come up again. When she does, you will be ready.'

On the grey boulevard of the Euston Road, among the youth hostels and union offices, St Pancras Station stands like a red-brick fairytale castle: a lofty symphony of turrets and pinnacles, spires, mullions and arches. In the 1960s a generation that loved neither beauty nor fairy tales almost demolished it. But it survived, and now towers in newly restored splendour as England's gatehouse to Europe.

Behind the brick façade, near where the trains pulled in, a portly gentleman in an overcoat clutched his hat as he stared up at the great glass roof curving above him. He was a poet; snatches of his verse lay scattered across the floor in gold, as if they'd spilled out of his briefcase. He didn't move. His bronze eyes would never tire of the view.

The man beside him was much less serene. From a distance you might have taken him for the statue-poet's brother: the round figure made rounder by the overcoat; the spaniel legs and pug-nosed face. He even wore a hat. He scanned the concourse like a thief, glancing up at the huge clock every few seconds as if waiting for someone. Even that early in the morning, the station was busy with businessmen taking the first trains to Paris and Brussels.

He stiffened. A dark-haired girl in jeans and a sweatshirt, no coat, was walking towards him. She carried a backpack, but wore it across her chest the way anxious tourists sometimes do. He fell into step alongside her.

'You made it here. Thank God.'

She didn't reply. What was there to say that could possibly fathom the last twenty-four hours?

'You got it?'

She cupped a protective arm over the bag, like a mother-to-be cradling her belly. 'Can you tell me what it is, now?'

'Something we've been waiting a long time to get back.' He half-reached to take it, but she recoiled; he drew away. Clearly she wasn't ready yet.

'I can't tell you what an achievement this is.' He sounded like a headmaster at prize day. 'You've no idea how many men have failed where you've succeeded. It's an amazing . . .' He struggled for the word. '. . . victory.'

It won't bring my dad back. Or Mum.

'I tripped an alarm,' she said flatly. 'They know it's gone. They'll be all over London looking for it.'

Harry nodded. 'We had men watching the bank: it lit up like a Roman candle around two a.m. We feared the worst.' He glanced over his shoulder. 'Could they have followed you?'

'Not the way I came.'

Harry reached inside his pocket and pulled out a slim paper wallet. 'Not where you're going, either. I've booked us on the next train to Paris.'

'I didn't bring my passport.'

'There's one in the envelope. Your name's Jenny Morgan now. Once we get to Paris, we can go right across Europe without leaving a trace. We'll keep you safe, Ellie. I promise.'

They descended the escalators to the departure lounge and waited twenty minutes for their train to be called. After everything she'd endured, that was almost the hardest part. She watched the seconds tick over on the clock, counting them off until she thought she'd go mad. Harry bought her a coffee, but she let it go cold in her hands. At last the announcement came; they shuffled up a moving walkway on to the platform and took their seats on the train. Ellie stared out of the window, willing the train to move, watching the queue inch aboard. Everyone seemed to have vast amounts of baggage, which took forever to stow. Families with children going away for half-term; businessmen extending their trip to the weekend; backpackers on the next leg of their journey. And two men in long black coats and black leather gloves, who carried no luggage at all.

A weary dread seeped into Ellie's blood. She clutched Harry's arm.

'Those men. They're Blanchard's.'

Harry sat bolt upright. 'Are you sure?'

'They were at my mother's funeral.' She felt the same overwhelming helplessness she'd felt in the tunnel, unstoppable light bearing down on her. 'But how did they get here?'

'They must have followed you.'

Ellie stared at him blankly. 'They couldn't have.'

Harry glanced down at the bulge in her jeans pocket. 'You didn't bring –?'

She pulled the phone out of her pocket and stared at it, the black plastic so smooth and beguiling. Red writing gleamed under the mirrored surface as the phone began to vibrate. It was ringing.

Harry jumped to his feet and pulled her up. 'Get out of here, Ellie! *Go!*'

He ran down the carriage. A steward tried to stop him, but Harry pushed past, shouting something about forgetting his umbrella. He pulled a backpack off the luggage rack and dived onto the platform. Ellie hesitated just a moment, then grabbed her bag and ran the opposite way.

At the end of the platform, a guard in a peaked cap blew a whistle. The doors slid shut with a hiss. The signal turned green.

Tripping over outstretched legs and bags, Ellie reached the train door just as the door locked. She hammered at the button, but the door wouldn't open. The platform began to move: through the window, she saw Harry and the two Monsalvat men like mannequins in a shop window. Harry had been wrestled to the ground; one of the men crouched over him, while the other searched the backpack he'd stolen. She watched, a spectator at an exhibition, as the tableau drifted out of sight. She wanted to scream, but the sound wouldn't come.

Pinned to the platform, Harry looked up into his enemy's face and felt the needle slide into his vein.

'This won't kill you,' the man told him. 'We just want a chat.'

Beside him, the other man had finished digging through the stolen backpack.

'It's not here. It must be on the train.'

Harry heard footsteps running across the concrete, but he wasn't expecting a rescue. He supposed they'd have some kind of story ready. He could feel the poison creeping through his body: soon he'd be in no position to deny anything.

They'd pinned his arm to his side, but he could still reach his coat pocket. He slid his hand in and felt for the capsules. There were two: he'd meant to give one to Ellie, but there'd been no time.

His captor got to his feet and started explaining to the station staff how Harry was an escaped patient from a private mental hospital. He'd stolen someone's bag – was there any way of returning it to the poor victim? They'd sedated him; if the station guard could just help them lift him . . .

The movement loosened the grip that held him. It was all the time Harry needed. He ripped his arm free, and in an instant had the capsules popped in his mouth. He bit down on both, just to be sure, while his captors tried too late to wrench his mouth open.

With his last living thought, he prayed they wouldn't catch Ellie.

Ellie got off the train at Ebbsfleet. The staff tried to stop her, to explain you couldn't use the Eurostar for domestic journeys, but she screamed and wept about a family emergency and in the end they let her go. She scanned the platform, terrified that Blanchard's men might have anticipated her move and got there first, seen the commotion she'd made. But it had only taken fifteen minutes, and even Blanchard couldn't conjure a faster way to get across London. She watched the train pull out of the station, a wasteland of concrete, arc lights and chain-link fences that looked like some kind of prison camp. On board, in the luggage rack above Ellie's empty seat, her mobile phone emitted its invisible signal, describing her progress towards the Channel Tunnel and France. With any luck, it would be hours before they found she wasn't with it.

She stood in the station hall and stared at the departure

boards. Through her shocked and exhausted eyes, the names blurred into a meaningless void, a nowhere place. Her shoulders ached from the weight of the backpack; she wondered what was inside, but didn't dare take it out in public. What could possibly be worth so much violence and terror?

Her mind was drifting. She forced herself to focus.

You're carrying something on your back that your father died trying to get hold of, that Monsalvat are willing to kill to get back. Harry might have some friends, but he's almost certainly dead and you've no way of getting in touch with them. You're on your own.

Where do you go now?

XXXII

Île de Pêche, 1142

The Count's corpse lies headless on the floor. Blood pools around the altar. At the door, two of our men are battling back the guards who've arrived too late. Malegant rips open the lid of the golden reliquary, peers in, then hurls it at the window. The glass cracks; bones and dust fall out of the casket. It's not what he came for.

He gestures to a side door in the chapel wall.

'Through there.'

Four of us follow of him into a tiny vestry. A ring of keys lies on the table. Malegant snatches them up, then leads us out by another door into the courtyard. To our left, the guards are still attacking the chapel. We fall on them like wolves: trapped between the men in the chapel and the men outside, they're quickly slaughtered.

I feel something peck my face, too hard for a raindrop. A small crater's appeared in the wall in front of me, gouged out by a crossbow bolt. I hurl myself to the ground. The man beside me isn't so lucky: the bolt hits his shoulder, drives through the chain mail and lodges in his back. I think about pulling it out, but it would only make the bleeding worse.

More missiles rattle around us. They're coming from the windows in the keep.

'We have to get in,' Malegant says. We don't have shields, but Malegant grabs one of the dead guards and hauls him to his feet. He holds the corpse in front of him like a rag doll. Bolts prick it like a pincushion.

I have a better idea. I tip over a water barrel and roll it up the slope, crawling behind on hands and knees. Halfway to the tower, it no longer protects me: I kick it away and sprint the last few yards to the shelter of the wall. Crossbow bolts clatter off the ground behind me.

Malegant's already there, an arrow-riddled corpse beside him. He's lethal, but I want to keep him close. He has an aura, a sense of invulnerability that I hope will protect me.

The rest of the men are still back by the chapel. Malegant orders them forward. One of them carries the priest's silver-bound bible as a shield; another tries to swat away the bolts with an oar. The rest have to take their chances.

But they're only there as a distraction. Malegant leads me up a thin flight of stairs to the curtain wall. To our left, a small door goes through to the keep. It's locked, but one of the keys Malegant took from the vestry opens it.

The archers didn't expect us to get through. They're standing by the windows, taking aim at their targets in the courtyard. Malegant and I have killed two of them before they even notice us. Another turns, a tensed crossbow pointing straight at my chest. If he loosed then, I'd be dead. But Malegant's aura protects me. Fear makes the crossbowman's hand quiver: the bolt goes wide, so close the fletches almost brush my cheek. I cut him down.

Malegant's dealt with the others. There's nothing in the corridor now except corpses and blood and unspent missiles – and, halfway down, a pair of double doors.

We enter into a great hall, with a fireplace in its centre, and wooden benches pushed back against the walls. At the far end stand two high doors, one black as mulberries, the other ivory-white: they remind me of the goldsmith's chequerboard table in the vault in Troyes. One's ajar – I can see a white-sleeved arm reaching around to close it. Malegant takes a knife from his belt and throws. The Devil's with him today. There's a scream from behind the door as the knife pins the hand to the wood. He can't close the door now: his own arm's jamming it.

Malegant wrenches the door open. The man within gets dragged out in its wake. Except it isn't a man. It's the woman in the white dress I saw from the courtyard. Blood's running down her arm, soaking into the sleeve, spreading towards her elbow. She must be in agony but she doesn't make a sound.

I don't see her face – not as it really is. I'm back in Tourcy, at the chapel on the edge of the forest. Her hair and skin have become paler, her fine dress reduced to a torn shift. Ada.

Malegant pulls the knife out of the door and slits her throat.

Strange to tell, all I remember of that moment is what I see through the door. It looks like another chapel, though without saints or crucifixes. It must be built out on a promontory: clear glass windows on three sides look down to the sea, so that the whole room feels like a boat adrift. The ceiling is a rounded vault painted twilight blue, with golden stars in their constellations. At the far end of the room, under the windows, a white stone stands alone on an ivory table. A black lance hangs over it, suspended point down by a rope from the roof-beam. With the window behind showing only mist, it seems to float in space.

271

The woman sinks to the floor. Blood blossoms through her skirts like a rose. Something breaks inside me; I raise my sword. Malegant must be expecting it. He spins around – his sword strikes mine with a clang that echoes through the hall like a bell. My blade shatters. All that's left is a fractured stump.

'Peter of Camros.' Malegant laughs. 'I wondered when you'd remember yourself.'

I don't know how he knows that name. I'm lost in a cloud, waking from a nightmare into something far worse. I can hear the sounds of fire and slaughter in the distance as the rest of the castle is devastated.

I hurl the broken sword at his face and run. Across the hall, into the main stair. More of our men are coming up from below – I can't go down. I go up, chasing around until it ends in an ironbound door that – thank God – isn't locked.

After the darkness of the stairs, even the fog is blinding. I'm in an open guardroom at the top of the tower. I stagger across to the rampart. There's no bolt on the door, no way of keeping them back. Even if I could hold them, there's only one way out.

I unstrap my helmet and pull it off. I can hear shouts, feet pounding up the stairs. How long do I have? I try to remove my armour, but the leather knots have shrunk in the wet. I take my knife and cut the cords. The hauberk falls to the ground like a broken chain. The footsteps are close, lots of them. I rip off my quilted coat. I'm left wearing nothing but a thin linen tunic.

I perch on the battlements. White-capped waves champ below me like teeth. I feel dizzy. The door bangs open.

I jump.

XXXIII

Oxford

'Ellie?'

Doug peered out of the door into the darkness. A warm yellow light framed him like a halo; from inside, the mouth-watering smells of frying onion and bacon drifted out. Ellie realised she was ravenous.

'Can I come in?'

'Of course. Are you OK? Why haven't you been answering my messages?'

She glimpsed herself in the hall mirror and realised why he looked so shocked. Her face was grey and worn. Underground soot still made a streak above her right eye; tears had left long silver fingers down her cheeks, though she couldn't remember crying.

She toppled forward and Doug caught her. He brought her in to his sitting room and made her a cup of tea. He had an old-fashioned kettle that whistled when it boiled; the smells of gas and steam brought back memories of winter evenings in the kitchen with her mother. She started crying again.

'Why don't you clean up?'

He took her upstairs and ran a bath. Part of her protested that she didn't have time, it wasn't safe. The pressure was like a clock ticking inside her. But she didn't resist. The water was so hot it made her skin blush scarlet.

She lay there almost submerged, her face sweating in the steam, her hair fanned out in the water as if she were drowning. Doug sat on the floor next to the towel rail. With his fisherman's jumper and cup of tea, Ellie thought he looked almost absurdly comforting.

'I got your text about your mother. I'm so sorry.'

He said it cautiously, but he didn't hide the reproach. Ellie slid deeper into the water.

'When was the funeral?'

'Yesterday.' It felt like a million years ago.

'I would have liked to be there. I don't know what's going on with us, but –'

'It's not that. It's – crazier than you can imagine.' Tears began to flow again, mixing with the sweat on her face. 'What happened to Mum, that's not even half of it. It's . . .' She slid down so that the water covered her face completely, then broached the surface again.

'I need you to help.'

Doug leaned forward. His face brimmed with confusion.

'Can you tell me?'

She told the story from the beginning, though she didn't tell him everything. She wondered if he realised, if he noticed the places where the story went inexplicably vague, and if he noticed that those places were always when she was talking about Blanchard. Blanchard was the void at the centre of her story. She saw, as she told it, how little sense it made without him.

274

But perhaps it was so incredible that Doug didn't see the omissions. He listened in silence. When she was done, he had only one question.

'What was it for?'

Ellie stared at the ceiling. 'I don't know. I didn't dare open the box in public.'

Doug glanced to the corner, where her bag lay beside a heap of stripped-off clothes. 'Shall we?'

She found some old clothes left over from the summer and dressed, adding one of Doug's heavy sweaters. She liked the weight on her body, his scent around her.

They drew shut the curtains in the living room and knelt on the floor, like children at Christmas. Ellie opened the bag.

Was it all for this?

She could see Doug thinking the same thing. A cardboard box and a leather tube. Could they really be worth dying for? Rain rattled on the windows: a fearful instinct made them both glance towards it. She remembered something Blanchard had once said. *Money is a fiction, a suspension of disbelief. Value is only what two parties can agree on at any given time.*

Blanchard thought it was worth killing for. Her father had believed it was worth dying for. That was some sort of agreement.

Doug slit open the tape on the box with a kitchen knife. Ellie opened the lid. They both stared in.

London

Destrier had had some bad days in his life, some very bad indeed, but this was up there. He'd been awake since 1 a.m. and he still hadn't found Ellie. The lack of sleep he could deal with: the lack of results was a problem. He'd already been to

275

Paris and back that day. He'd waited at the Gare du Nord with his men, watching the passengers drain off the train until it was empty. The phone signal said she was still aboard, so he'd picked up a discarded ticket and talked his way on, pretending to have left his bag behind. He'd found the phone in the luggage rack: the station staff couldn't understand why he'd be so furious to recover his lost property.

It had been a long trip back to London to face Blanchard and Saint-Lazare.

He cracked his knuckles and forced himself to be calm. He didn't blame himself: he'd never been troubled by guilt. If he felt anything, it was pure rage – rage that these people had disrupted his carefully arranged life. He hated them for it, and the hatred spurred his desire for revenge. He'd find them and tear them apart, make them pay for what they done to him. Find Ellie, get the box back, everything would be fine.

But he had to do it quickly. It might not be his fault, but it was certainly his responsibility. And the men waiting in the war room on the fifth floor weren't known for their patience.

So where had she gone? Not back to Newport – he had men watching. Nor to the Barbican apartment. He'd pulled it apart and found nothing, though he hadn't really thought she'd be that stupid. Did she have a fallback meeting with the opposition?

He ran through her recent e-mails and phone calls, looking for anything out of the ordinary. Numbers she hung up on before they answered, calls that lasted under a minute. There was nothing. He had to admit, she'd been clever.

He paused as he found a number that looked strange. An Oxford dialling code. He entered it onto her phone and got the name straight away. *Doug.*

Hadn't she dumped him?

He found the recording of the most recent call she'd made

to Doug and listened. '*I love you.*' The giveaway pause. '*I love you too.*'

It wasn't much to go on, but he knew he was right. The feeling in his gut told him so. He took the lift to the basement parking and slid into the Aston Martin. He pressed the accelerator: the engine's growl echoed around the garage.

His satnav said it would take ninety-seven minutes. He reckoned he could do it in under an hour.

Oxford

Ellie squeezed her hands down the sides of the box and lifted out the contents. It was a cube, about a foot square. The surface was black, cold and hard like obsidian, smooth as glass. Ellie twisted it around on the carpet, looking for a hinge or a crack or a lid. All she saw was her own reflection skewed back at her. It was surprisingly heavy, though the weight wasn't evenly distributed inside. She could feel one side was definitely heavier, which she assumed was down.

'I've got a hammer,' Doug said.

Ellie didn't answer. She was remembering her first day at work, two slabs of black plastic left on her desk as if by some lost civilisation or alien intelligence. She rolled the box over to make it right-way up, then stroked her hand across the gleaming surface.

A red light shone up at them. It was the same as her phone: glowing numbers hovering in the darkness below the surface. Only instead of a keypad, it was a grid of letters, like a wordsearch.

'I don't suppose you know the password,' said Doug.

She shook her head.

'I've got a friend in the Maths department who does some work on cryptography. He might be able to tell us more.'

Ellie didn't bother to correct the assumption he'd made. She could see by the clock on the wall she'd already been here over an hour. The pressure-gauge inside her was redlining again.

She set the black box aside and pulled the lid off the leather tube. She reached in. A scrolled-up sheet of paper – no, vellum – supple to the touch. She pulled it out as gently as she could and laid it on Doug's coffee table.

For the first time since the jaws of the vault snapped shut, she felt a pulse of hope. Finally, something that might be worth something. It looked like a poem, eight lines written on the vellum in a bold, medieval hand that reminded her of Blanchard's handwriting.

'Is that . . .?'

'Old French,' said Doug. She caught the shock in his voice and looked up.

'What? Does it say something useful, some kind of clue?'

He shook his head. 'I've seen it before.'

'The poem?'

'This exact piece of vellum.' He gazed into her eyes, as confused as she was. 'I held it in my hands, just like you are now.'

Ellie stared at him. 'That's impossible. I pulled it out of the vault this morning.'

Doug pointed to a place halfway down the page, where the text nimbly diverted around a small hole in the vellum.

'You know how you make parchment? You pull it tight on a frame, like a drumhead, then scrape it with a knife until it's paper thin. The edges of the knife are curved, but sometimes a corner catches the skin and nicks it. The tension in the frame means even a pinprick gets stretched to something you could put your finger through.'

Ellie nodded. She knew.

'But vellum's expensive, especially in the twelfth century, so you don't throw out the whole sheet just because of a small hole. If you're the scribe, you work around it – literally. That hole in the eighth line was there when the scribe wrote it, and it was there three months ago when I examined it myself.'

Ellie still didn't get it.

'You remember Mr Spencer and his Scottish castle?'

Did she? So much had happened since then.

'The old man in the wheelchair. The poem he wanted me to look at.' Doug stabbed his finger at the vellum sheet; his finger-tip hovered a millimetre above the surface. 'This was it.'

Mr Spencer. The Spenser prize. She'd wondered about it at the time and dismissed it as coincidence.

The Spenser foundation. Legrande Holdings. Saint-Lazare Investments (UK).

She rolled up the vellum and slid it back in its tube. It made a hollow thud as it hit the end, a decisive sound. Doug didn't understand.

'Don't you want to know what it says?'

'We need to leave.'

'Where to?'

'Anywhere. The man who owns that vault, my client, Michel Saint-Lazare – he must be the same as your Mr Spencer. I don't know why he got you involved, but he obviously knows all about you. He must know about you and me, too. They'll come here.'

She twitched the side of the curtain and peered out at the street. The lines of parked cars stood like sentinels all along the pavement, their wet windows reflecting the orange glow of the streetlamps. Was someone waiting inside one of them?

'There won't be a train for another hour.'

'No public transport. They'll be watching all the stations and airports. We'll need a car.'

Doug opened his hands and made a hopeless gesture. *And?* Neither of them owned a car.

'We might be able to hire one at the station.'

'We can't hire anything. No credit cards.' She caught the look he was giving her. 'Don't you get it yet? These people can snoop everywhere, and if they find us, they'll kill us. If you think I'm crazy, just say so and I'll go by myself.'

Doug's gaze strayed to the leather tube with the poem inside it.

'Let's go.'

'Can you find us a car?'

'I think so.' He looked reluctant so say anything else, but the ferocity of Ellie's stare battered down his reticence.

'Lucy has one she let me borrow once.' He headed for the stairs. 'I'll just pack my things.'

XXXIV

Bay of Morbihan, France, 1142
How did he know my name?

It isn't the most important problem facing me, but I can't let it go. My thoughts have detached themselves: my mind floats serene, while my body flails and kicks against its fate. I'm Jonah, fighting the water, the sea, the fundament itself. I know I can't win, but I can't stop trying. If the God wants His victory, He'll have to earn it.

How did he know my name?

From the boats, the sea seemed so calm. Now that I'm in it, even the gentlest waves come higher than my head. In the troughs, all I can see is water; from the peaks, only fog. I've lost my armour, but it's taking all my strength just to stay afloat. The water's freezing. My body rises and falls on the waves: each time it falls, the water comes a little higher. Soon I'll drown.

Something strikes my shoulder, harder than a wave. I'm so numb I only half feel it, but it still enrages me. I don't want to be rushed. I look round. A dark mass glides past, like an enormous fish broaching the water. Except instead of scales, the stripes on its flanks are wood and tar.

It's a boat.

I stretch out an arm and clamp on to the hull. It probably frightens the life out of them, but they haul me aboard. Three men: by their ages and their faces I guess it's a father and two sons. They fillet me with their eyes and find nothing good. I lie in the bilge, breathing in salt and blood and dead fish. They don't speak to me.

We pull into a rocky bay. Green weed trails off black stones. The sons wade ashore to check their fish traps. The father gives me a black stare: he doesn't want me on his boat. Half-drowned and almost naked, I'm still trouble. He's rubbing the amulet he keeps nailed to the transom to fend off evil. I think he might try to kill me. I vault over the bow and splash ashore. Barnacles and oyster shells are like razors under my bare feet. The men at the fish-traps watch me go. Nobody tries to stop me.

Night falls. The mist cleared in the afternoon, but now a thick fog comes rising off the ground. I stumble on through the darkness. I daren't stop. I'm freezing – my wet shift clings to me like sin. If I lie down to sleep, I'll probably never wake up.

Thump. I've walked straight into a stone. I reel away, clutching my knee. *Thump.* Another stone clips my elbow. I step back, and almost fall over a third.

The moon comes out from behind a cloud. I'm standing in a field of stones, rectangular slabs all facing the same way. It looks like a churchyard, though there are no markings. They stand in tight echelons, rank upon rank reaching deep into the fog that swirls around them.

I know where I am. I'm dead. It's a relief to know. I wonder

282

if I died in the castle – if the fisherman was a spirit ferrying me to the world beyond – or if I've died since I came ashore. It doesn't matter. I'm a ghost now.

Is this heaven? It doesn't look like hell.

I hear a noise in the fog. The jangle of armour, the thud of someone walking into a stone and a low curse.

There's someone else here. Is he an angel? A demon? Another ghost? I drop behind a stone, burying myself in the fog.

'Peter!' he calls. 'Peter of Camros!'

I don't recognise the voice. It isn't Malegant's.

How did he know my name?

God knows everything. I'm not sure if the angels do, too, but I assume God can tell them the relevant facts.

But he cursed when he hit the stone. Angels don't curse.

Am I really dead? I'm not so certain any more. Saint John says of heaven: *There will be no more pain, neither sorrow nor crying*. Surely I shouldn't have stubbed my toe in heaven. Surely my heart shouldn't beat so fast.

The fear convinces me. If I were dead, I'd have left that behind. But if I'm not dead, where am I? And who is he?

Another noise: the rattle of chain mail, like coins shaken in a purse. I look around, trying to judge where the sound came from. All I see is stones.

An owl calls, far off in the trees to my left. I think my pursuer must be distracted. I pull myself up on one of the stones and peer over the lip.

For a moment, the moon is bright and clear. A few dozen paces away, a dismounted knight stands waist-deep in the stones. He's bare-headed, but the links of his armour gleam like fish-scales in the moonlight.

'Peter?' he calls.

How does he know my name?

The moon goes behind a cloud. He disappears from me – and I from him. I drop down and start crawling away.

I might not be dead, but I'm certain I'm in a nightmare – trapped in that endless, featureless graveyard, scuttling about on my hands and feet, chased by an enemy I can't see. In my headlong flight I career into stone after stone. I run straight into one and feel a splitting pain through my skull. But I'm getting away. My feet are silent on the wet grass; he can't move without an iron chorus singing his every step. I weave between the stones, following the owl towards the trees. The knight's sounds grow distant.

I run into the forest. The terror I felt among the stones has me full in its grip. Sometimes I find snatches of paths and follow them; sometimes I just blunder through. Branches rip and tear at me: soon even my shift is gone. I rush on.

A tree root catches me and I sprawl on the ground. My head feels splintered; my skin is bruised and torn; my limbs are bloodied. I lie there, naked, wondering if I'll ever get up.

Something snaps and rustles in the undergrowth. I hear a snuffling sound. Is it an animal? A fox or a wolf? I imagine it savaging me, gnawing my entrails out of my stomach while I'm forced to watch. Perhaps I have arrived in Hell after all.

The creature shuffles out of the thicket. He bends to look at me: I can feel his breath warm on my cheek. I feel a hand or a paw on my back.

He rolls me over. I stare into his face.

XXXV

Oxford

Destrier left the car at the end of the street and walked back to the address he'd been given. He forced himself to walk at a moderate pace – he didn't want to draw attention to himself. The Aston Martin was memorable enough.

He found the house. The curtains were drawn but the lights were on – good. He slipped a pair of brass knuckles over his right hand and knocked with his left.

No one came.

He got out Ellie's mobile and dialled Doug's number. He lifted the letterbox flap and heard the phone ringing inside. There was no answer, and no sound of movement either.

He waited through another minute's silence and decided to go in. It was a college house, used by generations of students: the lock was a joke. It took him thirty seconds to get in, another ninety to establish no one was home.

But only recently. The kettle was still warm. In the bathroom, steam still fogged the mirror; wet footprints walked across the carpet, and the towel on the door was damp. In the corner, beside the laundry basket, he found a woman's sock.

He ran outside and looked up and down the road. It was empty.

Three streets away, Doug and Ellie sat in a borrowed Nissan and waited for the windscreen to demist. On the pavement, a petite girl in tight jeans and a figure-hugging top watched anxiously.

'She's just a friend,' Doug said. Ellie hadn't asked. She sat in the passenger seat, hunched forward, willing the wall of fog in front of her to clear. She wasn't going to judge Doug.

A half-moon gap appeared in the windscreen. Doug rolled down his window.

'Thanks again,' he said to Lucy.

'Drive carefully.'

They pulled away before she could have second thoughts. Halfway down the street, Doug jammed on the brakes.

'What is it?' Panic was never far from the surface.

'I left the lights on at home.'

'Leave it,' Ellie pleaded. 'I promise you, I'll pay for it.'

If we ever come back. She didn't say it, but Doug picked up the sentiment. He put the car in gear and started moving.

'Where are we going?'

MV Noordwind, North Sea

They sat at a plastic table and picked at the food in front of them: eggs, beans, anaemic bacon and sausages, slowly congealing in grease. Outside, a grey swell heaved and pressed under a grey sky.

It would have been faster to go from Dover, but Ellie insisted on avoiding London and the motorways. Doug rolled his eyes, but didn't argue: he drove through the night, crossing the country on B-roads and backroads until they rolled into Harwich with the dawn. The wait for the ferry had been agonising, sitting in the concrete lanes constantly checking the mirrors while Doug got some sleep. She'd almost been sick when they had to show their passports, though the immigration officer had barely glanced at them. Only when the bow had slammed shut, when she'd scanned the faces of all the passengers coming up the gangway and watched the piers recede behind them, did she allow herself to relax.

Doug squinted at a piece of sausage and decided it was worth the risk.

'Let me get this from the beginning.'

Ellie put down her coffee. 'There are two sides to this. There's Monsalvat, Blanchard and all them – and there's . . . a rival organisation.'

Call it a brotherhood, though we've nothing against women.

'Behind Monsalvat, there's a French billionaire named Michel Saint-Lazare. Your Mr Spencer. Whatever's in that box, Saint-Lazare's ancestors took it from the brotherhood centuries ago.'

'According to your friend Harry.'

'I have to believe him.' Two months ago, she'd never have believed she'd be saying that. 'I can't do this by myself.'

Doug gave her a weary look. Exhaustion bruised the skin around his eyes; his face looked grey where stubble poked through, but he still tried for a smile.

'You're not by yourself.'

Ellie reached across the table and squeezed his hand. 'I know. But we won't survive on the run for long. We'll run out of money, for a start. All my bank cards come from Monsalvat. As soon as they work out I'm with you, they'll probably find a way to cancel yours too – or track us if you use them.' Doug looked sceptical. 'They're a bank, remember. They can do that

287

kind of thing. Whatever we stole from them, they'll move heaven and earth to get it off us.'

'You could give it back.'

'I've chosen my side. This organisation, the brotherhood, whatever you call them – they're the only ones who can protect us.' She crossed her fingers and prayed that was true. 'We have to find them.'

'How do we do that?'

Ellie sipped her coffee and made a face. It tasted of detergent.

'I don't know,' she admitted. 'Harry was my only contact.' She'd tried the phone number he'd given her three times from the pier at Harwich. *If no answer, leave a message for Harry from Jane.* The voicemail had kicked in, but she hadn't left a message.

'Now he's probably dead – or worse.'

The boat rocked up and down in the swell. A toddler with a yellow balloon staggered down the aisle between the tables, fell flat on his face and started to wail. Ellie felt a kick of sympathy.

'There's a company in Luxembourg that Monsalvat have just taken over.' *A mid-ranking European industrial concern. By an accident of history, they own something that belongs to us.* 'They've got something that links to Harry's people. If we can find it, maybe we can find our way to them.'

'*If we can find it?*' Doug repeated. 'Are we just going to walk in there and ask if they've got an address for an ancient, secret brotherhood?'

Ellie allowed herself a pale smile. 'Something like that. Unless you've got a better idea.'

But across the table, Doug's eyes had closed and his face nodded forward. Driving all night had exhausted him; he couldn't stave off sleep any longer. Ellie shot out her arm just in time to stop him toppling into his breakfast.

Near Bastogne, Belgium

Doug drove; Ellie sat with two sheets of paper laid out on the map book on her lap. One gave a transcription of the poem, the other was a translation.

'Mr Spencer asked me to make the translation,' Doug explained. 'I wanted to keep the form of the original, so it's written in rhyming octosyllabic couplets. Eight syllables per line – it's the standard form for early French romance poetry.'

'Romance as in . . .'

'As in romance language. In ancient Rome there was written Latin and there was a bastardised, colloquial form called *Romanice*. As the empire fell apart, Latin stayed pretty much the same, but Romanice devolved into the languages that became French, Spanish, Italian and so on. In the twelfth century, when people started writing in those languages, the stories they wrote were called romances, to differentiate them from stuff written in Latin. Nothing necessarily to do with romantic love. Even today, the French word for a novel is "*roman*".'

'OK.' Ellie bent forward and read the translation, trying not to feel carsick.

> On mazy paths a Christian knight
> Sought noble turns: it was his right.
> From Troy to Carduel he rode,
> A maiden met him at the ford.
> She raised the bowl, he threw the spear,
> Her blood fell like a ruby tear.
> So now he scratches taut parched ground:
> The treasures sown will not be found.

The car bumped over a pothole. For some reason, Ellie found herself overcome by bleakness.

'What do you make of it?' she asked.

'Well for one thing, I think I know who wrote it. Chrétien de Troyes.' He saw her reaction. 'What?'

Blanchard gave me a book of his for Christmas. But Doug didn't know she'd been in Switzerland for Christmas, didn't know she'd been there with Blanchard, and certainly didn't know why he'd have given her a twelfth-century manuscript as a Christmas present. A manuscript she'd left behind, along with everything else she owned, at the Barbican apartment.

'I saw a book of his poems at one of Saint-Lazare's houses. What made you think of him?'

'Well there's the language and the metre, which are the same style as Chrétien wrote in. The subject matter, too: knights and maidens. Carduel is one of the places, in the romances, where King Arthur had his court. We think it's modern-day Carlisle.'

Doug broke off to concentrate as a white van overtook them. They were driving through the Ardennes, the road dipping and rising over steep ridges and wooded valleys. An easy landscape to imagine knights errant questing for damsels and treasure.

'But the real clue's in the text. Look at it. *A Christian knight . . . from Troy.* Chrétien is the French for "Christian", and Troyes is how they spell the ancient city of Troy. Chrétien de Troyes.'

'If you say so.'

'The whole poem's a riddle. When Mr Spencer said he believed it hid the secret to a lost treasure, I thought he was crazy. But the more I've thought about it, the more I think he's right. The *taut parched ground* is parchment, and the poet – Chrétien – is scratching at it with his reed pen like a plough.

He's sowing something in the parchment, hiding it in the poem.'

'How?'

The first two lines sound as if they might be a clue to something. *Mazy paths . . . noble turns . . . his right . . .* maybe you're supposed to find a maze and always turn right.' He saw the look Ellie was giving him. 'Or something.'

'You're cherry-picking words and trying to make them mean something.' Ellie closed the map book, shutting the poems away. 'Anyway, if your Mr Spencer was actually Michel Saint-Lazare, what's he looking for? The treasure was already in his vault.'

'Then why did he come to me?'

'Because of me. Everything Blanchard's done, he's been trying to draw me in closer. He recruited me. He took me down to the vault. Getting you to look at the poem must have been part of the same plan. He knew we were together. He must have guessed you'd tell me about it.'

'Why?'

It was the question she'd been asking herself ever since the stiff envelope dropped through her letterbox in Oxford. *Why me?* Now she had an answer.

'He was using me as bait. He knew my father had been part of this brotherhood. He must have thought that by bringing me into Monsalvat, dangling all these pieces of the puzzle in front of me, he'd draw the brotherhood into revealing themselves.'

'Which they did.' Doug reached the top of the hill and shifted into a higher gear. His gaze fixed firmly on the road ahead, though it was wide and empty.

'Except now you're not the bait. You're the quarry.'

*

Luxembourg

It was odd being back in Luxembourg – the same feeling she used to get going home to Newport from university. Like visiting a ghost town, except that the town carried on and she was the ghost.

An eerie quiet gripped the Talhouett building. Ellie had seen the bid documents: she knew that in six months the building would be sold, half the employees out of work and the other half moved to an office park on the edge of town. She wore a black polyester skirt and a jacket that almost matched: they'd been cheap when they were new, and cheaper still in the charity shop where she found them. Tights from a service-station vending machine completed the outfit. It wasn't much to look at, but that and her Monsalvat card got her past the front desk and into the Operations Manager's office. She hoped the receptionist didn't see her trembling.

'Tell me everything you can about Mirabeau.'

Claude Doerner, the Operations Manager, sat back in his chair and frowned. He was a middle-aged man with a middle-aged sprawl: his toothbrush moustache was the trimmest thing about him.

'What is Mirabeau?' he asked.

'Don't mess me around.' Fear sharpened her manner. *What if Blanchard guessed she'd come there? What if they were watching?* 'I'll be working on the integration team,' she lied, 'evaluating which personnel are going to be able to deliver the corporate synergies we need. Any cooperation you can give me will definitely be taken into account.'

'Are you threatening me?'

With a confidence she didn't feel, Ellie sat down and crossed her legs.

'Just tell me about Mirabeau.'

292

'I promise you, I have never heard of it.'

Perhaps he was telling the truth. Ellie glanced at the computer on his desk. 'Can you log me in?'

Doerner swivelled the monitor around. He tapped his password on the keyboard, then pushed it across the desk to her.

'Be my guest.'

Ellie found the search box and clicked. Doerner moved round the desk towards the door.

'Where are you going?'

'To the bathroom. Or do you have to sign a paper to allow that too?'

She blushed. 'Of course.'

As soon as he was gone, she typed in 'Mirabeau' and set the computer searching. Doerner came back sooner than she expected. He settled himself in his chair and played with his tie.

'Will there be much bloodshed?'

'I'm sorry?'

'The sackings.' He made an effacing gesture. 'Apologies. I should say, "the synergies".'

She couldn't see any point in lying. 'It's going to be bad. They – we – promised the Luxembourg government not to do anything until the next election, but after that they'll swing the axe pretty hard.'

He grimaced. 'You know, twelve hundred years ago Duke Siegfried built Luxembourg as a castle. I wonder how much has changed.'

Ellie watched the progress bar crawl across the screen. Every second was like a knot tightening around her throat.

'For all our technology, the only organising principle we recognise is the dominance of the strong. Feudalism. Workers

293

don't want to be empowered. They want safety: a steady income and protection from the vicissitudes – this is the word? – of the world. For that, they allow themselves to be exploited. They know their lord only cares for them because they generate income, but it is better to be abused by one tyrant than by many. And when a new master takes over through war or conquest, they know they will suffer.'

He drained the last of his coffee. 'I'm getting philosophical. Perhaps I should accept the no-doubt-inadequate early retirement offer they will make me.'

Ellie had stopped listening. She was staring at the screen.

Aucune légende correspondant aux critères de recherche n'a été trouvée

Translation: *nothing*.

She turned the monitor towards Doerner. 'What is this?'

His phone rang. He held up a finger and took the call.

'*Oui? J'attends.*'

When he put the phone down, his face had changed. He looked happier, almost eager to please.

'Can I get you a cup of coffee?' he asked.

'Not unless you can tell me about Mirabeau.'

He shrugged. 'No more than the computer.'

'Michel Saint-Lazare has just spent over a billion euros buying this company because of Mirabeau. You can't tell me no one knows anything about it.'

'Of course, someone will know, if it exists. But to find this person, it is not easy. Talhouett is a big business: we have many operations in many countries. There is probably no one in the company who knows everything.'

'I need you to let me in to your archives.'

'All the files are still in the data room. It has been locked for the duration of the takeover battle.'

'Then take me there.'

'If you can just wait a few moments. My secretary has gone out with my keys.'

Ellie waited ten seconds – long enough to assure herself that the smile on his face was 100 per cent false. She rummaged through her bag as if looking for her lipstick, until she felt the handle of the kitchen knife she'd bought that morning.

In a single motion, she whipped it out of the bag and held the tip to Doerner's throat. Doerner went very still.

'You're not really working for Monsalvat,' he said.

'No. I'm much nicer than they are.'

She watched him, wondering if there was any sort of panic button or alarm he might press. But these were administrative offices in one of the most boring cities in Europe: they didn't expect people to walk in and hold knives to their throats. Not literally.

'Who was that phone call from?' She jerked the knife: she'd only meant to scare him, but she was so tense she broke the skin. He winced. A drop of blood seeped in to his starched shirt collar.

'Your boss. Christine Lafarge.'

She almost took his head off. 'Where is she?'

His eyes sidled round to the window, though he didn't move his head. 'She said she'll be here in five minutes.'

For a split second, Ellie really thought about killing him. She saw the choice in black and white: him or her. She'd slit his throat, take his keys, leave his body for Christine Lafarge to find. Show them what they were dealing with. It would be so easy.

A second later, shame overwhelmed her. *What sort of person are you becoming?*

'Give me your keys,' she ordered him. 'And your mobile.'

He'd dropped the line about his secretary having the keys. He reached into the suit jacket on the back of his chair and deposited a ring of keys and a mobile phone on the desk. Ellie swept them across and picked them up.

'Stay there.'

She used the knife to cut the cord on his desk phone, and the cable going into his computer. She couldn't see anything else he might use to communicate with – and she didn't have time to look.

'Which is the key to the data room?'

'The one with the yellow ring.'

'And for this office?'

'The blue.'

She stepped out of the office and locked it. *Five minutes*, he'd said. How many had gone already? She ran down the corridor and found a bank of lifts at the back of the building. *How long?*

The data room was just as she remembered it, though somehow more forlorn. She locked the door behind her and turned on the lights, taking in the cheap tables and the long ranks of mechanical shelves. There must be a million pieces of paper in here. She'd have five minutes, if she was lucky.

But at least she had an idea where to start. She was sure she'd seen Mirabeau doing the due diligence. She ran to the shelves and punched in the rack she wanted on the keypad.

'Open sesame,' she murmured to herself.

The shelves rumbled into life, like giants woken from their sleep. They groaned and clattered, rolling themselves apart so that an aisle opened between them. Even that seemed to take forever.

Ellie pushed in before they'd finished moving. There'd been

stacks like this at university: she'd never quite shaken the fear that they might suddenly to decide to spring shut and crush her. Now that was the least of her worries. She found the accounts folders halfway down the aisle and started pulling them out. *Mirabeau.* Where had she seen it? She'd always had a good head for archive work, a recall that allowed her to find things again. She'd never needed it so desperately.

She turned the pages, searching for something to jog her memory, forcing herself not to go so quickly she'd miss it. She felt as if a giant fist had clenched around her heart, squeezing each time there was a noise in the corridor. She saw a jagged graph shaped like a mountain range and thought it looked familiar. She slowed down.

Two pages later, she found it. A single line in the budget for one of Talhouett's French subsidiaries. Mirabeau Exploratory (Ref 890112/A/F2727).

She knew the way their record-keeping worked. F2727 was the file reference. She consulted the shelving list. *F2650-F2900: Stack 7.* She went back to the keypad on the end of the stack and pressed the button to open up the new aisle.

A fraction of a second before the shelves started to move, she heard a noise at the door. The handle was turning. Time had run out.

Christine Lafarge snapped the door open and pushed Doerner through. He stumbled in. Nobody stabbed him. He gazed around the empty room, unused chairs at dusty tables.

'You said she'd be here.'

Doerner had never heard a woman growl before. He remembered Ellie: *I'm much nicer than they are.*

'She said this was where she was coming. And the lights are on.'

A book lay open on the floor. Christine Lafarge picked it up and swept her gaze over the page. A long fingernail rasped down the entries – and stopped.

'Mirabeau.'

'I told you. She wanted to know all about it.'

'What did you tell her?'

'Nothing. I have never heard of this project. Talhouett is a big company. We –'

'What does this reference mean?'

'It's the file location.' A pause, a consultation. 'Stack 7.'

Five feet away, in Stack 4, Ellie lay hunched up on the empty shelf under the accounts folders and tried not to shake it with her trembling. She lay there, entombed in paperwork, and listened.

Doerner's footsteps proceeded down the aisle. She could hear him counting off the file numbers under his breath. She clenched her fists, digging her nails into her palms in frustration. She'd led them right to it.

Doerner knelt. She heard the shuffle of files – and then, unexpectedly, a curse.

'The file – it's gone.'

Ellie went still as stone.

'She must have taken it.'

'How long since she left your office?'

'Five minutes. Maybe ten.'

'Did you tell Security to stop her at the exit?'

Doerner, plaintively: 'She took my phone.'

'Is there any other way out of this building?'

A silence as Doerner thought about it. 'There is a fire door at the back of the south corridor. It is supposed to be alarmed, but we disable it for the smokers. She maybe could have got out that way.'

Ellie could only imagine the look Christine Lafarge was giving Doerner. She almost felt sorry for him.

'If she has escaped, every person in this building will be out of a job. Do you understand?'

Ellie heard the clack-clack of high heels receding, Doerner's footsteps squeaking behind. The door opened and closed. She was alone.

She waited two minutes to be sure they wouldn't come back. She would have waited longer, hours if necessary, but she had a more pressing concern.

How am I going to get out?

The aisle was between stacks seven and eight. She was in stack four. There were three shelves of files between her and freedom, and no other way out. She could wait for someone to come, but the room hadn't been used in months, might not be used for months again.

And if anyone does come, I probably don't want to meet them.

She'd thought she'd already squeezed up as tightly as possible, but she found that if she pushed herself back she could make a small opening at the head of the shelf. That gave her space to reach through to the next shelf and start manoeuvring the files through, filling them in around her.

She felt like a worm, gobbling the earth in its path and squeezing it out behind. A bookworm. That's what her mother always called her. The memory spurred her on. She pushed herself over the divider into the cavity she'd dug out and started attacking the next shelf.

The second stack went more quickly than the first, and the last was easiest of all. With a couple of heaves, she pushed through, spilling a cascade of paper across the floor and slithering down on her stomach like a polar bear coming out of its cave. Dust and paper dandruff covered her. Her mouth tasted of paper, and she couldn't be sure when Christine Lafarge might come back. All she wanted to do was go.

But there was one thing she had to check. She moved along the aisle to where file F2727 ought to be.

Doerner had been right. There was nothing – only a thin gap where file F2726 leaned against F2728.

Who took it? Not Doerner. Not Christine Lafarge, or Blanchard.

She felt ill. So much effort, so much danger – for nothing. A gap on a dusty shelf. She crouched down and stared at the space, as if she could will the file back into its place.

A small bump on the shelf caught her eye. She reached in a finger and felt it. The waxy hardness of dried chewing gum.

XXXVI

Brittany, 1142

The abbot isn't happy. He sticks his hand in the pockets of his white habit; he blows out his cheeks, like a cat fluffing its fur to make itself seem bigger. He looks at the hermit, a biblical figure in his brown tunic and long white beard; and at the man beside him: the scars, the nose that didn't set right after a shield boss broke it, the strength in the arms.

'The monastery is full,' he says.

He's a fat man in a lean land. He didn't get that way by taking in monks who couldn't earn their keep. He wants younger sons from established families: youths who'll bring donations, patronage, bequests. He doesn't want an orphan grubbed out of the forest – disruptive, burdensome, and with who knows what sins on his conscience. But the hermit carries spiritual weight. The abbot has to at least pretend to listen to him.

'What is your name?'

'Chr . . . Chrétien.' The name doesn't fit me yet, though I'm determined it will. The abbot makes a face. He thinks I'm trying to impress him with my piety.

He stares at my head. The hermit cropped my hair almost to the skull, but there's still a remnant of the false tonsure I had for the assault. Does he think I'm a miscreant monk who fled his former home? Or has he heard of the men who dressed as murdered monks and slaughtered the garrison of the Île de Pêche? I think probably not. I doubt Malegant left witnesses.

'Have you taken orders before?'

'Minor orders. A long time ago.'

I look around the Abbot's room. He may be fat, but he isn't prodigal: the room is as Spartan as you'd expect. The only indulgence I can see is books. He has the usual literature of his office – Bible, missal, breviary and account books – but also many more: fine volumes bound in leather. I can see Vergil, Ovid, Cicero and Caesar.

He follows my gaze. He wonders if I'm planning to rob him.

'I can read and write,' I volunteer. 'Both Latin and Romanse.'

The abbot licks his lips. 'Brother Edward, who worked in the scriptorium, died two months ago. It's hard to find someone to replace him around here.'

'At least take him as a novice,' the hermit suggests.

I still don't understand what happened in the field of stones – if I left this world for a time, like the men in my mother's stories; if I dreamed it; or if, even more strangely, it might have been real. However it transpired, Peter of Camros died that night.

The birth-pangs of my new life were hard and painful. The hermit served as midwife. He found me in the forest and took me to his home, a turf cell by a spring. For six days I lay on a fern bier delirious with a fever. He kept me alive with honey and bread dipped in milk; he used his arts to make salves, which he

302

spread on my forehead; he whispered prayers in my ear.

When the fever left me, he suggested I make a confession.

'Something inside you is blocking your heart like a stone. You have to remove it if you want to be whole again.'

His hair grew wild, matted and long and streaked with mud. But there was a profound stillness in his deep brown eyes. A trust.

I knelt in front of him in the forest. I told him how for years I had hated God, how I wandered blindly without knowing where I was going. How everything I did was evil. I confessed it all. My adultery with Ada. The men I killed, from Athold du Laurrier to the Count's guards on the Île de Pêche. Long before I finished, tears were streaming down my face. The sins had taken deep hold on my soul, but I tore them up by their roots and cast them out for the hermit to see. I wondered if there would be anything left to hold me together without them.

The hermit heard me out in silence. When I had finished, I looked into his eyes to see what he thought. He'd closed them: but even his powers of self-will couldn't mask the horror on his face. A hermit, not a saint.

'Terrible crimes,' he murmured.

The words struck me like a lance. My face grew hot. Part of me wanted to hit him, to break his sanctimonious body and beat the forgiveness I craved out of him. Part of me, perhaps the greater part, knew I didn't deserve it. I curled over, rocking on my knees.

Something fluttered against my forehead like a moth. I reached up to swat it away, but it resisted me. I opened my eyes. The hermit's hand was trembling with the effort as he laid it on my head.

'God is Love, and according to the Scriptures, whoever abides in Love, abides in God, and God in him.'

303

He stared into my eyes. I could see the conflict inside him.

'Will you abide in Christ? Will you show love to the loveless, charity to the destitute, pity to the pitiless?'

I nodded. He made me repeat the words and I did, stumbling over them in my eagerness. I needed his forgiveness like a seed craves sun.

'Christ forgive you all your sins, and make you perfect in every way.'

He took the wooden bowl he used and scooped it in the spring. I remembered a story my mother used to tell, about a magic spring that summoned a knight to do battle if you drank from it. The hermit poured the water over my head. It ran down my face and washed away my tears until I could no longer taste the salt.

Almost to himself, I heard him whisper, 'Blessed are the merciful, for they shall have mercy.'

So Chrétien was born.

I wanted to stay with him, but he wouldn't let me. Day by day I saw his impatience growing, though he did his best to hide it. I had blundered into his solitude: he had shared it with me for a little while, but now he wanted it back.

When I was strong enough to walk, he took me down to the monastery.

It's easier being a monk than I thought it would be – not so different from being a knight. The monks are soldiers of Christ garrisoning the wildest frontiers of Christendom: the abbey is their fortress. They've diverted the river to make a moat; they've built high walls and watchtowers; they've cleared a swathe of forest so no one approaches without being seen. An internal wall divides the compound into an inner and an outer ward. I work in the scriptorium in the inner ward, off a cloister bounded on one side by the church and on another by the refectory and the dormitories. I rarely have to leave the cloister, let alone the inner ward.

As I novice, I share a cell with boys half my age, whispering in the dark. It's like being back at Hautfort. We joust with words and try to outdo each other in feats of piety, but otherwise there's little difference. I'm a child again.

But children grow. For a time, I bask in my redemption; I'm like a parchment that's been scraped clean, unwritten. But the shadows of the old words still remain stained in the skin. If you look between the glossy lines of new text, you can see the ghosts. Sometimes I wake up screaming in the dormitory, drawn back to the castle on the island or the chapel by the forest. The girl in the castle and Ada haunt my dreams – sometimes one, sometimes the other, always pierced through the breast, too late for me to save. The other novices think I harbour a demon.

Months go by. Each day, I sit at my copy-desk transcribing someone else's words. Errors start creeping into my work; the Librarian scolds me; I stare out the window and nurse old memories back to life.

Peter of Camros. I wondered when you'd remember yourself.

Peter's dead – I'm Chrétien now. But even the monastery's stout walls and safe rituals can't keep out my past. All my life I've been pushed down this road I didn't choose. I've failed in every bond of love or duty I ever undertook: my family; my lord Guy; Ada. To lock myself in the monastery now won't redeem me: it'll bury me.

I need answers. I need to find Malegant.

One day the Abbot comes to me. He wants me to travel to our mother house, the priory near Châteaubriant. The Librarian there has given him permission to copy certain works they hold. He almost salivates as he describes their library, listing the manuscripts he covets in loving detail. I'm given a list, a mule to carry the books back and a small purse to pay for vellum and ink. I don't have to worry about travelling alone. The Cellarer and two of his assistants will be taking a cart of wool to the cloth fair.

We travel east. The other monks pretend to ignore me, though every so often I catch them giving me nervous glances. They talk freely when they think I'm not there, and fall silent when they see me. I keep my eyes on the road and don't take it personally. When you've killed as many men as I have, the good opinion of your fellow-travellers doesn't matter so much.

All the way to Rennes, I pretend to myself that there's nothing special about this trip. I'll copy the manuscripts, load them on my mule and trudge back. I know it's a lie, but it helps contain my fears. South of Rennes, as the road takes us up the River Chère valley, I start to admit the idea. Day by day, step by step, it overtakes me until I can't conceive any alternative. By the time we reach Châteaubriant, I know what I have to do.

The abbey is only two days away from the town. The Cellarer and his assistants will stay there to sell our wool, while I travel on alone. I make a brief and insincere goodbye. As soon as they're out of sight, I double back into the market. The cloth fair has brought plenty of tailors to town, all vying to offer the best price. The coins the Abbot gave me for ink and vellum easily stretch to a new tunic, hose and coat. For an extra few pennies I buy a cap that comes low down the sides of my face, and a pair of stout boots.

I've got a long way to go.

XXXVII

Luxembourg

The door said 'ALARMED', but Doerner had told the truth: it was disabled. Ellie slipped out across a no man's land of cigarette butts and rubbish bins, down an alley and into freedom. No one saw her. She found Doug parked down a sidestreet where she'd left him.

He looked at her dishevelled hair, the dust-streaks and the blood where the paper had cut her. 'What happened to you? I was about to call the police I was so worried.'

Ellie slumped down in the passenger seat so that only the top of her head showed. 'Just drive. I'll tell you later.'

'Did you get what you wanted?'

'Let's find a phone box. Somewhere out of the way.'

Directory enquiries gave her the number she wanted and put her straight through. 'Mr Lechowski, please. It's Ellie Stanton.'

She supposed he could have been anywhere, but luck – if you could call it that – was on her side. Lechowski came on the line.

'Ellie – this is an unexpected surprise. I thought perhaps you forgot me.'

She shuddered; she almost slammed the phone back in its cradle. Lechowski was her past, far too close to Monsalvat. Just talking to him felt like stepping into the jaws of a trap.

What if Blanchard's got to him?

'The acquisition's gone through. I'm ready to honour our agreement.'

She tried to sound businesslike, like it was no big deal. Down the line, she could almost hear Lechowski licking his lips. Perhaps it was just the sound of his chewing gum.

'You are staying at the Sofitel? Will I meet you there?'

'I was thinking we could go somewhere more . . . intimate.'

He laughed. 'You are worried about reputational risk. Lechowski is not offended.' He named a restaurant in the old town. 'I look forward to our evening.'

Ellie put the phone down and wanted to vomit. Even in the Underground tunnel she hadn't felt this dirty.

You did it with Blanchard, she reminded herself. Somehow, in a way she didn't want to consider, that had been different.

She turned around and saw Doug watching her warily.

'What was the deal?'

She was too tired to lie. 'He had leverage over the Talhouett takeover deal that could have derailed the whole thing. I told him if he let it go ahead, I'd sleep with him.'

The bleakness on Doug's face was almost too much to bear. *Right reaction, wrong reason.* She reminded herself of Lucy, and found herself getting impatient. 'Don't be such a boy scout. I'd never have gone through with it.'

'But now you are. To get the Mirabeau file.'

'To get to the brotherhood. Without them, we're really screwed.'

The restaurant was bright and busy, filled with corporate types. Ellie scanned the room from the door, looking for danger. Lechowski might have been on the other side of the Talhouett deal, but that didn't mean a thing. If Blanchard had offered him a price, he'd give Ellie up in a moment.

Lechowski was the only face she recognised, and he wasn't hard to spot. He wore a black-and-white check sports jacket, so loud it made Ellie's head swim, though it had probably cost several hundred pounds. He ordered for her without asking what she wanted.

'All seductions succeed through audacity,' he remarked, with the authority of something he must have read in a book. 'As soon as the seducer hesitates, he breaks the charm. "There is not one woman who does not prefer a little rough handling to too much consideration." You know who said that? A woman.'

Ellie had never been out with a man who gave her a running commentary on his tactics. She squeezed her legs together and tried not to think of what was coming.

The waiter brought champagne, which Lechowski tasted with a great show of fussiness. He tipped his glass to her.

'So why are you in Luxembourg?'

'Talhouett.'

Lechowski took a gulp. Champagne dribbled down his chin. 'Now you have won your prize, you have come to poke around her.'

The innuendo was entirely intentional. Ellie took a sip of champagne and wondered how she'd manage to stay sober that evening.

'I'll tell you a secret.' She leaned forward, giving him an eyeful of her cleavage. 'Blanchard bribed the president of the privatisation commission to tell us how much you'd bid. You were always going to lose.'

Lechowski spluttered; champagne sprayed on to Ellie's cheek. 'If I was recording this conversation, you could go to prison for saying that.'

The mock outrage on his face dissolved into a smirk. 'But since we are being honest, I will tell you a secret in return. We never bid for Talhouett. An hour before the final offers were due, we informed the president of the commission that we had withdrawn our interest.'

Was it the champagne? All Ellie could do was stare at him in confusion.

'If we had made this public, our withdrawal, it would have been a scandal. Very embarrassing to the commission, that they reduced the field to two bidders and then one dropped out. To preserve appearances, we agreed we would submit a bid five million euros less than whatever Monsalvat offered.' He ripped a bread roll in two and dabbed butter on it. 'Whatever he told Blanchard, it was a fiction.'

She still didn't understand. 'Why? To avoid the Romanian lawsuit?'

'Mr Lazarescu, the obliging judge? So keen to tell me about his case.' Lechowski stretched back in his chair. His shirt-tails pulled loose from his waistband, showing a tuft of hair sprouting above the belt buckle. 'You think Lechowski is such a fool he cannot smell the rat?'

'If you knew the Romanian problem was overplayed, why not bid?'

'I found something everyone else missed – so secret, even the management did not know about it. A liability that could destroy the company.'

'What?'

Lechowski opened his mouth – then snapped it shut with a cruel grin. 'You own the company – you find out. If you can find the file.'

'Is it Mirabeau?'

Lechowski went very still.

'It seems we both underestimated each other.'

'Taking the file was a bit of a giveaway.'

'You still bought the company.'

'That makes the file my property.'

A waiter brought the food. Ellie put on a pretty, blank smile while her mind raced. When the waiter was gone, she straightened herself.

'If you never meant to buy Talhouett, then our deal is void.'

Lechowski dug into his food. '*Caveat emptor.*'

'Material non-disclosure.' She reached across under the table and trailed her hand across Lechowski's thigh – then suddenly pulled it away. 'I'm entitled to withhold payment.'

'You wouldn't do that,' he protested. But she could see he believed her. *As soon as the seducer hesitates, he breaks the charm.*

She toyed with the food on her plate. She swirled the champagne in her glass. She forced herself to go on. 'Perhaps we can amend our deal. You withheld Mirabeau from me, fair enough, but the deal's done. It's not worth anything to you any more.'

Lechowski stared at her as if she were naked. 'I wouldn't say it's not worth anything.'

Holding his gaze, she reached inside her blouse and straightened her bra strap. Her fingers brushed the top of her breast.

'I can make it worth your while.'

'You promised me that last time.'

'And now I'm here. I'm good for my promises.'

Lechowski didn't blink. 'I have the file in my office. We can go there tomorrow morning.'

'I'm flying out first thing,' she improvised. 'Can't we get it on the way home?'

'I think I prefer to see some evidence of your good faith.'

Ellie swallowed a gulp of champagne, then leaned across the table and kissed him. His tongue flicked out at her like a lizard's; she forced herself not to recoil. He tasted of chewing gum and too much aftershave. She took another deep swig of champagne to try and drown the taste.

'Is a down payment good enough?'

'We can get the file on the way back to my hotel.'

She stiffened. 'Are you in the Sofitel?'

'The Hilton.'

Lechowski had a sports car which he drove like a maniac, presumably because his book said it would impress her. She waited in the car, double-parked outside his office, while he went in for the file. Her breath fogged the windscreen; the seat leather was like ice against her thighs.

She knew at once it was the genuine file: she'd seen enough of them that day. She could see the F2727 stamped on the spine. She began to flip through the documents, but Lechowski slapped it shut.

'Everything is there. Lechowski is as good as his word.' A leer. 'I trust you are as good as yours.'

'You'll find out soon enough,' she mumbled.

As long as they'd been in the restaurant, she'd been able to ignore what was coming. In the car, the illusion began to waver; when they reached the hotel, she couldn't deny it any longer. If any doubt remained, it vanished when Lechowski draped his arm around her as he sauntered through the lobby. His hand swept proprietorially over her chest; his fingers wandered down her top.

She made herself walk to the lifts without screaming. In the lift he was all over her, pressing her against the mirrored wall and rubbing himself against her. She didn't resist. The moment they were inside his room, he started fumbling with his belt, while the other hand pawed at her buttons.

Ellie pushed him away and went back to the door.

'Where are you going?'

She didn't miss the edge in his voice. *You think Lechowski is such a fool he cannot smell the rat?* He might play the buffoon, but he was used to getting his way. She remembered what Doug had said, back in the summer. *The first sign of weakness, they'll tear you limb from limb.*

She waved the plastic Do Not Disturb sign at him, and hooked it over the outside door handle.

'We don't want any interruptions. I'm not in any rush.' Her mouth was dry; she hoped it came out husky rather than croaky.

'I thought you had a flight first thing.'

'Monsalvat can afford another ticket.'

She closed her eyes. Lechowski had undone her top: he buried his face in her cleavage and squeezed her like something he could get juice out of. If he noticed that she was as limp as a doll, he didn't complain. Perhaps he liked it.

There is not one woman who does not prefer a little rough handling to too much consideration.

'I knew it.'

Ellie's eyes snapped open. Light from the corridor flooded in to the dim room. Doug stood in the doorway, his face twisted in fury.

313

'You little slut.'

'Please, Doug.'

Ellie stepped back. Lechowski stared. His flies gaped open. 'Who –?'

'Shut it!' With a move straight from the rugby field, Doug dropped his shoulder and sent Lechowski sprawling back on the bed. Before Lechowski could react, Doug picked him back up by his shirtfront, and threw him down on the floor.

'If I ever hear one word that Ellie was here tonight, I'm going to hunt you down and make you wish you'd never touched her! I'll cut off your cock and make you eat it! Do you understand?'

He grabbed Ellie's wrist and dragged her towards the door. She just had time to snatch up the folder on the dresser on her way out.

'"Make you eat it?" That's disgusting. Where did you get it from?'

They were back in the car. Outside the windows, the grey blocks of suburban Luxembourg dragged by. Doug, driving, looked embarrassed.

'Must have come from a film or something.'

'You were great. Really scary.' She squeezed his knee. He flinched.

'Seriously, don't ever do that to me again. It was horrible.'

'It wasn't any better for me.'

Doug drove on, staring stiffly ahead. A sullen silence gripped the car.

'Stop here.'

He glanced at her, saw the look on her face and didn't argue. He pulled over in front of a mini-market. 'What?'

She reached across the car, cupped her hand around his

head and pulled him towards her. She kissed him hard, feeling the warmth of his mouth against hers. He tried to pull back after a decent interval, but she refused to let him go until she felt the muscles in his neck relax, until his eyes shut and his arms closed around her. She wanted him to understand.

'I'm sorry.'

She didn't say for what. If he'd asked, she'd probably have told him everything. But he didn't. The strain on his face seemed to loosen a little. He attempted a smile.

'I suppose we taught that creep a lesson he won't forget. Where now?'

Ellie opened the folder. Three pages in was a map.

'South.'

XXXVIII

France, 1142

> This is the tale of Erec's deeds,
> Adventuring with fair Enide,
> Which some poor storytellers dangle
> Before Kings and Counts – and mangle.

I bow towards my audience. Laughter goes round the hall. There are no kings and few counts among them, but they appreciate the flattery.

> This story that I now begin
> Will last as long as men do sin,
> A tale to sit in memory:
> So much does Chrétien guarantee.

My boast gets their attention. They lean forward to listen, to see if I can deliver on my promise. I'm sitting to one side of the fire, my face half in the light and half in shadow. They don't see me: their eyes are full of the knights, castles, kings and damsels I'm conjuring for their imaginations. But I can see them. I scan their faces, searching for one I recognise.

I need to get back to Troyes to find the man who recruited me, the goldsmith with the silver hand and the sky-blue eyes. But Troyes is a long journey from Châteaubriant, and the money I took from the abbot won't get me far. So I'm following the tournaments again, a ghost in my own former life, scraping pennies and lodging where I can as I wander east.

I don't ride in the battle line any more – I've kept that much of my promise to the hermit. In the mornings, I serve as a herald, announcing the knights as they parade past the stands. Everyone watches the knights: no one sees the man standing right in front of them, calling out their names. A herald's job is to know everyone. The night before the contest, I ferret my way among the tents and through the town's lodgings, asking the name and arms of every knight. I visit the lists and the rings to see the single combats, and the men who watch them. Malegant found all his knights that way – surely someone will return to their old paths.

I miss my old life. I miss the horse swaying under me, the smells of oil, resin and hot metal. I miss the thrilling fear of waiting for the charge, and the bond with the men beside me. Sometimes, I can barely resist throwing myself into the ring with the other knights. I don't. The promises I made the hermit are vague, but they definitely preclude fighting for gain.

In the evenings I go to the banquets and tell stories, of knightly deeds long ago, when Arthur was king. The knights like those stories. They imagine themselves as the heroes, and feel vindicated.

*

Back in the hall the candles have burned low. The audience leans in. I tell them how Erec saw Enide and fell in love at first sight; how life in the castle bored them; how they went adventuring together and learned to trust each other. I tell how they fought a hundred knights, and two giants; how they freed the kingdom of King Evrain from a murderous custom. And, at last, how Erec brought Enide to Carduel and installed her as his queen to live happily ever after.

When you're telling the story, you can choose how it ends.

> Thus Chrétien ends his tale of deeds
> Done by Erec and fair Enide.
> We leave them kissing by the door,
> The story ends – there is no more.
> And should a man say otherwise,
> I promise you: he's telling lies.

Laughter and applause ripple around the hall. I watch the faces change as the lords and ladies come back to the present. It's as close to magic as I've seen in this world. Speak the right words, in the right way, and you can change their hearts.

The story ends – there is no more. They want to believe it. They want to inhabit a world of certain endings, of happiness fixed forever. In all my tales, it's the biggest fiction of all.

Minstrels come in; benches get pushed back for dancing. The audience mill about. Some leave to return to their lodgings, or relieve themselves, or meet lovers in draughty stable-blocks. I watch the doors, scanning faces. A man in a cloak embroidered with lions looks as though he's paying me close attention – I keep my eye on him for a moment, until he gets drawn into conversation with the lady beside him. My gaze moves on.

And there he is. A grey, one-eyed face I've seen before,

standing by a ring watching men sport. *I work for a man who's always interested to see good fighters.* He wore a black coat that day – now he's dressed in scarlet – but the face is clear in my memory. That puckered socket isn't one you forget. Has he recognised me?

He's going out the door. I disengage from the crowd around me and hurry after him. By the time I get out he's already on the far side of the courtyard, a shadow in the braziers' smoky light. My footsteps seem too loud on the flagstones, but he doesn't look back.

The town is built on a hill, with the castle at the summit and the houses sloping towards the river. I follow the one-eyed man down. Tournament crowds still throng the main street, drinking and singing: it's easy for me to hide among them, harder to keep him in sight. Twice I think I've lost him. I try and close the gap.

The houses end at a stretch of open ground just inside the walls. Normally, the townspeople pasture their sheep here, but tonight it's become a makeshift encampment for the makeshift army who've descended on the town. I battle back memories of the nights Ada and I spent in these camps – maybe in this very town.

The one-eyed man seems to know where he's going. He turns between two tents, down a narrow, muddy path. He'll see me if I follow him. I go on and slip between the next row of tents, paralleling his path. Stakes and ropes reach out of the darkness to snare me.

Ahead, the glow of a campfire flickers on canvas. I crouch and edge forward, peering around the tent wall. Four men, still in the quilted tunics they wore under their armour, are sitting on logs roasting songbirds on sticks. The man I followed crouches beside them, trailing the hem of his expensive mantle in the mud, and talks in a low voice. I can't hear what he's saying, but the gestures he makes are sharp and urgent.

I creep forward to try and listen in. A purse changes hands.

'. . . bring it to me there.'

'And how –?'

But the one-eyed man isn't listening. He's staring past the fire, straight towards me. The puckered skin around his blind socket goes taut, as if a phantom eye is stretching to see me. But there's no problem with his other eye – and in trying to hear him, I've been drawn into the light.

'*That's him.*'

Too late, I realise he's hired them to kill me. I could hardly have made it easier for them. The knights snatch weapons from around the fireside and jump to their feet. Just for an instant, fear keeps me fixed to the spot – not fear for my life, but fear that if I lose sight of my quarry now, I'll never see him again. Never find Malegant, never find answers.

But I won't find him if I'm dead. I turn and run through the campsite, hurdling ropes in the dark, pushing past onlookers before they can stop me. I see the road ahead and swing left, through an arch and across the bridge. A gatehouse guards the far side – beyond that, I can surely lose them in the forest. I grab a ring in the gate and heave.

The gate's locked. The castellan must be worried about brigands drawn to the tournament. I bang on the door, but there are no lights in the barbican tower. The gatekeeper's probably gone to enjoy the festivities. He doesn't realise he's just signed my death warrant.

I turn, pressing my back against the gate. A single lamp hangs over the arch: the four knights prowl like wolves just beyond the ring of light. They all have swords in their hands.

I promised the hermit I wouldn't fight: I'm not carrying so much as a paring knife. I look for help, but the only other man on the bridge is a beggar, stumbling forward tapping his staff. One of the knights gives him a warning gesture, a hand slicing across his throat.

'Why do you want to kill me?' I shout. The night swallows the sound.

The nearest knight shrugs. He doesn't know why. All he knows is what he's been paid to do. He puts up his sword to strike – and pauses. The beggar's still coming, his staff tap-tapping the wooden bridge. Maybe he's blind. The knight makes a sign to one of his men to get rid of him. I want to shout a warning, but the words won't come.

Chaos and shadow make it hard to see what happens next. There's a blur of movement, a rush and a splash. Suddenly, there are only three knights on the bridge. The beggar seems to have grown six inches: he's thrown off his cloak and holds the staff like a cudgel. Two of the knights run towards him. One gets hit in the chest so hard I hear the ribs crack. He drops like a stone. The man behind him trips on the body and stumbles forward, into the path of a scything blow that sends him reeling to the parapet. Another prod of the staff tips him over the edge.

Now it's just three of us standing on the bridge. The beggar lowers his staff like a spear and walks slowly towards the remaining knight. The knight edges backwards until he comes up against the parapet. He's got nowhere else to go. He weighs his chances and makes his choice. He jumps in the river.

All this time, I've stayed rooted in place. Have I been rescued? The beggar turns towards me.

'Peter of Camros?'

The voice is familiar, though I don't know where from. I

stare. Now that his cloak has come off, I can see a wine-coloured tunic embroidered with lions. The man who was watching me in the hall.

How did he know my name?

'I'm Chrétien. Peter is dead.'

'Not to us.'

Something strikes the side of my head. Like a candle being pinched out, I sink into the darkness.

XXXIX

Chalon-sur-Saône, France

Ellie wanted to avoid the motorways and drive through the night. Doug resisted and won on both points.

'They don't know our car, and they don't know where we're going. They can't put watchers on every bridge in France.'

'They won't take long to work out where we're going. Someone inside Talhouett must know about Mirabeau. The moment they find that person, they'll be all over it.' She remembered Saint-Lazare's private jet. 'They move quickly.'

'That's why we should take the motorway.'

She surrendered. And when, halfway through the night, Doug turned into a service area and parked up at a motel, she didn't argue. She snuggled up to Doug and was asleep almost before he'd turned out the light.

People who rhapsodised about French cuisine had never eaten a 6 a.m. breakfast at a roadside rest stop. While Doug got the food, Ellie tried the number on Harry's card from a payphone again. All she got was the voicemail, a recorded epitaph.

They chewed greasy croissants and read over the file they'd taken. Juggernauts thundered past on the motorway, the heavy cavalry of commerce.

The file was in English, though it didn't help much. Most of it was so impenetrably technical that even Ellie couldn't get much sense from it. It seemed to be about a huge coal seam near Lyons which Talhouett was mining. There was only one reference to Mirabeau, near the end. Doug found it while Ellie was getting a refill of coffee.

Project Mirabeau : Unconventional Hydrocarbon Exploration
CONFIDENTIAL
Following environmental concerns regarding the hydraulic fracturing process, this project has been terminated.

'Is that all?'

Doug flipped through a few more pages. 'There's an Environmental Impact Assessment.'

They read it together. There was nothing about Mirabeau.

'What about that?'

Halfway down the page, under the heading 'Sites of Historic/Cultural Interest', Ellie read:

Submerged CHAPEL of Saint Donatian, Norman, XII-XIV(?) Century.
Map Ref: D5
Risk: Low

'At least it's medieval,' she said doubtfully. Doug had a strange look on his face. 'What?'

'It's three hundred miles from anywhere the Normans should have been building at the time.'

'You trust a mining company to know the difference? And what do you suppose it means by "submerged"?'

Doug consulted the map at the front of the file. His finger came to rest on a blue patch near the middle of the page.

'D5 is in the middle of a lake.'

They turned off the motorway and headed east, a long road winding its way through dark pine forests into the hills. Sometimes they'd come round a bend and glimpse the jagged peaks of the Alps far in the distance, before the hills closed in again. It reminded Ellie how close they were to Saint-Lazare's castle, not far over the border in Switzerland. She twisted round in her seat and stared out the rear-view mirror. A tremor in her stomach told her Blanchard couldn't be far away.

'I think this must be it.'

A chain-link fence had appeared on their left, running along the side of the road, penning in the forest. Strings of razor wire spiked the top of it. At first all they could see behind it was trees, but as the road climbed higher they found themselves looking down a steep escarpment into a bowl between the hills. It must have been a natural dip, but heavy industry had gouged it out to make a black pit, vast terraces sinking into the earth. Heavy trucks ground their way up a track like a scar through the trees.

A black haze hung over the valley. There was no sign of a lake. Ellie checked the map.

'The site entrance should be at the top of the next ridge. There'll be a track from there leading down to the lake.'

'Are we just going to drive in?'

'Let's have a look.'

The road took a hairpin bend and climbed towards the ridge. Ellie could see a guard hut, and the red-and-white stripes of a barrier post sticking up beside it.

Doug slowed. The gate was open. A black Mercedes 4x4 sat in the entrance, engine running. It must have just got there, though Ellie hadn't seen it on the road.

'Keep going.'

Doug glanced across. She gripped his arm. *'Just go.'*

If anyone was watching, it would have looked so obvious. One moment the car was slowing down; the next it was accelerating away as quickly as the small-bore engine could manage. Had they spotted Doug and Ellie? Had they noticed the car had UK plates? Ellie craned her head round and looked back: she thought she saw a man standing in the road, gesturing after them. Then the car went round a corner and she wasn't sure if it might just have been a tree.

'Wrong entrance?' Doug asked.

'Bad feeling about that car.' She thought she'd seen a Swiss flag on its number plate.

Doug checked his mirror. 'No one behind us yet.'

They crested the ridge and started down the opposite side. The trees grew thicker, hiding whatever might be coming after them. The chain-link fence continued unbroken.

'Pull in there.'

On the opposite side of the road a forestry track led off into the trees. Doug braked hard and nosed the car in. They couldn't go far – a rusted gate blocked the way – but it hid them from sight of the road.

'Let's get going.' The fear that had stalked Ellie since the moment she stepped into the vault was beginning to close around her again. 'If they saw us at the gatehouse, we don't have much time.'

Doug took the backpack with the box. They jogged down the side of the road where the trees gave them cover, examining the fence for a way in. They hadn't gone far when the baritone throb of an engine intruded on the silent forest.

'Get down!'

They lay flat on the ground and waited. Half a minute later a car roared past and vanished round the bend. With her face buried in moss and pine-needles, Ellie couldn't get a good look at it. They waited until the sound died away, then carried on, faster now.

Ellie quickly became aware that something had changed in the forest. Before, the trees had been an unbroken wall of drab green: now, most of them were brown. Dead needles clung to dead branches; dead trees pulled on their dead roots. Several had succumbed completely and torn themselves out of the ground.

'There.'

On the far side of the fence, one of the dead trees had toppled over, making a precarious bridge across the razor wire. Doug made a stirrup with his hands and hoisted Ellie up: she hooked her arms around the trunk and hauled herself on. The stumps of broken branches scraped and scratched her. One almost clawed her eye out.

'Will it take your weight?' Doug asked.

She wriggled along the dead tree. She was halfway along when she heard the sound of an engine coming back up the slope. She tried to go faster. She lifted herself up and crawled forward like an ant, tensing her hands and feet in the clefts of the branches.

With a horrifying crack, the branch she was holding snapped off. She threw out a hand to balance herself and grabbed a handful of razor wire. It stopped her falling, but sliced a bloody gash across her palm. She screamed, but if she let go she'd lose her balance and fall, probably slice her neck open.

'*Hold on!*'

Doug pulled himself on to the tree and crawled towards her. The engine was getting louder. Gently, he reached round and cupped his arm around her waist so she could disentangle herself from the fence. Wet blood ran down her hand and dripped on to the ground. When she tried to put weight on it, she could hardly stomach the pain.

'I've got you.'

With Doug supporting her, they edged forward. The engine was just round the corner now.

But they were too much for the fragile deadwood. The tree cracked: not a branch, but the whole trunk. In the split second before it broke, Doug threw his weight forward, carrying both of them beyond the fence. They fell in a tangle of limbs and branches and hit the ground with a thud.

The black Mercedes cruised past, driving more slowly this time. Ellie held her breath. The fence swayed. Could they see it? She felt sure they must hear the echo of the tree falling. All she saw was the tyres. She didn't dare look up for fear of making eye contact. Was it slowing down?

It disappeared out of sight. They lay there until the sound had died away completely.

Ellie got up and brushed pine dust off her face. 'How will we get out?'

'Cross that bridge when we come to it.' Doug pulled out a handkerchief and tied it around her hand to stop the bleeding. He picked up the backpack and slung it on his shoulder. 'If there is a bridge.'

They left the road behind and walked into the forest, heading down the slope. The pine-needle carpet muffled their feet like snow. The deeper they went, the browner the forest became. Whatever blighted the trees had spread to almost all of them. Ellie remembered the file. *Environmental concerns regarding the hydraulic fracturing process.* What did that mean?

Ahead, the forest darkness began to lighten to the flat grey of open sky. They hurried on. The trees thinned, then stopped abruptly in a hard line. They both stared.

'What happened to the lake?'

They'd come out at the bottom of a long, wide valley, a hollow cupped among the hills. Once it might have been a pretty spot: now it was a wasteland. Black mudflats stretched from one hillside to the other. Dead trees ran back up the slope like debris from an explosion. In the centre of the desolation stood a sandstone church with a square tower and no roof.

'Is this Mirabeau?'

'This is where the map says. That must have been the submerged church.'

They slithered down a steep embankment and walked along what had once been the shore of the lake. Doug took a tentative step on to the mud. It looked firm, but as soon as he put his weight on it it oozed away, sucking him in. Ellie grabbed his arm with her good hand and pulled him back.

'Perhaps there's a way across further round.'

The desolation overwhelmed Ellie. The more she stared, the more she saw the detritus of the lakebed littered across the mud. Boots and buoys, blackened tree-stumps and rocks. In the middle of the lake, the rotted hull of a rowing boat had a strand of weed trailing behind it like fishing line. Most of all there were the bones: the carcasses of unnumbered fish picked clean. The birds must have gorged themselves.

A gust of wind blew through the pines. The dead-brown

forest shivered: from somewhere up the slope Ellie heard a noise like a small explosion as another tree let go its roots. The grey sky didn't blink.

'What's that?'

Doug had stopped dead. Ellie, watching her footing, walked straight into him and almost knocked him over.

About ten feet into the lakebed, a flat stone lay embedded in the mud. It didn't look like much, until you looked beyond it and saw another about three feet further, and another beyond that, a string of dull pearls leading across the mudflat to the church. Too straight and regular to be there by chance.

'Stepping stones,' Ellie said. 'But how do you get to the first one?'

'There must be a million dead branches around here.' Doug ran up to the treeline. He came back almost at once with a quizzical look on his face, dragging a long plank behind him.

'I found this just inside the woods. Someone left us a drawbridge.'

Ellie gazed around the wasted landscape. 'Who?'

'Probably not your colleagues.' Doug threw the plank on to the lakebed. Mud spattered and slopped around it. 'They wouldn't want to get their feet dirty.'

They made their way out into the lake, jumping from stone to stone. As they came closer to the church, Ellie could see a brown line on the tower showing where the lake level had once been. Only the very top of the tower would have showed. She didn't like to think that where she was walking had once been under twenty feet of water.

'When did this happen?' she asked aloud.

'The Environmental Impact report was dated a year ago. It sounds as if the church was still submerged then.'

The last stone was still a little distance from the church. The

330

ground around it looked higher than the surrounding lakebed: they decided to risk it. Mud squelched under their feet, but not far below they felt the hard grip of rock.

'It would have sunk if it wasn't built on something solid,' said Doug.

'But who built it?'

Doug had doubted the file when it called the church 'Norman', but in fact it was a textbook example: the crenellated square tower; the concentric arches around the door; the shark's-tooth pattern that made you feel as if you were being swallowed whole. The door had rotted long ago, though the rusted hinges still grasped out into space. Through the opening, Ellie saw a twin row of columns leading towards a raised stone dais. It reminded her of the Monsalvat vault.

'It's so well preserved,' she marvelled. 'It must be almost a thousand years old, drowned for God knows how long. But all it needs is a new roof and a scrub.'

'The Normans built to last.'

They walked down the aisle towards the dais. She stared at the capitals on top of the columns. Submersion had softened the carvings to smooth ripples, like the contours of a seabed, but occasionally she could make out the shape of an eagle or a man or some fantastic beast. Were they important?

At the transept they found more carvings. Stone humps pushed out through the mud that caked the floor: at first she thought they might be fallen masonry, but they were too regular for that. When she bent closer, she could make out the vague outlines of human figures lying flat on their backs.

'Effigies,' said Doug. He pointed to one, better preserved than the others through some quirk of the stone or the water. 'That looks like a shield across his chest. They were probably knights.'

'Could there be anything inside?'

They crouched and tried to lift the stone. Water had defaced the carvings so thoroughly there was nothing to grip: try as they might, they couldn't move it.

A noise sounded behind them: not a falling stone or a frightened bird, but the mechanical click of steel. They spun around.

Half-hidden against the mottled walls, a man in camouflage fatigues stood in the corner and pointed a rifle at them.

XL

France, 1142

'A lot of people have been looking for you, Peter. You're lucky we found you first.'

I assume he's being ironic. My hands are shackled together above my head and looped over a hook in the wall; I have to stretch my toes just to touch the floor. My legs ache, my arms burn, and half my face is covered in dried blood. It still feels as if my head's split open.

My captor sees the disbelief on my face. 'You don't know what the others would have done.'

I squint through the one eye that isn't crusted with blood. I'm in a round stone chamber. Arched windows ring it, but all I can see beyond is bright blankness. Grey light drills into my skull. It feels high up, a tower. I can't see a door.

'Who are you?'

My interrogator steps back. He's an impressive man: tall, powerful and solid. He's probably ten years older than me, but there's a solemnity in his face that's ageless. He reminds me of my father.

'I belong to a holy order.'

I can't think of anyone more different from the reedy, God-bothering monks I lived with.

'A brotherhood. A group of men bound to protect a secret.'

I spit blood on the floor. 'What have I got do with it?'

'You've been part of it your whole life.' He folds his arms and stands inches away from me. Even dangled from my hook, I have to look up. His grey eyes hold me like a fist. 'Your father belonged to our order.'

He's too close, his voice too loud. I wish he would curtain off the windows – the light's killing me.

'My father?'

'The men who killed him were after our secret. The secret we kept on the Île de Pêche.'

I spin on my hook like a corpse on a gibbet. I know what he's going to say next.

'You helped Malegant take it. You betrayed yourself and everything your father stood for. You betrayed a secret we've kept for generations.'

My legs give way. I slump towards the floor, but the chains hold me back. They dig into my wrists – my arms almost pull out of their sockets.

Strong hands clamp around my side and lift me upright. His strength is incredible – he holds me as easily as a child.

'The treasure Malegant stole is beyond all reckoning. We've killed men for less, Peter of Camros.'

At last I realise where I've heard his voice before. 'That night in the fog. In the field of stones. That was you.'

'We heard about Malegant's plan and came to stop him. We were too late. All we found were corpses.'

The anguish in his voice cuts me worse than the chains. I can taste salt on my tongue: blood and sea air. *No one escapes.*

'After the attack, Malegant disappeared. You're the last man left alive to have seen him.'

'What happened to the others?'

He ignores me. 'Malegant's been looking for you the length and breadth of Christendom.'

'He knew my name,' I murmur.

'He knew everything about you. It amused him to involve you in his abomination. To rub the salt of your treachery in our wounds. Now that you've escaped, he's terrified you'll lead us back to him. That's why you're lucky we found you.'

He raises me up to unhook me, and lowers me gently on to the floor. I bury my head in my hands.

'Why don't you kill me?' I'm almost pleading with him.

'Because you've got what so many men never get – the chance to atone for your sins.'

Troyes

My heart skips a beat as we pass through the Porte de Paris inside the city walls. The blood sings in my veins, like the morning of a battle: the world is full of brilliant colours and every sound, every movement, explodes on my senses. It makes me feel sick. I scan the crowds for faces from my nightmares, for the goldsmith with the silver hand, for Malegant.

I'm by myself, but not alone. Hugh, the knight who captured me, is ahead dressed as a Flemish cordwainer. Two more of his men are behind me, always watching. They could save their energy: there's no danger I'll try to escape. As long as Hugh's leading me to Malegant, to the secrets he stole from the Île de Pêche and to some answers, I'll follow him into the jaws of Hell.

I go to the goldsmith's quarter and look for the shop under

335

the sign of the eagle. The sign's changed – it's a golden cock now – but the clerks are still sitting at their tables out the front, sliding coins across the chequered cloths like chess pieces. A fat man in an ermine cape oversees them, prowling back and forth, checking their counting. Wine splashes out of the cup in his hand as he barks his commands. I tell him I'm looking for Malegant de Mortain.

'Never heard of him,' he says. He doesn't notice I'm trembling when I say the name; he's too busy watching his money.

'How long have you had this shop?'

'Six months.'

'And the man who had it before you?'

'The shop was empty when I took it. A merchant, a Norman, arranged it.'

I improvise. 'My family had a cup stored in the vault here. Where can I find it?'

He shrugs. 'The vaults were empty when I took over.'

I drift away, but keep watching. From the corner of my eye I can see Hugh standing in a doorway. He's pretending to haggle with a man selling fish pies. I concentrate on the goldsmith's shop. The owner might have changed but the commerce is the same: Italian merchants bring their native coins, and go away short-changed. Some of them leave with even less. They deposit their coins, and take nothing in exchange but a piece of paper.

I turn my attention to the clerks. Two of them are Italian, bantering with the merchants in their own language. The third doesn't join in, but keeps his head down and frowns furiously at the accounts. There's something familiar about him: when the shop closes for lunch, I follow him down the street and accost him in the square outside the church of Notre Dame.

'I saw you at the goldsmith's.'

Suspicious eyes watch me closely. Goldsmiths, even their clerks, don't like strangers prying into their business. I try to smile.

'Let me buy you a drink.'

I take him to a tavern. Hugh follows us in and takes a table by the door.

'I visited that shop a few months ago, when it was under the sign of the eagle. You were working there then.'

He doesn't deny it.

'I want to know about the man who owned it. An old man with sky-blue eyes and a silver hand who sat in the crypt.'

A look of terror passes over his face. He's suddenly very aware of the other men in the tavern.

'His name was Lazar de Mortain.' He stares at the table. 'I only saw him twice. Most of the time he left his steward in charge.'

'The one-eyed man?'

The clerk nods. 'Alberic. He told us what to do.'

'Do you know where he came from?'

'Normandy, I think.'

'But you don't know where he went?'

He shakes his head. I change tack. 'The merchants who give you money and just get paper in return – what are they doing?'

The question surprises him, but he's glad to be on less treacherous ground. 'The papers are bills of exchange. They confirm that the merchant has deposited a certain sum with us. The merchant can go home, take it to our corresponding bank in Pavia or Piacenza, and they will give him the money.'

'If they take in paper and give out gold, won't they soon end up bankrupt?'

'We're doing the same in the opposite direction. A French

merchant coming home from Italy will give the corresponding bank his money, and bring us the paper. Twice a year, we add up how much we've paid out and how much we've received. The Italian bank does the same, and then whoever owes the other sends the money. Usually, the difference isn't much. It saves dozens of merchants all taking gold over the Alps and falling prey to robbers.'

'Did Lazar issue bills of exchange?'

'Yes.'

'But now he's gone. If I held one of these bills – if I came to you today and demanded the money you owed me, what would you say?'

'Guillermo – the master – would pay you. At Ascensiontide he'd send the bill by messenger to a money-changer in Bruges.'

I grip the table. 'So Lazar is in Bruges?'

'No. The man in Bruges is another correspondent.'

I'm beginning to get lost in this web of money, all these pieces of paper with their promises of riches. No doubt that's what Lazar intends.

'Do you know how the money finally reaches Lazar?'

A sly smile spreads over the clerk's face. 'When the Bruges moneylender sends us his bills, I enter them in the ledgers. Once, there was a mistake – he sent us a bill that he should have kept. There was no name on it, but I recognised the writing.'

'Did it say where it came from? How it got to Bruges?'

'It came from London.'

XLI

Mirabeau site, France

The man edged forward. His red hair grew long and wild, matted into impromptu dreadlocks. Leaves clustered on it like velcro. His face seemed to have deep clefts scored into it, though as he came closer Ellie saw it was actually camouflage paint. His eyes were wide and round like an owl's. He had a camera slung around his neck.

'Put your hands where I can see them.'

He spoke English with an accent, German or Dutch. Ellie and Doug put their hands in the air.

'Are you with the Brotherhood?' she tried. 'A friend of Harry?' He didn't look much like Harry – he looked wild. 'I'm Ellie. I broke into Monsalvat.'

Nothing registered. He jerked the gun. 'Are you with the company?'

Yes? No? What was the right answer? He didn't look like a security guard.

'Not any more.'

The gun barrel inched a fraction higher. She'd never imagined the absolute terror that came from looking down the barrel of a gun. She could almost feel the tension of the finger on the trigger, the tiny movement that was all that stood between life and death.

'I used to work for the company that owns Talhouett. I heard some rumours – I thought they might be doing something bad here.'

'OK.' He considered that. Ellie began to think he was as confused as they were. But he had the gun.

'Who are you?'

'Joost is my name. I belong to an organisation, the Green Knights. You've heard of us?'

Ellie mumbled something noncommittal.

'We're an environmental group. You know the old story, right? The Green Knight cuts off your head if you tell lies or do bad things? We do that for companies.'

'You're spying on Talhouett?

He tapped the camera. 'Documenting them.'

'Then we're on the same side.' Cautiously, Doug reached into the backpack and pulled out the Talhouett file. The muzzle followed him all the way. Doug tossed it on to the floor between them.

'That's their file on this place.'

Joost crouched, angling the gun towards them, and leafed through the file. Under the camouflage and dirt, Ellie saw his face soften.

'This is gold. Geological surveys, invoices, environmental reports. Risk assessments.'

'Risk of what?' Ellie said. 'What's happened here? Where did the lake go?'

The gun tilted down a bit. 'Hydraulic fracturing.' He saw it meant nothing to them. 'Talhouett have a coal mine here, OK? The concession expires soon – they have to decide if to renew it, but they've taken all the coal out of the ground. But they think, maybe there is something else here. You know shale gas?'

'What's that?'

'Natural gas trapped in rocks, like you use for cooking or whatever. But the rocks are impermeable, so you have to break them open to let the gas out. You pump water and chemicals deep into the rock to make a fissure. Hydraulic fracturing. Sometimes it goes wrong.'

'Talhouett have been doing that here?'

'Very secret. Very illegal. They do not have a permit, but they want to know if there is gas before they renew the concession. But they make a mistake. They drill too deep, they disturb something. Suddenly, the water vanishes.'

'Exposing the church,' said Ellie. 'So when Saint-Lazare started sniffing around Talhouett, the Brotherhood got worried he knew about it.'

'So what's in here that's so valuable?' said Doug.

Ellie looked around the roofless church, the green scum on the walls, the effigies of the knights with their faces washed away. 'There must be something.'

Joost jerked the gun. Another bolt of fear flashed through Ellie.

'You think Talhouett have hid something here?'

'They're desperate to protect it,' Ellie said. 'But we don't know what it is. Something old.'

Joost considered this. His round eyes drifted to Doug's back. 'What's in the bag?'

'Something we took from the company.'

341

'Let me see.'

A prod from the gun gave them no choice. Doug unshouldered the bag and unzipped it to reveal the square cardboard box.

'What is it?'

Doug lifted out the cube. His breath fogged the glossy black surface.

'What the hell is that?'

'I wish we knew,' said Ellie.

'Don't fuck with me, you people. It looks like a bomb.'

'We stole it from the company's vault. We don't know what it is. We think there might be a clue in this chapel.'

Joost's eyes bulged wide. 'You guys are crazier than me. If you're telling the truth. Maybe if we put a bullet in it something happens.'

He raised the rifle. Instinctively, Ellie moved to put herself between the gun and the box. Joost gave a manic laugh. 'So it's valuable.'

'To someone.' Ellie looked around, wondering desperately where Harry's friends might be.

'Give it to me.'

If she'd been braver, or watching the scene play out on TV, she might have wondered if he'd really shoot her. Standing in the cold, muddy chapel on the wrong end of a gun, her heart almost bursting out of her chest, she didn't doubt it. Even then, she hesitated. Joost squinted down the barrel of the rifle like an old-time gunfighter. She stood stock still, frozen like the stone knights on the floor.

Nye Stanton died trying to get it back.

She felt Doug's hand on her arm, tugging her away. She thought of her mother: her long, lonely years because her husband had thrown his life away. For what?

Swallowing her anguish, she closed the bag and slid it across the floor to Joost, who hooked it over his shoulder. She ached like a mother surrendering her child.

'So where do you find your clue?' Joost asked.

Concentrate. It helped take the pain away. She looked at the knights' effigies.

'They don't open,' Joost informed her. 'I tried. In case there was treasure inside, right?'

She felt dizzy. She leaned on one of the columns for balance. The massy stone reminded her again of the Monsalvat vault.

Where's the most valuable place in a church?

Towards the back of the chapel, the mud floor sloped upwards. Ellie supposed there must be a dais underneath where the altar had once stood. She walked on to it and knelt. Damp seeped into her jeans. She dug her hands into the mud, feeling it ooze around her skin.

On her right middle finger, something shifted. Blanchard's ring – she'd worn it so long now she'd forgotten she still had it on. She took her hand out of the mud, slid off the ring and shoved it in her pocket.

'Did you find something?' Doug asked.

She plunged her hand back in the mud. 'Not yet.'

Halfway down to her elbow, she felt something smooth and solid. She dug in with both hands, scraping like a dog. Doug joined her. Soon they'd excavated a small hole in the silt, down to the old church floor. Through the film of mud that caked the stones, she saw faint lines, like a diagram or a map.

'There's some sort of picture under here.'

They redoubled their efforts, scooping away mud to reveal the ghostly outline beneath. Eventually, they'd cleared a hole about a metre square. Joost brought a water bottle and splashed it over the stones. The tide carried away the last residue of mud, revealing the underlying mosaic as clear as the day it was laid.

They all stared. It looked like a knot, but with straight lines and sharply geometric corners that radiated out like the points of a star or a crown. There was a symmetry to it, almost mathematical, as if it plotted some unknown equation.

'It's a labyrinth,' said Doug. '*On mazy paths* . . . This must be it.'

'But it isn't a maze,' Ellie objected. 'There's no path. The lines criss-cross each other all over the place.'

She knelt in the mud and tried to scrape the edges of the mosaic clean. She took a nail file out of her bag and scratched at the stone, feeling for any sort of crack or lip she might lift.

A shadow fell over her. Joost held the camera pointed at the floor, his face screwed up as he stared at its screen.

'What are you doing?'

'Documenting the site. This is art, right? It's valuable.' Joost edged around to get a better angle. 'We're in France. If the politicians don't care that Talhouett fucked the environment, maybe they care about the culture.'

Scratching it to pieces with a nail file isn't going to look too great

344

on TV. Ignoring the camera, Ellie kept prying at the stones. They wouldn't budge. The mosaic tiles were almost seamless.

'Maybe there?' Still filming, Joost pointed to the middle of the design where the lines made a blocky cross. 'X marks the spot, right?'

But try as she might, she couldn't get them loose. She was concentrating so hard she didn't hear the throb of engines, not until Joost grabbed the collar of her coat and pulled her up. He dragged her to the glassless window. On the far side of the lake, a black 4x4 and two red pickup trucks jolted down a track between the trees.

'Did you bring them here?'

Ellie was trembling so hard she barely managed to speak. 'They want to kill us.'

The absolute terror in her voice dispelled any doubts Joost might have had. He let her go. On the far edge of the lakebed, the vehicles pulled up at the top of the slope. Half a dozen men jumped out: they surveyed the wasteland below, then began sliding down the embankment towards the mudflat.

'Are those guns they're carrying?'

'I told you, what they're doing here is very illegal.' Joost stuffed the camera into the backpack and slung the rifle over his shoulder. 'If they get caught, it costs hundreds of millions of euros. You think your life is worth more to them?'

'What about the mosaic?' Doug scrabbled on the floor, desperate. 'We haven't found anything yet.'

'You want to be around when they get here? Be my guest.'

Ellie peered out the window again. The guards were still stuck on the shore, tentatively testing the mud to see if it would hold them. They'd come down on the far side of the lake from the stepping stones: it would take them a while to work their way round.

345

'Is there another way to get here?'

'Not unless they have a helicopter.'

From somewhere unseen, a low tremor disturbed the air. It echoed around the bowl of the lake like gunfire. Ellie stared at Joost.

'I hope you were joking.'

A small helicopter in Talhouett colours swept over the ridge and touched down next to the cars. Two men clambered on to the skids.

'Now what?'

In the corner, Joost was fumbling something out of his bag. It looked like a pistol, though with an absurdly wide barrel, like something out of a cartoon. He tucked it into his waistband.

'Excuse me, but I think we should get the fuck out of here.' He ran to the walls and made a stirrup with his hands. 'Through the window. They see us if we go out the door.'

Doug took a last look at the mosaic. Ellie didn't wait. She put her foot in Joost's hands and let him lift her up to the sill. She squeezed through the narrow Norman window and dropped down on to the rock. Doug followed a moment later, pausing in the gap to help Joost after him.

The church blocked their view, but the sounds told their own story. Ellie could hear the pitch of the rotors rise as the machine lifted off; the *whomp-whomp* of the blades as it flew low over the lakebed towards them. It seemed impossible that she could outrun it, but she knew she had to try.

The stepping stones seemed further apart than before and more treacherous: each time she put a foot down, she thought it would skid out under her and pitch her into the mud. She looked back, to check that Joost was still with them.

Joost hadn't come. He was crouching behind the church wall, fiddling with his outsize pistol. Ellie hesitated. The

346

helicopter noise was all around them now, almost on top of her. But Joost still had the backpack.

A wall of air hit her as the helicopter came up over the church. It almost knocked her flat on the ground. One of the men perched on the skids saw her and aimed his rifle. She put up her hands. *I surrender.*

But they hadn't seen Joost. Tight against the wall, almost directly below the hovering aircraft, he was invisible to them. The helicopter banked, looking for a place to set down. Joost stepped out from his cover.

A bright light whooshed out of his hands, straight into the helicopter. The cockpit lit up like a supernova. Time seemed to slow down. The helicopter thrashed the air like a dying bird, then plunged to the earth.

Hypnotised by the dying aircraft, Ellie didn't see what hit her. All she felt was the impact – the next thing she knew she was flat on her back. Wet mud sucked her in; it seeped up her back; it trickled in her ear. The ground shook. A bright light seared the sky and a crashing roar enveloped her. Hot breath blew against her.

Then Doug was over her, reaching down, putting an arm under her back and hauling her up. Joost was there too. Behind him, a pillar of flames and black smoke seethed out of the shell of the church. The Normans had built to last, but even they couldn't withstand that impact. The old walls, eroded by their long immersion, collapsed. The fire swallowed them, belching out the fragments it couldn't digest in a series of secondary explosions. A piece of rock the size of a fist flew past Ellie's head, inches wide. A smaller one grazed her face.

She crawled forward, bounding from stone to stone like an animal. Debris peppered her back. Shielding her face with her arm, she glanced over her shoulder. Through the smoke, she saw the men from the cars had come down to the shore. Light flashed from the muzzles of their guns.

'Don't shit yourself!' Joost called. 'From this range, they're shooting wild!'

More shots came. Not far away, Ellie saw the bullets cutting plumes of mud out of the lakebed.

'Keep moving.'

They leaped off the final stone and staggered up the incline to the trees. Ellie's lungs ached; blood was pounding in her ears. She thought she heard a car up the hill to her right, but she carried on regardless. Joost's hand on her shoulder spun her round.

'Our car's that way!' she shouted.

'So are the bad guys.' Joost slipped off the backpack and gave it to Doug. 'This is too goddam heavy. I need my arms free for shooting, OK?'

'How are we getting out of here?' Ellie had been so fixated on crossing the lake, she'd forgotten about the fence.

But Joost was already heading through the trees. She followed blindly, hoping he knew where he was going. A car door slammed in the distance; a minute later a volley of sub-machine-gun fire ripped through the forest. Branches snapped; lumps of wood erupted from the dead trees.

Joost slid to the ground in a narrow defile, in the shadow of a fallen tree trunk. He aimed the rifle and squeezed off two shots. The gunfire stopped for a moment, then came back with renewed ferocity. Several bullets hit the tree trunk, but didn't get through.

'I think there's only two of them,' Joost announced. 'You said you have a car?'

'We left it in the woods on the other side of the road.'

He jerked his head back. 'Two hundred metres that way,

you find a tree with a red ribbon tied on it. Behind it there is a hole in the fence. Get your car: I meet you there. The camera's in the bag. If anything happens to me, you send those pictures to the Green Knights, OK? They know what to do.'

'What about the men with guns?'

'I take care of them.' Joost fished in the pockets of his flak jacket and pulled out a glass beer bottle filled with clear liquid, a cotton handkerchief and a cigarette lighter. He opened the bottle and poured some of the fluid over the handkerchief, then stuffed it in the bottle's mouth. Ellie smelled petrol.

'What sort of environmentalist are you?'

'A pissed-off one.'

He flicked the lighter. Flames flared up from the rag in the bottle. He got to his feet, crouched like a quarterback and threw.

The bottle hit a tree trunk and shattered over a pile of brushwood. The dead forest lit up like a tinderbox: flames raced through the dry grass and pine needles, spreading in every direction.

'There goes my carbon footprint,' said Joost. He aimed the rifle through the flames.

Only afterwards did Ellie realise she'd heard the shots before he pulled the trigger. At the time, all she felt was a surge of confusion, a sense that the order of the world had broken down. A second later she saw why.

Joost reeled backwards. Blood bloomed from three holes punched in his chest. The gun fell to the ground, and Joost fell with it, sprawling into the undergrowth. He hadn't thrown his firebomb far: already, the flames were licking back towards him.

Doug stared, hypnotised. Ellie pulled him away.

'We'll be next if we don't get out of here.'

They ran up the hill to the fence. They found the tree, a plastic red ribbon hanging limp from the branch, and behind it a small segment of fence which came away when they tugged. They crawled through, sprinted across the road and into the forest on the far side. Ellie found herself scampering like a hunted animal, bounding through the woods on all fours as she tried to keep low. Smoke began to drift across the road.

She saw a flash of silver ahead and changed course. There was the car – undisturbed and unguarded. She almost wrenched the door off its hinges. Doug reversed on to the road, changed gears and floored the accelerator. The smell of burning rubber was lost among the smoke of a far greater inferno building behind them.

XLII

Our boat glides up the Thames. Around Woolwich bend we see London like a blot on the horizon. A white stone tower guards its approach, looming over the whole city. It dwarfs everything. Cranes and scaffolds around it show tributary defences still under construction.

'The city's well protected,' I say.

Hugh, standing by the bow wrapped in a dark cloak, grunts. 'The tower isn't there to defend the city. It's there to dominate it. Even the colour is foreign – the Normans brought white stone across the sea from Caen to build it.' He grunts. 'Literally, putting our land under theirs.'

We've travelled together for six weeks now, but the facts I know about Hugh would barely fill eight syllables of verse. He's English. His family must have made some compromise with the Normans, or he wouldn't be a knight, but every so often I glimpse the hatred he has for them. I don't know if he counts me as a Norman. He has so many other reasons to hate me, it's hard to tell.

351

It's almost eight years since I was last in England. Back then, the country was in its springtime – ripe fields, safe roads, handsome towns and well-loved King Henry. Now, winter has fallen. Civil war has split the country open, and the wound is festering. King Henry died without a son: his nephew, Stephen, seized the crown, but Henry's daughter, the Empress Maud, contests it. They've been trading blows, gaining and losing territory, these past four years.

As we travel upriver every town we pass has its gates barred and fires set in the watchtowers. Occasionally, we see strange mounds erupting from the flat landscape, the mottes where castles have been thrown up and thrown down again during the war. Some still show the scorch marks: blackened lumps, bruises on the body of the country. Severed heads, in various degrees of decomposition, shrivel on spikes along the riverfront.

London looks as if it's preparing for a siege. So many ships crowd its wharves that we need three hours just to reach our mooring. The sheriff's men ask us hard questions when we land – even the barrel of wine we give them doesn't deter them. But they don't find the false bottom in our hull, the mail shirts, shields, swords and spears that give the boat its ballast.

We find lodgings at an inn on West Chepe. Hugh takes a room on the first floor, across from the mouth of an alley, and pays the innkeeper handsomely to have it to ourselves. He draws two stools up by the window – hour after hour, we sit there and watch, listening to the drinking, gambling and fighting which drifts through the floorboards. London is a city of constant noise and motion – like Troyes at fairtime, but every day and magnified a hundredfold. The smiths and pewterers and carpenters and masons hammer their metal, wood and stone; the hawkers shout in the markets to be heard over the smiths; and the merchants shout to be heard above the rest.

Down the alley, according to the clerk in Troyes, is the house where Lazar's debts are settled. I want to go and see it, but Hugh's worried I'll be recognised. Two of his men, Beric and Anselm, go and report that the building is locked and shuttered. They pass by twice a day to see if anyone arrives, while I stay confined to the inn, watching men pass beneath the grimy window, trying to make out the features beneath hats, scarves and collars. Even our meals get taken in the room.

Hours stretch into days. One afternoon I ask Hugh, 'What did Malegant steal?'

I've been working up my courage for the last hour to say it. I expect him to tell me to shut up. He stays silent so long I think he's decided to ignore me. At last he says, 'There are things in this world we can't understand.'

'You mean you won't tell me?'

He frowns. 'I mean you won't understand it.'

He stretches out his legs. 'There are objects in this world which have powers we can manufacture. A bucket has the power to draw water. An axe cuts wood. But there are other things we can't explain. The way a single seed contains an entire tree, or a woman's belly produces a life.'

I pick a lump of eel out of the grail-dish on the table and feel it slither down my throat. I lick the salt juice off my fingers and remember the first time I met Ada. She was carrying a dish like this that night.

'You're speaking in riddles.'

'Because I don't understand it myself.'

'Then why try so hard to get these objects back?'

'Because I know what they can do, even if I can't explain it. Their powers are terrifying.'

'Have you seen them?'

'I have.'

'Can you tell me what they look like?'

'Commonplace. They could be any of the objects in this room. But they have powers . . .'

He's beginning to irritate me. 'What sort of powers?'

He waves his hand out the window. 'Look at England. Ten years ago, this was the happiest country in Christendom. Now it's a wasteland. That's the sort of power Malegant stole.'

And then I see him.

It's a Friday afternoon in late January and Hugh's gone out: I'm sitting on my own. A man comes up the alley and stands there a moment, sniffing the air like a pointer. A beaver-fur hat covers his face, but he's too cautious. He looks up, alert to danger from any direction, and as his gaze passes over the inn I see him full on. A grey face wrapped in furs, a single eye scanning the street.

I stifle the urge to draw back. He can't possibly see me in the dark window, but he might notice the movement. He stands there another moment, then eases forward into the crowds.

I rush out of the room, down the stairs and into the street. The sun's almost disappeared, but I can just glimpse the crown of his hat weaving through the throng. He turns right towards the river, along a street that stinks of fish. Fish guts clog the gutters; fallen scales make the cobbles slippery. Half-dead fish flop and flounder in crates stacked by the fishmongers' doors.

The one-eyed man ducks into a wine shop on the corner. The Thames flows just beyond, though I can hardly see it through the fleet of vessels jamming the docks. I stand aside to let two porters go in, then step smartly in after them. If the one-eyed man looks up as they enter, he doesn't see me behind them.

The room is low, dim and smoky: the few tallow candles the landlord's put out cast more shadows than light. I look to the darkest corners and get a vague gleaning of a man taking off his fur hat. I edge around the room towards him. I'm halfway there when he looks up – straight at me.

I freeze. I'm unarmed, and the wine shop looks like the sort of place where brawls are commonplace. A corpse spirited out the back and dropped down a hole into the Thames probably wouldn't trouble the owner.

A man shoulders his way past me and clasps the one-eyed man's hand. *He wasn't looking at me.* My heart starts to beat again.

'Alberic,' the other man greets him. His voice is loud, a London voice trained in its markets and trading-halls.

'Alderman.'

The new arrival takes a seat facing Alberic. White curls bloom from the sides of his cap like hyacinth. His nose droops, his cheeks blush with broken veins. He takes the drink Alberic offers and sips it while he listens. I can't hear what Alberic says. He's facing away, and he speaks like a man well used to conspiring in dark corners. But I catch the reply.

'London supports King Stephen. We were the first to recognise him. When the Empress Maud came to London, we drove her out as a tyrant and a usurper.'

Again, I don't hear Alberic's reply, but I see the alderman's face change.

'London's true loyalty will always be to commerce. War is bad for business.'

Alberic swills his drink. His head moves back and forth as if he's laughing, though if he is, it's too soft for me to hear. I drag my stool slightly closer.

'War is excellent for business. We've never made so much money as we have since Maud and the Angevins invaded. The weak are crushed; the strong charge what they like.'

The alderman looks alarmed. 'I thought we were talking about peace.'

Alberic takes his arm, soothing. 'We are. When Stephen's victory is secured, all we want is to protect our privileges.'

'And my consideration?'

Alberic reaches inside his hat and extracts a limp piece of vellum. 'I thought in a place like this, a bag of gold might be too obvious.'

The alderman smiles. He pulls out his own piece of parchment and slides it across the table.

'This will get you your audience.'

The two men down the last of their wine. The alderman leaves; Alberic waits a few minutes, stroking the parchment thoughtfully, then goes out. I daren't follow immediately, and when I do go I find my way blocked at every turn in the crowded room. By the time I reach the street, he's vanished into the night.

XLIII

Near Lyons, France
'Now what?'

Doug and Ellie sat in a tiny restaurant well off the main road. She didn't even know where they were: an anonymous town, a pretty main square besieged by the usual engines of modernity: hypermarkets, warehouse stores and fast-food outlets. The streets were dark, though it was only five o'clock. She devoured a steak frites and asked for a second helping of chips – their breakfast on the motorway seemed a long time ago. Doug drained a beer and gave the bar a thirsty look.

'I think I've worked out the story so far,' he said. 'We've stolen something, we don't know what it is – on behalf of some people, we don't know who they are – and we're trying to give it to them, but we've no idea where they are and no way to contact them. Is that pretty much it?'

Ellie nodded blankly. 'Mirabeau was all I had to go on. Now . . .' She mashed a chip with her fork. 'I don't know where to go.'

'There must have been something in the Mirabeau chapel.

357

Something the Brotherhood wanted to protect from Monsalvat.'

'If only we'd found it. At least Joost would have died for something.' The guilt turned inside her. If she let herself think about it, she'd go mad. First Harry, now Joost: men on their quests, who stumbled into her and ended up dead.

Dead to save me. Was she the villain of the story, the woman at the roadside with long hair and wild eyes drawing men to their doom? She looked at Doug across the table. Her stomach flipped so hard she almost lost her supper.

I can't do that to him.

'What are you thinking?' she asked, to fill the silence.

'I'm thinking about poems and mazes.'

She despaired. 'We're totally lost, and you want to find a maze?'

'The poem hints at some sort of labyrinth. There was a labyrinthine design on the floor. It's something.'

'It wasn't a labyrinth, it was a geometric shape. It could be anything – just a pretty pattern.'

'Maybe it's a pattern that gets you through the maze.'

'And where is this maze, anyway? Carduel?'

Doug's shoulders slumped. 'I've been staring at this poem for the last three months. I've tried everything I can think of. I've had maps out with pieces of string, drawing lines between Troyes and Carlisle – which is ridiculous, because at the time he wrote this poem those sort of maps just didn't exist.'

'There's nothing else in the poem? No clues?'

'I think the whole poem's one big clue.'

A catch in his voice grabbed her attention. She looked up from her plate and gave him her best don't-hold-out-on-me stare.

'What?'

Doug looked almost embarrassed. 'You know what Chrétien de Troyes' greatest contribution to western civilisation was?'

'Romance poetry?'

He took a deep breath. 'The Holy Grail. It all starts with him. He's the first person ever to mention it.'

It was so ridiculous she almost laughed out loud. But Doug wasn't smiling. Ellie grappled for something sensible to say.

'Didn't the Bible get there first? I thought the Holy Grail was the cup of the Last Supper, the one they used to catch Jesus' blood on the Cross.'

'That's part of the legend that grows up around it. In Chrétien's original poem, *Le Conte du Graal*, it's just a mysterious dish that appears to Sir Perceval while he's feasting in a remote castle one night. A beautiful woman carries it, and behind it comes a lance with blood running down from its tip.'

'The holy lance that stabbed Jesus on the Cross, right?'

'Chrétien doesn't say. Again, that's part of the legend that attaches to it.' Doug leaned forward. 'It's hard to overstate how little Chrétien gives us. There's a grail – not a cup, incidentally, but a serving dish – and the spear, and that's it. No explanation. Perceval watches them go by, and specifically doesn't ask what's going on, because he thinks it would be rude. The next morning he wakes up and the castle's empty. He spends the rest of his life trying to find the Grail again.'

'Does he?'

'Not so far as we know. Chrétien didn't finish his poem – it breaks off mid-line. We assume he died writing it, but again we don't know. Some people think he deliberately didn't finish it. It certainly adds to the mystery.'

Ellie squeezed her eyes shut; she wondered if she was dreaming. When she opened them, Doug was still staring at her, waiting for her response.

She lowered her voice. 'You think this poem holds the secret to finding the Holy Grail?'

It sounded insane. She was almost relieved when she saw Doug shaking his head.

'I think the poem's got something to do with finding the Brotherhood.'

'And the Grail?'

Doug stretched his leg forward under the table, as if he was playing footsie. He gave the backpack under her chair a light kick.

'I think we've already got it.'

Mirabeau site, France

The shoes were miniature works of art. On the Boulevard Saint-Michel in Paris, a wizened cobbler had personally measured the feet, cut the leather, stitched them by hand and polished them until he could see his client's satisfied face reflected in their toe-caps. 'Every pair is as individual as the man who wears them,' he liked to boast. If he could have seen them now, almost buried in silt and ash, he would have wept.

Blanchard didn't care about his shoes. If he even noticed the mud soaking through the hand-tooled leather, ruining them irreparably, he didn't show it. He stared at the rubble of the chapel, the tail-fin of the helicopter rising out of it like a twisted cross.

Night had fallen, but there were no stars: they were hidden, or perhaps they had fallen to earth. The rim of the lake had become an unbroken ring of fire, the wastes of the dead forest still smouldering. Overhead, rotor blades thumped the air where his own helicopter hovered, unable to land. The downdraft blew smoke in his eyes.

The Talhouett security chief came up beside him. 'There

were three of them. Our guards shot one, but two others escaped.'

'Did they chase them?'

'Our job is to protect the site – not be the police. My men tried to put out the fire.'

Blanchard took out a cigar, then put it back in his pocket. There was too much smoke already.

'I want this church completely excavated. Bring in cranes, dredging equipment, whatever it takes.'

'It will be some time before they can get through, Monsieur. The fires are still blocking the access roads.'

'Then fly them in. Or bulldoze the trees. Money is no object. I want to see every stone that survives.'

The security chief was a blunt man who'd served twenty years as a paratrooper in the French army. He'd spent half his career in Africa, overthrowing tyrants and defending democracy, or vice versa, as his government demanded. It had brought him into contact with some of the most brutal megalomaniacs in the western hemisphere. But even in their air-conditioned palaces, with machete-wielding bodyguards cocained up to the eyeballs, he hadn't felt this afraid.

Out of an old habit he thought he'd forgotten, he saluted and ran off, talking urgently into his radio.

Blanchard stared at the devastated church. Billions of euros blown to nothing by a cowboy helicopter pilot and a flare gun.

The improbability of it nagged him. Why send Ellie here, when they knew how hard he, Blanchard, was hunting her?

And what was the Luxembourg break-in about? Again, why Ellie? It was almost as if they were trying to draw attention to the thing they wanted most to hide.

Was it a bluff? A trap gone wrong? Or –

'She's on her own,' he murmured to himself. A smile spread across his face. 'She's looking for the same thing we are, and she doesn't even know what it is.'

Near Lyons

Ellie reached her foot under her seat to make sure the bag was still there.

'You think I've got the greatest legend in history sitting in a cardboard box under my chair?'

Doug nodded. The sheepishness had gone: his face was alight with purpose. She could see he'd convinced himself. For herself, she wasn't sure she even believed it existed.

But what if it does? a voice inside her demanded. *What if it's all true, right there, in your bag? The greatest legend in history – and you've got it.*

'So what do we do with it?' It seemed like such a feeble question.

'Save the world? Achieve spiritual union with the Godhead?' Doug tried to smile, but his tension was manifest.

Ellie slumped in her seat. The magnitude of it was overwhelming.

'I stole it,' she murmured, almost a whisper. 'I went down there and I stole it.'

Another realisation: dark clouds rushing in, piling up like a thunderhead. 'Monsalvat are never going to let us get away with this.'

'We have to get it to the Brotherhood. If only we knew how.'

Ellie pushed back her chair – carefully. 'To start with, let's find an Internet café. Whatever else is in the bag, we've still got Joost's camera, and he died to get those photographs out. The least we can do is send them on to his friends.'

The only Internet café they could find had big windows and bright fluorescent lights, which lit it up like a TV screen. Ellie and Doug paid three euros and took a machine near the back. It didn't take long to find the Green Knights' website. The homepage showed a scan of a legal firm's cease-and-desist letter, with FUCK YOU scrawled over it in red crayon.

Doug took the memory card out of the camera and slid it into a slot on the computer. A folder opened on screen.

'There's a ton of stuff on here – lots of video, too. If we try to upload it we'll be here until next Thursday.'

Ellie clicked through a few more pages on the Green Knights' website. 'There's a post-office box in Utrecht listed. We can send them the card in the post.'

'What about us? That card's got the only pictures we're likely to get of the chapel.'

A sign above the cash register advertised discs, memory sticks and other peripherals for sale. Doug bought a replacement memory card and started copying the files across. Ellie went to a newsagent across the road and bought a jiffy envelope. When she came back, Joost's video of the chapel was playing silently across the computer screen. There she was, scrabbling away with the nail file. She was glad Joost had stayed behind the camera. The memory of his death was too raw.

The camera swooped around and zoomed in until the mosaic filled the screen: a sharp tangle of black lines. Doug hit pause and took a screen capture. Twenty cents bought him a printout of the image. He picked it up off the printer and stared at it. Ellie watched him.

'What are you thinking?' A crease had appeared above the right side of his mouth, a little tic Ellie had seen so often when he was poring over some notes, or staring into space at the dinner table.

Doug looked up, caught in the act. 'I was thinking of a woman called Annelise Stirt. She's an expert on Chrétien and the Grail legend. When I was studying the poem for Mr Spencer, everything I read seemed to lead back to one of her books or articles.'

'Did you contact her?'

'I wanted to, but I'd signed Mr Spencer's non-disclosure agreement.' A rueful grin. 'I don't suppose it applies any more.'

'Where can we find her?'

Doug tapped the computer. 'The all-seeing eye of the Internet.'

He went to a search engine and typed two words.

Holy Grail.

The pointer hovered over the Search button.

'If only it was that easy.'

He added 'Annelise Stirt' to the query and clicked Search. A couple more clicks brought up a page from the Literature Faculty at the Université de Reims Champagne-Ardennes. It listed an e-mail address and a phone number, beneath a photo of an owlish woman with round glasses and long grey hair.

Doug checked his watch. 'Six o'clock. Let's hope she works late.'

The café had headsets you could use to make phone calls over the Internet: Doug thought it would be pretty much untraceable. He bought some credit, hooked on the headset and was just about to dial when Ellie grabbed his arm.

'Are you sure this is a good idea? You said she's the world expert on Chrétien de Troyes. What if Monsalvat know about her?'

'We're running out of options.' Doug turned out his wallet on the tabletop. 'I've got seventy-seven euros and change. You?'

Ellie checked her purse. 'About fifty.'

'That's a couple of tanks of petrol, or maybe a couple of nights in a hotel. And we need to eat. Unless we can find the Brotherhood soon, we're going to end up out of money, out of time and out of luck. Then what do we do?'

Ellie thought, burrowing through her memories for any clue Harry might have given her. All she found were blank walls.

'Mirabeau didn't pan out,' Doug said. 'The box isn't going to open any time soon. All we've got to go on is the poem.'

He squeezed her shoulder. 'Look on the bright side. Monsalvat don't know how desperate we are – they probably think we're safe with the Brotherhood. This is the last thing they'll be expecting.'

Reluctantly, Ellie nodded. Doug pressed the button and made the call.

'Annelise Stirt.'

She sounded friendly enough. Perhaps it was the Scottish accent.

'My name is Dr Douglas Cullum. I'm a fellow at St John's College, Oxford.'

'I don't think I'm familiar with your work.'

'I'm researching the poetry of Chrétien de Troyes. I've made a rather extraordinary discovery that I'd like to get your opinion on. I think you might like to see it too.'

A pause. 'What is it?'

'It would be easier to show you.'

'Can you come by?'

'We're some distance from Reims at the moment.' Doug

checked his watch. 'We couldn't be there before about ten o'clock tonight.'

'Even I don't work that late.' She sounded amused. 'But I'll still be up. If what you have to show me is that important, why don't you come to my house?'

Doug took down the address, printed off a map and disconnected. His eyes met Ellie's. Somehow, through the tiredness, they managed to share a smile.

'This is mad,' she said.

'I'm beginning to lose my ability to tell.'

XLIV

Near Winchester, England, 1143

I almost get a dagger down my throat for my pains. When I go back to the inn, Hugh has me pinned to the wall virtually before I've stepped through the door.

'Where were you?'

He thought I'd left him. He thought I'd betrayed him to Malegant again. After what I did on the Île de Pêche, I can't blame him.

I wait for him to take his arm away, then tell him what I heard. His body relaxes, though his face grows grimmer.

'I didn't understand it,' I confess. 'One moment, Alberic was preaching war; the next he was talking about the king's victory.'

Hugh strides round the room, putting his few possessions into a bag.

'Does it make sense to you?'

'It does.'

'Then what are they doing?'

I don't expect an answer – at best, another riddle. Instead, Hugh turns and looks me straight in the eye.

'They want to kill the King.'

And now we're riding through the night, borrowed horses on borrowed time. Four knights, two pack horses loaded with our armour – and me. The wind sings in my ears.

Somewhere in the depths of the night I find myself riding beside Hugh. We're pushing our horses as fast as we dare, but there's a long way to go – at the moment, our pace isn't much more than a trot.

'Why are we doing this? I thought we were hunting for Malegant.'

'We are.' Two battling lions are traced in brass on the bow of his saddle. Their outlines make an eerie glow riding beside me. 'What Malegant stole is a weapon of extraordinary power. Now he wants to use it.'

'To kill the King?'

'Malegant hates order. He wants a lawless, broken world where his evil can flourish unchecked.'

'Will killing the king do that?'

I wait. When Hugh speaks again, his voice is fainter, distant like a prophet.

'Power flows through the world like water. Sometimes it evaporates; sometimes it pools in deep reservoirs. It accumulates in people, but also in objects. Some of those objects and people bind the fabric of our world together; others try to rip it apart. When two come together, in violence . . . The wounds never heal.'

He falls silent. Afterwards, I can't quite be sure if I dreamed it.

At dawn we find ourselves riding through a broad valley. It looks familiar, and then it hits me with a great pang of loss. I've been here before – years ago, a young squire fetching a bride for his lord. Then it was summer; now, a white hoar frost covers the hedgerows and the trees. In the darkness, I didn't recognise it. Not so far from here must be the hall where I first met Ada, where she braided her hair with gold and carried a grail-dish like a servant.

The sun rises behind us, licking away the frost. Up on the ridge, it touches the flanks of a gleaming white horse carved into the hillside, as big as a church. I wonder who made it, who keeps it so white. I wonder if in the night I crossed the invisible boundary into a different world, a world of signs and marvels. I wonder if I'll ever escape.

We reach a village, a wretched place near the river. Even the church is miserable: all that distinguishes it from the surrounding hovels is that its roof is intact. The other buildings languish half-open to the sky, as if someone started to rethatch them all at once and then abandoned it. But who thatches a house in January?

'What happened to the roofs?'

'They pulled the thatch off to feed their animals.'

I glance around. 'I don't see any livestock.'

'Then maybe to feed themselves.'

It's a town of living ghosts. As we ride in, villagers creep out of their homes to watch us pass. The clothes they wear aren't nearly enough to keep out the January cold. Ahead, a knot of them spills into the road, blocking our path. I tighten my grip on the reins, but they don't look hostile. They're so thin, even my tired nag could skittle them out of the way.

'Where are the women?' Anselm murmurs.

He's right. Their bodies are so thin it's hard to tell, but when I look closer I realise all the villagers are men. Even the ones carrying children, some only babies: scrawny, whimpering bundles barely distinguishable from the rags they're wrapped in.

We halt in front of them. The sullen crowd eyes us in silence. One, with a fur-trimmed cap perched incongruously on his head, steps forward. I assume he's the reeve, the headman.

'Where are your women?' Hugh asks.

It's like throwing corn to geese. A torrent of answers erupts around us, all deference forgotten. I can't hear the words for the noise.

Eventually, the headman quiets them. 'The Earl took them. When we couldn't provide him crops or tithes, he took our women instead. He put them to work spinning and sewing – he sells the clothes they make for a fortune, while he pays them nothing. If they don't produce as much as he wants, he strips them and beats them. They live locked in a cattle stall. Three of them have died there already.'

'Who is your earl?'

'The Earl of Wantage. Jocelin de Hautfort.'

Perhaps I should have anticipated it. Perhaps I *have* crossed into a different realm – a world where my past comes to life and piles on top of me. Scar tissue accumulated over years falls away in an instant. My wounds are as raw as the day Ada died.

'*Who?*'

'Jocelin de Hautfort. His estate was in Normandy, but he lost it when the Angevins invaded. King Stephen compensated him with English lands that belonged to his stepmother, and an invented title.'

The headman's eyes sidle to our pack horses. We've removed the points from our spears, but it doesn't do much to disguise them. One of the sacks has pulled open, showing the dull metal of chain mail inside.

'Are you knights?'

'Travellers,' says Hugh shortly. 'And you're blocking our way.'

A shiver goes through the peasants. They press closer around Hugh. Up on his horse, he's an island in a sea of desperate faces. The headman takes the horse's bridle and leans in. Hugh has to bend his head to listen.

'These lands are exhausted – you can see for yourself. Jocelin gets nothing from them. The only fertile ground he has left is this road. He harrows it like he harrows us.'

'What do you mean?'

'He watches the road. He'll be waiting for you. Half a mile up this road, where it passes through a thick stand of trees, you'll find a burned-out cart blocking the way. You'll get down to clear it, but it's loaded with river stones. More of you will dismount. The next thing you'll know, you'll have a dozen spears at your throats.'

'Why are you telling us this?'

'Look at us. There isn't an ear of corn here that Jocelin hasn't taken. There's nothing left.'

Hugh tugs his bridle out of the headman's hands. 'If we stopped to right every wrong we passed on the road, we'd never have got out of London. We'll find another way round.'

'*Please.*' The headman drops to his knees in the mud and flings his arms around the horse's leg like a child hobbling its mother. It's a piteous sight. He's lucky the horse is too weary to kick him. 'If you avoid his trap, Jocelin will know that we warned you. He'll destroy us – and our women. There are worse things he can do than make them spin cloth.'

'He doesn't know we're coming. Unless you told him?'

The headman bares his teeth, though half of them have fallen out from hunger.

'He watches the road – I told you. He's seen you. He rode through here fifteen minutes ago.'

We lace on our hauberks and devise a plan. I haven't worn armour since I tore off my old coat on the Île de Pêche. A shudder convulses me as it slips over my head, swallowing me. A moment later it feels like my own skin.

We make our preparations. While Hugh and the others withdraw a little way down the road, Abelard and I clamber into the rafters of houses where the thatch has been stripped back. I'm trembling all over. All I can see is Ada tied to the tree, the blood running down the shaft of the spear. An angel sings inside me, the seductive bliss of revenge. Jocelin was never patient: I wonder how long it'll be before he comes to see what happened to his quarry.

And suddenly there he is.

It doesn't take much to be an earl these days. His retinue is two knights, and a dozen serjeants who don't look much better than brigands. At least he's been enjoying the fruits of his estates. His face has grown jowls; his body bulges under the armour, which has a stripe down the back where new links have been added to enlarge the mail shirt.

I clench my fists. Blood beads on my palms where my nails break the skin.

He rides up to the headman and puts his spear against the man's throat. I almost choke on the memory of Ada.

'Where are they?'

Even his voice sounds fat. A slow, uninflected drawl, none of his father's subtlety. A man content to stuff himself on easy pickings.

'They took a different path.' The headman keeps his eyes

372

downcast. A wide scar, crusted black, runs down his cheek. The mark of Jocelin's lordship.

'*Liar!*' Jocelin wheels his horse round. 'There is no other path. Did you warn them?'

'We told them nothing.'

Jocelin tickles the man's neck with his spear. 'You betrayed me. I warned you, but you disobeyed. Now –'

A shriek tears through the village. A piglet comes out of one of the houses and gallops up the road. Smoke trails behind it: someone's tied a burning bundle of straw to its tail.

With whoops of delight, the serjeants break ranks and race after it. Some of them even drop their spears. Jocelin laughs and doesn't try to stop them. He reverses his spear and strikes the headman hard against his skull.

'How is a lord supposed to live if his serfs betray him?'

The smile withers on his face. Suddenly the street is full of men pouring out of the houses and surrounding the serjeants. The weapons they carry are primitive – knives and sickles, billhooks and mallets, even roof-timbers from their own houses – but their attack is lethal. They surround the serjeants. Some men act as living shields, soaking up the blows with their bodies, so that the men behind can get through. They beat and bite the weapons out of the soldiers' hands; they drag them to the ground; they tear them to pieces.

Jocelin and his knights spur forward. Gornemant once said: it's not birth that makes a man a knight, or training or skill – it's his horse. A mob of brutalised villagers can take down a whole host of foot-soldiers, but even three knights can put them to flight.

A pile of rubbish and rubble sits in the middle of the street – carefully laid there an hour earlier. The knights split around it like water round a rock, so close to the houses they almost brush shoulders with the thatch-poles. Praise be – Jocelin comes my way.

I count off the paces. Too soon, I'll be trampled underfoot; too late, I'll just bounce off the horse's rear. I time it to perfection. Just like we used to do in the orchard at Hautfort, I hurl myself off the roof, hug my arms around the rider and let my momentum carry us both. Jocelin comes off the horse; I tuck my head against his chest to protect myself as we both crash to the ground. Something snaps as he lands on a loose rock, though it isn't me. I'm winded, but unhurt.

Across the road, Anselm's unhorsed his opponent: they're wrestling on the ground. Further on, Hugh and the others have the third knight surrounded. I pick up the shield Jocelin dropped and pull my spear out from the thatch where I hid it earlier. Behind me, I hear a clang. Jocelin's ripped off his helmet. He staggers to his feet.

So many years I dreamed of revenge, but now that it comes it happens almost too easily. I've lost some muscle since I gave up fighting, but I'm lean and strong. Jocelin probably hasn't used his sword in years. The boy who delighted in physical courage has grown fat and slow, a bully throwing his weight around in a badly fitting coat of armour. And he hurt himself in the fall.

He draws his sword. I sidestep his lunge and punch him in the face with the boss of my shield. Blood trickles from his nose. I see Ada again, the blood flowing out of her. I grab his sword arm, twist it around and chop it with my shield rim. The bone cracks. He steps back – but his spur catches in the ground. He sprawls flat in the mud, flapping like a fish stranded above the tidemark.

I put my foot on his throat and raise my spear. It hovers over Jocelin's face. He goes cross-eyed trying to look at it.

374

'*Look at me.*'

He can't see beyond the spear tip. I draw it back to strike. Jocelin's pupils pull apart as if tied to a string.

Will killing him heal my wound?

The weight of the spear in my hand tells me *yes*. It tugs at my shoulder, coaxing me to strike. I want to believe it.

But my arm's numb – it won't move. I remember the hermit – *Will you show love to the loveless, pity to the pitiless?*

I killed Ada. I thought I could play Tristan to her Yseult, and write unhappiness out of our story. I forgot that for every Tristan, there's also a King Mark. If I'd wanted to kill Jocelin, I could have found him any time I liked. The real reason I didn't, why I drifted around tournaments and mercenaries nursing my fantasies of storming Hautfort, was that in my heart I knew it was my fault.

Jocelin stole her and tied her to the tree. It was Jocelin's man who threw the spear. If I was lying in the mud now under his blade, I'd already be dead. How much of my life have I spent waiting for this moment?

Pity to the pitiless.

The spear's like lead in my hand. My arm's trembling. I can't hold it still any longer.

It's easier just to plunge it down.

XLV

Annelise Stirt lived in the Champagne country south-east of Reims: a land of rolling valleys with vineyards on every hill. Ellie and Doug passed through village after village of squat, sandstone houses: shuttered windows and locked doors in the moonlight. They saw no one. Just as Ellie decided they'd missed it, Doug pulled up at a pair of wrought iron gates, framing a long gravel driveway.

'Are you sure this is right?' Ellie had imagined that all academics lived in houses like Doug's: cramped, shabby places mainly meant to accommodate books. Dr Stirt's house was a full-on chateau: a three-storey mansion with tall bay windows, a gaggle of subordinate outbuildings and a turret hanging off one corner.

'This is where the map says. It looks as if she's still awake.'

The drive had taken longer than they'd expected – it was after eleven now – but light still shone from the downstairs windows. Ellie scanned the shadows around the house, wondering what they harboured.

'Let's leave the car here,' she said.

'If anyone's there, they'll already have seen us.'

'That's not exactly reassuring.'

'I'll go up and have a look. If anything happens, drive like hell.'

I've already put you in far too much danger, Ellie wanted to say. But Doug had opened the door and slipped into the night. Ellie watched him stride up the drive, his lanky silhouette moving with purpose. If he felt any fear, he didn't show it. Ellie was trembling all over.

You don't deserve this, she whispered to him. *You don't deserve what I've done to you.*

Doug reached the top of the drive and looked around. Ellie watched him go left, then right, peering around the corners of the house. Her heart went into overdrive as he vanished behind an outbuilding, some sort of garage or workshop, but a moment later he was back, waving the all-clear to her.

She drove up the driveway and joined him at the door. Doug lifted the knocker – but before he'd let it drop the door swung in. A tall woman stood in the doorway, prettier than her photo on the website. She wore her greying dark hair loosely tied back, framing a heart-shaped face with round cheeks and a dimpled mouth.

'Dr Cullum?'

Doug shook her hand. 'This is my colleague, Ellie Stanton.'

As they shook hands, Ellie realised how filthy she must look. She'd washed her face at the restaurant, and brushed off all the mud she could, but there were still big stains down her jeans where she'd fallen in the lake, and her hair stank of smoke.

'We had a flat tyre. I tripped and fell in a ditch while I was changing it.'

'You poor thing.' Annelise Stirt put an arm around Ellie's shoulders and steered her through into a flagstoned hallway lined with paintings of hounds. 'Do you want to change? Have you eaten?'

Doug demurred. 'We've already kept you up far too late.'

Annelise led them into an elegant drawing room. A log smouldered in the hearth; a pair of gleaming shotguns were mounted above it, and long brocade curtains draped the windows. All the furniture looked at least a hundred years old.

'I'll just put the kettle on.'

Annelise disappeared. Ellie perched on the edge of a golden-upholstered chaise longue and hoped the mud wouldn't stain it. She felt like a lost soul finding an oasis in the desert, unwilling to believe its shimmering welcome could be anything more than a mirage. Everything around her seemed so soft and warm and comforting she thought she might cry.

Annelise came back carrying a tray. As well as the teapot and three mugs, she'd brought a plate piled with cured meats, sliced baguette and a steak pie cut into quarters.

'I had a rummage in the fridge. You look as if you could use feeding up.'

Ellie gave decorum about five seconds, then descended on a piece of pie. 'It's a beautiful house,' she mumbled through a mouthful of crumbs.

'My father was Scottish and my mother German, but both of them wanted to be French. This house was their way of achieving it.' Annelise sat back in a deep armchair and curled her legs under her. 'But you didn't come here to admire my home.'

'We wanted to talk about your research interests,' said Doug.

'You can say it – the Holy Grail. I know it's a bit of a dirty word in academic circles.' She settled back in her chair. 'Actually, I'm rather glad to see you hesitate. So many of the people I come across are fanatical on the subject.'

Ellie spread thick butter on the bread and added a slice of ham.

'In this field, there are two kinds of people: scholars, and crazies. I try to avoid the crazies, but you can't be a scholar – a proper scholar – and not come up against them from time to time. They talk about the Knights Templar, tarot cards, the bloodline of Jesus, Freemasons, all that conspiratorial stuff. Sometimes you have to admire their ingenuity, but it's still complete rubbish.'

'We're more interested in Chrétien de Troyes and his poetry.'

Annelise nodded, thoughtful. 'I looked you up when you said you were coming, Dr Cullum. Your field is French poets and their classical models. You haven't published anything on Chrétien.'

'It's a recent development.'

'You said you had something to show me?'

Doug glanced at Ellie. Ellie pulled the leather tube out of the bag and unscrolled the parchment. She passed it to Annelise, together with Doug's translation.

'Where did you find this?'

'A friend of the family found it in an attic,' Doug said. 'He knew I studied old manuscripts, so he gave it to me to look at.'

Annelise put on her glasses, which she wore on a red cord around her neck, and read over the manuscript. A glow came into her face.

'You think this is Chrétien's work?'

Doug nodded.

'And you're convinced it's genuine?'

'We wouldn't have troubled you if we weren't.'

'The language seems right. The Champenois dialect, some of the vocabulary. It's obviously Grail related. All those allusions: the bowl, the spear, the maiden. But that much you've surely seen yourselves. What did you think I could tell you?'

'We think it's some kind of riddle.' Ellie rushed out the words, then blushed. 'Now you must think we sound crazy.'

'To misquote Henry Kissinger, just because you're crazy, it doesn't mean you're not right.'

Annelise took off her glasses and rubbed them on her shawl. She squinted at the parchment.

'Some scholars – bona fide scholars – think Chrétien's poems are full of riddles. In the manuscript of *Lancelot* there's a totally unnecessary illuminated capital letter on line 4401. The whole poem is 7118 lines long. 7118 divided by 4401 gives you 1.62, the golden ration. Phi. Coincidence? No one knows.'

She stirred her tea with a finger. 'Have you considered chess problems?'

Doug shook his head, surprised. 'Why?'

'Chrétien has a thing about chess. It features in several of his poems – I'm sure you know this – and lots of examples of chequered floors, horses that are half black and half white, black and white coats of arms, a chessboard used as a shield...'

She gave them a probing smile, waiting for them to catch up. Ellie got it first.

'The poem's a grid. Eight lines by eight syllables. Like a chessboard.'

Annelise looked at Doug's translation.

'On mazy paths a Christian knight
Sought noble turns: it was his right.

'The word you've translated as "turns" –'
'I thought it might refer to tournaments,' Doug said. 'But it wouldn't fit the metre.'

'You could also translate it as "tours". Have you ever heard of the Knight's Tour?'

Ellie and Doug both shook their heads. Annelise unfolded herself from her chair and opened a silver laptop that sat on a gilded side-table. She tapped into a search engine.

'The Knight's Tour is a chess problem. The goal is to move a knight across every square of the board in turn, using only the regulation move – two up and one over.'

'Can it be done?'

'Easily. The problem's been known for centuries; the earliest solutions in Europe go back to the Middle Ages.'

'What does that –?'

'Your poem's a chessboard – each square is a syllable. Perhaps if you read them in the order the knight moves around them it would spell out something new.'

'How would you know which order that is?'

Annelise tapped the computer. Ellie and Doug stared. A geometric pattern had appeared on screen, a spiky tangle of black lines criss-crossed into sharp points and overlapping triangles. It wasn't the same as the Mirabeau mosaic, but the family resemblance was unmissable.

Annelise, with her back to them, didn't see their shock. 'This is what one of the solutions looks like.'

'*One of the solutions*?' Ellie repeated. 'How many are there?'

Annelise moved down the page on the computer. Text replaced pictures. 'More than you'd think.' She read a little further, then gave a rueful laugh. 'According to this website, no one knows how many possible paths there are. Something over one hundred trillion is the latest estimate.'

She gathered up the mugs and piled them on the tray. 'I'm afraid I haven't been much help.'

'Not at all,' said Ellie. 'You've given us lots to think about.'

'It's probably all nonsense. There's something about the Grail that provokes fantasies, even in a hardened old cynic like me. Eight hundred years ago Chrétien de Troyes described a jewelled serving dish. In the next generation it became the cup of Christ. In the German tradition it's a stone that fell from heaven. Now people want you to believe that it's the body of Jesus' love child, or esoteric wisdom. Did you know, there are scholars who argue that Chrétien intended his poem to be as infuriating as possible? He piles up these dense, allusive symbols like a dream, and never tells you what they mean; his plot spins out of control without resolution, and then he leaves the whole thing unfinished. Perhaps it's just a joke, to drive people mad with wondering.'

'You don't think it's a joke,' Ellie said. She tucked the leather tube back in the bag and stood. 'But we've kept you up much too late.'

'Do you have somewhere to stay?'

'We'll find a hotel.'

'Not around here, at this time of night. Stay here. You'd be very welcome.'

Ellie glanced at Doug. A vision of bed, of clean sheets and soft covers and hot water, danced before her eyes.

'It's very kind of you –'

Annelise made an embarrassed gesture around the grand house. 'I've plenty of rooms.'

The room she gave them was warm and snug. Doug had to physically drag Ellie out of the shower so he could have a turn. She left her clothes in a corner and curled up naked under the heavy duvet. Her head sank into the pillow – when Doug joined her ten minutes later, she was already almost asleep. He curled around her and wrapped her in his arms.

'That Knight's Tour . . .'

'I know . . .'

'I've got it in the bag. We could . . .'

'Shhh . . .' She didn't want to think about it.

Ellie woke in darkness. The luminous hands on the bedside clock glowed quarter to four. She lay there a moment, remembering where she was, savouring the dark peace of the night. She was safe and warm; she had nowhere to go. She listened to Doug's breathing soft and even beside her, like a mother with her sleeping child.

She needed a pee. She slid out of bed and padded across the wooden floor. The toilet was at the end of the corridor, dark except for spandrels of moonlight coming through the window. She couldn't find the light switch.

I feel like a ghost, she thought. *A pale figure, flitting through the old house*. It was hardly more fantastical than anything else that had happened.

She fumbled for the flush. The toilet had an old-fashioned chain to pull, dangling somewhere in the dark. As she swiped for it, something outside the window caught her eye. She looked out.

Lights were coming up the driveway.

XLVI

Vale of the White Horse, England, 1143

The spear quivers in the mud, a hair's breadth from Jocelin's face. Blood flows from a scratch on his cheek. It went very close. Even as I let it fall, I didn't know which way I would go.

His eyes are so wide I think he might have died of fright. For the first time, he looks at me properly.

'Where did you come from?' he whispers.

There's nothing to say. Now that I've made my decision, I never want to see him again. I stumble into the shadow of one of the houses and puke into the mud. Anselm watches me – he can't understand why I did it. I don't understand myself. All I can point to is a feeling, a glimmer in my tangled emotions that one wound won't heal another. Perhaps mercy will.

Five miles up the road we find the farm where Jocelin's keeping the village women. The guards leap to attention as we approach, but when they see their lord being led by a rope they quickly throw down their weapons. Anselm breaks down the

384

door with an axe. The women who hobble blinking into the light are pitiful: their hair loose, their dresses untied and so threadbare they hide nothing. Their necks are gaunt, their faces pale from hunger. And yet their fingers drip with gold – golden yarns they've been stitching into dresses for noblewomen to wear at court. Each thread must be worth more than Jocelin spends in a month on keeping them alive. It makes me almost wish I'd killed him after all.

Anselm cuts Jocelin loose. 'If I ever hear you mistreat your vassals again, I'll stuff that thread down your throat until you choke on it.' He jerks his thumb towards me. 'I'm not as forgiving as my friend.'

We leave them in the farmyard. Jocelin looks as dazed as the women. None of them knows what to do now they've been freed.

It's late afternoon, the sun already touching the horizon, when we find the court. It's at the frontline of a war, but there's not much fighting going on. Looking down from a ridge, we can see a patchwork of red and green tents dotting the fields, all the way from the forest to the edge of a river. A siege is in progress: on the riverbank, the army's set up a mangonel. Every ten minutes or so, it quivers like an insect and a rock sails towards the town on the opposite bank. Some fly over the walls to disturb someone's dinner; some splash into the water. A few hit their target, though with no urgency.

Half a mile back from the river stands a manor house. Two flags flutter from its tower: the two lions of England, and a gold banner beside it.

'Stephen gives his queen equal standing,' Hugh says. There's admiration in his voice, though not for Stephen.

'At Winchester, it was Queen Matilda who directed his

army into battle and routed the Empress Maud,' says Anselm. 'Strange times, when women lead armies against women.'

'Strange times,' I agree.

We ride through the sprawling camp. There'll be no winter grain from these fields. An army moves like a giant: wherever it steps, it presses its boot into the ground and crushes it. These giants have been marauding across England for years now. The imprint will remain long after they're gone.

We reach the manor house. A peg-legged man sits on the grass outside the gate, whittling a piece of ash. The yard is busy with all the business of a court – so busy, no one thinks to challenge us. We dismount and walk straight into the hall.

I've never seen a king before. If Anselm didn't point him out, I probably wouldn't have recognised him. In a long wide hall a dark-haired man sits dejectedly at the head of the room, while the knights at the tables gossip among themselves. They don't make nearly as much noise as they should. Even without hearing what they're saying, I can sense the conversations are sullen and disheartened.

'He used to be the most powerful monarch in Christendom,' mutters Anselm. 'Now look at him.'

Hugh murmurs something to an attendant, who disappears through a serving door. A few moments later, he returns with a man in a vivid blue robe and long fur coat.

'Henry, Bishop of Winchester and Abbot of Glastonbury,' the servant announces.

'A friend of ours,' Anselm whispers to me.

The bishop looks like an older and plumper version of the man on the throne. His fingers are almost invisible under the quantity of rings he's wearing – gold and silver, set with stones that are all the colours of a summer garden. They tinkle like bells whenever he moves his hand.

He recognises Hugh and greets him, then gives me a pointed look. 'Who's this?'

'One of Malegant's men who changed his ways.'

'Can they?'

Hugh answers with a nod. 'Malegant's coming here. We need to warn the king.'

The bishop glances over his shoulder. The King is still slumped in his chair, staring into the golden cup in his hands. A king should be the heartbeat of his kingdom, the locus of all its energy. There's something dreadful about seeing him so alone.

'You'd be better speaking to the Queen. My brother isn't himself today.'

We find the Queen in a cold, square room facing the river and the siege. She's more regal than her husband, with creamy skin and hair so fair it's almost white, hanging in long tresses to her hips. She's wearing a white silk gown, delicately woven with golden flowers.

She listens as Hugh outlines his fears. He doesn't mention objects of power or incurable wounds: he just tells her that a man is coming to kill the King. She plays with the clasp of her bracelet, but otherwise she doesn't show emotion. From the moment she became queen of England, people have been questioning her husband's right to the throne – usually with the weight of an army behind them. What's one more man?

And Hugh's story confuses her. When he's finished, she asks, 'But how can they kill him? He's the King.'

It's a sensible question. Last year, the Empress Maud captured Stephen at the battle of Lincoln and held him captive for months, until Matilda captured Maud's brother and forced a swap. I'm not party to an Empress's inner life, but I'd bet Maud never dreamed of murdering Stephen.

'Caesar wasn't so great that Brutus couldn't stab him.'

The Queen's an educated woman – she understands the allusion. 'But that was in pagan times. To kill a monarch consecrated by God . . .' She shakes her head. It's not that the idea's abhorrent – just unthinkable.

'These men aren't nobles,' Hugh presses her. 'They're godless brigands. They killed the Comte de Pêche; now they want to plunge the whole kingdom into anarchy.'

'Killing a king is not the same as killing a count.'

Hugh acknowledges the point.

'And have you seen the state of our kingdom?' She gazes out the window. Night's fallen, but a crimson glow patches the horizon where someone's house or field is burning.

'Crops fail, barons menace their tenants, bodies go unburied and every son turns against his father. Some priests say Christ and all the angels have abandoned England for good.'

Hugh nods soberly. 'And if King Stephen dies, those same priests will look back on this as a blessed time – a golden age compared to what came afterwards.'

There's something close to despair in his voice that cuts through the Queen's composure. She turns to Bishop Henry. 'You know these men? You trust them?'

The Bishop nods.

'Then fetch me William.'

Hugh and I withdraw to an antechamber. There are still onions hanging from the rafters – it must have been a storeroom, before the manor became an impromptu palace. Hugh paces the room, while I stare out the window. More fires have sprung up – the whole kingdom seems to be burning.

A golden age.

The door opens. William of Ypres, the captain of the army, sweeps in and strides through to the Queen's chamber. We follow. He's a tall, handsome man, with strong features and a commanding gaze. The grey that feathers his dark hair adds to his air of authority, while a lopsided smile makes you want to gain his confidence. I know him by reputation – for years, he was the most feared mercenary captain west of the Rhine. Now he's captain to a king. Strange times.

'These men have come from London,' the Queen tells him. 'They claim a one-eyed merchant is coming after them to attack the King.' A royal shoulder gives a discreet shrug, disclaiming authorship of this ludicrous tale. 'Can you review the arrangements and make sure the King is well protected?'

She's speaking as much to Hugh and the Bishop, for their benefit: she doesn't notice William's reaction at first. The handsome confidence drains away; his face goes grey.

'The one-eyed man arrived an hour ago. He had a letter from our backers in London – and a sack full of gold for our cause. He wanted to help.'

'Where is he now?'

'He asked for an audience with the King.' At that moment, William looks as frightened as a ten-year-old squire. He almost whispers, 'I thought it would cheer him up.'

Guards are summoned; lamps lit. The whole manor is turned inside out. It takes fifteen minutes to establish the crucial fact.

The King's gone.

XLVII

Near Troyes, France

Two cars, black Mercedes, coasted up the gravel drive. They pulled up in front of the house, boxing in the Nissan. Doors opened; half a dozen men got out. One was tall and commanding, with a silver head of hair that shone in the moonlight.

Ellie ran back to the room and shook Doug awake.

'Blanchard's here!'

'How –?'

'Doesn't matter.' Ellie was pulling on her clothes. The stink of mud and sweat that she'd so gratefully scrubbed off in the shower closed around her again. Doug jumped out of bed and started getting dressed.

'How would she have known to call Blanchard?'

'You can ask him yourself if we don't get out now.'

Ellie checked their window. At the back of the house, all was still – long lawns and box hedges bathed in moonlight. Below her, the wall was sheer and bright, unbroken by any drainpipe or decoration.

'Can we jump?'

Ellie shook her head. 'We might not break our necks, but we wouldn't be able to walk away.'

She grabbed the backpack and slipped out on to the landing. A light had come on at the bottom of the stairs. Low voices drifted up from the hallway; shadows swayed on the flagstones, though the staircase hid the people who made them.

Doug joined her. Three floors down, Ellie heard a stair creak.

'We're trapped.'

A bleak desolation overwhelmed her. To have come so far, only to be caught so easily. She should have known it would end like this.

But Doug was hurrying down the landing, checking the doors. Ellie followed after him.

'We can't hide,' she hissed. 'If we're not in our room, they'll tear the place down.' The footsteps had reached the first floor – the awkward sound of big men trying to tread softly.

'A house this big must have had back stairs for servants.'

Doug reached the end of the corridor and felt around on the wall. It was painted white and panelled, indistinguishable from the other walls.

'There's a hole here under the moulding.' He stuck in a finger. With a click and a squeak, the wall swung in.

'*Et voilà.*'

Doug's phone had a torch built in. He turned it on and held it forward. In the diode glow, Ellie saw a spiral staircase dropping away, too steep for the light to make much impact. She pulled the door shut behind her and followed after Doug, chasing the phone's orb of light as it spiralled down. Generations of servants had worn the stone smooth: when she glanced back, she slipped and almost pitched head first down the stairs. Doug caught her and put his finger to her lips.

'Careful.'

Ellie listened. She could hear voices again – below them, around the corner, too muffled to be in the stairwell. As they crept down, a bar of light appeared in front of them, pouring in through a round hole in the wall.

'It must be the latch for another entrance.'

Ellie knelt and put her eye to the hole. She was looking into the drawing room where they'd sat earlier. The fire had gone out, but all the lights were on. Annelise Stirt stood beside the fireplace clutching a brandy glass, looking at someone Ellie couldn't see.

'Twenty-five years since he showed it to me, and I still remember it like yesterday,' Annelise said. 'And I never lost your number. Just in case'

'Very fortunate.' Blanchard's voice, cool and unshakeable as ever. Ellie's mouth was dry as salt. 'Mr Spencer will be delighted to have it back.'

Annelise took a sip of her brandy. Her movements were snatched; the glass banged on the mantel when she put it down.

'You don't know how much I've wanted to see it again. Ever since Mr Spencer invited me to his chateau, I've been like a latter-day Sir Perceval. I spent a night in a castle and saw wondrous things, and ever since I've been trying to get back to it. Of course, I never breathed a word.'

'If you had –'

Shouts echoed through the house: through the hole in the door, and down the stair-shaft as well, so they seemed to come from all around. A thump echoed down to them. Someone was pounding on the door above.

Doug pulled Ellie to her feet.

'They know we've gone.'

More pounding. Ellie heard a creak, then a crash and angry shouts. She looked around. They were on the ground floor, but the stairs didn't end. There must be a basement. She didn't dare go into the drawing room with Blanchard there. They carried on down.

The light from Doug's phone stopped in front of an old door, thick timbers studded with nails and banded with iron bars. It wasn't locked – they pushed through. On the far side, they found a pair of heavy bolts. Doug slammed the door and shot them home.

'That should hold them for a while.'

'Where are we?'

Doug swung the light around, giving glimpses of brick vaults and cavernous spaces. A few dusty barrels sat in the shadows.

'These would have been the old champagne cellars. The chateau must have had a vineyard attached to it at one stage.'

'So where now?'

Doug shone the light around the room again, more slowly this time. 'Champagne ferments in huge barrels. There's no way they ever got them through the servants' entrance.'

Footsteps descended to the far side of the door and stopped. Ellie gazed at the bolts and wondered how long they'd hold.

'Are you in there, Ellie?'

Blanchard's voice. The sound of it was like a spell, gripping her throat so she couldn't speak.

'You're trapped, Ellie. Open the door.'

He waited.

'I always knew you were special, Ellie. You've done better than anyone in eight hundred years. You've led us quite a chase. But it's over now. You have some things that belong to us. Give them back, and we will have no hard feelings.'

Behind her, Doug was rummaging in a corner. Ellie still couldn't speak. Blanchard began to sound irritated.

'And you, Douglas Cullum. Did you come to rescue your friend? How chivalrous of you – especially considering how she treated you.' A dry laugh. 'Perhaps she did not tell you? She betrayed you. She gave herself to me completely. You were nothing to her – until she discovered she had a use for you.'

Ellie felt as if she were made of glass, as if a hammer blow had just shattered her into a million pieces. She glanced over her shoulder. Doug had half-vanished into a recess between two pillars, struggling with something in the wall.

'My patience is not infinite, Ellie. Open the door.'

She heard some noises she couldn't decipher – a shuffling, a murmur, a click. What –?

An almighty explosion detonated through the cellar, echoing off the vaults until Ellie thought her head would crush in. The door shook: dust billowed off it like an old carpet. But it didn't give.

Someone grabbed her from behind. She screamed, though with her ears still ringing from the blast she barely heard it. It was Doug, grim-faced. He was saying something, but the words wouldn't register. He dragged her to the recess in the wall, where a wide low door stood open. Another blast shivered the door – Doug mouthed something that looked like 'shotgun'.

He led her down a low, stone-walled tunnel that ended in a wooden ladder and a trapdoor. An open padlock had been hooked through the hasp: Doug pulled it off and pushed the trap door open.

They'd come up in one of the outbuildings. Through a window in the back wall, Ellie could see the chateau standing tall and proud about twenty yards away. The building must have once been part of the winery: now it was a garage. A green Land Rover filled the room, and the walls were loaded with gardening tools. A set of car keys on a champagne-cork key ring hung from a hook. Doug threw them to Ellie.

'You drive.'

'Where are you going?'

'Just be ready.'

Doug took a rusted sledgehammer from one of the shelves. The look on his face was so fierce she was relieved when he hurried outside with it. Ellie climbed in the Land Rover and started the engine.

For a few moments the night was unutterably still. Ellie sat there in the dark, shaking so hard she wondered if she'd be able to drive. She looked at the backpack on the back seat, scuffed and muddy from their ordeals. She thought about throwing it out of the car, leaving it for Blanchard and just running away, somewhere they'd never be found.

The sound of smashing glass broke the silence. A second later, Doug came haring into the garage. He threw himself into the passenger seat, gasping for breath.

'*Drive!*'

Ellie jammed her foot on the accelerator, The garage doors weren't quite open – she clipped them as she went out, spun on the gravel and careered down the driveway. The rear-view mirror lit up as floodlights came on outside the chateau. She glimpsed movement, figures running to the cars. To her horror, the cars started moving.

'I thought you broke them.'

'I smashed the headlights. They can't chase us far if they can't see where they're going.'

The gates loomed ahead, and the road beyond.

'Which way?'

'Whichever.'

She reached the road and turned right. She accelerated so fast she didn't have time to look back.

Destrier skidded the Mercedes through the gates and stopped. He wouldn't get far on those country roads without head-lights. He leaped out of the car and ran round to the boot. From a canvas bag he took a long rifle with a telescopic sight. He steadied it on the roof of the car and aimed. The speeding Land Rover zoomed into focus, tail lights heading towards a stand of trees. The high-beams threw up a curtain of light in front of it so he had a clear silhouette of the driver.

His finger tightened on the trigger.

XLVIII

Wiltshire, England, 1143

At least there's no body.

Hugh says, 'They're keeping it somewhere safe. They'll take the King and use it there.' He doesn't say what *it* is.

The sentries get called in and questioned. Everyone's seen something, even if he's just made it up to please the Queen. Precious hours go by while we sift the facts from the lies. Scouts ride out in every direction. All they know is that they're looking for a one-eyed mercer – the Queen won't let anyone know the truth.

'You can imagine the value the Empress will get out of his plight if it comes out he was kidnapped by a merchant.'

What she means is that half of England no longer believes Stephen's the legitimate king. If word of this gets about, he'll be finished. If we get him back alive.

Servants bring logs: the fire burns all night. The Queen and Bishop Henry sit up in the Queen's apartment, while Hugh and William stride around the manor fetching men, provisions and arms. I loiter by a tapestry and don't get noticed. A company of knights is assembled in the courtyard, but there's light in the sky and they still don't know which way to go.

Just before dawn, one of the scouts gallops into the courtyard. He's found a herdsman on the Monmouth Road who saw six men riding quickly towards Wales. Three rode abreast, one wrapped in a hooded cloak held between the others. He remembers the man at their head, a giant of a man in black armour, mounted on an enormous black charger.

It's enough for William. We clamber into our saddles and ride out.

We can't go in force – we'd move too slowly, and alert the King's enemies that something was wrong. William's chosen thirty knights, together with Beric, Anselm, Hugh and me. I think about this weapon Malegant has, that he intends to use on the King, and wonder if we're enough.

The roads are almost empty. Whoever's abroad, they hear our band of knights, swords flashing, armour jangling, and assume the worst. Everywhere we go, the hedgerows shiver and the trees whisper with the echo of just-vanished voices.

Early afternoon brings us to a river, so wide even an arrow couldn't get across. We're near the sea: curlews pick at worms in the sand, and rank smells drift up off strands of weed. It looks so foreign that when Hugh says the name I can hardly credit it. *The Severn*. The last time I saw this, I was a ten-year-old orphan on my way to Hautfort. And I was in a boat.

'They can't have crossed here.' William circles his horse on the riverbank. There's no way a horse could swim it. There are mooring posts for a ferry, but the only boat is a waterlogged hulk, almost submerged.

Anselm points to the hull. There are holes in the bow, the

axe-marks still visible. It wasn't done today: the splintered wood has rotted black.

'Someone doesn't want us crossing.'

We ride along the shore, until we come to a large boulder blocking our path. We splash into the shallows, and as we come around it we see a boat with two men aboard floating a little way off. We pause, waiting for the current to bring them towards us, but they stay perfectly still. They're anchored fast. At the front of the boat a man baits a fishing line with a minnow and casts it into the river.

Hugh rides out as far as he dares and hails them. 'Is there a ford or a bridge across this river?'

The fisherman frowns and puts down his line. Hugh's frightened the fish.

'Nothing.'

'A boat?'

'None bigger than this one.' He eyes the knights gathered on the foreshore. 'There's no way to get a horse across for twenty leagues.'

'Have you seen another group of knights come this way? Five men and a prisoner?'

'They came through this morning.'

'Did they cross?'

'Not here.' He extends an arm, pointing upstream. 'That way.'

The river shrinks as we follow it. The tide's going out: long sandbars surface in the water. Hugh keeps glancing at the river – I can see he's tempted. But the sandbars have their own hazards: they push the water into narrow channels, where it flows fast and deep.

Eventually, Hugh calls William to halt. 'We can cross here.'

William shakes his head. 'It's too dangerous.'

'So's delay.'

The bank on the far side is almost sheer where the river's carved away the sand. But the channel looks narrow – I'm sure I've jumped wider before.

'Let me try.'

I strip down to my tunic so the armour won't weigh me down, draw back a little way, then touch my spurs and come springing forward at a gallop. The horse leaps. His back rises under me, lifting me in the air. I lean forward, gripping his flanks with my knees, dizzy with the speed.

With an enormous splash, we hit the water. I've misjudged the distance – but not the horse. He strains forward, his head tipped back. His powerful legs churn against the current. For a minute I feel I'm straddling a barrel: it's all I can do to keep from rolling over. Then his body stiffens. He's touched bottom. Water cascades off his flanks as he digs his way up the bank, spraying sand behind him. He reaches the top and collapses to his knees, his lungs groaning.

I'm not much better off. I scramble out of the saddle and turn back to face the others. I cough the water from my chest, then shout, 'You see?'

Thirty-odd faces stare back at me with a mixture of admiration and disbelief. Even at that distance, I can see no one's going to follow me.

'Stay with the river,' Hugh shouts. 'Look for the place where they crossed – there must be tracks. We'll find it from this side and join you there.'

I don't like the plan. Night's coming, the day's cold and I'm sodden. I don't know how much further my horse can go, and I don't have any armour.

Hugh throws my spear across the river. 'Take this. Don't delay.'

I stand there on the sand and watch them ride off. When they're out of sight, I unbuckle the saddle and lay it on the grass to dry. I take off the saddle blanket and mop the water from the horse's back, flanks and legs. When he looks as if he's regained some strength, I slip his bridle back on and lead him away.

A few hundred yards inland I find a farm track running broadly parallel with the river. I scan the fields for any sign of a farm, but there's nothing. With a sigh, I turn north. I've forgotten Malegant, the King, Hugh's treasure – all I want is a bed for the night and a warm plate of food.

I come into a copse of birch and thorns. It's dark in here, though the birch bark seems to glow with a silver light. No birds are singing – I wonder where they've gone.

A twig snaps. I spin around. A man's standing in the trees, watching me. He's wearing a dirty smock and queer rabbit-fur buskins, but I don't think to mock him. He's holding a bow, and the nocked arrow's pointed straight at my throat.

XLIX

Near Troyes, France

The Mercedes rocked as the passenger door opened.

'I've got a good shot,' Destrier announced. He turned slowly, following the car with the gun. 'Do I go for it?'

It wasn't often that Blanchard hesitated. Destrier opened his left eye and looked at his boss. 'Do I?'

Blanchard stared after the car, the brake lights like jewels in the night. He said nothing.

Destrier got agitated. 'I'm about to lose them in the trees.' No answer. 'Fuck it, Blanchard – do I shoot?' He twisted a dial on the scope to correct the distance. His finger curled around the trigger. 'I'm going for it.'

The gun jerked in his grasp as a firm hand gripped the barrel and pulled it upwards. The shot flew at the moon.

Destrier put the gun down and gave Blanchard a look of pure, unvarnished rage.

'Just because you fucked her . . .'

The slap caught him clean on the jaw, so hard it left him numb. He tasted blood in his mouth. He wasn't used to being hit. It took all his discipline not to smash Blanchard's nose with the butt of the gun.

'That's none of your business.' Blanchard's breath steamed in the night. 'If you want to keep working for Monsalvat, you never mention that again.'

At the far end of the valley the Land Rover had vanished into the trees.

They drove for an hour and didn't say a word. Ellie's eyes flicked between the mirrors and the road ahead; she didn't dare look at Doug. Only when they saw a sign for a twenty-four-hour supermarket did Doug say, 'Turn in here.'

The store was virtually empty. In the stationary section, they found graph paper, tracing paper, and a child's geometry set. On their way to the checkout, Ellie added two boxes of biscuits, some instant coffee and a six-pack of Coke.

'Is there a hotel near here?' they asked the cashier.

'If you follow this road, you have a camping in five kilometres.'

Dawn had begun to crease the sky, blood-red beams splitting grey clouds. They found a sign for the campsite and turned down a muddy track. After a few hundred yards a plastic chain dangling a NO-ENTRY sign barred their way. Beyond it, they could see a clutch of caravans jacked up on bricks, a squat cinderblock toilet and an empty field beyond. A dog-eared sign pinned to a tree announced the site was closed until April.

Doug got out and unhooked the chain. Ellie rolled in and parked behind the caravans, out of sight of the road. Doug took his penknife and fiddled the lock on one of the caravans until it gave.

'That's a useful skill.'

'Misspent youth.' He didn't smile.

The caravan was like a museum: nicotine-yellow walls, orange lino floors and brown formica surfaces. A bare, mouse-eaten mattress covered the far end. Ellie drew the curtains, leaving just enough of a gap to see anyone coming. Doug took their stationery out of the shopping bag and spread it over the table. He nodded at the kitchenette built into the bulkhead.

'Do you think that works?'

She thought the tension might snap her.

'What Blanchard said . . .'

'A coffee would be great.'

She went outside so he wouldn't see her cry and found a gas cylinder nestled under the caravan. Water dripped from the trees; a flock of ravens perched on a power line. To her surprise, she heard a hiss of gas when she opened the valve.

By the time she went back inside she'd composed herself. There was no kettle, but she dug out a pan and a book of matches from under the sink and heated some water for coffee. Doug pored over the papers.

First, he drew an eight-by-eight grid on the graph paper and wrote out the poem in the original French, syllable by syllable. It filled the grid exactly. He drew the grid again on a sheet of tracing paper, then took the printout of the Mirabeau mosaic and used the ruler to copy the path on to the grid.

'Did they have tracing paper in the Middle Ages?' Ellie asked.

'You could treat vellum with water to make it semi-transparent. Or maybe they just used a pencil. Or maybe no one's ever done this.'

Doug laid the diagram over the poem and lined them up so that the two grids merged into one. They fit together perfectly – the syllables connected in a new order by the moves of the knight's tour.

But something wasn't quite right. 'It's an infinite loop,' Doug realised. 'You could start reading from anywhere – and go in either direction.'

'Start there.' She held up the original manuscript and pointed to the gilded *E* at the beginning of the fifth line. 'That explains why he put that elaborate initial halfway through the poem. And if you look at the inside of the *E* there are spirals turning counter-clockwise.'

'Most medieval church labyrinths go counter-clockwise.'

Turning back to the grid, Doug took a clean sheet of paper and wrote out the poem in its revised order, starting with the first syllable of the fifth line and ending with the third syllable of the line below. Ellie watched over his shoulder, double-checking his copy.

The stove hissed as water slopped over the edge of the pan. Ellie found a pair of chipped mugs and made coffee, trying not to spill as she poured. She put one down on the table next to Doug, who grunted his thanks. *Like two little children playing tea parties in our Wendy house*, she thought. His unyielding calm was crushing her.

Doug put down his pen and sipped the coffee. 'I still can't make sense of it. There must be some sort of secondary code.'

A wave of exhaustion broke over Ellie. She fought back a yawn and lost. Doug's face narrowed.

'You should get some sleep. I can work on this for a while.'

There was a rug in the back of the Land Rover. Ellie spread it over the mattress and wrapped herself in one of the caravan's moth-eaten blankets. She pretended to close her eyes, watching Doug bent over the table. He sucked his pen; he tapped a fingernail against his coffee mug. She wished she could throw her arms around him and bring him to bed with her.

At some point her eyes stopped pretending and closed for real. Doug got up from the table and entered her dreams. Some were ecstatic and some were dreadful: afterwards, all she could remember was sadness.

Her first thought on waking was that she'd hardly slept at all – the crack of the world she could see through the curtains still looked like dawn. But when she checked her watch the dial said four o'clock. She'd slept right through to dusk.

The caravan was empty. Doug must have gone out, come back and gone again: a new grocery bag sat on the table, beside a neat stack of papers and a green book. The two coffee mugs stood next to the sink, washed and dried.

Ellie went over to the table. The top sheet of paper was covered in scribblings, random syllables ordered and reordered, letters circled, lines connecting them and crossed out. In the middle of the page, boxed in heavy lines, a single word leaped out at her.

LOQMENEZ.

The book was a Michelin guide to Brittany. A strip of paper marked a map of the western peninsula. *Finisterre* – the end of the world. Some distance inland from Brest, in an empty quarter of the map where the only legend was *Montagnes Noires*, Doug had pencilled an 'X'.

X marks the spot. X is a kiss. X as in Ex.

She peered out of the window. The Land Rover was still there, but she couldn't see Doug. Had he gone shopping? Gone for a walk? His coat hung over the back of a chair – he obviously meant to come back.

She knew what she had to do, though she hated it. *Now you know who I really am*, she told him silently. *I won't inflict any more on you.*

She gathered up the papers in the guidebook and stuffed them into her backpack, fumbling in her haste. She didn't want him to come back and find her there. She knew he'd insist on coming with her. *You'll be safer this way,* she promised him. It was the last, only good thing she could do.

She took the bag of food and hoped he didn't mind. She left twenty euros on the table so he wouldn't go hungry, together with a quick note scribbled on a piece of graph paper. There was no time to say everything she felt – so much gratitude, so much guilt. She simply wrote:

I'm sorry for everything.

She drove away and didn't look back.

L

Caerleon, Wales, 1143

The bow is rough and gnarled: not horn or yew, like the Normans use, but unstripped dwarf-elm. That won't stop it from killing me. Welsh archers can hit a bat's eye in the dark.

I drop my spear and raise my hands in surrender. It's a wise move. More men melt out of the forest. In their green-brown smocks and muddy faces, they look like trees come alive. They bind my hands and lead me away.

We march through the night. Whatever dangers lurk by the roads, these men don't fear them. To be a prisoner is to be trapped in a long, lightless tunnel. I stare at my feet, never looking more than a yard in front of me. I don't think about the King, or about Malegant – I don't care. Instead I think about Jocelin. I remember the weight of the spear in my hand and the tremor of the point as it hung over his face. I remember the flash of mercy. I wonder why I did it. The rope chafes my wrists and I ask God, '*Is this how You repay me?*'

At dawn we reach a city on a river surrounded by woods and meadows. Sea-going ships unload on wooden piers, while a lofty stone tower overlooks stout walls. But if you look closer, the picture changes. The town is like an old fur coat patched with homespun cloth. Holes in the masonry have been filled with mortared rubble, or merely barricaded with palings, while the handsome red roofs sprout straw where the tiles have fallen through. At its centre stands an enormous roundhouse, like a pavilion: stone walls topped with a cone of thatch. The stones look ancient; the thatch is still yellow.

'Whose castle is this?'

My captors ignore me. Dredging words from the depths of memory, I repeat it in Welsh. They look surprised.

'Morgan ap Owain, King of Morgannwg.'

They lock me in a wattle enclosure that smells of pigs and leave me to rot. An icy wind blows rain through the woven branches, though I still haven't dried out from my plunge in the river. I curl myself in a ball and fall asleep.

Hours later – I don't know how many – the guards return. They tie my arms behind my back and slide a rod through my elbows, then drag me like a plough along the street to the roundhouse I saw earlier. Huddled in front of the gate a wretched group of prisoners waits in the rain. I don't recognise them without their armour, until I see Hugh.

'Are these your friends?' one of the guards asks. I nod; he whips the rod out from my arms and pushes me in with the other prisoners. I almost sprawl headlong into the mud, but Hugh catches me.

'They captured me just after I crossed the river.'

'Us too. We found the ford Malegant used. Two minutes later, we were surrounded.'

'What are they going to do to us?'

'Give us an audience with the King of Morgannwg.'

He says the name with scorn. I know from my childhood that the Kingdom of Morgannwg hasn't existed for fifty years. When the Normans conquered Wales they abolished it along with all the other old kingdoms. I assume that now, in the anarchy of the civil war, some enterprising local lord or bandit has seized power, resurrecting an obsolete title to buttress his authority.

William's standing just behind Hugh. 'Don't mention the King,' he hisses to me as I go past.

The guards take us through a double gate into King Morgan's hall. It's circular and entirely open, except for a central pole supporting the roof. A round table circles the edge of the room, with knights and barons seated at it like judges in a court.

The hall is filled with kings – rather, the same king again and again, woven into the cycle of tapestries around the room. A young king, a gold circlet on his head, receiving prophecies from a white-bearded old man. The same king, crowned and older, killing a swarthy giant; defeating a Roman emperor; locked in a great battle; finally, laid in a boat tended to by women in white. And, at the head of the table opposite the door, seated in majesty on a throne carved with dragons and lions.

The King moves. I blink. The smoky hall's deceived me: the last hanging isn't a tapestry, but cloth-of-gold, hung in the space where the eighth tapestry should be. The King sitting in front of it is entirely real: a flesh-and-blood man about my age, with a neatly trimmed beard and a gold crown on his head that looks very much like the one in the tapestries.

I don't know how he claimed his title, but I have to admit he looks more the part than King Stephen did. He lounges back in his chair and studies the prisoners. William has slipped back into the middle of the group, keeping his face down to avoid being recognised. Hugh stands at the front and meets the King's gaze.

'Who are you?'

'Knights from England. An enemy stole something from us. We followed him here to get it back.'

The King presses his fingertips together. 'You should have appealed to me for help. What was it he stole?'

Hugh stays silent. That doesn't impress the King.

'If the king of England wants to invade my kingdom, I'll give him a fight. I'll push him all the way back to the sea, reclaim all of Britain as it was in Arthur's time.'

He's exaggerating. It's a fine castle, but Stephen's army could reduce it in a week. If Stephen hasn't crushed this pretender already, it's only because he's had more urgent concerns. But Morgan's men love it. They're on their feet, shouting and clapping. Some of them pelt us with scraps from their plates. I duck a crust of bread and listen to what they're saying. One name, chanted over and again.

Arthur. Arthur. Arthur.

At last I understand the tapestries, the crown and the throne. Morgan's an opportunist, a usurper papering over his theft with a grandiose title that's fallen out of use. But the title he's claiming is more ancient and profound than the dilapidated kingdom of Morgannwg.

Morgan raises his hand and the hall goes quiet. Hugh's about to say something, but before he can speak I step forward, feeling for where the different torches overlap to make the brightest place. It's a trick I learned as a troubadour – no one listens to a man in shadow.

'I can tell you a tale.'

The King's gaze switches on to me. 'I want answers. The truth. I have the best minstrels and harpers in Wales to tell me stories.'

'Not like mine. I have the greatest story that was ever told in a royal court.'

Another troubador's conceit. No one pays to hear about the moderately interesting.

'My story is the story of Perceval the Welshman. A story no one has ever heard before. A story of secrets.'

Our eyes meet; he's intrigued. He nods.

'Tell me your tale, and I'll see how I like it.'

I lift my shoulders, tugging against the rope. 'It's easier to tell with my hands unbound.'

A guard cuts the rope. I rub my wrists, then walk over to the table and take a cup of wine to wet my throat.

'Long ago, when Arthur was king . . .'

I make it up as I go along. Sometimes I catch myself digressing, or repeating too much, but each time some instinct draws me back to the story, like a blind man feeling the edge of the path with his stick. I watch the King's face the same way I watched Ada's when we sat by the river at Hautfort, catching the things that please him, amplifying them where I can. Some of it comes from the stories my mother told me; other pieces from scraps I've heard in other halls, or half-remember from the books I studied as a child. For the rest, I take the coarse threads of my life, dye them vivid colours and weave my own tapestry to hang in the hall.

I tell the king how Perceval was born in the waste forest of Wales. How his father and his brothers were Arthur's knights, all killed on the same day. How his mother raised him with no knowledge of knights or chivalry, to protect him from the same fate – but how the moment he saw a company of knights riding through the forest, he knew it was his destiny.

I tell how Perceval went to Caerleon where Arthur kept his court. I make great play of looking around the hall.

'It wasn't a particularly great or magnificent court . . .'

Morgan flushes, sensitive to any insult.

'. . . only three thousand knights or so.'

They all laugh. Morgan thumps the arm of his chair and nods his approval. The energy in the room lifts and channels into me.

I tell them more. How Arthur dubbed Perceval a knight, and how Perceval set out to find adventures. How he met the Lady Blancheflor, saved her castle from the wicked Clamadeu and made her his sweetheart, though not his wife. In my story, there's no husband to get in the way.

The hall's growing dim – the servants have forgotten to replace the candles. I shift position; I crouch to keep my face in the light. I tell how Perceval set out again and came to a broad river and met a fisherman. How the fisherman directed him to a castle in a hidden valley, and how that night at supper he witnessed marvels he did not understand.

As Perceval and his host were talking, a squire entered the hall carrying a lance. He walked in front of the fire, so that everyone there saw the wood and the iron point. A single drop of blood rolled down from its tip and touched the squire's hand.

Then two more squires entered carrying golden candle-holders, each with a dozen candles glittering off the enamel inlay. A girl came behind them – beautiful and nobly dressed – and in her hands she carried a grail. The dish was made of purest gold, studded with the most precious jewels in earth and sea, and the light from within it was so bright that the candles were swallowed up in its radiance, like the stars at sunrise.

The grail passed by like the lance and disappeared into another chamber. The knight watched them go, but didn't dare ask who or what purpose it served.

413

*

Afterwards, I couldn't tell you how it came to me that way. All I know is that at that moment there isn't a man in the hall who would not stay there until dawn to find out what the grail and spear mean.

I tell them how Perceval woke the next morning and found the castle deserted. How as he was riding over the drawbridge it closed behind him. How he never found the castle again – how the quest drove him mad. How he lost his memory so totally that he no longer even remembered God. He wandered for five years, forgetting everything, until on Good Friday a hermit took him in and restored him to sanity. How he vowed he would not spend two consecutive nights under the same roof as long as he lived, until he had found out why the spear bled, and what the grail contained.

How –

I break off suddenly. Morgan thinks it's a dramatic effect; he waits a moment for me to continue. When he realises I'm not going to, he rises forward like a man woken from a dream.

'And?'

I shrug my shoulders. 'I don't know the ending. The story hasn't finished yet.'

LI

Blanchard sat in his office and stared at the chessboard on his desk. It was late in the game: the only surviving pieces were two kings and a white knight. He toyed with the knight, testing possible moves.

Which way now?

He was a good chess player – not formally brilliant, no automaton, but hard to beat. He knew that you had to read play not just from your perspective, or even as a textbook might judge it, but as your opponent understood it. *Where does he see his strengths? His vulnerabilities? What will he do next?* On the rare occasions he played against computers, he did badly: he needed a man sitting across the table to dissect, to worm into and ultimately to defeat.

Take Ellie. The moment she'd walked into his office, even in her frumpy clothes and wide-eyed innocence, he'd known she'd be a formidable adversary. Saint-Lazare had called her a pawn: Blanchard saw she was a pawn who could become a queen. For all he respected her, he'd still underestimated her.

He'd failed to block her path. Now she was almost home.

He had one chance left, a single shot. The engineers at Mirabeau said that the chapel was beyond repair: whatever secrets had once adorned it had been blown to pieces by the helicopter. Ellie might resurface, but after their run-in at Annelise Stirt's she'd be careful about showing herself.

Which way would she go? Which way should he go?

He pushed the chessboard aside, toppling over the king with the sudden motion. He took out his computer. His white finger hovered over a button, then stabbed down.

In twenty-four hours, he'd know.

Caerleon, Wales

Thirty-five knights crammed in a stockade makes for an uncomfortable night. There's not even space to relieve ourselves, except by pissing through the palings. At least we stay warm.

Around midnight the King's seneschal unlocks the door and brings us back to the hall. The fire's smouldering, the guards have gone. The King sits alone, wreathed in smoke, as if the dragons on his throne have started to stir.

'You can have your horses, your arms, and safe conduct out of my kingdom.'

Hugh starts to speak, but Morgan cuts him off.

'I'll also give you some news. The men you want left Morgannwg this afternoon, heading north-west. They stopped at an inn to feed their horses – the stable boy heard them talking about a place called Cwm Bychan. It's in Gwynedd, near the sea. Three days' hard riding through the mountains.'

Hugh gives a slight bow. 'Thank you, your majesty.'

A terse smile. 'Make sure you keep your storyteller safe. I want him to tell me how it ends.'

*

416

For three days and nights we ride, snatching sleep and food where we can, never more than half an hour, then back in the saddle and on again. The pace is brutal, the terrain unforgiving. I understand why the Normans never really conquered Wales – why Morgan ap Owain could overthrow them the moment the King's attention was elsewhere. It's a wild land of sheer valleys, icy swamps and dark forests that stretch to the horizon. It punishes the horses. One by one, they go lame or collapse with exhaustion. We leave the riders behind, though it's a long, dangerous journey home.

It feels as if the land is swallowing us. Each day the valleys grow deeper, while the peaks reach further towards the clouds. Snow blankets the upper reaches, vast heights where only God and eagles roam.

On the second afternoon we pause at the top of yet another ridge. Hugh reins in next to me and turns round in his saddle, looking for something.

He points back. 'Can you see them?'

I strain my eyes, but don't see anything. 'Who?'

'The riders. They've been following us all the way from Caerleon.'

'Malegant's men?' I look again; I still can't see them.

'Morgan's.'

'Has he changed his mind? Are they chasing us?'

'Stalking us.' He gives a grim laugh. 'Did you really think your story was so powerful it moved Morgan to mercy? He understood what you were saying, for all you disguised it. He knows we're after something powerful – a weapon. He wants it for himself.'

I scan the long valley behind us, the ranks of trees like furrows in a field. Browns fade to greys as they fall in the mountain shadows. It feels like the end of the world.

*

At dusk on the third day we come to a long lake nestled in a valley. High summits loom all around it like sleeping giants. On one of them, at the eastern end of the lake, a fire glows against the sky.

Hugh slips off his horse. 'That's them. Please God we're not too late.'

We dismount and leave the horses drinking from the lake. We don't need to tether them – they don't have the strength to wander far. We're not much better off, but we don't have a choice. We jog along the dusky lakeshore, hoping the men on the hill don't hear the sound of our arms.

Even on foot, the hill looks too steep to climb. But at the far end of the lake, we find steps cut in to the mountain face, climbing towards the pass between two summits. It doesn't surprise me. I remember what my mother said, how Wales is a wild realm on the rim of the world, how every rock and tree might hide the door to an enchanted land. Stones stand upright like trees; sometimes when the tide goes out, whole forests appear on the seabed. I think these steps must be the same, a hidden road that's opened by a beam of moonlight, or the song of a wren.

Scrambling up the stairs in the dark is agonising work. There isn't a muscle in my body that doesn't ache from so many long days in the saddle. The moon's behind a cloud: we scuttle like crabs, ungainly in our armour, testing every rock to make sure it won't make a noise. Distant thunder rumbles across the valley – a storm's coming. Above us, the flames on the mountain sway into the night.

The last few yards are the hardest: an almost vertical climb up a damp rock face. There must be another way, but Hugh doesn't want to run into any sentries. We strap our swords to our backs and cling on with numb fingers, praying the fire masks the noise we make.

At last I haul myself over the lip of the cliff, and flop belly-down in a patch of heather. I tilt back my head and stare at the open hilltop.

France

The Land Rover had a satnav, but Ellie turned it off. She didn't think you could track a car through its GPS, but the idea of a chip sending a signal into space, broadcasting her position, made her too anxious. Instead, she studied the map book and made a list of waypoints, then set out following the road signs. She stuck to secondary roads as much as she could. She wished Annelise had owned something less conspicuous – a Renault or a Citroën.

She'd never realised how big France was. She drove for hours, but when she checked her progress on the map she still had dauntingly far to go. Around 3 a.m. she almost dozed off – her eyes had closed without her realising it. The shock took her another few miles, but when she felt her eyes starting to droop again she had no choice but to pull over on a farm track and curl up in the back seat. A tractor rumbling past woke her at dawn.

Now she had a new worry. The fuel gauge on the car was edging inexorably down. She stopped at a small petrol station and spent the last of her euros on a few more litres. The needle barely budged.

She crossed into Britanny and kept driving. The main roads followed the coast, but she found one that cut straight through the middle of the peninsula, a winding valley overshadowed by a spine of hills. Even in France, she knew it was considered a wild region – a place with its own language, its own customs, its own ghosts and magic. The needle touched red.

She almost made it. On a road so minor she'd almost missed it, five kilometres short of where Doug had indicated on the map, the engine cut out. She coasted down the hill and nosed the Land Rover on to the grassy verge. After so many hours being carried along by its sound, the silence was eerie. She sat in the car for a few minutes, drawing up her courage. Then she got out and walked into the trees.

The forest was an otherworldly place. Whereas the Mirabeau forest had been dead and brown, this one burst with life. Green ivy hung from the trees and crept over their bark; moss carpeted the floor in a spongy mass that soaked up her foot-steps. At first Ellie found it comforting, a glimpse of spring in the depths of winter, but the further she went the more oppressive it seemed. The colour became alien, not vibrant but poisonous, stifling everything.

Black clouds began massing in the sky. The forest darkened. Thunder rumbled in the distance. Soon the rain began to beat down, and the leafless trees were no protection. It drizzled down her neck and soaked her clothes. The pack on her back felt twice as heavy. She began to wonder if she'd ever get out, or if she'd die of exposure in this lonely forest. Sheets of rain washed over her face, blinding her.

The sky seemed lighter up ahead. She plunged on, slipping on the moss and the slick rock underfoot. She came out of the trees on the edge of a ridge and stared. Below her, a narrow valley plunged away like a scar in the forest. Few trees grew there. The entire valley was choked with boulders, a jumble of vast lumps of granite, each taller than she was, piled up like giant golf balls. A stream flowed around the rocks, sometimes dammed into pools, sometimes spilling over them and falling in cascades, sometimes disappearing into hidden channels below. Moss covered everything.

Something gave inside her. She sat down on the embankment, oblivious to the rainwater that seeped into the seat of her jeans, and stared down into the rocky chaos. She was too tired to cry. She'd been running for days – months, it seemed – and she was spent. Whatever might be down there, or near there, or perhaps not even there – she'd never find it.

She rubbed a trickle of water from her eyes and stared. In the wash of green and grey that filled the valley a bright flash of colour had appeared out of nowhere. A man in a red anorak stood in the middle of the boulder field, dwarfed by the stones, looking as if he'd always been there.

He waved, then scrambled down from the boulder and began climbing the slope. He could have been anyone – a hunter, a forester, a lost hiker – but Ellie didn't think so. She didn't have the strength to run any more. She sat there and waited.

Halfway up the slope, he paused and looked up.

'Ellie Stanton?'

A dumb nod.

'We've been waiting for you.'

Cwm Bychan

A dozen men stand around a huge fire. They're staring at an upright finger of stone on the far side of the knoll. The King's tied to it, dressed only in a white linen tunic: he's on the far side of the fire from me, so that the flames seem to lick around him. Between him and the fire stands a flat rock, like an altar – there's something on it, but the flames hide it from me. Two men stand in front of it – one immensely tall and broad, suited in black armour; the other slighter and stooped, his head buried in the hood of his cloak. I can't see their faces, but

Malegant I'd recognise anywhere. The other, I think, must be the goldsmith with the sky-blue eyes and the silver hand, Lazar de Mortain.

Malegant picks up a black lance from the rock-altar and advances. The King's eyes go wide with uncomprehending terror. Even now, he can't really believe anyone would actually kill a king. Malegant levels the spear.

It's the scene from every nightmare I've had in the last five years. The bound victim, ghostly white; the executioner and the spear. I can't let it happen again. I dig my palms into the soft ground, push myself up and launch myself forward like a wolf. Malegant's so close to the King I'll never reach him in time. I pull a dagger from my belt, grip it by the tip and throw it – straight through the flames. It strikes Malegant in the back and bounces off him, too weak to penetrate the chain mail, but hard enough that he feels it. He spins around.

So does the man in front of me. He saw the knife fly by his face and turns to see where it came from. The fire lights me – standing there, empty-handed, I don't look much of a threat. He steps towards me.

I reach up to my shoulder as if I'm surrendering. My hand closes around the hilt of my sword, strapped across my back for the climb. The knight can't see it. I wait until he's in range, then whip the blade out of its scabbard. I run him through the throat in a single motion.

Forgive me, I whisper to the hermit.

The hilltop becomes a battlefield. Men move like shadows around the firelight, hacking and punching and kicking. Some of William's knights have gained the summit, but not enough. It's all they can do to keep from being driven back over the cliff. At the far end, I see Malegant grab a man by the scruff of his coif and hurl him over the edge.

Malegant turns back to the king, but he's under attack again. Hugh's managed to get through. He charges at Malegant; Malegant sees him come and puts up his sword. The two trade blows: Hugh's a big man, but Malegant dwarfs him. The first strike shatters his shield, the second almost takes off his arm.

I run towards them. I'm halfway there when someone steps in my way. I see a grey face, red in the firelight, and the puckered eye-socket like a screwhole. Alberic. He's got a sword, but I doubt he knows how to use it. I make the merest of feints, then reverse direction and drive the sword into his shoulder.

I suppose he screams, though in the fury of the moment I don't hear it. I just remember his mouth, stretched almost to breaking; his good eye wide open; the skin around his dead eye pulled so tight I think it might rip apart. He wheels away, and in my surprise I let go of the sword. Straight away, I lunge to get it back – but Alberic's staggering backwards. All I do is push him further. One more step, a horrible second as he teeters on the brink, then he's gone.

So's my sword. I spin around. It's impossible to say who's winning the battle, only that it's still as furious as ever. Malegant has Hugh pinned against the rock altar in front of the fire. Hugh's clutching something to his chest with his left hand, while fending off Malegant's strokes with his sword.

You've got what so many men never get – the chance to atone for your sins.

I grab a brand from the fire and run towards them. Malegant beats Hugh's sword aside and pins his arm back against the rock. With his other hand he wrests away the thing Hugh's holding, an egg-shaped white stone. Hugh bucks and writhes like a bird in a trap, but he can't get free.

As casually as if it were a piece of fruit, Malegant tosses the stone aside. His gauntleted hand pulls away Hugh's sword, reverses it, and puts it to Hugh's throat.

The brand in my hand blazes like a comet. Malegant sees it and steps away, turning to face me. He has a sword in each hand now, a death-angel coming to claim me. Away on the next mountain, a flash of lightning illuminates the sky. I power on, swinging the torch wildly towards him.

Those swords could have cut off my head like a pair of scissors, but Hugh launches himself up and crashes into Malegant, hugging him so tight the swords can't touch him. Malegant tries to shrug him off, but Hugh clings on. The two men wheel away, locked in their embrace.

Now it's my turn to rescue Hugh. But as I run on, my foot catches something on the ground. I fall forward and land on my knees. In the flow of battle I almost ignore it, but some sixth sense makes me look back to see what tripped me.

It's the lance.

Malegant must have dropped it when Hugh attacked him. I reach down and prise it out of the mud. Almost before I have it in my hand, I sense a movement from my right. The whole hilltop is a mêlée of breakneck violence and motion, but I have an instinct, honed in the chaos of the tournament field, for when it's coming at *me*. I wheel round.

Lazar is running towards me. His hood's fallen back; his bony face looks skeletal in the firelight. He moves quickly, despite his age. His silver hand presses the white rock to his chest; the other holds a curved knife.

Sheer reflex makes me lift the spear. It's heavier than I expect – I don't know what it's made of, but it seems to soak up the light. Lazar doesn't see it in the flickering darkness. All I have to do is hold it steady. Lazar does the rest.

Loqmenez

424

Ellie followed the man down the slope. There were no marks that she could see, but he led her unerringly between the rocks to a hollow on the far side of the valley in the shadow of a vast boulder. A torrent of water poured down over its face and vanished into a crevice. Peering down, Ellie saw white foam bubbling far below.

'It's a bit of a squeeze,' her guide apologised. 'Try not to touch the water.'

She gazed uncertainly into the hole. 'You want me to go in there?'

'It's not as bad as it looks. I'm Leon, by the way.' He stuck out his hand and Ellie shook it. He was older than she'd expected, probably in his fifties, but thin and wiry. With his thinning hair and his rimless spectacles, he reminded her of her fifth-form geography teacher.

'You've done an extraordinary job. We're almost there now.'

Following his instructions, Ellie knelt down on the rock and slid her legs backwards until they dangled into the hole. A weathered groove gave her a handhold in the rock – she wondered if it was natural. Her legs hung in the void. Icy water spattered her calves where the waterfall roared down inches behind her.

'Let go.'

She stared up at him, his anxious face staring down against the dark sky. He gave a worn smile. 'Trust me.'

She dropped – but not as far as she'd expected. A couple of feet, no more, landing on a ledge invisible in the darkness. Through her shoes she could feel criss-crossed lines hatched into the rock, giving her grip.

A red-hooded head appeared above her. 'If you shuffle in, you should find a tunnel.'

Ellie crouched and stretched a hand in front of her. She touched nothing but air. She crawled forwards, sweeping her arm in broad arcs to check the way. She heard a thud and a splash; the dim light at the opening disappeared completely as Leon dropped in after her, then came back artificially bright as he switched on a torch.

'You can stand up now.'

She did, feeling gingerly for the roof. She walked on; she counted thirty paces, then felt a change. The air was colder and somehow clearer. She could sense space around her.

Leon came out beside her. The head-torch strapped to his forehead played over the space as he looked around, showing flashes of carefully mortared stone walls, fragmentary images of knights and damsels rendered in plaster, lancet windows filled in with earth, fan vaults spreading into the inky darkness above.

Ellie gasped. 'Where are we?'

'The Chateau de Loqmenez.'

The torchbeam came down again, crossed a flagstone floor and came to rest on a shiny petrol generator sitting in an alcove. Leon bent over it and yanked back a cord. It coughed three times, roared into motion, then settled into a regular hum.

The room came to life. Bare bulbs strung between the walls filled the space with light. They seemed to be in some sort of great hall, with a fireplace at one end and a carved stone doorway opening on to the tunnel they'd come through. The only sign of modernity was the lights, and the tangle of cables around the generator. Further back, she could see a tower of stainless-steel scaffolding on wheels. She wondered how they'd got that in.

'Is this a castle?'

'It was buried in a landslide two hundred years ago. Even then, it was already derelict; afterwards, people forgot it completely. But credit to the builders, they built to last.'

Ellie nodded, though she wasn't looking at the architecture, or the fragments of plaster murals still clinging to the walls. She was staring at the far end of the room. A black spear hung in mid air, floating weightless above a stone table.

'Is that . . . *the* lance?' Her voice trailed off. She felt giddy, as if *she* were suspended in space. The world seemed to have been pulled inside out, a mirror-realm of strange enchantments.

An unreadable look crossed Leon's face. 'Chrétien used poetic licence. The blood that flows from the tip – I don't know where he got that from.'

Captivated, Ellie reached to touch the lance. Leon's sharp voice drew her back.

'*Don't touch!*'

Ellie stepped away and gazed around the empty hall. 'I thought there'd be more of you.'

'We haven't used this place in years. It was only after we heard about what happened at Mirabeau that we guessed you might make your way here. We've been scouring half of Europe for you.'

'I'm glad you found me,' she said. She wasn't sure she meant it. Leon's manner unnerved her, so breezy and offhand. He didn't seem to have any idea what she'd been through. And there were too many things that didn't make sense. She felt like the victim of some monstrous hoax, that if she shone a bright light on this castle she might find it was all made of cardboard. She looked at the floating lance again. Now that her eyes were used to the gloom, she thought she could make out thin wires holding it in the darkness.

'What about the poem? The pattern in the chapel?'

427

'The poem's a feint – a ploy. When Chrétien published *Le Conte du Graal*, we needed something to distract Saint-Lazare's people while we worked out what it all meant. It was only a stopgap – we never imagined that it would obsess him so long. Or, eight centuries later, that you'd be using it to try and find us.'

He offered her an admiring look. 'You're the first person ever to solve that particular riddle.'

I didn't do it alone. She wished Doug was there. She could feel his absence, a pain in her chest.

He's safer out of this.

Leon looked at her backpack. 'What about the other thing? Did you bring it?'

Ever since she'd crawled out of the Monsalvat vault with the box in her hands she'd been desperate to get rid of it. Every minute since, she'd felt the burden of it dragging her down. Yet now, she was surprised to feel a pang of loss as she unzipped the bag and handed over the ebony-black box. The red symbols glowed into life as Leon's hand touched the surface.

'Can you open it?' she asked. Suddenly she was bursting to know what was inside.

Leon shrugged. 'We've been waiting almost nine centuries to get it back. We can afford to be patient.'

She tried not to let her disappointment show. 'What's inside – is it . . .?' Even now, she struggled to say it out loud. '. . . the Holy Grail?'

'It isn't holy – not in the Christian sense – and it isn't a grail. But it's what Chrétien was writing about.'

'Was Chrétien de Troyes part of your brotherhood?'

A dark look, impossible to read. 'He was like you. He was never one of us, but he got . . . mixed up. I don't know if he ever saw the Grail, or just glimpsed it, but it obsessed him for the

428

rest of his life.'

A flash of insight. 'That's why the poems don't finish. That's why his symbols have driven readers crazy for centuries. He didn't know himself what the Grail was.'

'He invented it,' said Leon. 'And ever since, it's been like a game of Chinese whispers down the generations. From a serving dish to a cup, a cup to a stone – tarot cards, esoteric wisdom, everlasting life . . .'

He carried the box to the head of the room. Ellie expected him to put it on the stone table, but instead he stepped around and laid the box in the fireplace. The hovering spear swayed as he went past.

Ellie shifted on her feet. She was freezing.

'So is that just a legend too? Everlasting life and all that?'

Give me something, she thought. *Anything. A reason for what I've done for you.*

His face twitched. 'It has certain powers.'

'*What* powers? What does it *do*?'

'More than you can comprehend.' Standing behind the stone table, the spear hovering in front of his eyes, he looked like a priest at an altar. 'There are two principles in this world: life and death, creation and destruction, whatever you want to call them. There are certain objects which govern them, like a magnet moving iron filings on the table. There aren't instructions, no buttons to push or triggers to pull – but by God they're real.'

Creation and destruction. 'So the lance destroys . . .?'

'Think of it like an atom bomb. A chain reaction ripping through the fabric of the world.'

'. . . and the Grail . . .?'

'It heals. It's like a wave breaking over a beach. However rutted and chewed up the sand gets, the water smooths it

429

whole again. Monsalvat want the lance because they thrive on chaos and disorder. We want the Grail so we can try to do some good in the world. For eight hundred years we've been stalemated. We had the lance; they had the grail. Now, thanks to you, we've got both back together.'

His intensity frightened her. 'Is it magic?'

'Have you ever seen a baby playing with a remote control? They think that's magic – and they're right. Magic's just the name we give to powers we can't understand.'

'It doesn't make sense,' Ellie murmured.

'That's the point. Do you know what *rational* means? It means you can divide things up, one into another, ratio to ratio. For three hundred years we've been obsessed with mechanics: taking things apart into smaller and smaller pieces to see how they work. But life isn't a *thing*. If you dissect it, *rationalise* it, it's gone. That's what Chrétien got right. If you pursue the Holy Grail as a quest, as something to be owned and possessed, you're doomed to failure like Gawain and Perceval and all those other inadequate knights. *That's* why it drives us crazy – because we can't *have* it.'

In his red parka, the head-torch still strapped to his forehead and his eyes glowing with righteous fervour, he looked terrifying. Suddenly, Ellie was desperate to get out.

'Where do we go now? Harry said you could take me somewhere safe.'

'Soon. We just –'

He stopped. From down the tunnel, they heard a rattle like a stone or a pebble being kicked along the ground.

'Is anyone else coming?'

'No one who likes us.'

Terror seized her. 'No one followed me, I swear.'

'Did Blanchard give you anything?'

She shook her head. But even as she did, a horrible thought began to gnaw at her. Her hand strayed to her jeans pocket and felt a lump, a small bulge digging into her thigh.

Her mind flashed back to the vault at Monsalvat. Blanchard, sliding the cold ring on to her finger. '*A ring of power.*'

She tugged it out of the pocket and held it in her palm. 'He gave me this.'

Leon wasn't angry. A strange look had come over his face, a serene calm. Almost as if he'd expected it.

A small object sailed out from the doorway that led to the tunnel, bounced once, and rolled across the floor to the centre of the room. It sat there innocently, like a drinks can tossed from a passing car.

'Cover your eyes!' Leon shouted.

LII

Cwm Bychan, Wales, 1143

A bolt of lightning splits the world from the heavens to its core. Thunder rolls over the hill and hits me like a wave. I feel weightless, snatched off the hilltop, caught in the sound. I see the whole hill, a single instant of the battle frozen in the blue-white light.

Then the light goes out. Lazar reels away screaming, clutching his side in agony. Something stings the back of my hand. I think it must be a raindrop, but when I look down I see blood. Is it Lazar's? A little way off, a spent arrow lies on the ground. But none of Malegant's men were archers.

Something plucks at the sleeve of my hauberk. Another arrow. I don't know where they're coming from, but if I don't find cover it won't matter. I dive behind the rock altar. Behind me, Hugh's crouched by the stone pillar cutting the King loose. The moment he's free, they run across and join me.

An arrow rattles off the surface of the stone. Grit rains down on us.

'What –?'

'Morgan's men.'

There's a broken shield lying on the ground behind me. I reach back and drag it to me, then lift it over my head and peer over the rock. Two arrows strike almost at once: the shield shudders as they stick in it.

The battle seems to have been decided. The only men I can see are ours. It's a pitiful sight – of the thirty who set out, only a dozen are left, crouching under their shields as the arrows rain down. Corpses litter the ground around the fire. Some twitch as the falling arrows make redundant wounds.

I can't see Malegant anywhere.

'Where –?'

'He escaped.' Another flash of lightning seizes the hilltop. Arrows seem to hang in mid-air. The thunder follows, more slowly this time. The storm's moving on. A cool wind brushes my cheek; I can smell rain coming.

Hugh gestures to the lance lying at my knees. Trampled in the mud, it looks like any other weapon lost on the battlefield.

'Take that and make for the coast. We'll follow when we can.'

'What about the King?'

'William can take him to Harlech – the garrison there are loyal.'

'And you?'

Hugh wipes his sword and rises to a crouch. 'You didn't kill Lazar. He's still got what we came for.'

Loqmenez, France

Even with her arm shielding her face and her eyes screwed shut, Ellie saw the brightness of the flash. A white light more brilliant than anything she'd imagined, searing through her eyelids, like staring into a lightning bolt. At the same time, or so close she couldn't tell them apart, came the loudest noise she'd ever heard – not rolling like thunder, but a single sharp clap that went straight through her skull.

She smelled smoke and opened her eyes. Most of the lightbulbs had blown, while the ones that survived cast eerie beams through the dust and grit trickling down from the ceiling. Her nose was running – when she wiped it on her sleeve, she saw blood – and her ears were ringing. She could feel fluid in them, like water trapped after a swim, and wondered if that was blood too.

Ellie looked at the door. Five figures stood there in the swirling smoke, machine guns couched in their arms and torches on their heads. She tried to raise her arms, but she was trembling so badly she couldn't move.

One of the men stepped into the light and pulled off his head-torch. Through weeping eyes, Ellie saw the familiar, brutal contours of Destrier's face.

'In a puff of smoke . . .' He laughed. 'Got you at last, you bitch.'

He turned his head, as if he'd heard something down the tunnel, though Ellie couldn't hear a thing. Even his voice sounded impossibly distant, as if the words had been poured through some viscous liquid.

A new shaft of light beamed out of the tunnel. A moment later, Blanchard stepped through the carved stone doorway, a torch in his hand. He surveyed the hall, saw Ellie and smiled. But he didn't move. He seemed to be waiting for something else.

A wheelchair rolled into the hall and stopped. Ellie stared at the man in it. His body seemed impossibly frail – gaunt and pale as bone, his skin almost translucent with age – but the sky-blue eyes that stared at her were fixed with purpose. She wondered how badly he must covet what she had, to risk

434

crossing the boulder field and being lowered down that narrow crevice by the waterfall.

'Eleanor Stanton.' The box on his throat machined out whatever humanity survived in his ravaged body. The cough that followed sounded like a death rattle. 'You have done everything we expected.'

She realised the ring was still clenched in her fist. She opened her hand. Blanchard saw it.

'You kept it. My ring of power.'

For the second time that day, she found herself asking, 'Is it magic?'

Her voice sounded thick and sluggish. Blanchard gave her a pitiless grin.

'There's a GPS transmitter in it. A beacon, to help me find my little bird when she flies away. The battery is so small it only lasts twenty-four hours when activated, but it was enough.'

He crossed to the stone table. Beside Ellie, Leon stiffened, though the guns at the door kept him rooted to the spot. The lance still swayed gently from the explosion's aftershock. Blanchard reached out to take it – but paused. He pulled back his hand, stepped around the table and picked up the black box out of the fireplace. He smiled at Ellie.

'You brought it back. So thoughtful. We expected you would try and steal it – but even I didn't think you'd succeed.'

'Is that why you hired me – so you could use me as a pawn in your game?'

'Surely you didn't think we hired you for your financial expertise?'

He took the box to Saint-Lazare and laid it on the old man's lap. Saint-Lazare's withered arm shook, but his hand stayed firm as he pecked out a sequence from the glowing symbols on the lid. It swung open.

Blanchard looked uncertainly at the old man, who gave a curt nod. It was the first time Ellie had seen Blanchard defer to anyone. He reached in with both hands.

Cwm Bychan

Rain changes the face of the battle. As it falls harder, the arrows gradually disappear. Clouds of steam billow off the dying fire, which has sunk to a bitter red glow. The roar of battle gives way to spattering water, softening the ground and puddling with the blood.

I wait until the arrows stop falling, then run out from my shelter. I find a body – it isn't hard – and hoist him on my shoulder, then start the treacherous descent. I pray there'll be no more lightning. I try to go quietly, but on that slope, with the full weight of a mailed knight on my back and the lance trailing from my free hand, it's impossible.

Thirty yards down from the summit, I hear movement, the rasp of a blade being drawn. It sounds like a knife – I guess it's one of the archers. The rocks are steep and slick, and they don't know what's waiting for them at the top. They're in no hurry to storm the hill.

'Help me!' I shout in Welsh. 'He's wounded.'

He can't see me in the dark, but my voice sounds right. I see a figure coming towards me. I walk on, muttering encouraging words to the dead man on my back.

The knife slides back in the sheath. 'What happened?'

'He tried to go up there.' I let the body swing round. The archer puts his right arm under the corpse's shoulder, taking the burden.

'Christ, he's heavy.'

I shrug off the body so that the full weight suddenly falls on the archer. He's wearing armour, so I don't try to punch him.

436

Instead, I kick his legs from under him. He falls in a tangle with the corpse. I find the knife and whip it out of his belt. With my knee on his chest I press the blade against his neck. It would be so easy to kill him.

But too many men have died that night. Working quickly, before he recovers his wits, I take off his belt and knot his hands together. He has a cloth he uses to dry his bowstring – I stuff it in his mouth, then pull off his boots and hurl them into the darkness. It won't hold him for long, but it'll be enough. Finally, I take his shield.

Using the precious lance like a staff, I stumble down the mountainside. Rain drums against me. At last, the sound changes – I can hear the soft hiss of water on water. The lake. I slide down the final embankment and come out on the valley floor. The rain's stopped; the breeze shreds the cloud. Moonlight leaks out like a wound.

I can't see the horses. Have Morgan's men driven them off? My whole being is close to collapse – but before I despair I hear a whinny in the trees to my right. The horses must have sought shelter there from the storm. I call, and one comes trotting obediently towards me. He's already tacked up – we didn't have time to remove the saddles when we arrived.

I don't know which way the sea is, but I can hear running water. I track the sound to the far end of the lake, where a stream flows out. I follow it down a narrow gully between two hills, splashing in and out of the water.

Soon the stream grows into a small river. There's a track beside it, easier riding. I look back, but the hilltop where we fought is hidden from view. The fire's gone.

I let the river lead me to the sea. I know I should hurry, but a slackness has overtaken me, the let-down after the battle. I loosen the reins and let the horse find his own way. Soon enough, the earthy air takes on a new salt smell. Waves break softly ahead of me. The horse's hooves sound silver on the sand.

I dismount and take off the saddle. The horse lies down and I lie against him, drawing his warmth, one hand resting on the lance beside me.

The night's terrors aren't over yet. Malegant is still out there, and Lazar, and Morgan too. I'm supposed to be guarding the lance. But I've barely slept in four days. I've ridden, clambered, fought to the end of my endurance. The hot breath of battle drains out of me, leaving me empty and limp.

I fall asleep.

Loqmenez

Though she'd been warned, Ellie had still expected a cup – a gold chalice crusted with jewels, the image that a poet's words had seeded into the West's collective imagination for centuries. Instead, what Blanchard lifted out was an egg-shaped stone, about the size of a rugby ball. The stone was cloudy white, but even in the dull worklights it glittered with myriad points of light, like an infinitely multifaceted diamond. The reflected light glowed off it, making a nimbus in the dust and smoke that hung in the air.

As Blanchard turned it in his hands, Ellie saw that the tip of the stone was hollowed out into a shallow bowl, and the base was smoothed flat so it could stand upright. Blanchard carried it back to the stone table and set it down under the spear.

'These were separated in the twelfth century,' he murmured. 'We've been waiting for this moment ever since.'

'Why?' Ellie asked simply.

'The lance cuts and the stone heals. But only the spear that made the wound can cure it.'

As Blanchard spoke, Saint-Lazare's whole body seemed to lurch forward – almost as if he were about to get up from the chair and walk. The chill of centuries touched Ellie's cheek. She wondered how long he'd sat in that wheelchair.

Blanchard reached for the spear again. Again, Ellie sensed Leon go tense beside her. Blanchard, with his back to them, didn't notice – but Saint-Lazare missed nothing.

'Stop.' His face was drawn into a fierce scowl of concentration, hard as ivory. His blue, fathomless eyes turned to Ellie.

'You do it.' The artificial voice, uninflected and mechanical, was pitiless. Ellie stayed rooted to the spot.

Saint-Lazare jerked his head. Destrier marched forward, grabbed Ellie by her hair and dragged her to the table.

'Where I can see her,' Saint-Lazare rasped.

Ellie shook Destrier off and walked to the far side of the table, facing the rest of the hall. Destrier stepped away, keeping his gun trained on Ellie.

From across the table, Blanchard gazed into her eyes. She searched his face for any trace of warmth, any last lingering affection, and saw nothing. She felt tears stinging her eyes – not for Blanchard, but for so much waste. So many mistakes she'd never be able to correct.

Blanchard misunderstood. He shrugged. 'I'm sorry.'

Ellie looked past him to the hall beyond – like a suicide on the precipice taking one last look at the world she'd abandoned. Destrier, leering with triumph. Saint-Lazare's skeletal face fixed on Leon, who in turn was staring at Ellie. He mouthed something to her she couldn't understand; his eyes moved deliberately from the spear to the fireplace behind her.

Whatever he was trying to tell her, it couldn't make any difference. She looked down at the stone grail on the table, dull and plain in Blanchard's shadow, then up at the spear. It wasn't one piece, but two lengths of black iron, joined in the middle by a length of burnished wood. She could see the cables suspending it now, two wires snaking down from the roof. There were no knots: the wires disappeared right into the shaft of the spear.

Ellie put both her hands on the shaft. Her fingers closed around the iron. In the wheelchair, Saint-Lazare's eyes narrowed.

A shudder convulsed her; she felt an electric surge crackle through her body.

Then the room exploded.

Cwm Bychan

I wake at dawn. It wasn't the light that woke me, though I don't realise that at first. Grey sand stretches away to a grey sea at low ebb; wisps of grey cloud drift across a grey sky. The only thing that breaks the grey is a boat, a cockeyed hulk stranded by the tide.

Carried on the wind, I hear a sound – the clop of hooves on the shingle at the top of the beach. I leap to my feet, though it's clear at once that there's no danger. The rider's slumped over his reins, nodding as if asleep. He's kept hold of his lance, but it trails behind him like an oar. The horse isn't much better – he weaves and sways like a drunk as he ambles on to the sand.

My first thought is that he's no threat. My second thought is that he must be close to death. Then I realise it's Hugh.

I run across and grab the bridle. I try to lift him down, but he won't move: he's looped his belt around the cantle of his saddle to hold him in place. I unhook him and pull him free. There's a deep gash in his arm and another in his side, black wounds cut through his armour. I unlace his helmet. He squints at me, as if even that grey day is too bright.

'Chrétien?'

'Did you get it?'

A look of agony crosses his face. 'Lazar escaped. I tried to follow, but Malegant found me.'

'What about the others? Anselm, Beric . . .?'

'All dead.'

I stroke the hair back from his face. There's a flask of water in my horse's saddlebag: I fetch it, and pour some in his mouth.

There's no way we'll ride out of there. Even if I tied him back on his mount, he wouldn't last five miles. I cut off his hauberk and wrap him in one of the horse blankets. He still weighs as much as a pony. I lift him in my arms and stagger down the beach to the boat. Ribbons of weed hang off the hull; some of the planks have warped, but there's a pair of oars, a mast and a sail.

It's all I can manage to heave Hugh over the side and lay him in the bottom of the boat. I put the lance beside him. He feels it, and gives a grimace.

'At least they didn't get that.'

I put my shoulder to the boat's transom and make a half-hearted effort to push it into the water. It doesn't budge. It's too heavy for one man, and the sand holds it firm. I think about tying the horses to it, but I don't have a harness and I'd probably just break their necks.

I clamber back into the boat and kneel beside Hugh. I tell him how we'll wait for the tide to come in and then sail away. I don't know if he understands. His eyes are glazed; he barely knows me.

Loqmenez

It wasn't like the stun grenade. That had been over in a heartbeat – a flash and a crack, then nothing but blindness and

441

the ringing in her ears. This time it happened in slow motion: a percussive boom rumbling down from the roof, a torrent of sound that started loud and grew and grew until it was almost a solid presence, driving the air out of the room. She glimpsed flashes above and blooms of smoke, felt the first pieces of debris falling on her like knives. The floor shook.

She scooped the stone off the table and dived into the fireplace. The noise grew again, battering her; for a split second she saw the whole roof of the hall descending like a cloud, and Michel Saint-Lazare under it, powerless to move.

The world went black. She covered her head with her hands and curled in a ball around the stone; she felt her body being punched and kicked from every side, until the blows were so many they became indistinguishable. The world melted around her – sound and stone and flame became one roiling, furious mass pounding against her.

She couldn't say how she knew it was over. She couldn't even say she knew she was alive – only that she could identify some spark of life inside her, battling through the suffocating weight of numb flesh and bruises. She could feel something smooth and round and hard against her stomach, and that gave her confidence. She cracked open her eyes.

There was light. That gave her hope. She opened her eyes more; she tried to turn her head and found that she could. She looked around.

She was lying in the fireplace, half-buried under a cascade of earth and rubble that had spilled through from the hall. The fireplace itself seemed mostly intact, though a number of bricks had shaken loose from the chimney. She looked up. There was no light at the top of the chimney, but a hole gaped in the back wall where a cluster of bricks had been knocked out. Behind it she could see space – and light. It was a dim, dirty sort of light, but natural, not generated or kindled. Daylight.

She dug herself free. The hearth was so big, the chimney so wide, she could easily stand up in it. She found a piece of rubble and used it to hammer at the bricks, knocking them out one by one. The explosion had shaken the mortar loose: they came easily. Soon she had a hole big enough to crawl through. She posted the grail-stone through, then put her hands on the lip to haul herself up. She winced. Her hands were a bloody mess of scrapes and bruises. Two fingers seemed to have been crushed.

She heard a noise behind her, the rattle of shifting debris. Beyond the fireplace the whole hall was a symphony of ruination: sighs and clatters, cracks and bangs as the rubble shifted and settled. But this sounded closer. She looked down.

A hand had emerged from the mound of earth. She was sure it hadn't been there a second earlier. It twisted around, blackened fingers scrabbling at the rubble. The earth shuddered, and a second hand came out beside it. The gold bracelet of a Cartier watch gleamed on the wrist.

Ellie snatched at the wall and tried to haul herself up. The bricks wobbled under her grip; for a moment she thought they might bring down the whole chimney on top of her. Her arms burned, but she swallowed the pain and heaved. Broken stones cascaded behind her as Blanchard rose out of the rubble; something snatched at her foot, but she kicked free.

She flopped through the wall, landed awkwardly and rolled away. She was in some kind of stairwell, tumbling down the steps. She threw out an arm to stop herself, but before she could get a purchase she landed at the bottom with a bump. New shoots of agony ripped through her.

She pulled herself to her feet. A thin layer of earth carpeted the stairs, but otherwise they were clear. The daylight she'd seen seemed to be coming from above, though the tight-wound spiral hid its source.

She had to get there.

She picked the grail-stone off the floor where it had landed and began to climb. The light was barely clear enough to see by; some stairs were missing, others buried where lumps of the wall had fallen in. Her trouser legs tore open. Blood poured from the grazes in her skin, coagulating with dust and grit.

She reached a landing and paused. Her chest ached – she thought she might have broken a rib – and every breath hurt. She bent double to squeeze out the pain, listening to the sound of her breathing.

It wasn't all she could hear. Quick footsteps rose out of the darkness below – not running, but faster than she could manage. A weary tremor ran through her body.

She went on.

The air grew brighter and cleaner, drawing her up. The footsteps were getting close, but she hardly heard them: she was trapped in an ever-ascending world of her own, concentrating on the pain to keep despair at bay.

And suddenly she was there. She rounded the final turn and came out at the top of the tower. She stared.

After so long underground, the daylight was strange and foreign. The sun was setting behind the clouds, throwing a blood-red light over the landscape. Her eyes took a moment to adjust. When they did, the sight was still incredible.

She was standing on the top of a stone tower, dug into the side of the hill. Behind her, she could see shrubs and trees poking over the edge of an escarpment only a few feet higher than the tower itself. In front of her, there was only space.

The collapsing hall had brought down half the hillside, exposing the tower and leaving an enormous crater in front of it. A few pieces of masonry were visible, but most of the hall lay buried under the earth. Uprooted trees lay strewn across the surface.

Laboured footsteps climbed out of the staircase behind her. She heard heavy breathing, a pained sigh, then the clean, metallic sound of a bolt being snapped. She didn't look back.

'It's quite a sight,' Blanchard said.

'Is that . . . what the lance does?'

Blanchard gave a ragged laugh. Reluctantly, Ellie turned to face him. His white hair had become a crazed, mud-streaked tangle; his face and arms were a welter of cuts, and his clothes were shredded. A gaping wound across his cheek oozed blood; his right arm hung limp and useless. The only clean thing about him was the small pistol he gripped in his left hand, incongruously black and shiny.

'The lance was a lure – a decoy to trap us. Your friend, I think, rigged a detonator to it. When you touched both ends, your body completed the circuit.'

Ellie remembered the scaffolding, the wires running from the generator. 'The roof . . .'

'Explosives.'

A fit of coughing overtook him. The gun shook dangerously in his hand. He spat out a gob of blood.

'The lance was a fake.' He pointed to the white stone cradled to her chest. 'That, I'm afraid, is the real thing.'

Ellie had almost forgotten she was holding it. Instinctively, she pulled it closer, hugging it to her like a child.

'You did more than I ever expected, Ellie. More than your father – more than all these idiots have managed for centuries. But you cannot keep it.'

His broken lips twisted into a ghastly smile, encouraging her.

She almost gave it to him. But Blanchard's words bothered her. *More than your father.* She thought of him, the man she knew only from photographs, run down in a tunnel trying to rescue the stone she now held in her hands. She thought of her mother's long years of stoic widowhood and her lonely death, imprisoned in Blanchard's hospital. She thought of Doug. After everything she'd done, she was glad she hadn't brought him here.

She gripped the grail-stone tighter. 'No.'

Blanchard nodded. 'I understand.'

He shot her.

Cwm Bychan

There's no time on that beach. No sun or shadow, no church bells: only grey stillness and the lap of waves. The glassy tide never seems to move.

I examine the lance. I still can't tell what it's made off. It feels like stone, though surely stone would have shattered by now. Strange designs run along the shaft, engraved so finely I can barely feel the groove with my fingertip. I carry it down to the sea and wash Lazar's blood off the tip.

A tremor goes up my arm, a twitch like an adder. Maybe it was a muscle spasm, but I think it came from the lance. I put it back in the boat and cover it with the edge of the blanket.

Power pools in deep reservoirs, Hugh said. *It accrues in people, but also in objects.* If there are powers invested in the lance, I don't think they're good ones.

The day goes on. To kill time, I saw through the hawser that ties the boat to a rock. Hugh's sword is so blunt it can barely cut the fibres: I find a whetstone in his saddlebag and sharpen it. An easterly wind is blowing down from the mountains, but Hugh's face is glossy with sweat. His brow's hot to the touch. I fetch the flask, but it's empty.

We'll need more water if we put to sea.

We're not far from the river estuary – but I daren't go far unarmed. I strap on my armour and saddle my horse. I take the Welshman's shield, and Hugh's spear and sword. I leave the precious lance covered in the boat with Hugh. The tide's finally reached it. Waves race up to the hull, but they sink away almost immediately. I think it'll be an hour or more before there's enough to float it.

I trot over the sand dunes to the riverbank. The water's brackish, the flask isn't nearly big enough, but it'll have to do. I try to fill my helmet, but it leaks out through the rivets. I stare at myself in the river: gaunt, bloodied, filthy and lined with cares. This wasn't the sort of knight I dreamed of being. If my eight-year-old self saw me now, he'd run in terror.

Flies dance over the reflection, as if picking over a corpse. I put on my helmet and mount my horse one last time. The tide suddenly seems to be coming in faster: I don't want it to carry away the boat without me. I spur to the top of the dunes and look down.

The boat's still there – but it's not alone. A horse is cantering along the beach, a black horse with a black rider. He sees me and halts.

'*Peter.*'

The wind blows the name back at him. Giant though he is, the strain in his voice is obvious. He's been riding and fighting at least as hard as I have.

I ease my horse down the dune and trot out on to the beach. A bowshot away from him, I stop. Waves crash on the shore;

the wind snaps at the horse's mane. We might be the last two men on earth. We lower our spears.

Malegant pricks his spurs. I'm not wearing any, but my horse knows what to do. We charge together, as fast as our horses can manage. The wind sings in my face. I couch my spear and tilt it across the horse's neck; I crouch in my stirrups, knees bent, head forward, just the way Gornemant taught me.

The collision is immense. Against Malegant's lance, the archer's shield isn't worth two bits of bark. It doesn't even deflect the blow – the point carries on, cuts through my chain mail and slices open my arm, just missing the muscle. Malegant gallops on, his momentum tearing the shield off my arm. He almost pulls me off with it.

I'm shaking; I can barely hold on to my spear. But I have to get around before Malegant does. I haul the reins in, dragging the horse. This is why they call it the *tourney* – only now we're not fighting for ransoms or glory.

I'm fast – but Malegant can match me, and I don't have a shield any more. We start closer for the second charge, but the horses are slower: it seems to take an age to come together. Plenty of time to dodge Malegant's lance, though it means my own strike barely touches him.

We wheel again. Now we're so close there's no need to charge. We hammer at each other, blunt bodyblows without the power to pierce armour. My foot comes loose from my stirrup; my saddle starts to slip. I feel the girth snap. But my blows are beginning to tell too: Malegant's having just as much trouble staying upright. He slides back, his spear goes up; I see my chance and lunge, catching him high on the shoulder. He falls backwards out of the saddle and thumps down on the sand.

But the motion unbalances me too. Before I can press home

the advantage, the saddle slips round. I dive off, rolling away so as not to be dragged under the horse.

We both leap to our feet and draw our swords. To buy time, and gather my breath, I shout, 'What was I to you?'

Under the helmet, Malegant's lips draw back in a sneer. 'Nothing.'

'Why did you take me to the Île de Pêche?'

'To kill you.'

'Why me?'

'Unfinished business.' He laughs. 'I'd already killed the rest of your family.'

Afterwards, I'll always wonder if that was true – or just a lie told to provoke me. It certainly has that effect. Numb and dazed from the blows I've sustained, I don't question it. I'm ten years old again, back in the burning compound of my father's home. And like the boy I was, all I want to do is attack.

No fight is pretty, but this is worse than most. We're exhausted from last night's battle, and from the blows we've already traded. I lumber towards him across the sand. I swing at him, miss; he steps away, then scythes his sword at my helmet. I duck. Not soon enough: the blow catches it on the crown, snaps the laces and whips it off. My head's ringing like a bell. He raises his sword to split my bare skull. Instinctively, I throw up my shield arm

But I don't have a shield. I catch his blow hard on my forearm. The bone snaps; the arm hangs limp and twisted. Blood drips through the links of my armour and drizzles like rain on the sand. Under my sleeve I can feel the bone sticking out through my skin. When I try to move it, the splintered bone catches in the chain mail: I scream so hard I almost faint. Malegant laughs.

And yet, and yet – I still have the arm. His sword should

have cut clean through – bone, armour and all. The blow was certainly strong enough.

His sword's blunt: it lost its edge in the night's battle and he hasn't sharpened it. My blade is keen and well honed.

The pain brings clarity. I stagger backwards, my sword dangling from my good arm, as if I no longer have the strength to hold it. Malegant sees his chance and comes after me. He's as tired as I am and desperate to finish me quickly. I slow down; I start to totter. He quickens his pace and aims for my skull.

But though my body's swaying, my legs are firmly planted. Suddenly I kick off, launching myself forward: my sword comes up. He runs straight on to the blade. All I have to do is hold it firm and let his momentum do the rest.

The point pierces his armour and opens up his belly. He swings his sword, but I'm too close; there's no momentum behind the blow, and the blade's too dull to cut me.

I stand back, put my boot against his groin and pull the blade free. Blood leaks from his stomach, but he's still on his feet. A second blow slashes his helmet, smashing the nose-guard in to his mouth and breaking three teeth. He drops to the ground.

I cut the laces on his helmet and pull it free. He's still resisting me. A knife's appeared in his hand; he staggers to his knees. He no longer looks dangerous – just pathetic.

I grip my sword like an axe and swing. The strength comes: the neck severs. His head rolls down the beach and comes to rest just below the tide mark, rocking gently. At my feet, his open corpse pumps blood on to the sand.

Loqmenez
Ellie had thought she was immune to pain. For a second, she didn't feel the bullet at all. Then the pain exploded through her

side. She collapsed to the ground, shielding the stone with her body, while her blood gushed over it. Through the agonised haze she was dimly aware of Blanchard crouching on top of her, trying to wrestle her off. His polished, urbane mask was gone: he clawed and tore at her like a frenzied animal.

The ground shook again, though she didn't see what had caused it. Blanchard didn't look up.

A tall figure, silhouetted against the red sky, pulled Blanchard away from Ellie. Blanchard spun around. She saw Doug's face and cried out, though perhaps it was just a dream brought on by death. The gun came up.

Doug had seen it. Before Blanchard could fire, Doug dropped his shoulder and charged into him. Blanchard doubled over, stumbled back, and–

Flat on the ground, Ellie didn't see him fall. She just heard his scream echo off the valley, then die away.

Wales

Hugh lies straight in the bottom of the boat, his arms folded across the sword on his chest, his eyes closed. I lean down and whisper in his ear, 'We saved the King. We got the lance.'

He doesn't hear me. He'll never hear anything again. With clumsy, inexpert hands, I step the mast and rig the sail. It's poorly done, but it's enough. The wind catches the canvas and carries us out to sea.

LIII

Glastonbury, 1143

The monks watch me anxiously. There's no good way to hide what I'm carrying – I've wrapped it in sackcloth, but they can guess what it is. The covering only makes them more nervous, particularly when I announce that I want to see the abbot.

I've travelled a long way since that beach in Wales. Now I'm back in England. The kingdom's still at war – neither Stephen nor Maud can press home an advantage. Rather than fight each other, they lay waste each other's lands. If you can't kill the King, kill his kingdom.

I remember what Hugh said. *A blessed time – a golden age*, against what would have happened if the spear had killed the King. I have to believe he was telling the truth. Otherwise, so much was for nothing.

But here at Glastonbury Abbey the monks seem well enough – certainly fatter and more content than the brothers I lived with in Brittany. I think of them sometimes, like now, when I hear the drone of a psalm drifting out of church like bees on a summer's day. I wonder how my life would have been if I'd stayed there, locked in the library copying old words. Or if I'd taken the path laid before me when I was eight years old, when they cut the tonsure into my head. Would I have been happier?

The abbot receives me in his chapel. It's ornately decorated, as befits the richest monastery in England. A mosaic in the floor makes intricate, angular paths, criss-crossing each other in a web which has neither beginning nor end. Through the window behind him, I can see the steep slopes of Glastonbury Tor rising out of sight, the strange corrugations under the grass like some lost labyrinth or sunken castle.

'Tell me what happened,' Abbot Henry says. His eyes flick across to the sackcloth bundle. He looks older than when I last saw him. His cheeks have sunk, his hair greyed, but the stones in his rings are unchanged, bright and colourful as summer. They still tinkle like bells when he moves his hand.

I tell him almost everything. Our capture by Morgan ap Owain, the desperate ride through Wales and the battle on the hilltop. A lot of it he's heard before – from William of Ypres and the other men who came back, from his brother the King himself. But not from anyone who knew what happened afterwards.

I end my story on the beach.

'And the lance?' the abbot says. He knows the answer – his gaze hasn't left my bundle since I stepped in the room. My hand trembles as I give it to him. I hope he doesn't guess why.

He unties the cloth and pulls out the lance. The iron is black and mottled, forged in a rush. The smith who made it for me couldn't understand why anyone should want a solid iron spear. I hold my breath. If Henry's held the real lance before, he won't be fooled by my counterfeit.

He touches it with reverence. His eyes are wide with awe. I've got away with it – I try not to let my relief show.

'And the other . . . object. You saw what happened to it?'

'Lazar de Mortain escaped with it.'

A grey, distant look enters his face. 'We'll find him.'

There's a finality in those words, his mind already turning to other matters. I've served my purpose and he's a busy man. I don't know what function he serves in Hugh's Brotherhood, but he's also Abbot of Glastonbury, Bishop of Winchester, king's counsellor and royal brother. But just as he reaches the door, he pauses.

'What will you do?'

I don't imagine he's concerned for my wellbeing. He doesn't owe me anything. I may have brought him the lance, as far as he knows, but at best that's partial amends. And I know too much for him to let me go entirely free.

'I thought I would return to France.'

'You have land there?'

'No.'

'Family?'

'None.'

He frowns. Land and family are the levers of his world. Without them, he can't comprehend me.

'William said you were an accomplished storyteller.'

'I let my audience judge.'

He ignores the false modesty. 'My brother, the Count of Blois, enjoys stories. I think I can find you a sinecure at his court in Troyes. He isn't a member of my Brotherhood, but he's sympathetic to our cause.'

I bow.

Wiltshire, England

Even on the motorway you could feel the spring life bursting out of the earth on a sunny May morning. Ellie and Doug

454

drove down from Oxford and joined the M4 at Newbury, then headed west. They didn't speak much. Ellie stared out of the window, resting her hand on her stomach. Doug, driving, noticed the gesture.

'Is it the wound?' he asked.

'It's fine.' The bullet scar still ached when she walked, but she didn't notice it so much these days. It would heal. She gave him a smile he didn't understand. She hadn't told him yet – it would be another week or so before she could be certain – but she knew. She could feel the life growing inside her, a buried seed slowly germinating. She was happy.

They drove through the downs, where high-tech industries clustered on top of an ancient landscape: where standing stones signposted paths that had been walked for four thousand years, where carved animals branded the hills white. Ellie wound down the window and let the air blast her face.

Back in London, regulators and accountants were crawling over the Monsalvat offices, slowly dismembering its assets. There had been a few news stories when it collapsed, but not many. It wasn't the first bank to go under that year, and it wouldn't be the last. No one in the City was very surprised. Monsalvat had always been a loose cannon, they said, playing by its own rules – it was inevitable it would come unstuck. You couldn't get away with that sort of behaviour these days. Most of them, having been on the wrong end of those tactics at one time or another, were glad to see it gone.

The motorway divided – Doug took the M48 towards Chepstow. Just before the Severn Bridge he pulled off and drove through a small village, down a lane that came out on the banks of the river between an electricity substation and a sewage treatment plant. They sat there like a pair of lovestruck teenagers, staring out at the water.

'Is this your idea of a romantic day in the country?' Ellie teased.

'It depends what you mean by romance.'

She waited for him to go on.

'Leon – your man in the castle. You said – he said – the poem was a bluff. That the real clues to the lance's resting place were in Chrétien's *Conte du Graal.*'

Ellie nodded.

'In the story, when Chrétien's describing the Grail castle, he mentions two real places as metaphors. He says of the castle's tower, "From there to Beirut you couldn't find a better one." Talking about the galleries, he says, "They were more splendid than any you could see from there to Limoges."'

'OK.'

'Both Limoges and Beirut were once Roman towns. Limoges was called *Augustoritum*, Beirut was *Colonia Julia Augusta.*'

'Both named after the emperor Augustus.'

'Exactly. I looked up a gazetteer of Roman place names in Britain. There was one place here that was also called Augusta. It's now called Aust – I suppose it's a corruption of the old name.'

Ellie remembered the sign. 'The village we just went through.'

Doug gazed out over the Severn. The tide was low – brown sandbanks sloped down to the river, etched with crooked channels where the water ran off. A large boulder poked out of the stream.

'Just before Perceval came to the Grail castle, he reached a river. He looked at the deep and rushing waters, but didn't dare try to cross. The fisherman told him there was no bridge, ford or ferry for twenty leagues in either direction.'

He looked to his left, where the white cables of the suspension bridge swooped across the river.

'Luckily, we've got the motorway.'

They got back in the car and crossed the river. On the far bank, a painted sign welcomed them to Wales.

'The Severn's always been a border,' Doug said quietly. 'Between English and Welsh, Saxon and Celt. Rational civilisation and wild, ungovernable magic.'

Ellie laughed. 'I must have grown up on the wrong side of it.'

Doug took the next exit and drove a few miles through farmland. He pulled up on the edge of the road by a golf course and took two backpacks out of the boot. He handed her one.

'I brought a picnic.'

She didn't have to ask what was in the other bag. Since they came back from France it had been a constant presence, like a shadow or an odour. Neither good nor bad, but always there.

They found a stile in the fence. A fingerpost pointed to a footpath leading down into a valley.

'"Perceval turned back from the river and climbed to the top of the hill," Doug quoted. "Almost invisible in the trees, he saw the top of a castle."'

'I can't see any castle.'

'It's a mysterious place. It appears and disappears.'

They followed the path down into a shallow combe, walking single file. Birds sang; flies buzzed around and the sun was hot on her face. She paused to take off her cardigan and walked with bare arms, enjoying the touch of the sun on her skin, the long grass under her fingers. There was a spring at the bottom of the hill; she crouched beside it and scooped water in her mouth. The chill gave her a headache.

The valley narrowed; the path turned between two hills. Doug took a map out of his bag and consulted it.

'This should be it.'

He veered off the path and led her up a steep slope through the trees. The scar in her side pulsed, but she didn't complain. They crossed a field and came to a barbed-wire fence. There was no gate or stile: Doug held the strands apart for Ellie to squeeze between.

'Are we trespassing?'

'It's not the worst thing we've done.'

They re-entered the trees. After the glare in the field, Ellie's eyes took a moment to get used to the dappled light. Walls began to emerge from out of the undergrowth. An ivy-clad column she'd thought was a tree turned out to be the corner of a ruined tower, twenty feet high. Rough-coursed brown stones stuck out of the broken masonry like branches. Gnarled trees sprouted everywhere: further along, a chunk of wall lay tilted on its end, twined in the roots of a large old yew.

She turned to Doug. 'You knew this was here.'

'It's in the register of historic Welsh buildings. I found it online.'

'If only Sir Perceval had had the Internet.'

They walked across the site, picking their way among the trees, tracing the outlines of the old buildings that now barely poked above the forest floor.

'It dates back to the twelfth century, but it's been ruined for ages,' Doug was saying. Ellie wasn't really paying attention. 'If you look at the remains, you can see it was oriented east-west. A lot of people thought it might have been a chapel.'

'Do you think –?'

Ellie heard a rustling in the leaves behind her. She turned, drawing a sharp protest from the bullet wound, and stared.

A bearded old man had come up behind them. He wore green rubber boots and a quilted jerkin, with a flat tweed cap over his woolly white hair and an ash walking stick in his hand. He could have been any farmer or fisherman out in the country – or the landowner whose fence they'd crossed – but there was a gravity in his eyes that was neither curious nor angry.

'I thought you might come here.'

'Who are you?' Ellie asked. She'd almost stopped breathing, though she wasn't afraid.

He leaned on his stick. 'You can call me George. That's how Harry knew me – your father, too. He would have been very proud of what you've done, Ellie.'

He walked around a cluster of crudely mortared stones, tapping at them with his stick. 'If you're looking for the lance, I'm afraid you're a few hundred years too late.'

'Did Chrétien hide it here?'

'He did. He tried to hide it from us, thinking that would hide it from Saint-Lazare as well. He forged a replica and gave it to us, which had us fooled for a number of years. When we realised he'd written *Le Conte du Graal*, we followed the same clues you did.'

'Where's the lance now? The real lance.'

'Somewhere safe.' He picked up an acorn and rubbed it in his hand. 'Every few hundred years, we have one of these aberrations and someone outside the Brotherhood rescues one of the treasures in our charge. They always think it'll be safest hidden from us, but in the end, we get it back. It is best that way.'

He looked pointedly at Doug's bag. Doug backed away, a fierce look on his face.

'You could join us, you know. Both of you. You've certainly earned your spurs.'

'Join what?' Doug demanded. 'An organisation that can't protect its own members? That uses innocent people and then cuts them loose? You'd happily have seen Ellie buried under a French hillside to get to Saint-Lazare.'

Pain clouded the old man's face. 'We'd been stalemated with Monsalvat for eight hundred years. Unwilling to wield the weapon we had, unable to heal the wounds they made. You can't imagine how debilitating it became. Perhaps, in the end, we lost sight of who we are.'

'Then perhaps losing this is the price you pay.'

'Give it to him,' Ellie said quietly. Doug rounded on her.

'You're the one who got it out of the bank – you carried it across Europe and kept it safe. It should be yours.'

'If it has any power at all, if it can do anything good, it's better with him.'

Doug resisted for a moment longer, standing his ground and staring defiantly into her eyes. Then, with a sullen glare, he handed over the bag. Though she hadn't touched it, Ellie felt a great weight pass from her body and knew she'd made the right decision.

The old man nodded gravely. 'Thank you.'

A random thought struck Ellie. 'What do you call it? Can you tell me that?'

To her surprise, the old man actually blushed. 'Even we can't completely escape Chrétien's spell. We call it the Grail.'

They hiked back to the car in silence. At first Doug walked ahead, alone and stiff-backed, but gradually he slowed enough for Ellie to catch up. She slipped her arm in his and tilted her head against his shoulder. They walked up the hill together, parting only to cross the stile.

They reached the car, but didn't get in. They lingered on the roadside, unwilling to go. Doug leaned against the side of the car, and she hugged herself to him, burying her head against his chest.

'Do you feel it too?' she asked. 'That we'll never be able to come back to this place?'

Doug nodded slowly. 'In Chrétien's stories you have the staid world of the court, full of laws and customs and protocols; and the wild world of the forest, where the quests and battles and magic happen. I think we're about to leave that place. The story's over.'

'Some stories end,' she said firmly. 'Ours isn't finishing any time soon.'

But something still troubled her. She wanted to say it now, before the enchantment broke irrevocably. She pushed back so she could look Doug in the eye.

'About what Blanchard said – that night, in Annelise Stirt's basement . . .'

Doug silenced her with a kiss.

'I don't want to know.'

Bruges, 1184

The candle has burned low. I sit in a room in a high tower, scribbling myself blind. Over the years I've told many tales of men and women trapped in their towers. In the stories it's a challenge, an obstacle to be escaped. The reality is different.

I have outlived myself. My story finished forty years ago, but I've lingered on, a singer on the stage long after his audience has left. I served the Count of Blois, and his son the Count of Champagne – both are dead. The man I serve now, Philip of

461

Flanders, wasn't even born when my story happened. He pays my stipend and I flatter him: I write that he is more worthy than Alexander the Great. He pretends to be embarrassed, but secretly he wants to believe me. I praise his wisdom, his love of truth, justice and loyalty. I praise his generosity, particularly when my pay is due.

Bruges is a strange place. The men here are dour and humourless and care for nothing except commerce. Instead of roads they have canals – harder for walking, but easier for transporting their goods. The city exists because of sheep, but you never hear the bleat of lambs, or screams from the slaughterhouse. The sheep live elsewhere, beyond the walls, beyond the sea. Here they only exist in ledgers. They come here as sacks of raw wool; as bales of cloth, dyed and fulled; as skins for the tanners and hides scraped clean for vellum. All the Flemings shepherd here is money.

I'm no different. I stay in my tower, keeping the world at bay; I keep up with life through gossip and hearsay. I write second-hand accounts of second-hand lives, when Count Philip insists, but mostly I write my own story. Written and rewritten – for forty years. I don't know any other. Not one hour goes by that I don't think of the stone, and of the spear that makes wounds that never heal. I thought if I surrendered it I could be free of its power. Instead, it haunts my imagination.

I've taken some of those vellum pages and written my story, but the last pages are blank. When you're the storyteller, you can choose the ending. But I don't know how to finish it. I write and rewrite, but the final page remains incomplete.

A woman on the balcony heard the lamentations and ran down to the hall. She went straight to the Queen and asked her what was wrong.

What is wrong?

The story doesn't end. The quest isn't finished. All I can do is tell the tale, as far as I know it.

I put down my pen. A blot of ink spreads darkness across the parchment, but it doesn't touch the words.

I pinch out the candle.

NOTES AND
ACKNOWLEDGEMENTS

Chrétien de Troyes is arguably the perfect artist: unknowable, except through his work. All that survives of him are the five Arthurian poems he wrote in the second half of the twelfth century, which laid the foundation for the entire genre of Arthurian romance. Without Chrétien's imagination there would be no Camelot, no Lancelot and his illicit love for Queen Guinevere – and no Holy Grail.

It's almost impossible, now, to imagine a world where the Holy Grail didn't exist. Such was the power and mystery of Chrétien's elusive vision that within a generation his readers had begun a process of expanding, adapting and confusing it that continues to this day. Looking backwards, scholars have expended huge energy and ingenuity in trying to trace the Grail's mythic antecedents. For all their efforts, it's clear that while the life-giving vessel is a recurring archetype in human mythology, the specific instance of the Holy Grail belongs to Chrétien alone.

All the businesses featured in this novel are entirely fictitious and any similarities to actual companies or their employees are either wholly coincidental, or the result of a far deeper conspiracy than I can fathom.

Like Chrétien, I've drawn together my story from a mass of pre-existing material. I'm very grateful to everyone who gave me insights into the workings of the City of London, especially Mark Kleinman, Sophie and Marcus Green, Nick, Edward Sawyer, Don Simon Wapping and Mark Hallam. I've also benefited hugely from resources in the Bibliothèque Nationale de France, the British Library, the York Minster Library and the University of York library. The *Tristan und Isolde* described in chapter fifteen is based on an actual production at the Royal Opera directed by Christof Loy and designed by Johannes Leiacker.

At Random House, I'd like to thank the three editors who worked on this book – Oliver Johnson, who commissioned it; and Kate Elton and Georgina Hawtrey-Woore, who saw it through – as well as all the people who've helped design, produce and promote the book. In changing times one of the constants has been my agent, Jane Conway-Gordon, who continued her indomitable tradition of good cake and good advice.

Like my fictional Chrétien, I began writing to impress the woman I was in love with. My stories might not measure up to his, but my romance has been happier: my wife Emma is still the cornerstone of everything I do. Our son Owen accompanied me on a long, tiring research trip with astonishing good humour, and only the occasional croissant and *moules frites* by way of compensation.

Lost Temple

Tom Harper

For three thousand years, the world's most dangerous treasure has been lost. Now the code that reveals its hiding place is about to be broken . . .

Sam Grant is a disgraced ex-SOE soldier and an adventurer by trade. But he has a secret: six years ago, a dying archaeologist entrusted him with his life's work – transcripts of mysterious writing found in a hidden cave on Crete. Deciphered, it could lead to one of the greatest prizes in history. But the treasure is as dangerous as it is valuable. The CIA wants it; so does the KGB. Helped by a brilliant Oxford professor, and a beautiful Greek archaeologist with her own secrets to hide, Grant is plunged into a labyrinth of ancient cults, forgotten mysteries and lost civilizations. But time is running out.

The secrets of the distant past may hold the key to the newest threats of the modern world . . .

'In the tradition of *The Da Vinci Code*, a page-turner of a novel. Like Dan Brown, Tom Harper knows how to ratchet up the tension.'
Choice

arrow books

The Book of Secrets

Tom Harper

In a snowbound village in the German mountains, a young woman discovers an extraordinary secret. Before she can reveal it, she disappears. All that survives is a picture of a mysterious medieval playing card that has perplexed scholars for centuries.

Nick Ash does research for the FBI in New York. Six months ago his girlfriend Gillian walked out and broke his heart. Now he's the only person who can save her – if it's not too late. Within hours of getting her message Nick finds himself on the run, delving deep into the past before it catches up with him.

Hunted across Europe, Nick follows Gillian's trail into the heart of a five-hundred year-old mystery. But across the centuries, powerful forces are closing around him. There are men who have devoted their lives to keeping the secret, and they will stop at nothing to protect it.

arrow books

The Mosaic of Shadows

Tom Harper

Byzantium, 1096. When a mysterious assassin looses his arrow at the emperor, he has more than a man in his sights; the keystone of a crumbling empire, he is the solitary figure holding its enemies in check. If he falls, then the mightiest power in Christendom will be torn apart. Aware of the stakes, the emperor hires Demetrios Askiates, the unveiler of mysteries, to catch the would-be killer.

But Demetrios is entering an unknown world, a babbling cauldron of princes, slaves, mercenaries, pimps and eunuchs. From the depths of the slums to the golden towers of the palace, and from the sands of the hippodrome to the soaring domes of Ayia Sophia, he must edge his way through a glittering maze of treachery and deceit before time runs out. Nor are all the enemies within the city walls. With the Turks rampant across Asia, the emperor has sent to the west for mercenaries to reinforce his position. He gets more than he bargained for, however, when a great army, tens of thousands strong, appears before the gates. The first crusaders have arrived, intent on making their fortunes in war, and they have no allegiance to an empire they eye with jealousy and suspicion. As the armies of east and west confront each other, and the assassin creeps ever closer to his prey, Demetrios must untangle the golden web of intrigue which surrounds the emperor before the city – and the empire – are drowned in blood.

'Gripping from the first page . . . a fast-paced and exciting debut.'
Ink

arrow books

Knights of the Cross

Tom Harper

1098. The armies of the First Crusade race across Asia minor, routing the Turks and reclaiming the land for Christendom. But on the Syrian border, their advance is halted before the impregnable walls of Antioch.

As winter draws on, they are forced to suffer a fruitless, interminable siege, gnawed by famine and tormented by the Turkish defenders. The entire crusade is on the verge of collapse. His lord, the ruthlessly ambitious Bohemond charges Demetrios Askiates to find the killer. But as Demetrios investigates, the trail seems to lead ever deeper into the vipers' nest of jealousy, betrayal and fanaticism which lies at the heart of the crusade.

Praise for Tom Harper:

'Tom Harper writes with strident clarity in this epic tale of murder and betrayal, bloodshed and romance. Gripping from the first page, the reader is swept up in this colourful and convincing portrayal of an Emperor and his realm, under siege. Well-researched, and cinematic in its imagery, this is a fast-paced and exciting debut.'
Ink

'Harper effortlessly draws the reader into the court intrigues and conspiracies of 11th-century Byzantium in his outstanding debut.'
Publishers Weekly

'Scholarly but speedy narrative, steeped in medieval horrors ranging from flogging to famine, all anchored in what feels like a passion for history and spelling out the way things were.'
Literary Review

arrow books

ALSO AVAILABLE IN ARROW

Siege of Heaven

Tom Harper

August, 1098. After countless battles and sieges, the surviving soldiers of the First Crusade are at last within reach of their ultimate goal: Jerusalem. But rivalries fester and new enemies are massing against them in the Holy Land.

Demetrios Askiates, the Emperor's spy, has had enough of the crusade's violence and hypocrisy. He longs to return home. But when a routine diplomatic mission leads to a deadly ambush, he realises he has been snared in the vast power struggles which underlie the crusade. The only way out now leads through the Holy City.

From the plague-bound city of Antioch to the heart of Muslim Egypt, Demetrios must accompany the army of warlords and fanatics to the very gates of Jerusalem where the crusade climaxes in an apocalypse of pillage, bloodshed and slaughter.

'Scholarly but speedy narrative, steeped in medieval horrors ranging from flogging to famine, all anchored in what feels like a passion for history and spelling out the way things were.'
Literary Review

arrow books

THE POWER OF READING

Visit the Random House website and get connected with information on all our books and authors

EXTRACTS from our recently published books and selected backlist titles

COMPETITIONS AND PRIZE DRAWS Win signed books, audiobooks and more

AUTHOR EVENTS Find out which of our authors are on tour and where you can meet them

LATEST NEWS on bestsellers, awards and new publications

MINISITES with exclusive special features dedicated to our authors and their titles

READING GROUPS Reading guides, special features and all the information you need for your reading group

LISTEN to extracts from the latest audiobook publications

WATCH video clips of interviews and readings with our authors

RANDOM HOUSE INFORMATION including advice for writers, job vacancies and all your general queries answered

Come home to Random House

www.rbooks.co.uk